UNNECESSARY REACTIONS

Wayne Edwards

Published by
Llyfrau Cambria Books, Wales, United Kingdom.
Cambria Books is a division of
Cambria Publishing.
Discover our other books at: www.cambriabooks.co.uk

For my good friend Michelle, who reminded me of my childhood ambition, my family and friends, who tolerate my eccentricity, and my gorgeous wife Nic, who in spite of her intelligence and constant misgivings, continues to endure my foolishness.

Contents

Chapter 1: The Copper Kettle

Twilight faded quickly that early spring evening and above the orange haze of the modest streetlights, the South Wales sky was now pitch black. Those few cars that drove through the otherwise deserted town centre, all had their headlights on. Each passing glare harshly highlighted that another day was over. For Frank John, the once proud owner of the quaintly traditional *Copper Kettle Tearooms*, it had been yet another day without customers. He sighed sadly in recognition of that fact. Deep down he knew that he had made the right decision but selling his cherished business left a bitter taste in his mouth.

Frank had spent most of that last day idle, mindlessly staring through the large double glazed mock Georgian window, which pretty much filled all of the front aspect to his premises. White UPVC horizontal and vertical bars criss-crossed the grimy glass, creating a series of small square cells, peep holes to the outside world. A few were blocked out by stiff yellow coloured cards, desperately displaying untidy handwritten notes, each felt tipped marking proclaiming one of today's heavily discounted special offers. All were held in place only by the grace of thumb pressed Blu-tack putty. A cheap, temporary, and ultimately unsuccessful last-ditch attempt at marketing.

Turning away from the window, Frank stretched his left arm out and blindly flicked the catch, locking the front door one last time. He tugged at the hanging white plastic sign, twisting it around on its discoloured cord string to display the word "CLOSED" to the disinterested world outside. Then shuffling silently across the brightly lit rectangular room, his broad shoulders hunched, Frank dodged the vacant tables and chairs, until he reached the thick black arch shaped silhouette on the back wall. This was in fact a gap, a narrow passageway, leading to a dark shadow filled but otherwise empty, rear serving area and under used kitchen.

Instinctively, Frank navigated the sudden drop at the end of the passage. This single step down, between the higher front and lower back rooms, caught out most customers and staff, but never Frank, who despite his unsteady gait, could hobble quickly back and fore in darkness or light, without ever tripping or even tipping the (once upon a time) full tray of rattling cups and saucers. It was a skill developed in busier and obviously happier times. Back then the premises were always well lit, both front and back and the troublesome descent highlighted by two large "MIND THE STEP" notices, which Frank had displayed in clear view, for all to see. However, regardless of his warnings, both written and oft spoken, whether it was their first time or not, customers always seemed to misstep and comically stumble into the rear serving area.

Nevertheless, this back room had always remained popular with his older customers. It was well away from the draughty front door and the noisy traffic, which used to constantly roar up and down the once busy main road outside. The back room was also nearer the warmth of the kitchen and the young serving staff, whose forced but always polite company was strangely valued by the elderly. Here the "old dears" could sit "out back" for hours, snugly reading their newspapers or magazines, gently sipping their milky coffee and nibbling on a heavily buttered toasted tea cake; an order that was as predictable as their surprised stumble over the brightly whitewashed stone step.

Frank had always indulged his older clientele, even though they spent little. He told himself that a busy looking café encouraged passing trade. Yet, Frank never seemed to realise that

2

whilst it was busy "out back" an empty front always made the café look a little bit sad and desperate.

Once the neighbouring shops began to close down, fewer people passed by and whatever age the increasingly rare shoppers were, they had no time to spare, so they did not sit and drink his tea or coffee. Instead, most of those seen rushing passed were usually clutching a bucket-like-carton of coffee, probably purchased from the local petrol station's one-stop-shop. Over time, his loyal regulars grew too old to venture out and then, like his business, they died.

In the now closed café, tables and chairs stood silently to attention for their master one last time. Like Frank, they had all seen better days. At least the evening's increasing darkness helped disguise the shabbiness of the premises. Glancing around, Frank acknowledged each shadowy shape still guarding the empty room. He counted the tarnished copper kitchen utensils displayed high up on the walls. He even remembered the missing items, where now only faint off white outlines haunted the otherwise creamy wood-chip wallpaper. Frank recalled the enthusiasm his ex-wife had had, when she eagerly searched the local antique shops for those desirable objects. Quaint collectables that now all belonged to opportunist thieves. He knew that she had paid way too much for them. He had been angry with her, worried that she would fritter away their nest egg. How wrong he had been. Little did he know back then that it would be him and his stubbornness in trying to keep the business afloat that would waste their money.

Yet the business was their "dream" and what else would he have done with the money. That seemingly vast sum awarded to him by the Army Injuries Compensation Board. Perhaps he should have drunk it away, like so many of his former comrades had. Those who could not cope when finally forced to abandon their regimented existence in the service of Her Majesty. Those

3

who became increasingly desperate when faced with the temptations offered by a modern selfishly independent life on *Civvy Street,* where they tried through alcohol to anaesthetise memories of what now seemed to be considered (by those who had not fought) as an undistinguished service in foreign conflicts.

No! He was made of stronger stuff or at least that's what Frank had told himself. When the night terrors had come for him, he had seen them off, with beautiful visions of the future, and his bright determination to build a successful business for his children. A business that he had hoped would keep them close and stop them from needing to leave the apparent sanctuary of Aberfoist; the Welsh border counties town he called home.

Frank shook his head instinctively, trying to dismiss these increasingly regular and pointless reflections. He was still in disbelief that his daughter had grown up to hate the business he loved. A business he had sacrificed so much to establish and run. She did not want it! She resented the Saturday mornings spent helping her parents out, serving coffee to those smelly old folks, whilst her friends lay comfortably in their beds, messaging her constantly about the latest music videos, which they were all watching on MTV or You Tube. She had her own dreams, a modelling career in a distant big city, doing cool things, whatever cool things were!?! Her father would sneer at her, as she imagined herself surrounded by the beautiful people, whom she constantly read about in those glossy magazines; the ones that had been carelessly left behind by the forgetful old ladies. Those same old ladies whom she had tried so hard to ignore; the ones she struggled to talk with, well because they were so old. Obviously they had nothing in common.

Frank had grown angry with her immature fantasies. If only she had listened to some of those old customers, then his daughter may have learned that living a selfish "cool" life often reaped the reward of a lonely isolated old age. Anyway, he

4

believed that there was no substance to her ambitions, for as much as he loved her, he recognised that she was a plain looking girl, who had none of her mother's natural beauty. She was also overweight or well-built, just like him, and she always would be! Genetics! After all, she followed him not her mother. He had tried to tell her once, in a loving attempt to warn her off future disillusionment. She hated him for that attempted kindness and now rushed to the toilet after every meal to make herself sick and thin, just like the fake girls in the glossy photographs and trending videos she idolised.

Frank also sighed when he thought of his son. The boy had had it too easy and in Frank's opinion, also shared unrealistic ambitions. Well, no ambitions at all really, or so Frank had concluded! His son was like his dad, certainly no scholar! So Frank, with the hope of his own early retirement, had trained the boy to cook and run a business. Yet all the boy had done was to cook the books and spend the meagre profits on drugs. He had turned out to be a real disappointment, just a dope, only interested in getting high!

How had his children grown up with no work ethic? Frank just could not understand it. Perhaps his time away from them, when he was in the service of his country, or all the hours worked in establishing the business, meant that he had spoilt them instead of parenting them. God help them, for he could not now. His dreams had faded, as his traditional custom died off. His simple but just about profitable menu, was now as out of fashion as the town's once glorious shopping centre, in which the café still stood; only lately it was just surrounded by fast food outlets, charity shops and tattoo parlours.

So the decision had been made to sell up. The "Kettle", as everybody called his café, had gone off the boil. It was going to become another take-away outlet. A much needed kebab shop, on a street, which now seemed to have no purpose, other than to feed or ink the binge drinker.

The firm knock, sounding on the back door, told Frank that the soon-to-be-new-owner had arrived. Slowly taking the keys from his pocket, Frank felt for the large Yale on the steel ring and after grasping it, he began to unlock the security bolts on the back door. Frank thought about turning the lights on to make it easier, but he was too ashamed by the condition of the room and left them off. Finally Frank opened the door. Two men stood outside, their features hidden by the dark of the evening.

'Mr Lord?' Frank asked cautiously.

'Good evening! Mr John?' The first man, his dark outline, tall and broad, began cheerfully; holding out a big open hand as he confidently stepped forward.

'No power?' He asked, peering into the dim interior.

Embarrassed, Frank broke out of the firm handshake, reached over and flicked the grubby plastic switch beside the brown stained Formica door. The neon light stripes pulsed and then the tubes burst into life, brightly illuminating the sad looking room.

The second man, who was much shorter than his companion, now stepped into the room and let out a hiss of disapproval as he surveyed the dismal scene. Frank could see that the small man wore a smart pin stripped suit with a white shirt and formal navy blue tie. He carried a battered brown leather briefcase. His silver streaked frizzy shoulder length hair sported an unflattering comb over on top. When he spoke his accent had the sing song lilt of the Indian sub-continent and Frank seeing his prospective purchasers in the light for the first time could not hide his surprise. They were both Asian and not Welsh. Their voices, on the telephone at least, had sounded pure Valleys but now Frank was taken aback to see their brown skin.

'This is going to need some refurbishment, Sardaar Sarbaah Sar!' Frank heard the short man exclaim.

'No this is fine Purdil. Just what I wanted! Remember our business needs to be front of house not back room.' He laughed. Then turning to Frank the big man smiled broadly. 'Forgive Mr Khan, he is a rare being, both an accountant and a lawyer. Sadly these professions combine to make him far too cautious a man for us entrepreneurs eh!'

Frank looked at Mr Lord, if that was his name, and felt betrayed. He needed the money but an irrational anger and resentment began to build inside of him. His eyes scanned the tall man, taking in his black hair, which was greased into almost a quiff. Then there was the elegant, neatly trimmed, and possibly oiled beard. Frank also saw the black, steel toe-capped, cowboy boots, stone washed jeans, matching denim shirt, worn under the unzipped lime green leather Bikers jacket, and finally his eyes stared incredulously at the red silk, cowboy-style, neckerchief, which was loosely tied around the big man's thick-set neck.

Frank had always been prejudiced and unlike some of his comrades, his military service in Afghanistan had not changed his views on the people, whom he always generically and incorrectly referred to as *"Bloody Pakis!"* His horror at the prospect of selling his "dream" to foreigners must have shown on his face, for Mr Lord's easy smile had suddenly vanished.

'Is there a problem?' Lord or Sardaar Sarbaah Sar, asked bluntly. He was angered by the look he was being given. A look that he had seen too many times before, on those pale faces of the people in this supposedly welcoming land.

With an effort Frank controlled himself. He thought of the money. Maybe there was a natural irony in selling to people whose countrymen may have caused the injuries that gained him the compensation, which he duly used to buy his business in the first place.

'No! It's just that ... ... your accents! On the phone I thought you were Welsh!'

'I am!' Lord or Sardaar Sarbaah Sar replied indignantly. 'I am a Ponty boy!' He laughed. 'And my colleague is from Cardiff!'

'K-ar-diff's foreign to real Aber boys Mr Lord!' A new, local voice, called out, slyly, from the open doorway. 'Isn't that right? Frankie!'

The three men stood inside the café turned as one to see another three men looking in at them. The first was average height, pigeon-chested and paunchy; unshaven with close cut fair hair. He wore thick lensed black rimmed glasses that magnified and distorted his grey blue eyes, making them look as if they were peering in from behind a pair of fairground goldfish bowls. The other two were a real contrast. One was short and stocky. One was tall and wiry. Both wore black woollen beanie hats, pulled down tight on their heads. All three men wore similar black trousers and black fleeces, adorned with the same, glow in the dark logo, "Aberfoist Security Services", emblazoned across the chest. They strutted into the room as if they were the new owners.

'What the fuck are you doing here Flicker?' Frank snarled at the lead intruder.

Lord answered him instead and did not hide the growing irritation in his voice.

'Mr Pace is going to be my local partner and I took the liberty of asking him along to secure the premises on completion of the paperwork but he is a little early, I think!'

'A little early! I should coco!' Frank now had a target for the anger that had been building in him. 'You don't want to be going into business with this bastard!' Frank spat out.

'Now! Now! Frankie! No need for name calling, just because I upset you by offering to give your little girl her big break!' Pace licked his lips and continued. 'Can you believe it Mr Lord, old

8

Frankie here refused to let his daughter take the opportunity of auditioning for my wife's modelling agency and it was her dream you know!' Sneering, Pace then made a sarcastic tut-tut-tutting noise before continuing. 'But what Frankie didn't know was that she came to me anyway!' Ellis Pace paused for effect and licked his upper lip again before laughing out loud. He was enjoying provoking Frank John. 'Ha! She didn't tell you eh Frankie! Well she proved to be a natural, with a bit of personal coaching from me and the boys of course!'

'Bastard!' Frank roared and with fists clenched tried to rush at Ellis Pace.

The blow from Lord caught Frank hard in the solar plexus. Surprised and fully winded, Frank let out a low grunt and staggered backwards. Lord stepped quickly forwards and with one strong arm around the stunned man, steered him easily away from his provocation and directed him towards the nearest table and chairs. With his free hand, Lord dragged a chair from under the table and then forced the wobbling Frank to sit down on it.

'You're a big man, but you're in bad shape. With me it's a full time job. Now behave yourself.'

Lord allowed himself a long smirk after delivering his favourite and much quoted line from one of his beloved movies but his body remained rigidly *en garde*. The quote was lost on Frank. Always a man of action rather than words, Frank recognised the imminent threat from Lord's physical presence more than his mocking tone. Not that Frank felt able to respond, as the perfectly executed blow had not just been painful to his pride but had winded him so badly that he merely gasped for air, whilst inwardly seething and promising himself that he would kill Pace, whether what he said was true or not. He knew about Pace's side-line in pornographic movies and he had told Jan, his daughter, to have nothing to do with the pervert.

Lord addressed Khan. 'The contracts are in the bag? Yes?'

9

'Yes Sardaar!' Was his nervous reply.

'And the company cheque book?'

'Yes Sardaar!'

'Good! I think it best that Mr Pace takes you to that bar he told us of, so that you can agree the terms of the security contract in a more amicable environment, whilst I have a little chat with Mr John here and close our particular deal! Yes!'

Ellis Pace began to move his mouth and then thought better of whatever he was going to say and just nodded.

Khan put the brief case down on the table and the four men backed out. Without looking back Lord commanded them to close the door behind them. He then spoke quietly to the disabled man beside him.

'Now Mr John, I am sorry for Mr Pace but he is essential to my plans and I am going to er,' he paused briefly, before mimicking Marlon Brando's gruff accent from The Godfather movie, 'as they say *"make you an offer you can't refuse!"* Eh!'

Frank heard the door close and still breathing heavily, struggled to say something but could not.

'Now, first things first! Do you have a kettle in that kitchen?' Lord continued, talking matter of factly, as he casually moved away with the confidence of a man used to getting his own way. Switching on the kitchen lights, Lord began searching, opening cupboards and drawers, banging the pots and pans about until he exclaimed: "Ah yes this will do!"

Frank could hear the sound of the cold water tap being turned on as Lord began to fill an old, slightly dented copper kettle. It was one that Frank had once displayed in his front window, long before sunlight had tarnished the metal.

'You must indulge me my love of the movies Mr John! As you correctly spotted I have not always been a Welshman! Where I grew up English was not spoken much but the British and American soldiers left a fine collection of videos for me to study.

Perhaps, like your Mr Pace's movies, they were not the best influence on a young impressionable boy but I did learn a lot from them!"

Lord paused as if remembering something poignant.

"Later some of my actual teachers were unhappy with some of the words I learnt!' He laughed harshly. 'They beat me! Yes! They were cruel teachers, Mr John! But they taught me well. Not only proper words but they taught me how to make people not only say the words I want to hear but mean them too. Yes! I hope that I don't have to share with you all the lessons they taught me, Mr John!'

Frank could hear the burst of energy as Lord lit the gas and began to boil the kettle full of water. He still felt very angry but suddenly for perhaps only the second time in his life, Frank John also felt very weak and very alone.

Chapter 2: Isolation

'What you looking at?' The teenage girl aggressively spat out her unpleasant challenge towards the middle aged man, who was sat silently behind the teacher's desk just a few metres to her right. Her screeching voice had disrupted an otherwise silent classroom, startling the man out of his daydream. Nevertheless, he successfully resisted the natural inclination to immediately look away. Instead, he focused fully on her, for probably the first time that day. His quick study inevitably provoked a repeat of her exaggerated outburst.

'I says, what YOU looking at!?!'

He fought the temptation to reply that he was looking at nothing, nothing at all! Not that he would have intended to cause the offence such a statement should give. He did not mean that she was nothing! Regardless of how understandable such a sentiment might have been in the circumstances. He, like her, was just bored but unlike her he had simply allowed his mind to drift off, temporary escaping the confines of the stuffy classroom. His eyes were open but literally saw nothing. He really did not wish to admit that! Not to a pupil! Especially one he was meant to be closely supervising. So, he said nothing at all and merely gave her a seriously disapproving look.

'Ugh!' She grunted in frustration. Then she cried out again, this time even louder in her childish voice. 'Stop looking at meeeeee!'

There was no point in attempting to explain to her, particularly in her current frame of mind, that he was the teacher presently in charge of the high school's punishment room, the so called "Isolation Room" and as such he had a duty to watch all the pupils detained there in. Equally, he felt there was no point in trying to reason with her. Why should he have to explain that this duty was only to ensure pupils did not vandalise the tables or commit any other misdemeanours. That would have been putting ideas into her seemingly empty head. Anyway, why on earth would he want to look at her! Barely a teenager and dressed in a dirt-stained, washed out, school polo shirt, far too small for her chubby torso; her face and limbs unnaturally orange with fake tan.

The teacher glanced briefly at the only other pupil in the room. A slightly younger girl, who had obviously breached school rules by turning up that morning with bright blue "look-at-me" dyed hair. Now evidently distracted from her set work, the blue rinse girl was peeking furtively between him and his *provocateur*. She looked mildly embarrassed by the commotion but he suspected that she would soon warm to the distraction. He felt that he had to say something to the older girl, something authoritarian.

'How dare you!' He began in his most practised "appalled" teacher's voice. 'Who do you think you are? To talk to me, a member of this school's teaching staff, in that tone of voice!?! Now stop your nonsense, shut up and get on with your work!' It was all an act and sadly not a very convincing one.

'No-ooh! Stop looking at meeee!' The girl wailed even louder in response.

'I'm warning you! If you continue, you, you ...' he hesitated, his brain searching for something appropriate to say.

'You will be in further trouble!' He concluded, in an increasingly louder and naturally angry tone, which just made her laugh. She then gave him a look of utter contempt. This pushed the button and made him roar. He was usually very good at roaring down pupils, regardless of how ridiculous it made him, a grown man, feel! It was after all only a natural reaction, given the frustrations of the job.

'And you will get at least another hour in isolation! And perhaps even an after-school detention!' He knew that he had now raised his voice much higher than he had intended, in what was a futile attempt to drown out her increasingly boisterous laughter. Trying to sound firm and fierce often worked with less rebellious children. However, in reality, he felt totally impotent at the inadequacy of the threatened punishment and what's more the girl knew it.

'You can't make meeee! You can't do anything to meeee!' She responded, acutely aware of his position's limitations. This knowledge made her even bolder in her growing sense of outrage and injustice.

Well, sometimes it worked! He sighed silently to himself. Sadly this was not one of those times. At least the only other pupil in the room had now nervously turned away and was looking down, seemingly concentrating on her work, clearly intent on not sharing in any further sanctions that might be issued. She was also, sensibly, avoiding any eye contact with the loutish loud-mouth, who was inevitably grinning across, keenly looking for support or at least a suitably impressed audience to entertain further.

After eight years of teaching teenagers, ten if you counted his Qualified Teacher Status training course, Mr. Kane was used to this sort of verbal interaction. Abuse really or so the union kept claiming and whilst management would agree "it" was unacceptable, everyone in the profession would just shrug and say that "it" was all *part of the job!*

Nonetheless, first-hand experience was always unpleasant and exasperating; especially for a man, who was built like a front row rugby forward. Someone who could actually do anything physically he wanted to do to the small child, if he was so inclined. Someone who had been spoilt by years of wiser deference for his *larger than life* bulk, once so intimidating, in the real world. A world not governed by liberal education policies. A world, where provoking someone who looked like him, would be universally accepted as foolish. Now, of course, he had no effective way of dealing with such obvious goading. He was not allowed to do anything other than attempt to reason with the unreasonable. Like him, school sanctions had gone soft around the middle. Not that he actually wanted to do anything other than sit and daydream this onerous duty away. Perhaps that was it! Kids could always tell when you did not mean something! They had instincts that adults had lost.

Kane wondered if things were worse now than when he had first made the "exciting" career change into the always "challenging" world of teaching. The majority of children still got "it" but he was in no doubt that there was an increasingly "significant" minority, who were making everything he had previously enjoyed about the job, utterly miserable. Yet it was a living and nobody died (usually).

Of course, there were procedures available to him in his current predicament. He could send the girl back to her Head of Year. A small, pleasant woman, who although approaching her thirtieth year, looked and dressed like the teenagers she taught. In spite of being almost ten years his junior, she was in charge of discipline for 250 mixed gender pupils, aged thirteen to fourteen years old and without the burden of machismo, by and large did a wonderful job. The boys made no secret of fancying her and most of the girls wanted to be like her. The Head of Year might listen to the girl's complaint and try to persuade her to be reasonable before inevitably sending her back, to sit in the Isolation Room and sneer at him, as they both knew her rude outburst had gone unpunished. If the girl was not "reasonable" she could be sent to the School's Head Teacher, who would

15

ultimately negotiate time off "Isolation" for promised good behaviour or threaten the thing the girl wanted most, the "horrifying" sanction of being sent home! Such was the school policy. Such was all school policies these days.

Then again, the Head of Year might take the girl's side and Kane could find himself in front of the Head Teacher, awkwardly trying to justify his own behaviour, with only one, probably hostile, teenage female pupil as an independent witness. Kane imagined the possible reaction. "Staring and shouting at a child?" This was likely to be considered unprofessional conduct by most people outside of the teaching profession, especially those who remembered unjust punishments from their own inevitably stricter schooldays. Ever under pressure from such volatile and increasingly politically correct public opinion, who knew how the determinedly populist Head might react.

Nevertheless, Mr. Kane grumpily gave the formal warning required. If she continued to misbehave, she would have to go and see Ms. Singer, (her Head of Year). Well, it was no surprise that the girl laughed back at him. She appeared not in the least bit worried by this threat. After all (it was obvious to him), she just wanted out of the room. Her constant fidgeting had, probably, drawn his subconscious to her before she interrupted his temporary escape into that lovely daydream. It was understandable really; an inevitable reaction to her frustration with being condemned, on what was the last day of term, to three hours in the "expected" silence of the hot and stuffy port-a-cabin, (which budget constraints meant substituted for a proper classroom). Kane knew his professional challenge was to contain her for as long as possible. So he looked back down at the exercise book laid out expectantly on the desk in front of him, the one that he had been unenthusiastically marking with his red pen before the daydream rescued him, and he tried to focus on assessment work. Although ignoring her constant huffing and puffing, which was punctuated by her bitter *"this school is rubbish"* comments, was certainly a challenge.

Faced by his sudden indifference, the "terror" began to noisily scribble over her work books. Kane now felt obliged to actually do something. Putting his pen down, he slowly and dramatically reached for the telephone in front of him and called the more senior teacher's number. The phone went straight to voicemail, just as the girl began to mock him.

'What yer doin'? Callin' fer 'elp eh! Path-etic!' She gloated.

He tried another number. On the other side of school, a telephone rang in the empty office of the Deputy Head of Year. He was a bright and cheerful thirty-something, who liked the pupils to call him by his first name. After listening to another three voicemail messages, all telling him that each of the progressively more senior teachers were not available, Kane sighed and gave the girl one final futile warning. If she persisted in not being silent, he would send her to her Head of Year and she would probably be sent home! He immediately wished that he had not said that last bit.

'Good, I'm tired! I can go back to bed!' The girl sneered back between mock yawns. 'This school is rubbish!' She added again.

He did nothing and looked down at his marking. Furious at his lack of action, the girl began tearing her book apart. When this brought no reaction, she began tossing the resulting confetti up into the air, all the while chillingly laughing out loud whilst making comments along the lines of "Look everybody! It's snowing!"

Unable to ignore this destructive behaviour any longer, Mr Kane slowly stood up and moved passively to the door of the cabin. Holding it open, he loudly told the girl to leave.

'No! Make meeee! I ain't going an' you can't make meeee!' She sang out repeatedly in triumph with her arms folded in defiance. His head bowed, Mr. Kane stepped out of the room and strode as calmly as he could across the wooden ramp to the neighbouring port-a-cabin. Opening the classroom door he tried to contain the irritation in his voice as he called in:

'Excuse me Miss Royale! Can I borrow one of your pupils to go on a message for me, please?'

Having despatched the pupil to find and fetch Ms. Singer, he returned and stood by the open door, watching the exultant girl, who was continuing to amuse herself by flicking the pieces of torn paper off her desk. On seeing his return, she demanded at the top of her shrill voice, once again, that he: "stop looking at me!"

'You're sick, you are! 'Aven't you got anything better to do than look at meee? You're a paedophile! Yes you are! When I tell my mum, she'll come up the school and thump you, she will!'

When Ms. Singer eventually arrived, after what seemed like hours but was probably only ten minutes, the torrent of abuse had inconveniently ended. Kane had to explain the incident to his younger colleague in front of the now gloating girl.

'Oh! Well if that's the case, she can come and sit at the back of my room!' Ms Singer informed everyone coolly. 'Come on Tia.' The young teacher smiled sweetly at the girl, who grinned happily back at the casually dressed role model, with her mouth so wide that it seemed to stretch from ear to ear.

'Thanks Miss!' Kane heard the suddenly angelic child gush as she grabbed her bag. It was not a proper school bag, like a satchel or sports bag, but one of the ridiculously enormous and hugely expensive, high fashion designer handbags, so popular that year, with young girls, and their mothers. Kane suspected that it was a fake. An imported forgery, hawked around the pubs and bingo halls by track-suited chancers. He knew that it was the type of bag that was most definitely banned under the (apparently unenforceable) school rules. Kane sighed. As soon as she was through the door he could hear Tia Maria Sharpe confidently declare, at the top of her voice:

'He's a bloody "Paedo" Miss! Kept looking at me he did!'

Kane rolled his eyes but no one was watching. Slowly he moved over to Tia's empty desk and bending over began to pick up the pieces of torn paper that she had left behind, littering the floor. The air around her desk had the whiff of stale cigarette smoke. The stink had clung to her clothes and still wafted in her wake. He suspected the abuse that he had just suffered, was purely due to the girl needing her next nicotine fix. He sniffed the air again and for a moment wondered if there was perhaps something else he could smell mixed in amongst the tobacco aroma. Well, that would explain her paranoia he concluded to himself. Then after dumping the paper shreds in the large cardboard bin marked "Recycling only!" Kane sat back down at his desk. Twisting back, he took out a pink incident form, from the well-stocked tray on the shelf immediately behind the desk and slowly began the long process of writing up his report on the incident for the school records. Fortunately, the only other person in the room, kept her head down, leaving him to contemplate his detailed explanation.

At least he had only two lessons remaining that day, after this always painful duty concluded. Not that he would get to teach in those lessons, for they were the last lessons before the desperately needed Easter Holidays! No school for a whole sixteen days! Ten holidays! Two Saturdays! And two Sundays! Freedom! Yes! He could make it or so he told himself. However awful those DVDs that the pupils would demand to watch might be. Then, the phone rang.

'Isolation Room. Mr. Kane speaking.' He answered instantly and formally, as was always his way.

'Mickey?' He grimaced slightly, recognising the cheerily informal voice of Glenys, the school's receptionist. She always

19

called him Mickey, even though his given name was really Mykee. He had told her that Mykee should be pronounced My-Key! Not Mickey or Mike, as people persisted in calling him! Unfortunately, she never, ever, got it right!

When he was a child and then again as an angry young man, Kane had been fiercely proud of (what he had always assumed was) his first name's Celtic origins. He had literally fought to get people to pronounce his first name correctly. "My-Key! Not Mickey!" Now, he was older and thankfully a lot more mature, and tolerant, he had learnt to (just about) accept whatever mispronunciation, well-meaning-people spoke. After all, (as he knew only too well) life was short!

The matured Mykee Kane had also more recently researched his name and discovered a painful truth. One that caused him to cringe each time he remembered those wild, unnecessary reactions of his youth. He had been more than a little embarrassed, when he first found out his name's Hebraic origins, which meant that he, his parents, grandparents, and of course pretty much everyone in his direct family and circle of friends had been wrong. The name, according to most academic sources, should have been pronounced as "May-Kiy!" It was definitely Old Testament and not Ancient Briton!

'Yes.' He confirmed to Glenys that it was actually him. All the while trying hard but failing not to sound too grumpy.

'I've got a call for you! MICKEY! Do you want to take it?' Glenys, the receptionist asked uncertainly.

He frowned, thinking the enforced formality of the Isolation Room was not necessarily the best place to take any call but he could not help himself and he quietly asked who was it from?

'Oh! Sorry Mickey! I thought I said!' There was a pause and then the line went silent, whilst Glenys double checked who actually wanted to speak with him. Then the line went live again.

'It's a Mrs Wendy John!' Glenys said. 'She said you'd remember her and that she was really sorry to ring you in work but it was really important that she speak to you! She sounds pretty upset Mickey!'

For a few seconds Kane wondered whose parent was ringing him now and what had he done this time to get such an urgent call!?! These days mothers often had different surnames to their offspring. So he was constantly confused. The name sounded familiar though! Then it suddenly dawned on him why the name was familiar! He blushed. He should have recognised the name straight away. This was indeed a personal call! A call from an old friend but someone whom he had not spoken to for years!

'Ooh, er, yes! Please put her through.' Kane stuttered excitedly and then as an afterthought he added: 'Thank you, Glen!' He heard the line tone change as the external call was put through on the system. Kane took a deep breath before saying his "hello" softly and nervously into the receiver.

'My-Key is that you? Are you there?' The strange yet familiar voice burst out of the ear piece, releasing a tidal wave of memories that washed over him and swept all thoughts of formality away.

'Wen!?!' He gulped, suddenly oblivious to where he was sitting and the present company he was in. In his mind's eye he saw her, the beautiful girl; the one that he had known so long ago. He saw her long wavy bright red hair, as dazzling as her green eyes. He felt the awkwardness again. The embarrassment that he had not been in touch for such a very long time. The guilt! He had not thought of her in that long, long time. After all, she was the wife of his best friend! A best friend whom he had not seen for, Kane closed his eyes and concentrated. He was shocked by the realisation that it must be at least five years, if not more!

'Look My-Key, I don't know how to tell you this but I

thought you needed to know!' Her voice was strained. Hard and serious. No hint of the friendship (and close affection) they had once shared.

'It's Frank! My-Key!' Her tone wavered. 'He's dead! He killed himself in that bloody café of his!' The tears sounded in her voice now and probably drowned out his shocked and stupid denials as he protested that it could not be true! He felt sick to his stomach and stared straight ahead, blind to the room's other occupant, who although keeping her head down was obviously listening, intrigued by the half a conversation that she could hear.

Wendy John had suddenly composed herself and was speaking again.

'Look, there's nothing to be done but I just wanted you to know. I'll tell you as soon as we have a date for the funeral. I'm sorry to ring you at work but you had moved and we'd lost your new address and phone number!' She started to cry, sniffing and snivelling as soon as she realised that she had used "we'd"!

'Where are you?' He heard himself bleat.

'At home, of course!' She said distantly.

'Look, we need to talk properly. I know I haven't been there for you! But I finish work in a couple of hours. I can be with you by 4:30pm!'

'Make it 5:30pm! I can see you then. Bye.' She hung up. Kane heard the line go dead. He felt a fool. There was so much he had to ask. How? When? Why? He knew the Where!?! Yet Kane did not understand! He could not understand. His face was pale but he could feel his cheeks warm as he suddenly remembered where he was. He risked a glance at the girl to his left. Fortunately her head was down. She was still pretending to work but she was blushing too. He wondered how much of the call she understood. Too bad!

He suddenly did not care about anything anymore. His new world, the life that he had carefully created to escape his past,

22

none of it mattered anymore. He had to go back. He had to go home. Back to Aberfoist!

Chapter 3: Welcome Home

Kane had made this journey "home" countless times before. However, he had found little reason to do so recently. Since the passing of his mother and the subsequent sad sale of the family home, visits back to Aberfoist had become a rarity. Especially as he had no other relatives remaining in the area and the few real friends, those who had not already moved away for work like him, had their own increasingly busy lives, which could not stop just because the city slicker wished to honour the country bumpkins with a visit. Nevertheless, in spite of such off putting awkwardness, Kane could still pretty much drive the route on auto pilot and this allowed his mind to wander, if not wallow, in the past. His past!

The inevitable nostalgia inspired by the familiar scenery constantly swept over him, oddly generating feelings of anticipation, joy, and excitement. Kane tried hard to change his suddenly cheery and therefore inappropriate demeanour. Focusing his mind on the sad news would help. The bad news, which still seemed so unreal. Frank John dead! A suicide! It just did not make any sense to him.

Motoring along alone, Kane paid scant attention to the radio, which he habitually left on to disguise the increasingly tinny sound of his car's exhausted engine. The usual selection of bland pop songs, inane DJ chatter and urgent sponsors messages, blasting constantly out of his cheap speakers, went in one ear and out of the other. In spite of the broadcast professional's best efforts to engage with their listener, the frivolous talk and din of trendy music provided hardly any distraction to the mental puzzle of why his old friend had taken his own life. Only when Kane caught sight of the old factories, where so many of his former school friends had started apprenticeships, did he allow his attention to drift away from the perplexing problem. Kane could still vividly remember the proud faces, as the boys suddenly became young men and spent their first wages in the local pubs. Now, those works were all shut down and the jobs had been lost abroad.

Bold glass frontages, which previously reflected the area's glittering ambitions, had been cruelly shattered by macro economics. Although the actual stones that had been hurled through the dirty glass by disgruntled and redundant passers-by did not convey more than mere casual vandalism to the absentee owners and opportunist capitalists, who would ignore such pointless protests and as usual vote to protect their own selfish interests and maintain the status quo at the next election, regardless of any positive socially aware alternatives.

Most of these buildings were still boarded up. Cheaply painted "For Sale" signs hung optimistically where once bold household names featured. Others were regenerated into "enterprise zones" complete with brightly lit notices, advertising self storage units, a go-kart centre and a Mission Fitness Gym. Yet none of these ventures seemed to be truly satisfactory replacements for the mass employers, who had once produced iconic Great British goods for sale to the world market from this proud industrial corner of Wales.

Slowing down for a mini roundabout on the road ahead, Kane glanced briefly to his left. There he saw where the combined work's Sports and Recreation Centre had once been. He recollected playing football there so many years before. He was not the best with a ball at his feet but seemed to recall that the youth sports tournament, which he remembered so fondly, had been sponsored by the army. Had Frank been in his team that day? Had that been the event which led to his friend joining up? Or did just talking to those army recruitment people inspire an interest? Kane could not remember. He could not actually remember the last time he had spoken to Frank and he suddenly felt bitter at his memory's betrayal of such key facts. It was probably in a pub! Yes! They would have laughed about the good old days. The fun times that they had enjoyed together, as they downed a pint or three! Kane was overwhelmed with sadness then as he drove on, realising that there would be no new times now. Only fading, untrustworthy memories, of old and "better" days would remain.

Turning his attention momentarily back to the road ahead, Kane attempted to accelerate. His car needed to climb a steep incline. He was leaving a short stretch of dual carriageway, the factory bypass behind and the road was beginning to narrow, suddenly, dangerously, sharply, from two lanes to one. The run down buildings disappeared as he climbed higher up the hillside, replaced by farmland, and eventually on reaching the summit his car's endeavour was rewarded with a brief but magnificent view of the valley ahead. There, beyond the scruffy roadside boundaries of carbon soiled hedgerows, the landscape burst out wide with open fields stretching away to the right and left. At the far end of the fields, shrub covered hillsides rose up higher still, merging with slopes that became grim dark mountains, which blocked off the main South Wales Valleys to the west. In the east, the pretty rolling hills of Herefordshire were just about visible on the horizon. Then the Mazda began an almost roller coaster like descent, into the twisty, snaking, two way 'A' road and the views were blocked out by taller hedgerows and lumpy, grassy banked hillocks.

Further on the landscape opened out once again. The road ran into a river plain of wide lush green meadows, populated with a smattering of fat grazing, woolly white sheep. Then the

26

road became a straight black tarmac line, running down the centre of the valley. Dead ahead, at the very end of the line, Kane could make out a dull grey mass on the horizon. That was Aberfoist!

'Vroooom!!' The noise was sudden and incredibly loud. It came from nowhere but totally surrounded him. Shocking him to the core. He gripped his steering wheel tightly and instinctively touched his brakes. Checking his mirrors and swerving slightly, he shook internally as a bright green blur tore past him on the outside, his right hand side. Then, it was gone! Instantly, Kane recovered his composure and focused on the motorbike, now so far ahead of him, streaking away towards the town, way way down the road. He cursed the rider under his breath, shaking his head, slowly. Then he remembered. Back in his youth, he may well have done the same thing but not now. Not the sensible Mr Kane! The forty-something! The teacher! The bore!

Glancing up into his rear view mirror, Kane realised that he was still shaking his head in disapproval. He began to laugh at himself. How long had he been such a cautious old fogey. Frank John would have laughed at him too! He would have called his old friend a wimp! Or knowing Frank, Kane thought, he would have called him something much worse! Suddenly Kane was overwhelmed with sadness.

Back in the day, their day, this stretch of road had been infamous locally. All the boy racers knew to watch out for a police speed trap towards the end of the straight. "Dead Man's Straight!" They had called it, as if they were in some American movie. In his mind's eye Kane could still see the traditionally uniformed policeman, the British Bobby, purposely stepping out from behind the cluster of trees, the clump that he himself would see soon enough, way down on the left hand side of this straight road. The officer of the law would raise his right hand and carefully take aim with what was once, allegedly, a hi-tech speed gun and zap the speeding motorists. A few hundred metres further down the road, well it might have been yards back then, a blue and white police car, hidden in the lay-by, just around the bend, would have switched on its flashing lights and sounded it's two tone siren, before either giving chase or more usually ushering the offenders to pull over, and collect their speeding ticket from the navy blue clad constable.

Of course, in the modern era, there would be no Bobbies on this beat, only a large yellow box, containing a camera, stuck high up on a pole, and the ticket would automatically be served by post a few nervous days later. Kane naturally kept his own speed legal. He even slowed down to negotiate the blind bend that some dim-witted planner had inevitably and stupidly retained at the end of such a fast and straight stretch of road. Then his mood lightened and he laughed out loud. Kane could not believe it! The reckless motor-biker had, incredibly, been pulled over.

Standing beside the shocking green coloured machine, the biker appeared to be talking to two uniformed police officers. They were all stood in the very same legendary lay-by. The exact one that the boys in blue had traditionally used to catch Kane and his contemporaries, back when they were not so cool cruisers, tearing around in their parents cars.

Cheerfully motoring passed, Kane caught a glimpse of another man, who was perhaps five or even ten years older than the two young officers, who were already interviewing the still helmeted biker. This man was dressed in civilian clothes, loosely covered by a three quarter length, fawn coloured, MacIntosh coat. He was stood beside the back of the police car, a lighted cigarette in his mouth. There was something oh-so-familiar about that man but Kane was damned if could remember what it was! Perhaps it was merely the fact that this third man was wearing a traditional coat, much beloved by old fashioned TV detectives.

Kane was passed them in that instance and his mind began to concentrate, once more, on the town ahead.

Sometime, since Kane's last visit, the town council had obviously been tempted into trying to regenerate the area, but this had obviously been done on the cheap! A great mound of earth had been dumped strategically to block out the main road's view of the infamous eyesore that was the now dilapidated local bus station. Planted in the mound was an impressive collection of flowers, mainly daffodils, but all in early spring bloom. They attractively spelt out the Welsh word for welcome. "Croeso" might well cheer visitors with its various shades of yellow, green and white, but Kane was certainly surprised that this civic resource had not been fully utilised by locals during the recent Mother's Day celebrations. For a moment he thought that things must be looking up for his old home town. However, the optimism generated by this jolly greeting was sadly short lived, for little else had been done to improve the overall appearance of the town.

The once rather grand three storey Georgian buildings still flanked the road as it entered the town's main shopping centre. However, the upper floors had numerous estate agents' signs posted across their windows, worryingly indicating most dwellings were empty and available for rent. Down at ground floor level, a similar fate had befallen a multitude of retailers. Too many windows were sadly boarded up. Those few shops that appeared open proclaimed themselves as various fast food outlets. Then he saw it! *"The Copper Kettle Tearooms"* was there on his right. To Kane's even greater surprise, the lights were on inside his dead friend's premises. Instinctively, on seeing an available parking space, he immediately pulled over and stopped.

Looking suitably sad and rather lonely, the "Tearooms" appeared to be totally out of time and place in its current location. Possibly that was due to its lack of a "Lease Available" sign. Oddly, the only other shop window, on the whole right side of the street, missing the inevitable sign of the times, was next door. The tattoo parlour did not look open but that was probably because it had a ghastly, black painted frontage. At the heart of this was a large tinted glass display window, featuring the shop's simple pun of a name. "Tat4U" stood out in grotesque, almost dripping blood red lettering.

Kane got out of his car and crossed the road, intending to walk down towards *"The Kettle"* as everyone used to call his friend's café. He knew that he was too early for his promised visit to Wendy and it had always been his custom to call in at *"The Kettle"* every time he was in town, so why should he change the habit of a lifetime, just because he had been told that his friend, the owner, was dead! Then Kane noticed that just ahead of him, two schoolgirls were lingering outside the tattoo parlour.

The girls were taking a great interest in something inside. He assumed tattoo designs must be on display. Kane sighed, wondering if they were going to celebrate the end of term by getting inked. They were of course too young, but when did that stop anyone. At that very moment, the thinner girl was distracted from the window by a bleep from her phone. She said something to her friend, which may have been a yelp or a high pitched curse. He could not tell which! The other girl nodded, clearly understanding the inane statement. Both girls turned, took a few steps down the road and to Kane's utter amazement, they went into the café. Suddenly Kane was unsure what to do next. He did not want to follow those girls through the door. So instead he paused awkwardly and when a car drove passed he quickly pretended to look at the obscene designs, quite blatantly displayed, in the Tattooist's shop window.

More cars passed by, speeding up and down the road and causing Kane to wonder if their drivers happened to look sideways, what would they make of the overweight, middle aged

man, dressed in the smart but casually "uncool" grey Farah
trousers and washed out, once navy coloured, Millet's fleece,
apparently considering getting a tattoo!. They might have said to
themselves: "Poor fellow!" And thought him just some fool
suffering a mid-life crisis! Perhaps they would be right!

Kane could see his reflection in the dark glass of the shop
window. He was not impressed. He looked nothing like he
imagined himself to be. He looked old, tired and fat. The last ten
years of "normal" life had truly taken a toll on him. The life style
he had chosen was meant to be easier but it was not!

To his delight an "OPEN" sign was clearly displayed on the
glass front door of the café next door. A door left invitingly ajar
by the two school girls. Inside the lights were on but strangely it
seemed like nobody was home! Well certainly not in the front
serving area. The girls must have gone straight through to the
back room or so Kane thought as he stared at the empty tables
and chairs, which were still arranged so normally around the
room. There was no sign of mourning. No evidence of tragedy.
Kane even spotted the ornamental copper kettle, still on display
in its usual position, sat on the ledge right in the middle of the
bay front window. He remembered Frank nailing this particular
kettle to the window ledge after a light fingered customer had
made off with the original. Frank had laughed and later told
Kane that he always kept a spare copper kettle in the kitchen, just
in case another thief was successful. Kane had thought that it
was bad luck for the business to lose its emblem. However, he
had been careful not to share his superstition with his old friend.
Now he thought that maybe he should have! Forewarned is
forearmed or so Kane sadly reflected to himself, but now it was
all too late. He sighed and decided that he needed a coffee.

Pushing against the heavy double glazed, mock Georgian
UPVC door, Kane heard the familiar sound of the old tin bell
tinkle as the door opened inwards. The bell tinkled again when

he carefully closed the door shut behind him. Kane called out a faint "Hello" before striding over towards the open archway, on the far right hand side of the cream coloured, wood chip papered, partitioned wall. When he reached the artexed gap Kane was surprised by how dark the back room seemed to be. No lights were on in there but thanks to the natural light, which somehow managed to filter through the small, thickly barred, kitchen window, high up on the wall at the very back of the room, he could just about make out the shadows of a group of people, sat silently in the gloom.

Kane missed the step and stumbled forward, down into the lower level back tearoom. He cursed quietly to himself. Out in the shadows, on the fringes of the room someone chuckled and Kane felt the attention of the dozen or so people already sat in the room focus on him. Blushing slightly, he glanced around. Kane could just about see the oddest assortment of people. All shapes and sizes but really no more than dark outlines, sat on chairs arranged around the edge of the room. All the dining tables had been stacked, against the partition wall, on his left. The arrangement reminded him of a school drama lesson, where the class were perhaps waiting to audition performers for maybe an end of year show. His blush deepened, as he considered himself to have just won the part of class clown!

'What the fuck do you want?' The question was blurted out aggressively by a young man, who was sat immediately to Kane's right. His inquisitor, who could only just be in his twenties, had been almost invisible, because he was dressed all in black. Bewildered by the sudden hostility and momentarily disorientated by his trip, Kane was temporally struck dumb.

'Well?' A long tall man had stood up and was impatiently demanding that Kane answer the youngster's question. This bloke was so tall that he had to hunch to prevent his head touching the low traditional beams on the ceiling. He had a deep dull sounding voice that suitably matched his lofty stature. He was dressed in an identical black fleece and trousers to the younger man. There was a sudden blurred movement to Kane's right. His original interrogator had leapt up and impatiently repeated his question, just as nastily as before.

'Er! Umm!' Kane hesitated again, being equally deep and dull sounding, much to the obvious annoyance of the smaller man, who was now moving far too close for comfort. Kane suddenly heard himself saying: 'I thought you were open! I, er, wanted a coffee!?!'

Well, perhaps he was right! It was certainly much easier than trying to explain the unfathomable real reason of why he had felt obliged to visit.

His simple statement caused a few of the audience to burst out laughing. This seemed to irritate the small man even more. He stepped closer and started to tell Kane that the place was shut, using the broadest and bluntest Anglo Saxon terminology to colour his statement. Perhaps emboldened by his own aggressive language, towards the end of the one way conversation, the small man made the mistake of actually grabbing hold of Kane's right arm, by the wrist, probably with the intention of ushering Kane out.

Unfortunately, instinctively, and certainly without angry intention, Kane reacted. He pulled back for a second and then pushed his arm forward, which added momentum to the force the small man was exerting, as he also instinctively was trying to counter the initial, surprisingly strong, tug away. Then, lightening fast, Kane stepped slightly to the side. Instantly rotating his naturally straightened arm in a wide circular movement, he used the smaller man's force to gain momentum. This resulted in the grabber being rocked backwards and off balance. When Kane twisted his limb away, the aggressor lost his grip and was totally unbalanced. The small man went backwards, quiet dramatically.

This perceived slight caused the immature man to completely lose his temper. He blundered in towards Kane and swung a punch with his right fist at Kane's head. Luckily for Kane, in his haste the small man had not taken care to regain his balance and as Kane was still moving, adjusting from breaking out of the grip, the fist missed its target and smashed straight into the stone archway behind Kane. The contact made a solid and sickening thud against the hard wall. The small man let out a loud, high pitched cry of pain.

The tall man, on seeing and hearing his friend's hurt, gave an angry yell and mindlessly rushed at Kane, who still in shock at the sudden physical aggression, again unthinkingly, evaded the assault by just simply jumping back up onto the step immediately behind him. This left the tall guy grasping thin air at exactly the same moment as the shorter man, blinded by pain, pulled back. Maybe he was attempting to attack the same space where Kane had been stood just seconds before; who knows! The only thing the small man achieved was to barge into the tall man and send him spinning off balance. So much so that the long limbs flapped out and tapped against the first, poorly stacked table. Clumsily, trying to regain his balance, the tall man made a grab for his smaller colleague, with his other hand, hoping for some support but it was all too late!

Nothing seemed to happen at first, and then as if in slow motion, the irresistible laws of physics took over. The tall man fell down, dragging the small man with him. They hit the floor hard. At the same time, all of the tables were also falling over. They began to hit the floor and each other, with ever louder and louder crashes. It was like some oversized Guinness Book of Records, Great Domino Challenge, which had gone horribly and noisily wrong.

As the sound of the multiple impacts died down, the following silence was amplified by an almost audible sense of stunned confusion amongst the other people, those sat around the room. Then, from the back door, a man's voice rang out.

'What the hell is happening in here!?!'

A man had appeared at the back door entrance to the room. He must have been just in time to see the end of the chaos. He was dressed in the same black uniform as the other two. He was angry and his voice shared that rage perfectly with the room, whilst oddly being controlled enough to retain a strange air of authority.

Kane instinctive held his arms up, in a shrug like gesture. This mess was nothing to do with him! Or so he seemed to be indicating from his suddenly smug perch on the higher level, a step up and underneath the archway. Then, despite his shock at being attacked and shouted at, Kane began laughing. He was not laughing just at the chaotic and comedic scene before him. Kane's merriment was because he recognised the new man in black. For here at last, was someone whom he knew. Someone from his past! Someone that he knew only too well! Back in the day! Their days!

Chapter 4: Bad News

Ellis "Flicker" Pace was definitely the man standing at the back door. Never truly a friend, but certainly an old acquaintance. Someone who rarely used a front door, Flicker would always hang around with the young Frank and Mykee, whether they liked it or not, and usually they did not!

Of course both men had changed since the last time they had seen each other. Then it had been no more than a mere nod in recognition of their shared childhood. They had both grown older and heavier. However, Kane would always recognise those icy grey blue eyes. He could never forget them. They were still cold and calculating, and from the way they were nervously lurking like a sly and frightened animal's, a look weirdly magnified by the lens of those black rimmed spectacles, which sat high on the bridge of Pace's snub nose, Kane knew that Pace had not forgotten him.

Noting the paunch that had appeared below the puffed out chest, Kane could not help but breathe in himself. In the absence of a mirror, he briefly allowed himself the delusion that he was lucky; his waistline was not so large. In truth, his broader shoulders and wide legged standing stance meant that Kane did carry his spare tyres better. Pace on the other hand had always suffered from hunching his shoulders. This bad stance had not changed over the years.

Kane also noticed that Pace was wearing the same black uniform as the two slapstick comedians; the instigators of the farcical chaos, which had just unfolded before him. Both the short man and the tall one were now attempting to stagger to their feet. In that instance, Kane made out the wording on their fleeces. It read "Aberfoist Security Services". Maybe it was a release from the stress of being attacked, or simply a consequence of the way they had performed so clumsily around him, but Kane could not help suddenly roaring with laughter, again. His mirth was made all the more uncontrollable, because he had realised that the name, proudly emblazoned on the thugs clothes, could be abbreviated into "ASS"! How apt! Kane reflected to himself. For the Ellis "Flicker" Pace that he used to know was certainly, as the Americans liked to say, one hell of an ASS!

'Flicker!?!' Kane called across the room, albeit in a slightly higher pitched voice than he had originally intended. Familiarity, it seemed, was helping him quash the embarrassment that he had felt, and thanks to his quickly returning wicked sense of humour, Kane now had the bravado to boldly challenge them all, as if he were still the wild and arrogant youth of his past.

'Are these two donkeys with you?' Kane asked his old acquaintance, momentarily deepening his voice, as the two, now shame faced thugs, continued to dust themselves off in front of him, and their suddenly apparent boss. Behind the thin disguise of his sly smile, which had replaced Pace's initial frown, it was the turn of the man by the door to be totally stunned.

In fairness, Ellis "Flicker" Pace did well to compose himself. He had had years of practise. Pace had surveyed the comical scene of tipped tables. He had seen his men rolling on the floor and shared in the shock of the hushed audience, who normally should have added their laughter to Kane's. Yet something odd, fear perhaps, kept them in check. For Kane alone was the only one present who had not suffered from the nasty temperament of the Aberfoist Security Services men.

This shared experience had given those in the shadows better sense than to join in the joke at the expense of the two young thugs now standing in front of them. They knew that the duo might well be asses but they also knew that if given the chance by their unpleasant boss, they could certainly kick like mules. Kane had also picked up on the shadows hesitant body language and nervous demeanour. Pace's presence actually seemed to scare and inhibit the audience, more than his two men had, in spite of his far from intimidating physique. This certainly surprised Kane and as a result his defensive instincts tried to restrain him. The man by the door may have sensed the subtle change in Kane, for he now took the lead, and Kane recognised, much to his surprise, that his old acquaintance seemed to be a lot more confident than he remembered him ever being in their youth.

'Bugger me! My-key Kane is that really you?' Ellis Pace aka Flicker began bullishly. 'My God, but the years haven't been kind to you! Have they!?!' Pace sneered, matter of factly. Just as Kane was building up to reply, "nor to you", the short man interrupted them, his unpleasant young voice full of resentment.

'Fatty here was just leaving, Mr Pace.'

'Really Dylan!?! And what were you doing? Playing a quick game of musical chairs before he went? Or was it musical tables or what?'

A few unwise giggles broke out around the room at the sarcasm. They must have felt it was safe or even political to laugh with Pace. However, they quickly stopped when Pace frowned, and Dylan the short man glanced angrily around the room.

'I've gotta ask, what the fuck are you doing here!?!' Pace began again, almost apologetically, almost jokingly, but still conveying an odd sense of authority in his tone as he stared back towards Kane. Whilst always careful of appearances, internally Pace's initial composure was becoming overwhelmed by irritation, for as he spoke to Kane, his two men moved slightly and almost immediately tripped up again, this time over a fallen table. They regained their balance but only after angrily and clumsily and noisily, slinging the table out of their way, almost hitting a group of four teenage boys, who were sat by where it landed. The boys immediately began to protest with an outburst of four letter words, until Pace, shouted out an angry grunt, which could have been the simple command: 'Shut it!'

Impressed at the young yobs instant compliance, Kane chose to keep his answer simple, for Pace certainly seemed to have an authority in this room. A real presence and one that Kane would have liked to have projected in the "Isolation Room" at his school.

'Well, the sign said "Open!" So in I came for a coffee! Just like I always do when in town, and then Laurel and Hardy here started their nonsense!?!' Kane shrugged casually at the two angry young men. They now stood right in front of him, both obviously seething. The tall man opened his mouth as if he was about to speak. Kane sensed from the puzzled look on his face that he was about to say something back to Kane. Perhaps correcting him that they were not actually called Laurel or Hardy, but then the tall man stopped himself, just as if he could not find the right words to express his true feelings. This just made him look even more puzzled than before. Kane in turn, simply tried to look hurt and disappointed, owning his role as victim of their previous attack. The short man, Dylan, then growled something, which was difficult to make out. It may well have been along the lines of let me finish him! Pace completely ignored it. Kane chose to ignore the short man too. He did not really want to provoke further violence. He knew that he had been lucky before. He was unlikely to take the fit looking, much younger men, by surprise a second time. Then again, Kane knew that he had always seemed to be lucky in physical incidents like that one. It was perhaps one of the strangest things about him.

Pace barked an order, loudly telling his men to leave the tables alone and "for fuck's sake, just sit down!" Internally Pace was wondering if it was possible that Kane had not actually heard about Frank John's death. Although sensing that the danger might be passing, Kane still kept a loose guard up, whilst studying the changing reaction on the face of his old acquaintance. Pace had surprisingly paled slightly. The "Flicker" that Kane remembered had never been one to hide his emotions and now he was showing that he had thought of something, something that had unsettled him.

Pace had heard the talk about Kane maturing, settling down, getting married, having a family. Someone had said to him once, somewhere, sometime, that Kane was a school teacher now! Pace could not imagine that! Not the "Mad Mykee" he used to know! Not these days! What with the amount of abuse teachers were meant to endure in modern schools. Mad "Mykee" Kane was not the type of bloke to take abuse without reacting. Pace remembered him as the lad who would suddenly fly off the handle for the slightest thing. Someone who took offence easily, and Pace only had to look around him at the smashed and up turned tables to know that the destructive part of Kane was probably still true. God help you if you mispronounced his name back then. My-Key! Then again, Pace studied the forty-something man in front of him. Had his contemporary really gone as soft as he looked. Pace hoped he had! Yet, all these years later, a significant part of Pace's devious mind, was still scared of Mykee Kane. He was also worried about telling this now seemingly docile looking man, standing almost sheepishly in front of him, the bad news.

Then again, the other part of Pace, the overtly sly part, doubted this sudden appearance was a coincidence. Pace struggled to work out the best angle for him to deal with the threat he instinctively felt. The threat that Frank John's oldest, and allegedly best friend, could present to him and his new business venture. He decided, like Kane had, that caution was the best policy, at least for now. They were after all old friends, even though they had had their disagreements in the past. Now was not the time for Pace to take revenge for the slights he felt that he had suffered at the hands at the young Mad Mykee Kane. Maybe, Pace hoped, that time would come. Pace slowly let his tongue lick over his upper lip. By the time it had finished its journey, he had chosen his course of action.

'You haven't heard then?' Pace began softly, slowly scratching the back of his head, as he tried to look amicably puzzled. Then equally casually, Pace began to move slowly across the room towards Kane.

'Heard what?' Kane asked, determined to look even more confused than before.

'Hmm. It shouldn't really be me to tell you the bad news but ...' Pace hesitated, sounding almost compassionate, or as compassionate as his flat monotone voice allowed him to be. Kane listened quietly but his eyes followed the cold blue grey leer as Pace glanced over and up to an old oak beam, which lent atmosphere to the otherwise drab café. Both pairs of eyes followed the broad oak as it ran along the ceiling until, just above the whitewashed step, where Kane was now standing, it sagged slightly to leave enough of a gap between the wood and the plaster ceiling for a hand or a thick rope to run through. Without looking away from the bowed bow Pace spoke again. This time his voice was even quieter.

'Come on; let's go into the front so that I can tell you in private! Away from this gormless lot eh!' Pace suggested, finally meeting Kane eye to eye as he finished speaking. Kane shivered slightly as the cold eyes looked into his. He gave the dimly lit back-room and the odd assortment of people who sat there one last glance, before nodding slowly.

41

'Okay.' Kane said, still trying his best to look and sound innocently puzzled. He stepped back, away from the darkness, into the contrasting warm glow of the neon lit frontage and Pace moved slowly after him.

'So come on, tell me what's this bad news then Flicker?' Kane asked trying to sound as matey as possible, whilst at the same time being seriously intrigued, even though he suspected that he already knew what the bad news was going to be.

'You might want to sit down!' Ellis "Flicker" Pace suggested, almost kindly but though the gritted teeth, which were betraying his obvious irritation at the constant use of his old nickname.

'No, it's okay "Flicker!" Spit it out!'

Kane knew that he had always had a nasty side to his personality. He was normally quiet good at hiding it, or so he thought, but he could not resist the temptation to wind up his old acquaintance, even though the sensible part of his brain was warning him not to. Kane knew very well how much the young Pace had hated the nickname. It was a moniker that Frank John had given him. It was a name that had stuck throughout "Flicker's" formative years. However, a delayed anger at the unnecessary reactions of Pace's apparent minions, was building inside of Kane, who knew he had to vent his natural mean streak in some way or risk losing the control that had taken him years to master. Kane also resented the fact that Flicker knew more about his "best" friend's demise than he did. Kane remembered Wendy John's words. Those said on the all too brief phone call. The one he had received earlier that day. What was it that she had said exactly? "He killed himself in that bloody cafe' of his!"

'Er... ...' Pace paused. Then trying to sound all reasonable and businesslike, he blustered on. 'Look no one calls me "Flicker" anymore! And I'd be grateful if you didn't either!'

'That's not your "bad news" is it?' Kane felt a surge of anger, which matched a glint in the otherwise cold eyes that stared back at him. Pace almost triumphantly spat out the next words.

'He's dead.'

'Who?' Kane acted dumb.

'Frank!'

Kane could see a spark of resentment flash across Pace's eyes. He hoped that Flicker could not see the same in his own. Kane tried his very best to give, what he hoped, was a look of total surprise.

'Frank?' Kane said again, as a stupid, needless question.

'Yes Frank John!' Ellis "Flicker" Pace almost sneered when he said the full name. Then, feeling he needed to add more, Pace started to explain in a very matter of fact tone. 'He sold the business, to provide for his kids, I guess, and then let himself back in, and ...' Pace paused, before triumphantly continuing with the words 'hung himself!'

'What!?!' Kane found it easy to look shocked now. He had known that his old friend was dead. He had looked up at the beam and kind of knew in that instant, but to hear how Frank had killed himself, for it to be spoken out loud, the fact that his friend had hung himself. That statement was unbelievable. Kane reacted instinctively. Rather too quickly, too naturally, as his mind replayed Pace's reactions and behaviour. The leer upwards, just before the declaration. It was as if Pace was seeing Frank's body actually hanging from the beam.

'From that beam!?!' Kane's eyes looked passed Pace and back to the passage. 'The one you were looking up at just now?' Pace was studying Kane's reaction. Doing what he did instinctively. Pace was coldly calculating once again. Wondering if he was just telling Kane old news or simply telling him too much! At the same time, Pace was also still trying to work out why Kane had just walked into the tearooms and caused chaos. Why now? Why when Pace had such an important meeting to prepare for!

Pace quickly concluded that there was indeed genuine shock, and grief, in those blue eyes. The ones that were now staring back at him, questioningly. Under their strong gaze, Pace felt that he had to continue talking. So, determined to own the situation, as best he could, Pace carried on. 'Yes! So I'm told! You spotted that eh!'

Kane had a load of questions. All were spinning around in his head. All at once, but he forced himself to stay silent and listen to what Pace was actually saying. Listen to the clues! He told himself.

'I'm finding it hard to believe myself too My-key! That a hard man like Frank, the Frank we both knew, could just give up and do what he did to himself! But he'd changed My-key! He wasn't the man we knew! Not at the end!' Pace shrugged in apparent disbelief. They were both putting on a good show. 'My firm, Aberfoist Security Services, has the contract to look after this place. After Frankie sold it, of course, I was working with the new owner.' Kane could not help but wonder why Pace had added the "of course" but he managed to resist asking directly. 'In fact, I'm responsible for the whole block now!' Pace continued way too proudly. 'Anyway, my men came in,' Pace paused for effect. 'Just to inspect the premises last week, you know! And they found him, swinging, in there!' Pace gestured behind him, with an unfortunate jerk of his head. 'Dead! Nothing we could do but call the cops!'

'Dead!' Kane repeated softly.

Chapter 5: More Bad News

'So Little and Large found him!?!' Kane grimaced. At that moment his emotions got the better of him and he found it impossible to stop his irrational anger spilling out in childish name calling and he would have called the two clowns "Abbot and Costello" next if Pace had not cautioned him.

'Be careful taking the piss out of those two My-key! They can be more trouble than I expect you're used to nowadays!' Pace had been looking Kane up and down again, noting the changes time had made in his old acquaintance. Although still cautious of the much softer looking man than the hard nut that he had known in his youth, Pace had spoken with his habitual sneer. He was also unable to resist adding an unnecessary snipe at Kane. 'Those school dinners haven't done you any favours mate! And I think it's fair to say you've upset our young Dylan! So take care, mate!'

Kane shrugged as if he wasn't really bothered. Pace shrugged back likewise, before adding: 'He can be a really wild one!' The cold grey eyes glinted. 'That's Dylan Francis!'

Kane was not sure whether Pace had intended to sound as sarcastic as he did. Was the small man really more dangerous than he looked? Pace continued and Kane listened, with growing irritation. 'You know how they are at his age, don't you! I'm his boss and I like to think a bit of a mentor to him!' Pace allowed himself a smug smile. 'But there's only so much I can do!'

'Oh yes, I've always suspected that of you, Flick, er, Ellis!' Kane agreed sarcastically because Pace was busy reminding him why he had never really liked Ellis "Flicker" Pace. The contradictory self-effacing boasting, the snide, obvious digs, but Kane's instinct was to stop bickering. Polite patience might produce more useful information from an overconfident Pace. Kane was sure that Pace had just said "we" whereas before he had been careful to say that his men had found Frank, implying that he was not there! Given the bad blood, which Kane knew only too well had existed between Pace and Frank John, Kane could not believe that the old "Flicker" Pace, the small minded youth whom he had known, would have passed up the chance to gloat over his childhood rival.

Then, all of a sudden, Kane was absorbed by the imagery of the short man crudely laughing at the swinging body of his friend. Yes that's right, Kane told himself, "Flicker" Pace had stressed that the less than dynamic duo had found Frank, not hanging but "swinging" there! Inevitably another surge of anger took over Kane and he spat out his own taunt in unnecessary retaliation.

'Dull-one in there will get over me but he won't get over being an ASS will he!

'Oh very good My-key! I forgot that's the Welsh way of saying Dylan! I like that! Dull-ann! Dull-one! Very apt! I think I'll use that myself! It really sums up that little tool! Especially at er times like this!' Pace actually chuckled. Although he thought to himself that tools can be usefully if you know how to use them properly. Then with a real, surprisingly sharp, edge to his voice, he added: 'You and Frankie have always had a way with nicknames eh! My-key! Never gave one to yourselves though, did you!'

'Why did Frank do it?' Kane asked, ignoring Pace's implications.

'How the hell should I know!?!' Pace had not really intended to sound so angry and quickly shrugged, adding an insincere sympathetic smile for good measure.

'You two never got on really, did you?' Kane attempted to provoke a little more from Pace.

'He never respected me!' Pace said quickly and bitterly. 'But I tried to be a good friend.'

'Why?'

Pace thought for a moment and then said quietly without a hint of irony: 'Because I liked him in spite everything! He was old school, hard, yeah that was Frankie!'

The pale pink tongue flicked across the upper lip as if comforting the speaker or attempting to wipe away any trace of sincerity that might be left behind on the lips as they instinctively curled back into an unpleasant sneer.

'No, I meant why didn't he get on with you Flic – er sorry!' Kane tried hard to "play" nice now. He wanted to keep Pace chatty. He wanted to find out as much as he could from the man.

'Frankie never respected my "achievements". Since you left town I've built up a number of successful businesses. People depend on me. Frankie didn't like that! He soon found out, running a business these days is tough.'

'Running an "honest" business is even tougher!'

Pace pulled an even weirder face than normal. His cheeks reddened, the cold grey eyes narrowed, then just as quickly he regained control and his lips broke into a thin insincere smile.

'Now, now, that's uncalled for My-key! I run "legitimate" businesses. Nowadays!' Pace's tongue slipped out of the side of his mouth and flicked quickly over his upper lip. This time it left a glistening trail across the thin pale pink flesh.

'Security?' Kane suggested.

'Yes!' Pace nodded. 'Amongst other things!' He allowed himself another sly smile. 'You've seen the street outside. Most things are closed down out there. Empty buildings need protecting!'

'How does an arsonist get away with running a security business then?' Kane asked harshly.

Pace actually looked hurt and snapped back that "that" was a long time ago!

'You of all people should know, we made mistakes when we were kids!' A more thoughtful Pace added.

'Yeah, sorry, perhaps "that" was uncalled for; I've been away a long time.' Kane replied insincerely.

'Why are you back now then? It's a long way for a coffee?' The cold grey eyes narrowed into slits again.

'Believe it or not just visiting old friends!'

'That's nice!' Pace said sarcastically.

'It would be if they weren't dead!' Kane responded menacingly. He had heard those words somewhere before but could not place where, maybe in a film. Pace obviously did not like them. He had no come back. They both paused for a moment or two and looked each other up and down.

'What's going on in there then?' Kane broke the silence first, gesturing to the back room with a slight forward nod of his head.

The colour drained momentarily from Pace's face and his upper lip twitched slightly. Kane could almost hear the cogs whirling in Pace's head, as he thought long and hard before suddenly smiling.

'Job interviews!' Pace then added confidently: 'Fancy working in a Kebab Shop?'

'There are worse things!' Kane grimaced in reply. 'You running a recruitment company as well as your security firm then?'

Pace tried to look thoughtful for a moment.

'Not a bad idea!' He agreed but then shook his head.

'No the new owner asked me to open up and then texted to say he was running late! He wants to recruit some local staff. Clever really! He could've just brought in a load of workers from his other outlets; you know what these foreigners are like! Half his staff are related!'

'Foreign is he?' Kane asked.

'Yeah a Paki!' Pace said casually, showing a total lack of awareness that such a simple description might offend his client. 'They all are nowadays! Well at least the ones who make money from fast food anyway!'

'Frank must've hated that?' Kane suggested.

'Hated what?' Pace tried to look confused. He did not have to try that hard.

'Selling to a foreigner!' Kane explained.

'Yeah! He hadn't changed that much! He was always racist! Not into diversity like me!' Pace laughed.

Kane thought about defending his dead friend but had to let that dig go.

'What you gonna do now?' Pace asked, almost convincing Kane that he was interested?

'Oh I'd better go and see Wendy; she must have taken the suicide badly!'

Pace looked at him oddly; once again the cogs were whirling in his head. 'You don't know do you?' Pace began, fighting back another involuntary smirk.

'Know what this time?' Kane was truly irritated now.

'They split up!' Pace was almost jubilant as he shared this latest tit bit. He even licked both his lips as he savoured the obvious confusion on Kane's face, but Pace thought better than to laugh. Not at Mykee Kane. However soft Kane appeared to have become, Pace was really very aware that, despite what he had said, this "soft" Mykee Kane had made short work of a challenge from two of his best men.

'When was the last time you saw them together?' Pace asked instead, which to Kane was an equally cutting put down. A wave of guilt washed over Kane but before he could answer there was a shout from the back room. Someone was calling for 'Mr Pace!' The tall guy ducked his head under the archway. He had a rather nervous expression on his otherwise plain and simple face.

'Mr Pace! Mr Pace! Mr Lord's here!' He said.

'Thank you Dai.' The boss replied, suddenly allowing the annoyance that had been probably bubbling under the surface throughout his whole conversation with Kane to show clearly on his face. 'I'll be there now!' Pace spat out, before regaining control of his cool and turning back to face Kane. He gave him an almost genuine smile.

'I've gotta go! My most important client is here. Good luck with Wendy!' He winked and turned to go into the back room but suddenly stopped and turning around again, Pace reached into his fleece pocket. He produced a crisp white business card and held it out for Kane to take.

'Here's my number, give me a ring and we can have a chat about all this! Properly!' The cold eyes fixed on Kane's. 'And catch up on old times eh! I'll tell you my rags to riches story if you like, eh!' He gave Kane another wink. Kane took the card. Pace turned and disappeared down into the dimness of the back room.

Kane could hear Pace shout: 'Someone turn the lights on, for fuck's sake!'

For some unexplainable reason Kane followed Pace back through, stopping at the step, just in time to see Pace regain his balance after obviously miss timing the drop down to the lower level. He was now muttering something rude under his breath, as he tried, once again, to regain his composure.

Kane called out a polite but unconvincing:

'Thank you, Ellis, why not! I'll give you a ring! Cheerio!'

Kane then took a long last look into the back room, as the light came on and illuminated the previously shadowy gathering. Scanning the faces of the prospective kebab shop workers, Kane concluded that they looked like a motley crew of ne'er-do-wells, who would need an awful lot of training, particularly on hygiene standards!

Apart from Pace, the two silly school girls and the hate filled face of Dull-ann the Dull-one, and his partner, the blank expressionless tall Dai, there was only one other person that Kane vaguely recognised. It was the figure now standing by the back door. Tall and broad, wearing the bright green motorcyclist leathers! It was the biker! The one Kane had seen on the road to Aberfoist. He still wore a crash helmet but he had to be the reckless rider who had shot past Kane. The helmet visor was up now and Kane could see the facial features of a strong looking, dark skinned, possibly thirty-something, bearded man. So this was the new owner of The Copper Kettle Tearooms. A Pakistani motor biker!

In his hands the man held a sizeable, double pouched, black leather motorbike saddle bag. It seemed stuffed full, with odd shaped bulges in the tight leather. The man was looking around the room, frowning at the people present. He stopped to stare at the smattering of tables, still lying untidily about the floor. He took in little Dylan sat on a chair, obviously sulking and nursing his hand, the one that he had punched into the wall. Kane took pleasure in seeing the Dull-one's suffering. The biker looked beyond the approaching Ellis "Flicker" Pace, and Kane suddenly felt uneasy, as the dark eyes bore into him. Before the biker could say anything Kane heard Pace start a new charm offensive, greeting the biker, whom he seemed to be calling Mr Lord.

For a moment Kane thought that the biker's Anglophile name was a bit of an oddity. He had come across many men from the Asian sub-continent, whose native names roughly translated into the equivalent of Lord, King or ruler. He wondered whether the biker's family had simply adopted the English version of their family name, perhaps when they first arrived in the UK. The tall man had the bearing of someone of authority. Indeed not everyone could carry off lime green leathers!

Then Kane realised other eyes were on him. Pretty much all those gathered in the back room were looking directly at him. He sensed their curiosity at this strange man, who had blundered into their gathering, and caused chaos. A man who actually called Mr Pace by his first name and a man who had been brave or even foolish enough to call Mr Pace: "Flicker!" Pace must have realised this too. Briefly breaking off from his ostentatious greeting, Pace called out by first name to his taller employee, who hovered nearby.

'Dai, show my good friend My-Key out, and try not to knock anything else over eh! Alright?'

Tall Dai grunted by way of an acknowledgement.

Pace then added quickly. 'And make sure no other mistaken "customers" arrive to disturb our business with Mr Lord eh! Lock the fucking front door! Alright!'

With a quick but poignant look up at the exposed beam and one more glance around the room, which ended with him briefly returning the stare into Lord's now seemingly angry eyes, Kane backed out and left whilst he still could.

Tall Dai followed him to the front door, all the while maintaining a surprisingly respectful distance, given his size and earlier aggression. It was as if Tall Dai had forgotten his animosity as soon as his boss had given him the job of escort. He was simply trying to be a good escort.

Once safely outside on the seemingly deserted street, Kane turned around to look back at the tearooms. He saw the tall man staring blankly out at him, his face slightly distorted by the small glass squares created by the white criss-cross UPVC lining that ran through the window. Then Tall Dai, without any change of expression, reached out and slowly, purposefully, turned the

"OPEN" shop sign over to "CLOSED". He appeared to flick the latch, locking the door shut. Tall Dai was still standing there, impassively on guard, when Kane decided he had seen enough. Kane turned away and began the walk back up to his car.

Chapter 6: A Not So Brief Encounter

Five minutes after leaving the "Kettle" a rather perplexed Kane was stood outside the once familiar terraced house in Union Road. This was where he expected to find Wendy John. This was the home Frank had bought when he married Wendy and as far as Kane was aware until earlier that day, had lived happily ever after. However, when Kane tapped gently on the frosted heart shaped glass panel at the centre of the mock oak composite front door, he was taken aback to see a very different "old friend" answer it. He recognised her instantly. Even after all those years. Yet Kane tried hard not to show his surprise, mainly because he was embarrassed that she might mistake a look of shock on his face for an unkind reaction to the fact that her instantly recognisable and still pretty face was now so unexpectedly morphed onto such a grossly obese middle aged body.

Sue Ward-Davies, sounded exactly the same as she had decades ago. She giggled his name out in an over the top greeting. Her high pitched, girlie sing song, voice, which many might have assumed was a false put on affectation, had not changed since her teenage years. Then she coyly smiled at him. Oddly not shocked but seemingly simply bemused by his sudden reappearance after so many years. At the same time her sparkling hazel brown eyes grew large in an almost creepy, lustful look. A stare that uncomfortably reminded Kane of the way the young Sue's mother, the vivacious Mrs Davies, had looked at the young, much slimmer and fitter Kane, on the very few occasions, when he had been brave enough to call on Sue, back in the days when they dated, albeit briefly, during the first term of their Lower Sixth year at Aberfoist Comprehensive School.

'So what brings you to my door stranger?' She joked. 'You know I'm married to Griz now!' She added, rather too coquettishly for someone of her age and shape, rolling her cat like eyes, still bright and interested, under the colourful eye shadow of her heavily made up lids. Her many chins then wobbled uncontrollably, as she laughed out loud, because she had added, tartly: 'Mind you, he's working away all this week!'

Kane remembered Ben "Griz" Ward, mainly from their days together in the school rugby team. They had played, not surprisingly given their common stocky shape, as prop forwards, but Griz, short for Grizzly Bear, a nickname that suited the extremely hirsute young Ben in more ways than one, had not only physically but also mentally matured earlier than Kane, and therefore had excelled at the casual violence required of the front row. Accordingly he was quickly elevated to a regular slot in the first fifteen, whilst Kane who had, back then, been far too fair minded (and soft) to claw eyes and chew ears, was quickly dropped from the squad. Kane also recalled that Griz had been obsessed with lorries in his youth, and had got his HGV licence as soon as he could. For that reason alone, Kane assumed from what Sue said, that Griz was on a long continental road trip. Kane had a vague memory of meeting the older Griz Ward in a local pub, probably ten or maybe even fifteen years ago and being painfully polite as he endured graphic tall tales of female hitch hikers, who were allegedly prepared to do anything, absolutely anything, for a ride. For some bizarre reason, Kane also recalled Griz obsessing about the amazing fact that the toilets at German service stations were undoubtedly the cleanest in all of Europe!

There was no need for Kane to wonder what Sue now did for a living. She was dressed in green scrubs, the baggy and fortunately shapeless modern health-worker's uniform. The name of the local hospital was printed in white lettering across her bulging left breast. Sue frowned when Kane explained that he had actually come to see Wendy John. With a disappointed sigh, she patiently began what sounded like a well-rehearsed tale about "The Johns!" They had "moved" years ago. They had had to "sell" the house to fund the "business" and Wendy now had a "flat" up on the "council" estate. It was a terrible thing, Sue went on to say, her chubby fingers forming exclamation marks as she squeaked what she deemed to be "key words" throughout her story.

'Losing this house, their marriage, then the business, forced to "sell" they was, and of course now he's "lost" his life. It was a "terrible thing" but "perhaps" no surprise really. He was a "terribly proud" man and wouldn't "listen" to "reason" see! Poor Wendy, she still "loved" him you know! I was on duty the night they "brought" him in. Oh the bruises My-key! It was "awful" and not where you'd really expect them, you know, like not just around the neck! Mind you, he'd had a "load of accidents", even scalded himself with hot water! He had! That must've set him off "thinking" you know, if he couldn't use a kettle anymore what "future" for him! I guess! Not that I know like see, just "speculating" I am!'

One thing about Sue Ward-Davies, that hadn't changed, was her ability to talk. There on the doorstep of the Union Road house, she updated Kane with all the gossip he needed to know and much of what he did not need to know. She told him of Frank's boy's "drug" addiction! Griz found loads of "seeds and stuff" behind the skirting boards when he was decorating the back bedroom! She told him of how the girl fancied herself as a model, but frankly she had not got "it" really.

56

'Honestly I'd have more chance!' Sue had rolled her eyes again and then looked extremely hurt when Kane did not jump in to disagree with her!

She went on to tell Kane how Frank had gone "mad" and slapped "Flicker" Pace about one night because he'd heard that Flicker had offered Jan a "session" at his wife's photo studio. She continued, telling Kane all about how Flicker was "well known" for his side line in making porn.

'Uploads dodgy movies online or so Griz tells me!' She winked. Suddenly she remembered the time and screeched out in a panic. 'Oh Christ, I gotta go! I'll be late for my shift! Look pop round anytime. I'd "love" to catch up!' She gave him another wink before adding with a smirk: 'I bet we could make Griz jealous eh! Mind you, he'd have a "laugh" seeing you again.' Then suddenly she squeezed up her face into a puzzled expression. 'You teaching ain't you or something!?!'

Kane nodded, sadly, but before he could say anything more she blurted out the usual, almost inevitable comments, the clichés that he dreaded, when forced into mentioning his current profession.

'I don't know how you "do" that job! Kids these days!'

'Nor do I!?!' He smiled back at her adding heroically: 'Not all the kids are as bad as we were!'

She shook her head disbelievingly. 'My three were monsters! At least they're not so "bad" now they're grown up.'

Kane wondered how old her children could actually be! Doing the maths he thought the oldest could only be in their late teens. Maybe early twenties! Fortunately, before he could challenge her on that point, she sighed and began telling him that whilst this was lovely "and all that" she really had to get to work!

He suddenly remembered to ask her for Wendy's actual address. She hesitated and looked nervous.

'I got it written down somewhere, you know to send on her post like! We don't normally give it out! You wouldn't believe the number of "people" who came knocking after we first bought the house! You know like "bailiffs" and all that! No wonder they split up! I couldn't live like that! Could you!?!' Sue suddenly looked horrified, as what she had said dawned on her. Tears actually welled up in her eyes. 'Oh it was horrible, you know, what happened to him My-key! Poor Frankie!' She began to dab at her eyes with her swollen and stubby fingers.

'I reckon it was "the debts" that made him do it! They brought him in on my shift! I had to prepare the body for the post mortem, you know! I reckon he had been beaten up by bloody debt collectors. There were lots of bruises! You know!'

Kane flushed slightly, equally at her tears and at what she was telling him. He also wondered whether he should tell her that she was repeating herself. Each time she told him about the state that Frank was in, his blood began to boil! Inside he was raging at the thought of someone assaulting his old mate! They would never have got away with it before his disability.

'Who could've done that to Frank!?!' He eventually managed to ask her, when she stopped to breath.

'Oh My-key! Frank had changed; he wasn't as "hard" as when you knew 'im! You know, what with his injury and all that happened with the kids and the business!'

That hurt! *"When you knew him!"* Kane had ignored his old friends for too long. Somehow happy in the blissful ignorance that they were bound to be so much better off than him, still living in their home town, happily running their own business, he had conveniently lost touch with them.

'Oh I dunno but I hear things! That Flicker employs some right nasty people! He does!'

'Flicker!' The disbelief sounded in his voice.

'Oh yes! He's changed a lot too! Don't be fooled! Fingers in lot's of pies that one! He runs a loan shark business or so I'm told, like, by some of the other nurses, the younger ones, the silly ones!' She said without any sense of irony. 'They thinks he's harmless, they do! Lends them money and writes it off in exchange for, er, shall we say "favours" if you know what I mean! He fools some of 'em into thinking they can be models too!'

'Really!' Kane could not help but register his utter disbelief at the thought of his old acquaintance, the man he had just met again after so long, passing himself off as a "connected" fashion agent.

Sue Ward-Davies rolled her now suddenly dry eyes, comically giving him a look that with the mascara runs that had drizzled down her puffy cheeks was nothing less than weird.

'One of the younger girls even got the sack, like, after a "video" she made for Flicker found it's way onto the porters phones. Stupid girl! She wore her "actual" nurse's uniform! And name badge too! Well, kind of! She didn't have it on for long! You know what I mean! Oh no! I really shouldn't have said that!' She laughed.

Kane shock his head, partly trying to reassure her that it was alright to say these things to him and partly in incredulity at what she was saying. Of course, as he then went on to tell her, it really should not be a surprise to him, for as a teacher, the problems he had experienced in school, with girls, and boys "sexting" each other, then sharing the explicit pictures to all and sundry, caused no end of trouble!

'Oh they're all at "it" now!' Sue shrugged. 'We were so lucky back in our day! Polaroid's were crap weren't they! Mind you, My-key! I wouldn't mind having a few pictures of me and you back in the day, just to prove we weren't always past it eh!' She winked at him once more.

He actually blushed but resisted saying the naïve words *speak for yourself*, which were actually on the tip of his sadly deluded tongue.

'No, you remember what Flicker was like!' She continued, without a breather.

'We've had a lot of blokes down at A&E, who've suffered burns. I know we always get a lot but these guys are well, like, all on benefits and well, like, they can't explain why they burnt themselves or if they do, their story keeps like changing! One of the young doctors kept a file on it for a while, but, like, nobody was really like interested. Flicker, 'e's got a lot of "friends" on the police nowadays!'

Eventually, Sue Ward-Davies remembered, once again, that she had to: 'Bloody well get to work!'

She disappeared back into the house, shutting the door on him, despite their apparent intimacy, leaving him standing on the street alone. Although he was not really out there on his own. Kane saw the net curtains on next door's house twitch a couple of times whilst he waited and sensed more than one pair of eyes was now watching him. There was definitely a shadow behind the nets on the upstairs window of the house opposite. No doubt they were all eagerly compiling their own reports to present to Griz, when he returned from his travels; reports all about the strange man who called on his ever so "attractive" wife.

After an age, Sue reappeared, her make up suitably refreshed. She was carrying an immaculate Waitrose Supermarket plastic "bag for life" that was stuffed full with various biscuit packets, of all shapes and sizes.

'Not for me! They're for the girls on the shift!' She exclaimed when she saw him looking. 'I'm on a diet!' Or so she lied, as if trying to reassure herself. She then presented him with Wendy John's new address, scribbled onto the back of a torn envelope.

Sue opened her arms wide and he felt obliged to submit himself to a hug. She squeezed him tightly into her well cushioned body, so hard that he almost choked in the process, not from her grip, which was surprisingly strong, nor the smothering effect of the huge soft pillows that were her breasts, but the chemical attack that was the overwhelming scent of her cheap perfume. She sighed, when she finally had to let him go, and he stepped back, dizzy from the fumes.

'Oh it's so nice to see you, My-key! You're looking, well!' He could see her doubting that statement. 'I like a man with a bit of meat on him!' She added, as if to make up for her previous hesitation. He was not flattered but uttered a vague false promise that he would call round again. He added, loudly, especially for the neighbours' benefit; "when Griz is back!" She sniffed, fighting back more overly dramatic tears, before sighing once again, that it was all so sad!

'Give Wendy our love! Tell her if there's "anything" we can do, just ask, eh!'

Kane then watched her scurry away up the street. She was almost a green blur! He was relieved to see her go and more than a little amazed at how fast she could actually move, being the size that she was! He paused for a moment trying to absorb all the things she had said. Sue Ward-Davies always exaggerated. He had always known that. She had always told him how much she had "loved" him, when they dated, but he found out later that she had been seeing other boys at the same time as him. Apparently once she had gone to the cinema three times in the same week to "see" the same movie but with a different boy each time. Once with him and then the other times with two older, more worldly, boys! He wondered if she had changed now that she was "grown" up! He doubted it, what with Griz working away so regularly. Then he remembered the neighbours and retreated back down the road to where he had parked his car. It was just outside a shabby looking house, which was in a real need of painting. There was a large "For Sale BY AUCTION" sign fixed to it. When he drove away, a few more net curtains moved. The neighbourhood watch was certainly proficient in Union Road.

Chapter 7: Bitter Regrets

Wendy John sat slumped in a tall backed armchair, which stood stiffly upright in the middle of her rented flat's open plan living room. The chair's faded yellow plaid patterned weave was stretched thin over the upholstery, yet unlike the other simple but functional furniture, it indicated an uncharacteristic and out of place indulgence.

Everything else in the flat was functional but looked like she did, a little bit tired and sad. Just behind her, a small rough pine dining table had been pushed right up against the magnolia painted plasterboard wall. Three simple pine chairs were neatly tucked in at each of the table's three open sides. Three plastic coated floral placemats had been arranged neatly on the table, with three matching coasters and three basic sets of plain stainless steel cutlery beside them. All were ominously laid out in anticipation of the reduced family's evening meal.

Kane had smelt the overwhelming aroma of warm cheese and garlic, as soon as he had entered the flat. There was also the faint purr of an electric fan oven coming from just around the corner, out of sight, in what he assumed must have been the kitchen area of the squat L-shaped room. This all indicated to him that whatever was baking in the oven was almost ready and his visit was not expected to be a long one. Accordingly, he was now perched uncomfortably on a worn two seat, brown faux leather sofa, approximately ninety degrees to Wendy's right hand side. He sipped carefully at the chipped white china mug, full of boiling hot milky coffee, held uneasily by his right hand. She had presented him with the drink, as soon as he had arrived at the flat, in a scene almost reminiscent of the occasions when he had visited her and Frank down at *"The Kettle"* in happier times. However, there had been no other warm greeting and she had quickly retreated to the sanctuary of her chair, after the briefest acknowledgement that he need not have come so far.

In the awkward silences that regularly broke out between them, they both stared blankly at the large flat screened TV, which hung on the wall directly in front of her. A cheery early evening quiz was beaming out. Its bright colours illuminating the unlit room as outside the late afternoon dulled into evening. The sound had been muted when he had arrived but the set had not been turned off. Onscreen the smiley faces of the familiar looking host and supposedly celebrity contestants, contrasted dramatically with the pale looks on the faces inside the flat.

Once again Kane had been surprised. Here was yet another old friend, someone he thought he knew well, but someone who had changed almost beyond recognition since the last time he had seen them. It must have been at least five years ago, but in truth he could not recall their last meeting or his last conversation with her. To his horror, at some stage during that gap, Wendy John had cut her stunning long red hair into a short messy multi layered bob and worst of all, in his biased opinion, dyed it jet black. Her once strong athletic body now looked thin and frail. She had never been a girlie girl but neither had she been a true tom boy. Wendy just tended to dress casually and Kane was slightly relieved to see that her dress code had not changed as drastically as her hairstyle. Today she wore her usual uniform of faded jeans, a plain T-shirt, (today's was pink), and perhaps in a nod to the coolness of the spring that year, a pale blue cardigan, which was carelessly unbuttoned above the waist. On her feet, Wendy still wore her dirty brown, sheep skin fleeced, slippers. He had remembered as soon as he had seen them, that she had practically lived in them from the moment Frank had bought them for her. Kane had never liked them. He had thought they made her look common and to him she had been far from common. Nevertheless, he had always teased her, calling them "Granny Slippers" but she had insisted, with a determined glint in her eyes, that they were warm and comfortable, like her smile.

However, the Wendy of the present did not smile. She also now wore spectacles. A rather stern bright blue rimmed pair. Their hint of blue tint served only to neutralise her once vibrant green eyes. In spite of the tint, he could see that behind the dust speckled, greasy finger marked, lenses, her eyes were puffy and raw. He assumed this was the result of her constantly wiping away the tears. No doubt she wept for her late "estranged" husband but then again, the Wendy he knew in the past had been as hard as nails, and always kept her emotions in check. She had been so practical in dealing with all that life had thrown at her. She had had to be, being married to Frank John.

This new Wendy seemed to weep at anything. She had not smiled when she first saw him; instead she looked ready to cry. She had seemed settled when she gave him his coffee and first sat down, but she began to cry, with frustration perhaps, when she could not find the TV remote controller. The little things seemed to get to her. She had muttered, whilst fighting back the tears that she never learnt to use "the bloody thing" properly as "Frank always had it!" Then she had laughed out loud, a terrible demented laugh, when she finally found the device. It was in the kitchen! To his surprise, after all the fuss she made looking for the damn thing, she did not use it. She had just sat down again and stared at the silent screen, virtually ignoring him as tears rolled down her cheeks.

Kane had found the flat easily enough, using the address Sue Ward-Davies had given him. He knew the location by reputation from his youth. He had hoped that it had changed in the passing years. Like most things it had and it hadn't! Wendy had relocated to the heart of what the locals still persisted in calling "the council estate!" High on the cold north hill that overlooked Aberfoist town centre, it was still a bleak, out of the way location.

Most of the houses on "the council estate" were now in reality not owned by the county council. They were privately owned homes. Indeed, many of these ex-council built houses were in fact better looked after than the Victorian or Georgian terraced houses, which were to be found in the so called more "desirable" areas of town. However, scattered amongst the smart and tidy 1960's three bed roomed semi detached houses or the neat short rows of two bed roomed 1980's linked homes, were a few three or four storey apartment blocks, like the one he had found Wendy's flat in. According to the graffiti covered signs, they had been transferred from council ownership to privately run "charitable" housing associations a long time ago. Alas, it was this well meant "social housing" that was a constant frustration for the generally hard working and aspiring private home owners in this and (no doubt) most other former "council" neighbourhoods. For not only did the private owners have to put up with the regular anti-social behaviour of the few, dishonest and habitually work shy, often long term benefit claimants, who had been dumped in these buildings, but the private owners also knew that the presence of such "nightmare neighbours" was always going to limit their own properties re-sale values.

Admittedly alongside those undesirables, there were more genuinely unfortunate tenants. Those like Wendy, who had found themselves with no alternative, whether through indisputable economic hard luck or ill-health. They were now the deserving poor and rightly justified the welfare state. Nevertheless, these new arrivals suffered the same resentment and were never truly welcomed. Wendy's fall from grace had obviously hit her hard.

Kane did not doubt that she was aware of who some of the less savoury residents in her block were. She was after all a former Vice Chair of Aberfoist's Shopkeepers Neighbourhood Watch Group. In spite of her bold new image, he could see the heartbreak and discomfort that she felt, being stuck in her new surroundings. It was etched on her pale face and reflected in the manner of her unusually inhibited body language.

Listening to her hard luck story, Kane felt the guilt of being the worst type of absent friend. He had just assumed things were fine. He never looked beyond the annual greeting in the Christmas Cards nor bothered to make the time to visit. Yet in truth he wondered what he could have done to address the decline in his friends' relationship.

Wendy and Frank seemed to have worked harder, rather than smarter, but what else could they have done; apart from perhaps admitting defeat earlier! She told him, between snivels, that Frank had put longer hours in at the tearooms. He even tried to set up regular "special" club nights, for local artists, writers, poets, musicians, (which was not really in line with his down to earth no nonsense style) and at one stage, he had even tried to set up a "cyber cafe"! Eventually he had agreed to diversify the menu, to met new trends. Mocha and Latte replaced Hot Chocolate and Milky Coffee. She in turn took on extra jobs, but she lacked qualified work experience, other than being a military wife, mother and part-time tearoom helper, so much so that she had only found work in the time-rich/pay-poor roles of part-time cleaner and/or temporary guardian/supply carer for the elderly. What little she earned was spent so that her children did not miss out on the so called modern essentials. The frivolous luxuries required for twenty-first century teenage life. The time apart, due to work commitments, created a distance between them all, and their mutual stubbornness only increased selfish resentment.

Even when they had had to sell the house and Frank insisted they sink the limited equity into "his" floundering business. Wendy had compromised and tried all four of them living in the spare room at her sister-in-law's. "Just until things improved" and "the business turned the corner!" Kane had forgotten all about Janice, Frank's older sister. He made an immediate mental note to try and look her up before the funeral. She would have a view worth hearing about her little brother's demise and she had always expressed her views and opinions openly.

Of course, this cramped "family life" had been doomed to failure. The tension between sister-in-laws had exploded the evening when Janice was interrupted at the monthly local PTA meeting, which she proudly hosted in her pristine lounge, by her own young children, loudly complaining about the horrible smell coming from the spare bedroom, and Janice, who was even more straight laced than Frank, had discovered Kevin, (Wendy and Frank's eldest), smoking cannabis whilst leaning out of the back bedroom window.

Embarrassingly evicted by their own relatives, the Johns could ill afford the dreadful bed and breakfast lodgings, taken for a month or so until the housing association had offered Wendy her current three bedroomed flat. Frank had refused to move to "the estate" but she had swallowed what little of her pride was left and went ahead anyway, defying him for the first time in their relationship. She had expected him to come round, but he did not and when he started sleeping at the "Kettle", her "so called" friends started to talk to her of divorce!

Proceedings had started, after yet another cataclysmic argument, on the grounds of his unreasonable behaviour. She thought that the legal proceedings would shock him into begging for forgiveness. It should have but Frank was too stubborn even then, and she let the lawyers carry on, mainly allowing her to claim much needed welfare benefits for the kids, and possibly to help her avoid the increasingly likely personal liability and bankruptcy for business debts. She had even hoped that the end of their "partnership" would finally force him to see sense and sell. So now, after her desperate tactics had appeared, briefly, to have succeeded, she blamed herself totally for his sudden and unexpected death.

Kane tried hard to reassure her. She should not blame herself. He wanted to ask her about whom Frank had borrowed money off. He really wanted to ask her if Frank had got into debt with "Flicker" Pace!?! However, he found himself trying to alleviate her sense of blame by stupidly suggesting that there were so many other reasons why Frank "may" have killed himself.

'MAY!?!' She had said in a loud exaggerated tone whilst shaking her head.

Kane was pleased that at least she was still sharp enough to pick up on what he had hoped was the subtly of his point. Unfortunately, when he tried to develop this pet theory by mentioning that some of his army friends told sad stories of old soldiers who had done the same thing, she did not get angry, she just looked right back at him and simply scoffed at what was to her his obviously misguided hypothesis.

'Do you really think Frank did "it" because of bad memories from his army days!?! Frank loved his tours. He didn't have bad memories! No! Frank never had any hang ups about what he did! Certainly not for Queen and Country! He always took pride in his service!'

When Kane tried to say that it was not always about what brave men did but what they saw! She just silently shook her head from side to side.

Kane then changed tact. He began to express his doubts that the man he knew could just "give up on life!" That was another mistake. She immediately squashed any such suggestions,

69

this time laughing cruelly at him, telling him he didn't know Frank over the last few years. And then suddenly she was raging once again. She sobbed that "it" was all her fault! The tears came. This time they were much heavier than before.

It was at that stage her son, Kevin, appeared. Kane thought he must have been in his late teens. He could remember getting drunk (with Frank) to "wet the baby's head!" But Kane could not remember exactly how long ago that was! Without a word Kevin went into the kitchen. He got his mum a glass of water and some tablets from a brown plastic bottle.

'Just to calm her down.' He said in a soft and soothing voice, gently shaking the bottle so that the pills rattled around inside it.

The sweet tobacco stench, which Kane suspected was marijuana, clung to Kevin's clothing and hung about in his wake. It was the same stink that he had smelt on the girl back in the Isolation Room, so much earlier that day.

Kane studied the boy's relaxed movements, trying to listen as he talked quietly to his mother. He could not hear the words, only the boy's soothing tone. Kevin clearly took after his mother in looks, excepting his height and weight, which was no doubt his father's. He even had the same jet black dyed hair or perhaps she had chosen to match his, but he wore it chaotically, in a longer bushy, shoulder length, unkempt, style. However, the stubble on his chin, which was perhaps unshaven for a good few days, grew out ginger, hinting that he actually shared his mother's original hair colouring. The effect was not attractive. Kane did not understand why so many people, he observed, were now choosing to attempt to disguise their natural hair colourings. It seemed to him that everybody these days, wanted to be someone different to who they really were. Maybe he was guilty of that too!

Every now and then, as Kevin talked to his mother, he would briefly lose focus, before turning to Kane and repeating that his mum would be alright, once she had had her pills. Kane doubted it.

Gradually Wendy was calm again. Kevin told her he would check on "tea" and the boy slowly moved over towards the kitchen area. Wendy repeatedly told Kane that her Kevin was: 'such a sweet boy!'

'How's your boy? And Jill of course?' She asked vaguely.

Kane felt guilty when he told her that they were both fine. He quickly tried to change the subject from his family by asking her what she knew about the new owners of "The Kettle". Wendy shrugged and said she knew nothing. Then after another awkward silence, which had them both staring at the silent TV screen again, she muttered, as an afterthought, that a very nice lawyer, an Indian man in a smart pinstriped suit, had paid her a visit. He had explained that whilst Frank had signed everything to do with the business over to his client, a Mr Lord, the cheque did not appear to have been cashed. She became tearful again at that, recalling with frustration, that Frank was a hopeless businessman.

'Fancy that!' She groaned. 'Selling your own business and forgetting to get paid for it!'

'That Mr Khan was very good really. He was so keen to give me the money and put a stop on the original cheque!' She said.

Kane worried that the buyers had not paid for the business. He wondered, to himself, if the deal was void for lack of consideration or something like that. However, as he was about to try and sensitively raise that point, Kevin shouted from the kitchen, that his parent's solicitors, Gadsby & Co., had met with Mr Lord, and that Mr Khan, and everything was okay now!'

The use of the word "okay" upset Wendy and she snivelled that things would never be "okay" again. Kevin protested that he meant the deal was "okay" and that they had now been paid a tidy sum. Wendy snorted and laughed bitterly, before turning to her guest and whispering.

'Kevin thinks he'll get that money but he's in for a shock. Most of it will go towards paying his father's debts. The business owed tax going back years!'

Kane could not help himself and speculated out loud that if the business was losing money it should not have had to pay tax. Wendy went quiet at that, and Kevin shouted rather too excitedly from the kitchen area that he would speak to the solicitors again, first thing on Monday morning.

The room went quiet again, with everybody lost in their own thoughts. Kane and Wendy stared silently at the TV. The quiz show had ended and the Six O' Clock News was beginning.

Kevin called out from the kitchen.

'This Lasagne's done! It's going to spoil Mum! Where the fuck is Jan?'

'Language Kevin!' Wendy sounded horrified at her "sweet boy" swearing and then she said, in a distant far away voice, as if she was a completely different person: 'I have no fucking idea where your sister is!?! She should've been home hours ago!'

Kane cringed in his seat and drank back the last of his coffee. He could see the pills were starting to work. The blue tinted eyes seemed to have glazed over.

'I'd better be going now!' He said to Wendy and stood up.

Kevin shouted an encouraging 'Okay!' from the kitchen.

Wendy asked Kane if he would like to stay for tea but he quickly started making his excuses, as Kevin had let out a frustrated groan from the kitchen and was muttering that the Lasagne "wasn't very big Mum!"

She told both Kevin and Kane that she "wasn't hungry" but her "Sweet Boy" insisted that she had to eat something! Kane agreed with him. Kevin went on to bemoan the fact that just because Jan seemed to have stopped eating his mother shouldn't too! Truly embarrassed, Kane once again made a point of reassuring both of them that he really had to be going and making a great show of standing up, he asked them both if there was anything he could do to help.

Wendy simply said: 'No! We can manage!'

He doubted that but said a polite: 'Okay then!' He immediately cringed at his poor choice of words and moved over to her, looking he supposed, to give her a goodbye hug or kiss. When she did not react he simply bent over and gave her an air peck near her cheek. She did not respond at all and just carried on staring at the images on the TV.

'I'll give Kevin my mobile number in case you think of anything, okay!?!' He cringed again.

'Yeah that's okay isn't it Mum!' Kevin said as he carried two plates full of Lasagne out of the kitchen and dumped them loudly on the table. Kevin then quickly produced his mobile phone from his black jeans back pocket. Kane noticed that, unlike his own, it was an expensive looking iPhone, certainly one of the larger, and no doubt, latest models. They exchanged numbers by Kevin dialling the number Kane called out and then cancelling the call as soon as the shrill ring tone sounded from deep within Kane's fleece pocket.

'Psycho!?!' Kevin grinned at the stabbing musical notes that rang out from Kane's phone.

'Yes, it's a bit of an old joke!' Kane nodded apologetically.

'An old film too!' Kevin suggested jovially. The boy was certainly happy to see Kane on his way. And then with one last look back at Wendy, who was still sat in her chair, blankly staring at the silent TV screen, Kane left.

Chapter 8: Loa Fu

Kane sat in his car and stared blankly at the windscreen. He needed to compose himself for a moment or two before driving home. He saw nothing, apart from his own stupidity reflected back at him in the dust tinted glass. He did not know what he had expected to find when his old fashioned sense of duty had compelled him to travel back to Aberfoist. He was certainly not sure how he felt now that he had seen Frank's widow. Perhaps he would have got more closure out of seeing Frank's body! Although Wendy had insisted that there was no point in visiting the chapel of rest because the casket was closed, apparently on the advice of the undertaker. That in itself spoke volumes to Kane. Maybe Sue Ward-Davies had not been exaggerating. Kane had seen more than his fair share of dead bodies and if a modern undertaker could not present Frank's body, well!

He was still sat in his scruffy old car, where he had parked on the street just below Wendy John's flat, a good half an hour later, brooding on all that had happened since Wendy's telephone call earlier that day. Nothing seemed to make sense to him. Finally he roused himself and sought certainty.

Taking out his mobile phone, Kane rang his wife. Jill never answered her phone straight away. He suspected it would be buried deep within her handbag, as usual. He pictured her, with a slightly flustered look on her face, digging through the debris of old receipts and other oddities, trying to find it before the ring-tones stopped. She would be too late! She would then check the number, wonder what he wanted and eventually her curiosity would get the better of her and she should ring back.

Whilst he waited for the inevitable return call, his concentration further lapsed from resolving the puzzle of his friend's death, and he began to look around the dumping ground that Frank John had refused to countenance living in. Given the dreadfully reduced circumstances in which he and Wendy allegedly now found themselves, this surely was not that bad a place to live. Both he and Frank had certainly seen much worse places on their travels.

In the gloom, above the uniformly tiled rooftops of the cheaply constructed yet practical dwellings, darker grey clouds were gathering, casting their shadows across the picturesque high hills, which were being increasingly silhouetted black against the white light still running in a thin line along the distant western horizon. The hills to the east were already lost to the night but Kane knew their stark beauty would be stunningly displayed by the rising sun in the morning. He wondered how many of the residents gazed out and appreciated the natural wonders surrounding them. All there for them to enjoy for free. No wonder people from all over the globe were risking life and limb to come to this land of opportunities, if this was where the desperate and needy of society were placed by the generosity of the welfare state. And yet he knew not everyone was so lucky. There were families with pupils in his big city school, who would have loved to live where Wendy John and her children now did and where his friend Frank could not.

Kane looked around him again, appreciating how well the buildings were spaced out compared to modern newly built estates. The fading light may have hid the grime, which a closer inspection could have revealed, on the apparently unloved communal constructions. The dusk certainly merged the muddy paths, where locals took short cuts across the rough grass expanses of the supposedly council maintained landscaping. It certainly hid the soft mines of dog mess, no doubt left lying

75

where children should play, by those errant owners who merely released their pets to wander free rather than walk them responsibly.

Looking back, once more up at her flat, Kane watched as the glow of the TV flickered brightly against the dark glass of Wendy's lounge window. No blinds or curtains had been drawn to try to shut out the gathering gloom of that evening's twilight. A few electric lights had been turned on, in rooms belonging to other flats in the building, creating an irregular pattern of yellow and white dots across the darkening walls. He doubted that even the brightest bulb could have lightened the darkness in Wendy's room. Kane sighed and tried to gather his thoughts. Was there really nothing that he could do? He asked himself. Unlike Sue Ward-Davies, neither Wendy nor Kevin seemed to doubt that Frank had killed himself. Had Sue actually doubted the suicide? No, Kane decided, she had not, but he had. Were his own doubts based purely on her innuendo? He continued to wonder to himself.

Further up the road, a few cars began to arrive and park up outside the nearby linked houses. The drivers, all women, in their thirties or forties, were generally dressed in some form of "works" uniform. Most were showing their employers branding. There was a wide ranging representation of major retail outlets. Kane wondered to himself whether their employees residency in this street alone, was sufficient evidence to question the positive spin put on the household names low costs business strategy. Nonetheless, in spite of their probable low income, each woman carried at least two full shopping bags from their car towards their individual house. Some struggled with three or four bags, a luxury that would further motivate desperate refugees.

Nobody came out of the houses to help the women. Those struggling down their own pathway strangely did not acknowledge their neighbours endeavours. He would have expected a few inane comments, if not warm greetings, another week over, etc. So much for community spirit. He watched the women. They all walked as if they were weighed down by a lot more than their shopping. Their heads were bowed. Their eyes focused straight ahead. All looked tired and yet all were still rushing to get in. More jobs to do. Too busy to talk. A part of him felt guilty, maybe for not playing the gentleman and helping them but which one should he choose? And, if he did, would they not be suspicious of his kindness!?!

Just then, a few street lights burst on. Perhaps reacting to the growing dusk, or maybe just responding to an unseen automatic timer. They did little to light up the street, as only every other light came on. Maybe it was not truly dark enough for their faint economy setting to be effective. The "Psycho" ring tone, although expected, still made him jump, when finally it shattered the quiet reflection in the car.

'Hello? What do you want?' The familiar voice asked, in an irritated tone, when he eventually pressed the green screen icon to answer her call back. He started to up date her but she interrupted him.

'Look, I'm in the supermarket, doing a bit of shopping! Tell me when you get home. What time do you expect to be back?'

'Oh in about an hour.' He replied.

'Have you eaten?'

'No!'

'Okay, don't! I'll do something for later.'

'Okay, thanks! See you soon!'

'Bye!' She rang off.

Kane put the phone back into the cheap black plastic grip that was mounted on the air vent, in front of him. Then he reached for the key, already in the ignition, intending to turn the engine on. Suddenly he stopped. His attention was caught by a sight that he had not seen for years. Two young boys, probably about ten years old, were running down the road playing tag. It was not the boys or their game that made him freeze but he was fascinated by what they wore.

Both boys were wearing matching martial arts uniforms, consisting of bright yellow tops, black baggy trousers, white socks and black Chinese style slippers. The tops and socks stood out, almost luminous in the dimming light. The boys carried on running passed his car, oblivious to the watcher inside. He followed their weaving and swerving movements until they disappeared, darting into the entrance to a block of flats. The one's opposite Wendy's nearly new home.

When he was sure that they were not coming back out, Kane strangely felt sad, as if he had just lost an emotional link to his past. Then he stared out of his windscreen, looking ahead, back towards where the boys had come from. Straining his eyes to see through the rapidly increasing gloom, he cheered slightly, for he could just about make out three similarly yellow topped and white socked illuminated shapes. Other children were apparently gathering at the far end of the street in small groups, waiting across from the road junction. Kane smiled to himself. He was suddenly excited.

Even more children, all dressed in exactly the same uniform, were now appearing. On closer examination, the blurry figures seemed to be exiting from one particular single storey building, which stood alone at the very end of a narrow tarmac path that ran away from the main road, across another adjacent flat patch of grassy land. Kane must have counted over a dozen children now. Some were beginning to get into cars. He had not realised that there had been people sat waiting in the cars that had been parked along the side of the main road. Now engines were being turned on and headlights were blasting out beams of bright light, much brighter than the insipid low glow haunting the oddly lit street. Other children were being greeted by larger shadowy shapes, probably much older children or little women, who had suddenly appeared from around the corner. They seemed intent on winning individual tug of war battles, snatching onto the smaller children's hands, before dragging their wards away from their friends, and pulling them back out of his sight.

On the spur of the moment Kane was compelled to pull out his car key. Grabbing his phone from its rest, he quickly got out of the car. With a firm, reassuring, clunk of metal, he had slammed the door shut and eagerly began walking towards the low level building. An electronic bleep sounded behind him, followed instantly by a responsive blink of the Mazda's lights as he locked the car, without looking back, by instinctively pressing the oval button on his black plastic key fob.

Striding down the tarmac pathway in the poor light, Kane could just about make out the weather-worn sign above the doorway. It read: "North Foist Community Centre". He opened the door and stepped into a bright, electric light lit hallway. On his right were two doors, each labelled bilingually by cheaply laminated paper printouts. "Gwrwy/Male" and Benywaidd/Female" respectively. To his left was one door marked "Cegin/Kitchen" and straight ahead there was a set of double doors, with a simple monochrome black plastic sign stating: "Prif Neuadd/Main Hall". The doors were slightly ajar and he could see a whiter more natural but still electric light, illuminating the gap. Pushing the doors gently open, Kane instinctively bowed his head, respectfully to the room as he stepped in.

At first glance the room appeared empty of people and furniture. Then he saw him. A little old man sitting cross legged on the light wood block floor, to the centre left of the otherwise empty community centre hall. Kane could not believe it! After so many years, the old man was still there. Just as he always had been, meditating alone after class. Kane was instantly overwhelmed with nostalgic affection and his eyes became a little moist.

Dressed in an all black, loose fitting, light-weight, cotton, Chinese Style, Mandarin Suit, with wide white cuffs at the end of the jacket's three quarter length sleeves, the old man looked typically oriental, except for his pale white skin, and piercing light blue eyes, which starred blindly into space. His snow white hair was cropped short, close to his head, apart from a thin pig tail that weaved its way down his back, until it stopped and dangled between the man's prominent shoulder blades. Just like the children that Kane had seen leaving the hall, the old man also wore bright white socks and black Chinese slippers on his feet.

The old man had studiously ignored Kane's arrival; even though the hall doors had banged together the moment after Kane had stepped into the hall. In his excitement he had clumsily allowed them to swing shut behind him.

Kane was truly amazed at the impossibility of it all. The old man looked no different to when Kane had first met him, and that was almost thirty years ago!

***

'Why do you want to learn to fight?' That was the very first thing that the old man had ever said to him, when Kane's real "old man", his father, had dragged him, as a young boy, along to the self defence class at the local Leisure Centre. It had been less than a week since the ten year old Kane had returned home, from what was meant to have been a game of football with friends in the local park. Blood was staining his white T-shirt where it had flowed from a split lip. The basic boxing techniques, which his father had attempted to teach Kane from infancy, had obviously not served him well enough. He had foolishly tried to stop a gang of much older boys from stealing his football. Now,

80

with two black eyes and dry scabs on his lips, the young Kane was too shy to answer the teacher's question. His father impatiently huffed and puffed.

'Come on My-Key! Tell Mr Evans why you want to study Chinese boxing!' His father had urged. Ever the practical man, Mr. Kane had taken matters into his own hands, when his young son had been unable to confirm to his satisfaction, that the "other guys" looked worse than his own beaten up features. Almost immediately, Kane's father had collected Kane's even angrier uncle, and together the two men had retrieved the boy's football, after finding the gang of teenage thugs, still foolishly having a kick about with the proceeds of their crime.

Kane learnt much later from exultant witnesses, that his father had terrified the gang leaders and frog marched them one by one to their own parents' houses, insisting that their startled parents perform suitable corporal punishment on their unruly children or he would! Of course, that was back in the days before political correctness had nullified adults' authority over children. Nevertheless, although the antagonists now knew better than to pick on that particular little boy, the one with the mad father and even madder uncle, there were certainly other bullies out and about in a rough border town, who might be big, ugly and stupid enough to fancy their chances in the future. Kane's father was not willing for his pride and joy to come off second best, without at least inflicting a fair share of pain, if not humiliation, on any future adversary. Hence the decision was made that the young Kane would learn self defence. It was perhaps his good fortune that the advert for Kung Fu classes appeared in the local paper the very next day or Kane may have attended a different martial arts class, and never met his mentor, the old man who was to have such a profound and lasting influence on him.

At the time of their first meeting, the young Kane did not want to learn to fight. He certainly did not want to say that he

81

had to learn to fight or his father would go all ballistic again. So after an agonising delay, under the inscrutable stare of the martial arts teacher and the increasingly hot glower of his angry father, Kane had meant to say that he wanted to learn to fight to avoid getting beaten up again but somehow it came out that he wanted to learn to fight to avoid fighting! This mistaken statement seemed to please the old man, who nodded enthusiastically and said "Well done!" Over and over again. For some reason, Kane's father seemed pleased too.

The young Mykee Kane had been surprised that unlike the physically aggressive moves his father had attempted to teach him, most of the techniques practised in class were how to evade attacks, rather than strike others first. Over the coming weeks, months, and years, Kane had become more and more self confident as the techniques taught turned naturally into instinctive reactions. Certainly, after the first few weeks of high school, his ability to fight without fighting had ensured that he was never the target of local bullies again.

***

Still sat on the floor, the old man slowly turned his head to his right, and began to study the visitor, who was standing patiently at the door to the hall. The old man's calm peaceful expression did not change, but ever so subtly he made the slightest bow with his head. Kane responded by stiffly moving his left hand to his left hip, clenching it into a fist, then moving his open right hand, palm down, over the fist, before making a full bow, or at least as full a bow as his overweight body would allow. Straightening up, with a slightly embarrassing wobble, Kane smiled at his old teacher. The old man did not smile back.

'Lao Fu!' Kane called out in sincere traditional greeting, meaning "Old Father" and he stepped forward with his right

82

hand outstretched, as if intending to shake hands. The old man gave the thinnest smile of recognition. Then suddenly, as Kane neared him, he sprung up from his cross-legged stance, instantly standing, in one lightening quick move. The old man took a deft pace forward with his left foot, toes turned out. Then as soon as the foot touched the floor, the old man swung his right leg up, kicking in the air. Only the slightest movement of Kane's head, rolling backwards, prevented the right foot connecting with his chin. Even though the younger man was much taller (and obviously wider) than the old man the foot had flown higher than seemed possible. Then as his right foot came down, the old man controlled it and placed it about a half pace ahead of his left foot, with the right toes pointing out to anchor it on the floor. Immediately the left foot swung straight up, kicking high into the air, and hit the space where Kane's face had been but a second before. Kane had just stepped back in time. The left foot dropped down, half a pace ahead of the old man's right foot, with the left toes pointing out to anchor it firmly on the floor and once again, as one foot touched the floor, the other kicked up high, missing it's target by millimetres, as Kane continued to back off just in the nick of time.

The double kick dance continued until Kane felt the wall at his back. With no escape, he waited until the old man's left leg rose one more time. Then with startling speed for such a big man, Kane moved his own left leg forward, turning his whole body left and bringing his right foot parallel to his left, so that he suddenly stood sideways to the old man's kicking leg, and as it swung back down, Kane was able to use both of his now raised hands to push down on the dropping leg. This added momentum and the leg hit the floor, unbalancing the old man and preventing another immediate attack from a strong stance. The minimal time it took the old man to adjust, just about allowed Kane to sweep his right foot away, at a 90 degree angle, and then repeat the evasive movement with his left foot. Kane did this awkward movement twice more, so that he had somehow zigzagged away, creating a safe gap between him and his elderly, but supremely fast adversary. The older man laughed.

'Good!' He said, before continuing, in a deep, sing song, voice: 'You do remember something after all these years!' Turning to face Kane, without another word, the old man moved his left hand to his left hip, clenched it into a fist, then moved his open right hand, palm down, over the left before making a full bow. His light blue eyes watched Kane's sternly as he bowed. Then they twinkled brightly as he saw an exhausted Kane, slowly mimic the same move.

'I am old and slow!' The old man sighed. 'You have always been lucky with you evasions. Yes! I think it is still luck rather than skill because I believe you do not practice and without practice your luck will run out one day soon, My-key! But not today eh!' Kane busy wiping the warm sweat from his brow, still found time to nod in acknowledgement of his continued good fortune.

'You look like you need a drink, and I could certainly do with one!' The old man smiled. 'Come on buy your old teacher a pint, and you can tell me why you got so fat eh!'

Chapter 9: The Coliseum

A glorious pint of Guinness stood magnificently settling on the tall table next to an equally picturesque miniature half pint twin. The colours of the drinks soon matched the two-tone black and white swirl displayed on the small Taoist enamel pin badge, so proudly worn by Kane's old martial arts teacher. The two men were chatting enthusiastically about the good old days, whilst sat on high barstools, either side of the tall round table, in the middle of the last pub still open in Aberfoist town centre. When the young Kane had first ventured out into the night life of his old home town, there used to be ten public houses on or just off the main street, and four private members clubs, all busy with men drinking regularly every night of the week, but as the old man was saying, *"things ain't what they used to be."*

In the time it had taken Kane to walk back to his car and drive it up to the community hall, the old man had washed, using the sink in the men's toilets, changed into a smart pair of navy blue chinos, a matching casual polo shirt and an olive green hacking jacket. The white socks and Chinese slippers had been replaced by a casual pair of soft brown leather Timberland brand moccasins and the seemingly much younger looking dapper gentleman was locking up. Admittedly, Kane had taken time out to ring his wife, and after the inevitable unanswered call, he had had to resort to his slow thumb typing in order to text his warning that he was now going to be late for dinner, because he was going for a drink with an old friend.

Kane had found it strange at first to see his old teacher in "normal" clothes. So much so that he almost did not recognise the slight built man, who was hunched over fiddling with the door mechanism. Kane could not remember the last time that he had seen the old man wearing anything other than his martial arts kit. It was odd how ordinary this extraordinary man looked in the smart casual clothes, which could have been worn by someone forty years his junior. However, Kane found it even stranger when he was told that all of the public houses, which he had suggested they go to for "their drink" had all been closed down years ago. Kane was incredulous, when the old man had told him to drive to "The Coliseum" as this was the only pub still open in the centre of town!

The Coliseum had used to be the local cinema. Kane had vague but happy childhood memories of going to see blockbusters like "Back to the Future" and the original "Batman" movies there. However, *"the flicks"* as his parents used to call the old movie house, had closed down a long time ago. The old man had told him that after a few years of being a carpet warehouse and then an empty derelict eyesore, blighting the town centre, "The Coliseum" had been acquired by a new up and coming national pub chain. Re-launched as a cheap and cheerfully bland hostelry, its low prices and long opening hours caused the competition, the other more traditionally inclined town centre pubs, to close down one by one. A sad story to start the conversation between the two men but perhaps one that aptly set the tone, for they were inevitably nostalgic for past times and as the dark stuff was thoughtfully sipped, both continued to agree that times had not necessarily changed for the better. Nevertheless, they were soon lost in more cheerful nostalgia, happily remembering names, trips to tournaments and infamous challenges from past opponents.

Lao Fu, whose real name was the less exotic Keith Evans, had established his Kung Fu School in the seventies, when most of the films shown at "The Coliseum" had been made in Hong

86

Kong rather than Hollywood. He had adapted his classes over the years to meet the demands of the changing market place. Evans had taught Tai Chi, Oriental Medicine, Meditation and Well Being, even Kick Boxing; but Lao Fu had refused to run the most aggressive, yet increasingly popular, Mixed Martial Arts courses or the brutal Cage Fighting "nonsense" (as he described it), which had become increasingly popular in more recent times.

Kane listened, nodding in agreement, as his old teacher moaned on. The old man maintained that boys (and girls) today merely expected to pick up a few tricks to help them win a playground scrap or for the more insanely ambitious, a fight at the various mean "open" cage fight nights and such like, which seemed to be held monthly up and down the nearby valleys. A desire to become a "celebrity" fighter, like those the youngsters saw on satellite TV was not "the way of the warrior" Lao Fu endorsed. The contempt was clear in his voice.

'Most students these days don't want to learn an art or adopt a healthy lifestyle'. He sighed sadly into his now almost empty pint glass. Nevertheless, both men were happy to wonder out loud about why "this generation" had developed such deluded expectations. Kane trotted out his own pet theory that it was all the fault of reality TV and the fickle nature of modern celebrity. Constant programmes featuring so-called entertainment with instant superficial results all from minimum effort. He talked bitterly about his own experience as a High School teacher and the unrealistic demands placed on pupils (and teachers) by over-optimistic parents or government statisticians.

'Managing expectations! That's the trick!' Kane shrugged. He did try to end his rant on a positive note by saying that there were kids, he knew who had genuine ambitions and were prepared to work to achieve their goals. However, both men had to agree, as they finished their drinks, that too many lacked the rigour to really work at anything for long enough, so often failed to turn raw talent into consistent skills. However, Kane was quick to celebrate how good it had been to see a young class, in all the right gear, returning to the more traditional arts of Kung Fu.

Keith Evans grimaced briefly, as if his last sip of stout had suddenly gone off. He told Kane that he had always had a loyal class of about a dozen "much older" students, who still trained every week. He paused, staring mockingly at Kane's plump stomach. Then having attempted to make his point, apparently in vain, from Kane's non-reaction, he carried on, saying that it was mainly that group's grandchildren, whom Kane had seen leaving earlier that evening. Evans explained that the grandparents had begged him to teach their youngsters, in the hope that learning the ancient arts might instil some self-discipline and improve the kids' general behaviour. Kane could not resist interrupting by acknowledging that that was easier said than done these days. Lao Fu suddenly looked every year of his age. He sighed yet again and confessed to Kane that perhaps it was not the kids fault! Maybe he was too old to suffer the youngsters now! Their constant inability to take things seriously or listen or work at anything challenging was wearing. At least, he concluded, their grandparents made sure they wore the right uniform, and perhaps most importantly, paid their subs on time.

The old man did smile when Kane suggested in his most respectful tone that he was surprised that the "Old Father" had not retired years ago. In reply, Evans joked, that he was not as old as he looked, and in any event, he had never sorted out a proper pension, back in the boom times! He gave Kane a whimsical wink and then, staring shocked at his empty glass, added cheerfully, that if he wanted to keep drinking Guinness, he had better keep teaching the way of the warrior to all who could pay!

'Or find someone to buy your pints for you!' Kane teased before asking: 'Another?'

'I can still buy my round!' The old man said proudly. 'Do you want a pint this time?'

'No, I'm driving; I'd better have a Coke or Pepsi this time!'

'Not good for you, you know! Full of sugar!'

'Ah well!' Kane shrugged and tried, unconvincingly, to look miserable. 'As long as they're not full of alcohol!'

Picking up his own empty pint glass, Evans turned towards the bar, leaving Kane alone to glance nostalgically around the old cinema. In some ways the new layout was very different to the last time Kane had gone to see "the pictures" at The Coliseum. In others it was still the same. Albeit slightly refreshed. The colour scheme still used lots of red and gold but everything was fresh and clean. Not dusty and dirty like it had been in the past. The ceiling was not tar-stained and there were no clouds of smoke hanging in the air. Along the walls, beneath the mocked up posters of classic movie stars, were some of the original "cinema" style dark wooden seats. Oddly numbered, they must have been salvaged and their crimson brushed velvet cushions looked as if they had been re-upholstered into a refreshed retro reminder of past "glory" days. Kane remembered, that back in the day they had never been as comfortable as they looked, especially when he had had to spend two hours or so, sat fidgeting on them.

A few younger drinkers, (hopefully over-eighteen, maybe not, but definitely teenagers), were sat on the "cinema seats" now. Happily chatting to friends, who perhaps more wisely, sat on the normal, comfortable, upright chairs, which were just the other side of slightly smaller versions of the dark wooden drinks table that Kane, himself, was using. Kane's attention then focused on the three small, rectangular, glass panels, no more than a hand's breadth across. They were fixed high up on the red painted back wall, well above the bar. Behind that wall the projectionist had once lurked, shooting out through those little

89

windows, the flickering light, which would illuminate the dancing dust filled smog of constantly rising cigarette smoke on its way down onto the big screen. There was no "silver screen" now, just a plainly painted creamy gold coloured wall. No balcony or stalls, just one long levelled room, mostly filled with tall tables and cool stool-style highchairs, like the one he was sat on.

Kane's visual memory of the place was also complicated by the confusion of two glass double doors, added on what must have been the old cinema's side wall and fire exit. The closed doors were fitted in the centre of what appeared to be a large panoramic style window, which appeared to be all black glass, mainly because of the dark night sky outside. Yet there were occasional glows, flickering about on the other side. Kane realised that Aberfoist was not infested by fireflies but the individual dancing orange red and yellow spots were actually cigarettes in the hands of people, who had gathered together into a small shadowy group on the other side of the glass doors. Closer inspection revealed that the external assembly was stood on wooden decking, a balcony, which Kane reasoned, must serve as the pub's outside and trendily elevated, smoking area.

'My-Keeeey! It is you isn't it! Bugger me!' A deep rasping voice called out from somewhere behind him. Swivelling around on his stool, Kane looked left, in reaction to the loud call. He found himself gazing at a wild looking man, tall but far too thin. The man was slowly staggering across the pub towards Kane. From his unsteady gait he was drunk. His slurred but loud voice, continued to call out "My-key!?!" Fortunately, he appeared to be smiling, although his grin suffered from dark gaps due to missing teeth. Those few teeth that remained were chipped and either dirty yellow or rotten blue black. The drunk's grey hair was long and unkempt. He looked as if he were a ghost of an old heavy metal rock star, obviously down on their luck, not too dissimilar to the skeletal guitarist illustrated on the faded grey, possibly once black, T-shirt, that hung on the emaciated body. It proclaimed the legend "Rock 'n' Roll will never die!" The drunk also wore a long, much torn, khaki military style jacket, which hung open, mainly due to missing buttons rather than any sense of the wearers attempt at style. The skinny jeans were faded and split across the knees, through age rather than design, but the drunk also wore an impressive and expensive looking pair of silver snakeskin cowboy boots.

The unsettling smile was not improved by a cut and swollen upper lip. One eye was almost shut with freshly thumped, dark purple bruising, and a large graze mark reddened the left check. The unsteady rocker had not shaved, for a few days, if not a week, as his chin had irregular, untidy, tufts of white hair, mixed in with dirty grey stubble. Dangling down from his left ear lobe was a short gold chain, with an ivory white, miniature replica of a human skull, an earring that spun around on its chain just above his shoulders as he lurched vaguely forward.

When he eventually arrived in front of Kane, the drunk began, confidently telling him that he "My-Key" had made his day! Made his week! Made his whole "fucking" year! Of course, Kane looked puzzled at this and eventually his unsteady new friend picked up on Kane's perplexed expression.

'You don't recognise me do you?' The tall painfully thin man looked emotionally crushed for almost a few seconds. And then he decided it did not matter. 'But I recognised you! Straight away! I did!' He beamed. 'I said to me-self I knows 'im and then when you showed up that ...' the drunk paused, a disgusted look pulled on his pale face and Kane feared the poor excuse for a man was going to be sick. Fortunately, he wasn't and after a pause the drunk continued. 'That! 'That! Wanker!' He literary spat out. 'Dull-ann, Fucking, Francis! Well I knew for certain see! My-Key, Fucking, Kane! I says to myself! I did!'

'Hello Bernard!' Keith Evans spoke softly in his deep voice but almost made Kane jump off his stool in surprise. Evans had returned from the bar so quietly. The drunken man did jump back in shock. Putting the drinks down, carefully onto the two spare beer mats, on the tall table top, Evans stepped ever so easily and lightly around the table, so that seconds later he was standing, almost protectively, alongside Kane, blocking the now slightly swaying, shocked and shocking, unsteady man. Kane noticed, with slight irritation, that the old man had insisted on buying him another half of Guinness, instead of the unhealthy Cola he'd asked for, but he did not complain or say anything about it, for now. Instead, he found himself simply repeating, slowly, the tall, thin, raggedy man's name, almost as a puzzled question, asked back to his old teacher.

'Ber-nard?' And then, with stunned recognition, quietly, really just under his breath to himself, Kane muttered again. 'Bernard? Not Bernard Russell!?! Well bugger me!'

Chapter 10: Aberfoist Never Disappoints

Images from his past shot through Kane's mind as he silently mouthed the name "Bernard Russell" once again. First, he saw his own mother. Still youthful, she was busy with her housework and talked to him over her shoulder whilst vigorously working the thick white coating from the brightly coloured spray can into the dark wood cabinet with her damp yellow duster. Kane could almost smell the polish. He was a child again, playing on the floor with his toy soldiers. He heard her softly spoken voice telling him through the ages to be nice to young Bernard. "Bernard is a little bit special! You see My-key! The poor boy doesn't have a father! Be kind!"

Then Kane's inner eye suddenly saw two young boys, aged about seven years old, laughing and playing cricket together, using a broken tennis racket as a bat, hitting a hard rubber bouncing ball. They were sheltering from the rain, making runs up and down a long brick walled, concrete roofed alley, which barely separated two tatty end-of-terrace houses.

Finally, Kane saw an unsmiling teenager, dressed in a dark blue Wrangler denim jacket. Wild long brown hair tumbled down below the frayed jacket collar, like an out of fashion heavy metal rock star. The youth was squatting down, almost hidden behind a large, metallic bronze coloured car. It was the biggest car in the green field, and as such stood out amongst the smaller and shabbier cars, all neatly lined up in the County Showground car park. The long-haired youth was snarling, and swearing to himself, whilst struggling with a long metal crowbar. He was trying to force open the posh car's boot. Kane felt the shock waves again, the same ones his innocent young self had felt, a mix of fear and repulsion and excitement, just as he realised the real crime that he was witnessing! He had only been strolling through the car park and naively cried out the cheery greeting "Bernie!" All before being harshly told to "shut up", and "keep a look out!"

Maybe it was the alcohol on an empty stomach, but the much older Kane once again felt the wave of nausea and anger as he recalled how his younger self had recoiled from the unsettling threats. The venomous ones his once childhood friend had made. "Say nuffing!" or Bernie Russell would "'ave 'im!" Kane could see again the savage desperation in the youth, who had once been his friend. For a few seconds he keenly felt the confusion that aiding a criminal, however petty, had brought to him back then. And now as he looked on the wreck of that man, staggering about before him in The Coliseum pub, Kane felt a pulse of anger at the betrayal. However, it was not fear or threats that had kept the young Kane quiet, but a perverse sense of honour and duty to a friend. Nonetheless, Kane still felt the guilt and shame, the sorrow for the unknown victims of the crime and sadness too, with the realisation that Mykee and Bernie would never now be "real" friends again.

For a moment, the older Kane wondered, as he had done on previous occasions when haunted by his past, whether he could have, should have, done more that day in that car park. Had he abdicated his moral responsibility? The man he became and was today, surely would have done something else other than just turn and run away. Kane twitched nervously. Was he any different now to how he was back then. He had never told anyone about that incident. It was an unspoken secret between old friends, a secret probably forgotten long ago by Russell. Yet back then, just a week later, the young Kane had read in the very next edition of the local newspaper, with shame and guilt, that "security guards had stopped a local youth, who was attempting to leave last weekend's County Show, with a suspiciously clunking oversized black bag. They were duly pleased to discover an assortment of low value items, suspected of being stolen from cars alleged to having been broken into whilst parked at the show grounds."

Kane's acute relief that the victims goods had been recovered, was tempered with even greater guilt, when he found out, a few weeks later, that *good old Bernie*, had been sentenced to six months youth custody for his crimes that day. Bernie had ultimately returned home to Aberfoist, much later than the quoted six months, with an addiction to drugs, which inevitably contributed to him spending much of the next two decades in and out of various prisons, or so local pub-talk had informed Kane. A bad habit, which the shambles swaying before Kane still seemed to be very much in the grip of even today.

'What's happened to you Bernie?' Kane asked quietly and sensed the immediate disapproval from Keith Evans beside him. 'You fall over or something?' Kane added quickly trying to make the question more relevant to today's cuts and bruises, rather than the tragic history created by decades of self-abuse and neglect. However, Bernie Russell still looked confused. Then, all of a sudden, the wreck laughed, just as if he had got the punch line to some long convoluted joke. He put a hand to his right eye, testing it, like a child realising the hurt for the first time.

'Fall over!?! Nah! Dai Oaf did it coz I laffed at his little boyfriend didn't I!'

'Dai Oaf!?!' Kane asked puzzled.

At that stage they were interrupted by the pub's bouncers. Two solid broad built, almost identical looking young men, with thuggish looking close shaved heads. They had appeared, a bit like Keith Evans had, seemingly out of nowhere. The men had official looking plastic wallets, containing photo id-cards, attached to their right upper arms by elastic bands. Although given their almost identical appearance, how someone could tell which of them was in which particular photograph would have been an interesting dilemma worthy of any identity parade or "Real Life Detective" magazine quiz. Kane instantly noticed that both wore black fleeces, labelled with the now familiar Aberfoist Security Services logo. This time the words were neatly embroidered on the left breast of each zipped up jacket. There were larger transfers affixed across their backs. Kane still thought it was a shame that none of the labelling was abbreviated.

'Russell! You've been warned before 'bout coming in 'ere!' The closest man began.

'Come on get out now or we'll 'ave ta shifts yer!' The second man grunted.

'And tell Mr Pace!' The first man added seriously.

'And you know what 'e'll do!' The second man warned earnestly.

Bernard Russell winked at Kane using his remaining good eye, before turning his bruised face around to face the two tough looking young men. He began to pull himself up to his full height. An imposing stance, aided by the manic grin that was menacingly appearing across the battered face, as Russell spread his cut lips wide. The pose reminded Kane of another story from the past, one from way back in his school days. It had done the rounds of the playground and cloakrooms, building the legend of Bernie Russell. The story went that when Bernie had joined a notorious local gang, a gang made up of much older boys, part of his initiation had been to fight one of the gang's toughest lads. Not surprisingly the older, and much practised thug, had given the younger boy a right kicking, but instead of accepting his beating, and accepting his junior place in the gang's hierarchy, Bernie had lost it, and got mad and madder. Totally unhinged, he just would not give up. However savage the beating became, he kept trying to fight back. Eventually, he told the tough, that he (Bernie) was going to bite the older boy's ear off. The lad laughed and gave Bernie a few more slaps. Knocking him down but each time Bernie got up, again and again, until eventually, the exhausted older boy was left screaming, as the bruised and bloody younger boy, ultimately wrestled him to the floor and bit into his ear lob, tearing it off with his bare teeth, or so the story goes. Whether true or not, this urban legend worked well for Bernie, as it was universally believed by all who knew that *nutter* Bernie Russell. Kane never heard of any other local boys crossing Bernie, ever again. Looking at the stance his contemporary had assumed now, Kane could still easily believe the story.

'Flicker don't call the shots now!' Bernie spat out. 'We all 'ave a new Lord 'n' Master now boys! 'N' 'ee don't care wat I do so long as I sell 'is stuff!' Russell then laughed as if possessed by the devil himself.

In that instant the first man grabbed Bernard. The speed of his sudden action stunned Kane and by the time the twin joined in, the first man had already got Bernie in a strong "Half-Nelson" lock. A few seconds later the second man also had a firm grip on Bernie's right arm and they began dragging him out.

Grunting at first, Bernie seemed to suddenly regain his composure and after a few more yards, he cheerfully shouted back: 'Sorry Gents! I gotta go! Catch you again My-Key!'

Lao Fu still stood like Kane's personal bodyguard, watching the three men struggle down the steps towards the exit. Only once they had disappeared, out of the main door, did he ease himself back onto his stool. Shaking his head slowly, disapproval written all over his face, Lao Fu/The Old Man became the more relaxed Keith Evans and began to sip his fresh pint.

'He's still a *nutter* then!' Kane sighed. Shrugging, trying to make light of the incident.

'Sadly he's not the only one in this town!' Evan's sounded resigned and gloomy.

'So what's he doing, when he's not off his head?' Kane asked.

'Nothing! He's been off his head all his life.' A hard, suddenly disinterested, voice replied. 'He always was a hopeless case. A lad who has squandered every chance he was given!'

'The way I remember it he didn't have much of a chance to start with!' Kane suggested.

'We all have chances My-Key! Russell always made the wrong choices!' The casually dressed man briefly looked a lot more like Lao Fu than Keith Evans as he uttered the strangely unsympathetic and unforgiving words. 'Petty crime! Drug dealing and taking! People like him always want the easy option.'

'Nothing about that looked easy!' Kane interrupted.

'It never is!' Lao Fu shook his head again, before Keith Evans finally took an even bigger swig of his drink, leaving a line of froth across his upper lip.

'I remember his mother!' The older man continued surprisingly mournfully. 'She was a good girl but not very bright and always made the wrong choices too! I never knew his father. Nobody did!'

'Did you train those two?' Kane asked, trying to cheer his mentor up, gesturing gently with his head towards the doorway where the three men had exited.

'Once!' Evans nodded. 'But they, like so many young men these days, were too impatient. They ended up going to Karate, up in Brynmawr!'

Again Lao Fu Evans gave a disapproving shake of the head, before adding dismissively: 'A good sport if you like all that aggressive shouting!'

Kane was in no doubt that whilst Lao Fu must respect another Martial Arts tradition, the grumpy old man that was Keith Evans did not like the Japanese influenced fighting style!

'Your other mate, what's his name, Frankie something, he liked all that stuff didn't he!'

'Frank John?'

'Yes! That's right! The Late Tea Rooms owner. Now that was tragic! He ran a nice little business down the bottom end of town. I always used to call in and have a Green Tea once a week. Not many places serve just that nowadays! It's all buckets of frothy coffee and vegan muffins. It really was a surprise to hear people say he killed himself.'

Keith Evans assuming the manner of the old teacher he really was, looked up and made eye contact with Kane, before speaking slowly and purposefully in his deep voice.

'Frank John was a real fighter. However bad things were I didn't sense that he was going to give up. You know, he warned me that he was selling the business, and that he was going to use whatever money was left to get back with his wife, and sort his family out. No! That man wasn't a quitter!'

Kane nodded in silent agreement. He was about to say something to acknowledge that fact but was struggling to find the right words, when he was totally distracted by an incident. The two security men had reappeared and were in a rush. They were red faced, obviously angry about something, and had jogged quickly up the steps from the front door into the bar. Instead of slowing down, they ran aggressively across the bar floor, heading over towards the smoking area. They halted at the window and looked out briefly before glancing across to each other, nodding grimly, and then each took hold of one of the glass doors, deftly pulling them open, they stepped through in a perfectly timed move. As the doors opened, Kane could hear, for the first time, the commotion that was going on outside. Keith Evans also heard it and spun around.

'Oh dear! More trouble!' He suggested casually.

It was difficult to make out what was going on behind the glass, which was almost blacked out by the night sky. Dark shadows were cast by the light of the moon. There seemed to be a thick outline, a moving scrum of people, who presumably had been standing on the balcony outside. One of the "twins" soon reappeared. He had a firm grip on a young woman. She was screaming that his uncompromising arm lock was breaking her arm. He did not seem to be too worried about that complaint. A few people turned around from the bar. Some others looked up from their tables. However, they all seemed equally unworried about the girl's plight. On seeing who was causing the fuss, pretty much everyone turned away, just as quickly as they had looked up in the first place. Tears were causing a dirty stream washing smeared make up down her chubby cheeks. In spite of this and her smart clothes, Kane still recognised her immediately. She had been one of the two schoolgirls, who he had seen go into "The Kettle" earlier that afternoon.

A thin scrawny looking young man and another teenage girl now staggered through the glass doors, closely chaperoned by the second security twin. Kane recognised this girl too, because she was still wearing her long grey cardigan. She said nothing but followed in the wake of her friend, who was being pushed through the pub, towards the main exit. The young man was deep in conversation with the security guy. From his expression he seemed to be in the middle of a long apology. Kane noticed the security guy was holding a large chunky e-cigarette vapour device in one hand and a clear hard plastic container in the other. The container was about half the size of a traditional cigarette packet. It was half full of a bright yellow/green liquid. The liquid swashed around inside the clear plastic as the group continued to move quickly through the pub.

Just as they reached the top of the steps to the main doorway, Kane noticed that they were met by two young looking uniformed police officers. There was a brief group discussion before the security guys reluctantly handed over the chubby girl to the officers, who then had to drag her off as she began struggling and shouting for her friends to help her. The "cardigan" girl meekly followed her friend out but the young man stayed and began talking amicably to the security. Kane watched as the twins uncompromisingly shook their heads and the young man simply nodded, before turning and slowly walking out of the pub.

'Aberfoist never disappoints!' Kane said turning back to face Keith Evans.

'It does me!' The old man said sadly.

Kane was suddenly very thirsty and picking up his well settled half pint, he took a long swig of the thick dark liquid, performing a not so subtly, mock salute, in his mind, to the unchanged wild west nature of his old home town.

Chapter 11: Guilt

Guilt! That unbalancing emotional burden troubled Kane on his silent journey homeward. It sat sullenly beside him in the Mazda. His only companion as he drove on through what had become yet another pitch-black South Wales night. Now the empty countryside that had cheered him on his afternoon drive, hide its scenic distractions under a thick blanket of darkness and provided no relief from the quiet, constantly twisting, two lane country road.

Guilt nagged him about Bernie Russell's lifestyle choices. Guilt increased his sense of frustration about not knowing how bad things had become for Wendy and Frank. Guilt multiplied his sense of impotence at not having any solutions for them. And guilt spoilt his relief at realising he could just leave their troubles all behind him and return to his less complicated life away from the misery of Aberfoist. He even felt guilty at his anger and resentment at the smug Ellis "Flicker" Pace, and the perverse joy he had taken in provoking Pace's men.

Guilt! Almost blinding him, like the bright headlights of the odd occasional car, which infrequently flashed passed him, their inconsiderate drivers not bothering to dip the full beam. Such harsh interruptions increased his irritation, so much so that he almost stopped at one stage, intending to argue with the driver of a car that had suddenly appeared behind him. A car that did not push on and over take him, but a car that surprisingly accepted his modest pace, content to dawdle and even drop back at times. Yet every now and then, its intense full beam hit his three mirrors, dazzling him because of a misaligned headlight.

Nevertheless, Kane's intuitive auto pilot kept him driving on, allowing him time to fret over and over whilst sub-consciously navigating the slowly zigzagging route out of the dark countryside and on towards the distant orange haze of the busier South Wales Conurbation.

Guilt was not something Kane usually suffered from. Even when he had actually done something, something that others might consider to be wrong, he usually had the ability to justify his actions, at least to himself, with the convenient certainty that he was only doing his best, given the circumstances he found himself in. However, that evening, as his mind conducted the trial, in the dark isolation of his moving metal box court room, Kane found himself guilty on a number of charges, and he was sure, that this time, he was guilty, at least, of not doing his best. He also took into consideration a number of petty offences, which would all add to the weight of evidence against him.

He was guilty because if not actually drunk driving, he was certainly drink driving. His conscience, which over the last ten years had become a real pain as he tried to live a decent, law-abiding life, was regularly reminding him that this was something he had sworn never to do, (again). Although, Kane might have been just about old enough to remember when it was socially acceptable to have *one for the road*, at a time when serious, responsible, disciplined, real men, like his father, would not have had more than four pints on a night out, because after all they were driving! Kane was very much aware that he now lived in the age of designated drivers, when a mix of car keys and alcohol was universally taboo, and that disappointingly, he had drunk almost *two halves* of Guinness! Kane may have consoled himself that he was probably worrying about something and nothing, for given his body weight and the fact that he had left at least a third of his last half pint sloshing around the bottom of the glass, and as such was most likely to be still well under the actual legal alcohol limit, *drink driving* was still something he disapproved of, and something that he had certainly not done since the folly of his youth, well over twenty years ago.

He was certainly guilty because of the time. Earlier that evening, when he had noticed that it was almost 8 o'clock, and he had had to make his excuses to leave the old man, his former "Master" Keith Evans, who certainly seemed to be all set for a full night out, in the den of inequity that The Coliseum Public House and Restaurant, in Aberfoist town centre, was rapidly becoming, Kane felt strangely guilty for abandoning his old mentor.

He was also guilty at being late for the evening meal that his wife had promised him. Although this guilt was definitely losing the battle with the guilt of abandoning his drinking companion; especially as before he had actually left, another fight had broken out in the pub. This time, two young men, sat on the far side of the bar, had decided to slug it out over some unseen slight. It had certainly been a busy early evening for the two "bouncers" from the Aberfoist Security Services, as they rushed to efficiently remove the new offenders from the increasingly disorderly pub.

Kane also felt guilty for having stopped briefly, at the invitingly bright lights of the 24/7 mini supermarket, on the outskirts of town. He had visited its bakery and bought himself their last, over baked, flaky corned beef pasty, even though he was less than an hour away from the meal, which he knew his wife would be preparing for him. So what if he had not eaten since lunchtime, a good seven hours before, and the so called *food* snack, was allegedly needed to soak up the alcohol and ensure that he had a fighting chance of sobering up for the drive home. Yet, he had not needed to buy (and scoff) the "meal deal" extras, the large packet of crisps, the bucket of coffee, and the oversized bar of chocolate as well as the quick nibble. All eaten, Kane would allege in his defence, to ensure that he was (chemically) well and truly *under the legal limit*!

Then the orange bright urban world disturbed Kane from his increasingly irrational reflections. He had arrived in a lamppost lit built up area, with its dirty looking houses, all crammed together, beside the modern dual carriageway, which led down to the valley bottom and the quick, short, stretch of motorway to Cardiff. Kane consciously accelerated up the slip road and carefully negotiated his way onto the first inside lane of the three-lane motorway, which even at this late hour, was full of fast moving traffic. He pulled out into the middle lane, as soon as he was able, and quickly passed the slower moving traffic. There was a small Citroen van, an old Mercedes salon, and finally an articulated lorry that seemed to be cruising along at the head of the forty-five miles an hour convoy. Kane noticed the red lit needle, of his car's accelerator gauge, flicker just above the seventy MPH marker, at just about the same time as he registered the pulsing warning lights, flash "50 MPH" from it's stand on the central reservation to his right. Even though the traffic in the outside lane continued to trundle passed him, at what must have been well above the usual 70 MPH speed limit, he felt it prudent, especially given his recent alcohol in-take, to slow down and so gradually pulled back into the left hand lane. Now he led the convoy of cars, by cruising at a steady 50 MPH.

Kane had not really been surprised, when he first noticed, in his car's mirrors, that a dark Ford Focus, which had followed him up the slip road, and matched his initial acceleration, was now copying his compliant manoeuvre. However, he became increasingly irritated again when he realised it had a similar slightly misaligned bright headlight to the car that had followed him along the country road out of Aberfoist. He did not want confrontation now but itched to speed up and pull away from it. However, he was locked in to the left hand lane now, even though the speed restrictions seemed to have come to an end, trapped by another convoy of slightly faster cars trundling by, on his right, in the middle lane of the motorway.

Slowly it dawned on him that the Ford must have been behind him for most of the trip. Nothing strange in that, he told himself; where else would someone go from Aberfoist but to the bright lights of Cardiff at this time of night on a Friday. As a young man he would have made this journey himself. Kane casually tried to make out the car's passengers, by using his mirror. He wondered if they were a group of youngsters, heading out like he had done, to enjoy a night out in the big city. Given the entertainment options in Aberfoist, he did not blame them. He just wished that they had put their foot down and passed him earlier on, so that their headlamp was not distracting him. Kane tried hard to focus, once again, on what was bothering him. Guilt or grief! He could not decide.

After a few minutes of deep thought his "autopilot" alerted him to the fact that his exit was approaching fast. Kane concentrated again on his driving. He began signalling and slowed down just as the exit countdown signs appeared on his left. However, as he carried out the simple manoeuvre something else was bothering him. The misaligned headlight had followed him off the motorway but when he came to a stop at the red light on the roundabout, at the top of the slip road, the car had seemed to drop back, almost as if the driver did not want to get too close.

Kane almost dismissed such thoughts as merely his over-active imagination, a silly unrealistic reaction, caused by dwelling too much on the past. Yet something in his sub-conscious had instinctively triggered a strange awareness of the vehicle, which must now still be somewhere behind him. His reasoning told him that the driver had taken the wrong junction for the city centre. Perhaps the "*night-clubbers*" had turned off too soon, distracted by their merry *Friday nite-out* banter. Maybe they needed the nearby *"services!"* Although when he took the first left onto the link road, and cautious, because of his alcohol guilt, slowed to the new lower speed limit of 40 mph, the irritating light almost caught up with him. If they had wanted the *services* they should have taken the second left at the roundabout! Yes, it was dark, due to the council's energy saving restrictions on lamppost light pollution, but the "City Gate" motorway service station was well signposted! They had seemed to slow down obviously confused or so he reasoned and when he took a right at the next roundabout, intending to enter the housing estate, that was his short cut home across North Cardiff, he was pleased to see them spin around the roundabout, as if they were trying to head back to the motorway.

Kane then dismissed the oddity, relaxing back into his driver's autopilot mode once again as the car seemed to know its way through the familiar empty residential roads. A mature couple, quirkily wearing bright high visibility sashes over their coats, appeared slightly ahead of him on the right. They were walking their dog and caused him to stop at the pedestrian crossing. As he waited he studied the bright green pattern of the LED lights that pulsed around the dog's collar. He pontificated to himself on the preparation it must take nowadays to take your pet out for a simple stroll. His mind debated the necessary evil of carrying little black plastic bags every time you walked a dog. The woman smiled at him and waved her hand gratefully at him for his patience, a hand that contained a rather full looking dark plastic bag. It was well meant but a rather off putting gesture nonetheless. Kane tried not to think about the bag's content but he did not succeed and sadly he found himself resolving never to own a dog again. He then carried on driving up the hill, before turning right into the total darkness of the country lanes, which linked this new housing "development" to the next North Cardiff village, the one where he lived.

Although the lane was narrow, Kane inevitably drove faster as he approached the familiar home stretch of his journey. Nevertheless, he instinctively kept checking his mirror, glancing at it every few seconds. It remained dark. This relaxed him and telling himself that he was almost home, no more than five minutes or so he reckoned, he concentrated on the road ahead.

The full beam of an approaching car was illuminating a twist in the hedgerow a few hundred yards further down the lane. Kane slowed down and dipped his own headlights. The approaching car tore around the blind bend and bore down on him without a care. Idiot! Kane thought to himself, squeezing his car closer to the hedgerow that bordered the lane to his left. He held his breath. He heard a branch snap as it was hit by his nearside wing mirror. At the last minute the approaching car dipped its beam, then accelerated passed. Kane blinked and naturally exhaled. He was sure that the two metal boxes must have passed each other with only millimetres of fresh air between them.

Pulling back on the lever to switch his own headlights back onto full beam, he negotiated the bend, before pressing his right foot down on the accelerator pedal, enjoying the safety of the long dark straight section of lane ahead. The hedgerow was soon replaced by the wooden fencing of someone's gardens on both sides of the lane, until just as he started to climb, a stone wall replaced the fence on the right and a cultivated thicket ran along the left hand side. He could now see the start of a long line of yellow lighted lampposts illuminating the next urban area. Kane sighed. He was nearly home. Glancing in his mirror he noticed that way back at the start of the straight, a set of headlights flickered behind him. They were on full beam so he could not really tell at that distance if they were misaligned or not. The lights were gaining on him. More car lights appeared ahead of him on the brow of the hill and began the descent. The unseen driver flicked his beam on and off once in warning. Kane complied with the request, before muttering an apology at his lack of anticipation. His lights dipped, he adjusted his speed. The lane may have been wider on this stretch or the approaching driver must have been more sensible, for the cars passed each other with less drama. Kane glanced back, using his mirror, and waited to see if the following car dipped its beam. It did not and there was a flash as the car in the right repeated its request. Too late, the cars passed each other, and then the beam of the following car eventually dipped, too late. Kane checked ahead and then looked back in his mirror, taking longer this time. Much to his annoyance he could see quite clearly that the headlights of the pursuing car were misaligned.

When the lane ended, Kane would normally have turned right, at a mini roundabout, which filtered traffic into his home village. Tonight, he chose to drive straight on. Whilst a part of him was convinced he was imaging things, a strange foreboding was creeping over him, warning him not to lead the car with the misaligned lights to his home. He sped up and noticed the car behind matched him. Although not gaining or closing down the distance between them, it kept pace with his Mazda.

Kane knew the road ahead well. He waited until it twisted left, then right, and he knew that it would rise up to an almost blind right turn. This was the right turn he needed to take to head for home. He accelerated, recklessly shooting into the bends. A glance back, there were no lights. He looked forward. He was lucky. There was no approaching traffic. Kane gambled. He did not indicate and swung the Mazda right at the junction. The car swayed violently and with tyres screeching he accelerated again, disappearing up the rise into the residential housing estate that spread out and up the right-hand hillside. Kane took the next left and skidded to a stop. He turned his lights off. Breathing heavily, he hunched down in his car seat. Risking a hand movement, he reached up and adjusted his mirror. He could now see if any cars were approaching or passing by the last junction. He worried about the unavoidable noise. He half expected the house owners, at the main junction, to be looking out of their windows and wondering what rally car was tearing up their residential area, but he hoped the people in the following car would not have heard anything. He hoped they had their radio on.

Five minutes passed and there was no traffic. Sitting back up straight, he re-adjusted his mirror. Slowly, with no lights or indication, he eased his car forward, in darkness, and at the bottom of the street turned right. Kane knew that he could work his way up the housing estate, using the maze of side roads, rather than the main channel to get much closer to his house. He had decided that he should park two streets away from his actual house. There were only two access roads connecting the main road to this warren of side streets and there was no way to drive through to his street, but he also knew that there was a path, which he could use, on foot, to get from the neighbouring street to his own street. He would simply walk around the corner. He told himself if someone was searching for his car it would take some finding on the trendy, ecologically friendly, dimly lit streets, and even then, they would struggle to find his actual house, amongst the many similar styled houses on the estate. Of course, they might trace the registration number of his car to his address, and see the illuminated house number that he had proudly stuck on the wall last year but perhaps that was taking his sudden paranoia to a whole new level. Why follow him if they knew his address?

So why would someone follow him all the way from Aberfoist to Cardiff? Kane asked himself as paranoia replaced guilt in his self-analysis. He began walking through the neighbourhood. It was ridiculous but it was just a feeling he had.

He had not had a fight for, well, he could not remember when, and although he did not call the incident in "The Kettle" a real fight, the cuts and bruises on Bernie Russell's face indicated that Dylan Francis, if that was really the little man's name, was not taking the humiliation lightly. Kane's old instinct for survival told him that whatever Ellis Pace had said, Dylan would want to get even. Not that he was particularly worried about the little man. Whatever Sue Ward-Davies thought, Kane had experienced too much to truly worry about a vengeful little bully. However, so had Frank John! There was also something about the tall man. The one they had called Dai Oaf. Kane remembered the way that he had looked at him through "The Kettle's" window. He could not put his finger on what it was about that look, but it was more than a little unsettling, especially now, with hindsight. Then it occurred to him. The man had looked guilty!

Kane stopped for a minute and stood silently in the shadows of the pedestrian pathway that cut through into his own street. He was waiting, waiting for what he was not sure. All was quiet. He could hear the hum of traffic in the distance, as a few cars moved along the nearby main road. None were moving into the estate or were they. He gave it a few more minutes. Listening hard, he heard nothing. Then just as he was feeling silly and about to return to his car and drive it home, he heard the unmistakable noise of a car approaching.

From his hidden view point, Kane could see a car slowly entering the street and then steadily making its way up towards him, with its headlights oddly on full beam. The dark shadow in the driver's seat seemed to be moving its head around as if studying each house and examining each parked vehicle. The car looked like an old Ford Focus but then so many hatchbacks do! When the car reached where the Mazda was parked, it stopped. Kane held his breath. Then the car suddenly accelerated passed the Mazda until the dead end of the street. There it did a rapid

111

three-point turn, before returning to pull up abruptly, right in front of the Mazda. The dark shadow got out. Kane could not make out who it was but it was tall.

The shadow went to the back of the Ford and opened the hatchback. It reached inside and after what seemed like ages, it reappeared with a large insulated rectangular bag. Kane exhaled. The man, for the shadow moved awkwardly, like a tall lanky man, lurched across the road, away from Kane's hiding place. As he walked up the drive to the house, directly opposite Kane's parked car, holding the bag out in front of him, hidden security sensors worked their magic and the driveway was instantly flooded with bright light. All of a sudden Kane could see, quite clearly, that the tall teenager was dressed in a familiar blue and red uniform. The youth stooped to ring the doorbell and nervously stepped back holding out his fast food home deliver in readiness for the householder. Despite his snack earlier, Kane remembered that he was still hungry. He was also embarrassed.

Shaking his head in disbelief, Kane turned and walked away down the cutting towards his home. The false scare had almost done enough to persuade Kane that he was wise to leave his car where it was parked, just for tonight, just in case. He did feel silly about the precautions he had just taken, but no guilt. In his life he had learnt that it was always better safe than sorry!

Chapter 12: The Watcher

Sardaar Sarbaah Sar lent forward to look out through the circular window. His broad shoulders filled the diameter of the one way glass. The tall man had fitted this outlook inside his private office and he enjoyed standing behind his desk and spying down on the street below. Set at almost the highest point of the south facing gabled end to his grey, rubble stoned, polygon shaped, three storey building, this view point also allowed him to watch the approaching main road, which was the only access road up the valley, and as such, the only way down to and up from Cardiff.

At this time of night the road outside was quiet and the capital city was a mere twenty minutes drive away. Of course, if you had to try your luck during the morning rush hour, then the time somehow doubled or even tripled, as stressed commuters followed each other in single file along the congested escape route, out of South Wales' central valley, in search of prosperity to where (these days) the only reasonably paid employment was available to them.

Providing the only escape from benefit poverty was certainly not the intention of the original road builders. They had desired access to the rich resources found under the lush green green grass of the once scenic hillsides. Now, after centuries of exploitation and abandonment, it made perfect sense for anyone, let alone a man like Sardaar Sarbaah Sar, to a keep a close watch on what mischief might head up the valley.

His building had once upon a time been considered to be a nineteenth century sanctuary and was a perfect architectural model of a typical Welsh Baptist Chapel. A spiritual citadel, balanced worryingly on the edge of an untidily urbanised hillside. However, it had now been controversially "re-imagined" into a private members "sports" club; and according to the cheap, green neon sign, which hung outside, flashing brightly into the dark and wet night sky; it was hilariously called "The Potting Shed." The new signage almost obscured the once respectful, original stone masonry legend, "Libanus, Built in 1844". The conversion amused Sardaar Sarbaah Sar greatly. He often reflected on the many white Christian ministers, who in the past would have used such an Old Testament inspired base to lecture sternly against the evils of a misspent youth. A youth they traditionally feared might be corrupted in the snooker halls and bars of the locality. Now, his old chapel was the only such commercial den of inequity that actually remained open in the vicinity, and it was his club. A club for sinners not for saints! Here evil had cheerfully taken over the dead missionaries' once sanctimonious beacon of hope for a godly future.

In reality, the club was simply a cover. It was the perfect location and a grand base for his hidden illicit operations. Those that existed to service the desperate needs and wants of the nearby towns and villages. Sardaar Sarbaah Sar did not watch the northern route. He knew exactly what went up and came down that road to and from his club. He laughed. "The Potting Shed!" A name chosen ostensibly because the only genuine sports played inside were snooker and pool; and yet it was a name that caused many others to chuckle, mainly because they knew of the illegal, more cultivated herbal product that was also available inside on request, by the wrong type of customer.

The old congregation and their pastors were probably spinning in their graves at his oh so modern, commercial crusade, run from their once holy sentinel. In the past, the Baptists had been innocently worried about the corrupting influence of gambling over a game of snooker or billiards and the evil of alcohol fuelled distractions. Nowadays, Sardaar Sarbaah Sar was only worried about how he could ensure the supply of an altogether more toxic means of misspending not so much the natives' youth, but certainly their paltry income and bridging the gap in their demand for something, anything, to distract them from their limited economic opportunities and selfish hedonistic ambitions.

From his viewpoint on the upper floor, Sardaar Sarbaah Sar or Ed Lord, as he now insisted on being called in his adopted homeland by all but his closest allies, casually looked out at the rain, sweeping up the valley, battering against his expensively refurbished Victorian building. The bright spring day that had encouraged him to use his beloved Kawasaki motorbike for the first time since winter, had turned into another bleak and dark night, before finally fulfilling the regional obligation to rain; and it was certainly maintaining that tradition by raining hard on all who dared venture out that night. Coming from a generally dry country, Lord Sardaar Sarbaah Sar enjoyed watching the weather through his personal spy hole. Perhaps he was obsessed with the rain. No wonder really, for being cold and wet was a natural condition that he had seemingly endured constantly since arriving in this god forsaken country called Wales. Or was it "Wails!?!" He laughed to himself again. That was a joke, one which he had gotten straight away, back on that very first day, even with his limited understanding of English, when two years ago, some of his club's original members had tried to confuse the dark skinned foreigner, the tall man who had taken over from the hapless, and bankrupt, previous owners. The people of the valley may have resented him for being a foreigner but they had soon learnt to respect him, and many now depended on the unique products he supplied them with. In turn he tolerated them. Mostly, trying to be the *"good fellow"* that he knew they now called him mockingly behind his back.

115

Whilst Lord ran his own business as hard and unrelentingly as the rain was falling outside, the man who was Sardaar Sarbaah Sar had a begrudging respect for some of his new acquaintances. Well the older ones mainly. The proud ones, who like him, could remember working hard to make a living. The ones who knew you only got something if you made an effort. They tended to be tough old guys. He enjoyed the bitter humour, which they used to shield themselves from the truth of their situation and stave off the depression at being caught in a relentless economic and emotional trap. They had been betrayed too, just like him, believing that the outsiders, their invaders, the business owners and the absentee landlords, those whom their forefathers had made rich, through their hard graft, would honour their promises and obligations, instead of cutting and running, abandoning the communities their exploitation had built up, to their unfortunate fate at the very first sign of economic difficulty.

When Lord looked around him, at the so called sites of industrial heritage, which still scarred the land in this area, he recognised the history of exploitation. The greed of asset strippers, indulged in here, as equally as they had in his homeland so far away. However, this recognition merely motivated him in his solitary mission, making him determined to survive and prosper. This was the way of the world. It always would be or so Lord Sardaar Sarbaah Sar believed. He knew that he would and could do anything to achieve his goals. That man, the other week, Frank John, had learnt that lesson the hard way. Funny, Lord thought, how he had remembered the old soldier's name! Yes! That was the name of the latest fool, who had crossed him, and paid the ultimate price.

Lord did not feel guilty. He did not understand that emotion. He did feel regret, but it was regret for the inconvenience. In the end, that stubborn and deluded man had earned his respect. He had resisted the torture. Lord had never

116

known a man to manage pain like Frank John. If only there had been another way, he thought now with the benefit of hindsight. A man like that could have been useful to him. Instead, he had to rely on people like that odious buffoon Pace. Frank John had been too candid for his own good. A stupidly stubborn man but sincere in his prejudice.

It was all so unnecessary. John's reactions had made Lord lose his temper. Lord had beaten him. He had used the boiling water treatment, usually so effective with weaker men, pouring it over John's legs, again and again. Yes, the man had screamed. He had even wept when his trousers had stuck to his raw, scalded flesh, but as his skin flaked off, he had found the strength to threaten Lord. If only the fool had broken and signed the contract. It may not have had to end with John's death. Lord had become so angry with John's defiance (and overt racism,) that he had strangled him to death, using his red silk scarf. A skill he had been taught many years ago when training with the northern tribes of his homeland. Yet it was John who had encouraged him, telling him to pull tighter, eventually pushing him over the edge and the choke torture had turned into an execution. Shaking his head at the memory, Lord wondered why the dying man had got all biblical. At the end he had gasped something about Cain. The missionaries had told him that old story a long time ago. He could not remember the point of it now. All he knew was that Cain was a killer!

Pace might be a buffoon but he had his uses. He had been the one to suggest hanging the body up to make it look like suicide, rather than create another awkward disappearance. A simple ruse, that seemed to have worked well. Maybe, despite his misgivings, Pace may prove to be an asset. After all, Pace seemed to have influence over the local police or at least certain key officers; and if not, Lord gave a subconscious shrug and thoughtlessly touched the red silk scarf that he still wore around his own neck.

Lord may have regretted losing his temper but he certainly did not worry about seizing the opportunities the western world presented him. Many of the younger locals were a waste of space in his private opinion. He laughed at them behind their backs! All they did was moan a lot. They did not recognise the possibilities. The wonderful advantages their world presented them. They unbelievably moaned about how hard their lives were now! They felt entitled to the treats presented to them through modern multi media. Yet they had free education and were allowed to do pretty much anything they wanted but all they seemed to want to do was do nothing! Nothing but moan about why they weren't rich and famous! He felt they should be ashamed. They should see where he had come from. What being born into a real war zone was like! He certainly felt no guilt about what he was doing on this side of the world. No guilt about what they were letting him do to them. After all, as they and their adverts often told him, *they deserved it!*

Just then, as he sneered out of the window, his attention was caught by two passing pedestrians. The young men had obviously been caught out by the weather. They were both wearing the unofficial uniform adopted by students from the local college. Ripped jeans, white ink slogan labelled black T-shirts and ridiculously expensive trainers. Both students were soaked to the skin and struggling down hill against the wind and the rain. Their staggered movements also suggested a Friday night spent drinking in one of the two local pubs, found higher up the hillside, where the remains of a once vibrant town centre was generally shuttered or boarded up, like most small community centres in this economically distressed region of the Welsh Valleys. Here the shutters came down most evenings, whether the shops were open or closed. They were necessary to protect their windows from the over exuberance of revellers like these two.

118

Lord often wondered why smashing plate glass windows or general vandalism had become the thing to do to round off a great night out. Maybe it was the fact people resented seeing their reflections and despised themselves for being in such a state. Perhaps they were just "off their heads!" Watching the wet students staggering home below him, he could almost hear the excuses often made for such behaviour. "It's not them! It's the drugs!" Lord allowed himself a thin smile. Perhaps they weren't drunk. Maybe they were customers of his, albeit supplied by those he purposely recruited to act as frontline distributors.

It did rain in his original homeland of Afghanistan but never cold and constant like this. In fact he really could not remember it being anything other than dry and hot or cold as a child. He closed his eyes and tried to remember, fighting off the pain that thinking back would bring.

***

A beautiful lady, dressed in a dark blackish blue embroidered Balochi tribal dress, sat on the floor by an open hearth, bare footed, as water boiled in a metal basin on the middle of a crackling fire. He could smell the wood smoke. She whispered sweetly to him. He heard the sound but could not recall the words. Was she singing? Then he felt the fear. The scene changed in his mind. The woman was lying still, dirty and dead on the street. There were other bodies amongst the scattered wreckage of a car and a bus. He could hear nothing but as flames danced through the gaps in the walls and doorways of nearby buildings, he could still feel the sickening shock and terror of a survivor. It was far too raw an emotion, even after all those years.

Black smoke mixed with sand and brown dirt filled the air, clouding his imagination, as silent flashes of light exploded at the far edges of his inner vision. Like the other people in his village,

119

he knew to run away from the light. A sad man, who back then looked a bit like he looked now, had eventually come and roughly carried him away. He remembered walking with that man, across the dusty plains and struggling across uneven ground, stumbling over rocks, up and down hillsides, with sharp stick bushes, guided by starlight, and urged on by kind words, through the cold darkness of the night and then the dry heat of the day.

He imagined playing happily with other children at a large camp site. Then he remembered being left with a fierce looking old man, who wore his white beard long and beat him, with a stick if he cried because he was hungry. An old man, who shamed him by making him help the women, instead of letting him go out into the fields, with the older boys. An old man, who had refused to let him go back to fight the enemy, even when he had grown taller. An old man, who had a plan! An old man, who had taught him the best way to take his revenge!

***

On the wet pavement outside, (in Wales), the two students had paused, briefly hunching together against the now almost horizontal downpour. They were stuffing their mouths full with giant pizza slices, carelessly picked out from a soggy red and blue cardboard box. They seemed oblivious to the water already dripping from the doughy triangles, which must have left an unsightly trail of greasy tomato and cheese sauce on their lips, chin, and cheeks. They were also oblivious to the watcher, hidden behind the privacy glass window, on the upper floor of the building just across the road, diagonally behind them. One boy stooped suddenly, when a lump of meat fell from his over stacked slice. Down it fell, down to the dirty wet floor. Lord watched in disgust, anticipating that the drunk would try to pick up the droppings, but the boy was not that flexible. Instead he

120

swayed, from side to side, for what seemed like ages, before screaming out an obscenity, hurling the remains of the slice from his hand, wastefully down the short distance to the floor. Then, roaring with laughter, he was trying to straighten up and failing. Eventually, he lurched forward, still hunched, to try and catch up with his companion, who having abandoned his partner, was now making good progress down the increasingly steep hill to where, Lord knew, the nearby so called "university" halls of residence were located.

Lord was not stupid. He did not sell to his neighbours. He sold to someone who sold to someone who sold to them. He was not interested in cutting out the middle man. He covered his costs and made a healthy profit. He also knew that his product would generate demand. The demand of his customers would only increase as would his price, once their want turned to need. If they were clever enough, they would work this out themselves. Surely that was the purpose of educating them in the first place.

Education was something he envied them. The only thing he envied about their privileged lives. Mostly self taught, he had learnt a very basic English when as a teenager he was sent by his "uncles" to work at the nearby UN army bases. He tried to develop this rudimentary understanding by talking to the American and British soldiers he met. Most of his understanding of spoken English had come from sneakily watching video films at the barracks and then eventually through the abandoned DVDs he had acquired. Of course, now he was a successful businessman, he had amassed his own collection! Not surprisingly perhaps, given his history and chosen profession, they were mainly gangster movies or action films, like the ones the soldiers had been so fond of. They had been fond of him too and he them, until they had abandoned him and his family to the brutal war lords. Men of violence, who had ultimately chased those pretend protectors away. At first his language skills, albeit only oral, endangered him, as they made him a collaborator in the eyes of some factions. Yet they ultimately proved to be an asset, and he was taken into the service of a more enlightened tribal leader. Long before being sent to Britain, he had even attended night school, in Pakistan, and learnt to read and write in English.

When he had first arrived in the UK, he had been shocked to find out that his basic literacy was so much better than so many of the people he was required to mix with! They, the locals, seemed to either dismiss learning or simply saw the opportunities of higher education as an excuse to avoid work. A culture of over indulgence, whether it was alcohol or drug fuelled excess, had developed, and every effort was exerted into this decadence rather than learning to improve themselves like he had done. He now despised western society's casual acceptance that their children could misbehave and hence had no qualms about supplying them with the means to destroy themselves.

The irony of trying to enrich a generation's thinking, whilst allowing them, and even encouraging them, to consume a toxic mix of chemicals, as part of growing up, constantly amazed him. His mind recalled the sharp sting of the old imam's thin stick on his young hand, when fear caused him to nervously stumble over the sacred words of the Koran, in the dilapidated mosque, near the orphanage, which had briefly become his ramshackle home, in the days after the planes had bombed his village and killed all of his direct family.

Another group of four students were passing by below him now. At least one of these had a coat but he was not wearing it. The gang shared it as he held it aloft, over their heads, whilst they too staggered along, down the street, laughing and joking. One, with long black dripping wet hair, broke away from the group and began to vomit on the pavement right outside the front door of one of the terraced houses. This caused raucous laughter amongst the other three. Lord tut-tutted to himself and then gasped when he realised that the vomiting student was a girl. One of the three gave up the limited shelter of the coat and went to her friend's aid. She was another girl, short plump with cropped blonde hair. She wore dark denim shorts, lacy tights and baseball boots, with yet another slogan embossed T-shirt. Lord could not make out the white writing on her bulging chest but within seconds of moving out of the cover of the coat, she was soaked. She put her arm around the taller girl and steered her back to the group. The coat was hoisted again and the gang began to make their now not so merry way down the road.

His eyes lazily followed the groups' slow progress until he noticed coming up the road, the headlights of an approaching car. As it got closer he recognised in spite of the darkness, the two tone markings on the classic Mercedes Benz saloon. The students also recognised its familiar paint job and knowing it to be one of the black and white cabs that normally operated in the nearby city of Cardiff, they all abandoned the coat and rushed to the side of the road and began to vigorously hail it. The taxi cruised ignorantly passed them, just fast enough to create a giant wave of dirty water in its wake, as the extra wide, hi-performance, tyres splashed through one of the huge pools created by the inadequate drainage and large pot holes of the poor quality tarmac road. Soaked, the students retreated from the kerbside, yelling abuse, then they burst into fits of laughter and turned away to continue their sorry procession, presumably down the road towards their digs.

In the meantime, the taxi had slowed and signalled right, crossing the road, it pulled up in front of the club. A large man got out of the front passenger seat. His long bushy beard blew about him in the wind. He was holding a long unopened black golfing umbrella and dressed in the climatically unsuitable, baggy trousers and long loose fitting shirt of a traditional Shalwar

Kameez. Seemingly oblivious to the rain, the giant slowly walked around the front of the car and made his way back along the pavement to the back passenger door. Once there, he purposely opened the umbrella up and held it high but at a slight angle to combat the wind, which was causing his now damp long shirt to flap behind him. Only when he was truly satisfied that he could protect his passenger from the elements, did he open the door. Lord watched as a man in a well cut, light coloured, lounge suit, slide smoothly out of the car. He looked tiny compared to the first man but so would most people. They quickly moved out of Lord's sight. However, he was in no doubt that they were heading towards his club's main doorway.

Turning away from the window, Lord manoeuvred himself around his imposing double pedestal mahogany desk, with its high backed, dark red leather, executive chair. He strode across his office's thick pile burgundy carpet, taking the five paces needed to reach a reinforced white Georgian style composite door. Opening the door, by pushing the ornate brass handle down, triple locks lifted with a metallic clunk. Lord forced a smile on his face and began the decent down the dark wooden gallery style staircase, whilst calling out to those below:

'Look sharp now! Our guest is here!'

Chapter 13: In the Club

When the commanding voice boomed down from the top of the stairs, the two large men below, instantly stepped away from the full-sized snooker table, immediately abandoning their game. Regardless of their usual fierce competition and the fact that the player on the table was in the middle of a game winning break, they knew where their duty lay and both were disciplined enough to switch off from their match at the first sound of their master's voice. This was a trick they were used to doing, for the table was purposely positioned right at the bottom of the stairs, so that no one could have slipped passed or gained access to the stairway, without drawing even the most intense player's focus away from the green baize. However, such security was not needed tonight for they were the only players in the otherwise empty room.

Nevertheless, by the time Lord had reached the bottom stair, both had securely placed their snooker cues into the clip holders of the nearby wooden cue stand and were waiting, like soldiers on guard duty, either side of the stairwell. Their impressive physiques looked far more suited to the weights room of a gymnasium, with its brutal clanking of pumped metal, rather than the subtle whisper of the chalked cue tip and occasional clunk of ball on ball. Well defined muscles rippled under the tight grey flannel of their sweatshirts and matching jogger pants. The boys appeared to have a common mixed race heritage. They were possibly twins, not identical but certainly brothers. Their similarity was strengthened by the fact that they wore the same clothes and were of equal height. Both had shaved their heads and beards to a perfectly matching thin dark layer of stubble. In simpler times, they may have been described as Eurasian. However, their complex but perfectly natural genetic make up was perhaps best left open in these more liberal, transient times, for they had never met their father.

Lord began to stride purposely up the middle of the large rectangular room, right through the central pathway created by the other, symmetrically arranged, snooker tables. Without a word, the casually dressed men fell in behind him. Their soft grey suede training shoes silently slid across the heavy duty carpet, leaving no impression despite their bulk, unlike their taller and broader leader, whose sharp toed cowboy boots left a temporary Cuban heeled imprint in the thick pile of the expensively carpeted, wide open plan room, which took up the whole of the building's second floor.

In addition to the staff only table, located at the bottom of the stairs to Lord's office, the snooker room had eight full sized snooker tables. Four tables were spaced out to the left and there were a matching four to the right. At the far end of the room, on Lord's left hand side, there was a small drinks bar, with a sitting area extending out from the bar, to the right hand side of the club. This space was filled mainly by two comfy looking red leather sofas, sat either side of a low short smoked glass coffee table. There was also space for one, sky blue clothed, pool table, and four matching blue cloth armchairs. Four tall stools stood empty by the bar, and on the fifth, guarding the open gap left by the raised hatch of the dark varnished wooden bar top, sat a stern faced, long legged, slim but strongly built, mature woman. She had an extremely short, almost shaved, high fashion, pixie-cut hair style, dyed bright yellow. Her skin was varnished, almost as dark as the bar wood, through regular application of expensive false tanning product. She had dressed to please Lord, so wore tight fitting skinny white jeans and an equally provocative white, see-through lacy blouse, the top four buttons of which were

126

undone to reveal a firm heavily spray tanned cleavage, the dimensions of which seemed to be truly out of proportion to the rest of her petite but oddly muscular frame, and like her hair, her breasts were obviously not natural. She did not wear a bra. Perhaps the clothes she wore were once upon a time considered by some to be too young for someone of her advancing age, yet no one would dare say it. Her strong but slim physic had uncomfortably cheated time, no doubt as a result of an addiction to the gym and big city beauty clinics.

Lord winked and gave the woman a glimpse of his most confident smile. Her red lips widened slightly in what may have passed for a smile but had no obvious warmth, for the rest of her features remained Botox frozen. She may have been about to say something as her mouth opened slightly. Her brown eyes stared intensely straight back at him until she blinked, once, her long black, false, eyelashes fluttering briefly. However, a loud electronic bleep drew everybody's attention to the main door to her left. It was now opening slowly.

The large bearded man, in the now rain soaked traditional clothing, held the door open. Leaning in, he glanced menacingly around the hall. The dark eyes above his large hooked nose, were darting from person to person and then flickering up and down, around the room, making him look like a savage bird of prey, searching for its next meal. They scanned right to the back of the room, before returning to the two bodybuilders. The cruel mouth broke into a wicked mocking grin. Then, seemingly satisfied with this brief examination, the hawk turned his head, with its long hair, dripping wet from the rain, back to face the waiting diminutive shadow that could be seen outlined beyond the frosted glass panel wall divider to the left of the door. A splash of water unintentionally flicked off the hawk's brow as the large man curtly snapped his head forward in a short bow to the shadow. He muttered something, before stepping aside, giving space for the much shorter man, elegantly dressed in a smart modern business suit, to enter the room. The large man followed his master in, shutting the door quickly and carefully behind him. With his back to the door, his bulk intentionally blocking all access in or out of the room, the giant hawk gave another glare that demanded respect. In his massive left hand, he held the closed golfing umbrella point up. It was still dripping, like a blood soaked sword.

'Khosh Amadid! Welcome Brother!' Lord spoke formally, nodding his head in what was unmistakeably a ceremonial bow.

The man in the suit broke into a broad smile.

'Salam! Sardaar Sarbaah Sar!' He replied, equally formally, and copied the ceremonial head bow. Then in a thick London accent, he added a cheeky familiar greeting.

'Alright Bro!?!'

The short man opened up his arms inviting a hug, which his host accepted with an even broader smile. As their escorts looked on awkwardly, the two men stepped towards each other. Lord was a tall man and had to hunch down before they could warmly embrace like long lost brothers. At the doorway, the giant hawk was a full chest, head and shoulders above the huddle. The shorter man spoke up.

'Cain't yer do anyfink 'bout vis bloody weafer Bro!?! It's worse van a fucking monsoon!'

The bigger man chuckled before responding.

'They tell me this is God's Country but he is always crying because of what you English have done to it!' Both men laughed.

'I jus knew you'd fucking blame me as soon as I stepped off of vat fucking train!'

Lord or Sardaar Sarbaah Sar as his visitor had correctly called him, turned slightly to face the bar and with his right arm still casually draped over his guest's shoulder, he waived his left arm in an almost theatrical gesture.

128

'What do you think of my club? Nice eh!'

'At least it's fucking dry!' The shorter man said with a wry grin.

'Dry eh! What am I thinking? Forgive me! Kim!' He called out to the woman, who was now standing to attention behind the bar with her thin but now unmistakably nervous smile straining her unnaturally taut face.

'Kim! Please offer our guests a drink!' Then calling behind him, to his two minders, he continued.

'Boys, get a towel so my friend's companion can dry himself and rack up a table so he can pot a few shots whilst I have a private chat with my dear friend here!'

He turned back and looked the shorter man directly in the eye.

'Well? What are you drinking?'

'Somefink fucking 'ot!' His guest replied, with a mock grimace on his face.

'Tea or Coffee then? We got the lot! Latte? Cappuccino? Flat White? Espresso? You name it we got it! My lovely lady, Kim, is a fully trained and qualified Barista!'

'I bet she is!?!' Came the almost sarcastic reply. 'Can she do a simple black filter coffee ven?'

'Of course, she can! Kim we'll have two Cafe Americanos in my office right away!'

He winked once more at his pet blonde, who now opened her mouth for the first time in the slightest of genuine smiles to reveal that a dazzling set of straight, brilliantly white teeth lurked behind the red painted lips. A gem set on her left upper incisor added sparkle to her smile.

'Sure thing Boss!' Kim acknowledged with only the slightest hint of irony in her thick deep and husky Welsh Valley's accent.

And then as Lord began to usher his guest through the club, he suddenly shouted back to her. 'And don't you forget to look

129

after his man!'

'Oh I won't forget, don't you worry about that!' She said rather tartly eyeing up the big man, who was still standing silently on guard behind them, his broad back blocking the doorway. He was looking on most disapprovingly at all the sudden familiarity. He glanced down and glowered at the dripping umbrella that he was still brandishing in his hand, like the drawn sword his uncompromising stance deserved.

'Now, now, Kim! Don't be a tease or you will embarrass my devout brother!' Lord reprimanded her, sensing the big man's awkwardness.

'It's okay Mo! Re-lax! We are amongst friends! Ga on knock yerself out!' The short man called back to his minder as he allowed himself, still arm in arm with his host, to be led towards the stairs at the far end of the room.

Once upstairs, in the privacy of the Lord's well furnished office, both men cooled their ostentatious ways and sat in two of the four bucket style leather chairs, which had been closely pre-arranged around a little smoked glass coffee table, in what was a small lounge-like sitting area to the side of Lord's main desk in his open plan office. There were three doors to the office. One to the landing, one to a private bathroom, and the other led to a small bedroom.

The men began talking quietly and seriously in their own language, a village dialect of Farsi, which many a linguistic scholar may have considered Persian or a bureaucrat labelled Dari, but in truth the tone and words used would have confused a none native eavesdropper, for the speakers instinctively used a multi-lingual mixture of words and phrases that truly reflected the historic confusion of their homeland's ethnicity.

Lord briefly confirmed that *"their"* business plans were progressing as well as could be expected, and in turn, his guest reassured him that the next "consignment" was safely and

130

securely deposited in their Cardiff storage centre. As proof of his statement, he produced from his pocket a simple Yale brass key, which was attached to a small black plastic computer USB fob. He held it out towards Lord but when his host reached for it he playfully tossed it up into the air before catching it sharply in his other hand. The short man then broke back into English, saying:

'Vis is all yours!' He indicated the key and fob with his eyes. 'Well as soon as the fucking accountants fucking confirm vat vee fucking funds are in our fucking account, yes!'

Before Lord could answer there was a loud warning knock on the office door and seconds later one of Lord's bulky boys opened it slowly to allow Kim to carry the tray of coffee in.

Both men held their breath as she silently placed the tray down on the table between them. Lord resisted the temptation to slap her bum, as he often did affectionately when they were alone, for she had deliberately bent over and cheekily presented it to him. However, he could not resist a smile when he noticed his guest's eyes staring directly down the open gap in her blouse at her firm cleavage, which again she had most deliberately displayed by ensuring her positioning and movement would achieve the maximum amount of male teasing. Money well spent, Lord thought to himself, as he remembered the night, in bed, when she had suggested he pay for her cosmetic surgery. She was not only his personal pleasure but a real asset to his business or so he thought.

Kim straightened up slowly, and knowingly teased both men again, this time by provocatively asking them, in her deep and husky voice, *if they wanted anything else!* The shorter man laughed out loud and tried to play it cool but still blushed during his reply.

'Nah fanks sweetness! Vat's more van in-nuf for me!'

She turned and smiled slyly at her boss (and lover), sensually running her empty hands, with their long, elegant fingers, and

131

glittery gold dust painted crimson gel nails, down from her slim waist to her slightly curved hips, emphasising the close fit of her skin tight trousers, before casually swaying out of the room, pleased that she obviously still had "it" at her age. Without looking back she knew that both men's eyes were following her from the room.

'Wow! Fucking hot stuff!' The young man beamed as soon as the door shut behind her. He pretended to fan imaginary steam rising from his large black coffee cup. His host acknowledged the fact, with what he hoped was a smug grin, rather than a dirty leer as he confirmed:

'Yes you can't beat experience! She serves a great cup of coffee!'

'I fucking bet! Nah wat you fucking mean "*as well as can be expected!?!*" Yer 'avin' a lauf or wat?'

Lord frowned and turning his hands over in a subconscious shrug, muttered in a low voice.

'These people, round here, they don't make it easy for themselves but persuading them is really no problem for me!' His right hand rose subconsciously to touch the red neckerchief that hung loosely around his neck.

'Yer still a fucking cowboy ven!' The elegantly suited but inelegantly spoken man nodded at the scarf, with it's silver Texas Longhorn Buffalo Steer Cow Skull clasp.

'Well it is like the Wild West down here!' He laughed.

'Fucking right!' The short man laughed too and then in his native language, he asked more reverently for Sardaar Sarbaah Sar to tell him all about it.

Chapter 14: The Brotherhood

Criminal gangs are usually given a name by the police or the gutter press, when their activities become noticed and there is a need to connect individuals to collective misdeeds or dubious practices and forbidden places. These are often so lurid that they are only then adopted by the less intelligent gangsters in what is an obvious show of mock bravado. Other names, which arise through gossip or folklore, are rarely publicly acknowledged by the usually offended villains. Only a few are worn as a badge of pride or infamy, because most such named gangs quickly become historic. Once identified, they have made themselves a target, not only for the authorities but also more worryingly, for their rivals. Therefore, it was quite odd that the organisation, which Sardaar Sarbaah Sar and his associate Amadid, were leading members of, had endured for decades under such an epithet, whispered amongst themselves, albeit initially chosen, to give them a bond, an identity, and vitally assistance, above and beyond a common sense of belonging. However, little did they know, back when they first organised, that the name their mysterious founder would ultimately choose, hoping to link them together and add gravitas to their association, would on translation, turn out to be the same name as that of a hugely successful but essentially cheesy, British pop group, from the late 1970's, the very era of their own unique genesis. Nonetheless, the original founders of the fearsome *"Brotherhood Of Man"* had certainly persisted with the name, no doubt in blissful ignorance, for those who became aware of the secretive network, were never brave enough to point out, what some foolish observers may have considered to be a hysterical, if not unprecedented, marketing gaff.

Indeed the creation of what in reality was a rather sinister criminal organisation, certainly predated Google, so in fairness, the leading players could not have performed a search check. It also seems unlikely that they were inspired by watching the actual Eurovision Song Contest. The chances of that particular light entertainment television show, bouncing off a satellite, onto a TV screen somewhere in the tribal lands of Afghanistan, must have been pretty slim back in 1976! As slim a chance, perhaps, as an *evil ne'er do* well, sitting around a camp fire and deciding with a cackle or two, that the whimsical song *"Save Your Kisses For Me"* would make a good theme tune or anthem.

Sardaar Sarbaah Sar, in his perhaps more appropriately re-branded name of Ed Lord, had at first been appalled, when he discovered Kim, sat in her pleasingly tight fitting clothes, at The Potting Shed bar, humming away, whilst watching an old re-run of the pop group, performing on a nostalgic late night TV show. Lord knew, because of his own linguistic struggles, that meanings were often lost in translation, but his initial concern at ridicule had evaporated as the "camp" song progressed. Eventually, he had become mightily amused by the irony that the name given to (in his opinion), such a sophisticated and vicious criminal gang, was a name that in the mind of any British authority figure of a certain age, would only conjure up images of flared cabaret suits and frilly fronted shirts, should they have even heard the *"Brotherhood Of Man"* mentioned in security despatches. That would certainly put investigators off track! Perhaps the name of a "hush hush" secret organisation, was not, and would never be, party to modern branding protocols. However, big, successful, and menacing it became! Maybe breaching copyright made them even more *bad ass!* Nevertheless, Sardaar Sarbaah Sar chose not to share the joke, especially when he attended meetings, with his *brothers*, like the meeting he was currently in tonight.

134

The Brotherhood had survived in spite of the name, rather than because of it. A survival mainly due to their secrecy and the proven ability to regenerate members, who often appeared to be no more than individual crooks or totally discrete gangs, and as such could quickly disappear with no obvious continuity in their successors. Yet there usually was a connection, and those who rose to fill the void, often became absorbed into a group that was indeed a brotherhood.

It was possibly more likely that the founding members were heavily influenced by that other, allegedly secret, yet hopefully less sinister and certainly more charitable organisation, The Free Masons, who apparently enjoy referring to each other as *the brotherhood*.

Not unlike *that* international brotherhood, the criminal *"Brotherhood Of Man"* had their own *"traditions"* and strict rules governing *"brothers"* conduct. Since they had grown out of the desperate disillusionment of a few refugee Afghan tribesmen, men who had had enough of fighting for fanatics and promises of a better afterlife, men who now sought to profit in the here and now, from the continued chaos in their homeland, regular meetings between cell leaders, links on the loose chain, were a fundamental rule of their organisation and essential in avoiding conflicts of interest and ensuring continuity in their disparate "business" affairs.

In the modern age of digital information communication technology, maintaining their organisation's adapted version of the centuries old *Balochi Oral Tradition*, or put simply *Afghan storytelling*, had proved vital and unlike certain Western organisations *"their brotherhood"* did not fear spies or hackers, as ultimately all communication was oral. Quietly spoken exchanges, no less than once every three months, in their almost impenetrable dialects, meant successful eavesdropping was unlikely. Their organisation's strict code, together with its lead

135

members inevitable indoctrination to the benefits of profit, rather than the words of the prophet, had created a fierce loyalty, which also meant that betrayal or whistle-blowing was equally unlikely. Without such breaches or any actual paper trails, it was considered almost impossible for investigating authorities or other interlopers, to substantiate anything other than a mere coincidental connection behind their seemingly arms length transactions.

Infiltration was also deemed to be equally unlikely. Potential *"brothers"* were secretly observed as they pursued their own individual nefarious activities and their suitability ultimately assessed by the unknown, shadowy *"father figures"* before any *"orphan"* could be adopted into this exclusively covert male family.

Participating in this model oral "tradition" also provided a psychological benefit for these unlikely *"captains"* of criminal industry. In sharing their secrets with peers, they found, for probably the first time in their lives, that they were not alone. Their misdeeds did not alienate or horrify the listener, who usually gave unquestioning support or at worst constructive counselling; so that each shared *"confession"* ultimately produced a bond, through a sense of belonging, at long last, to a *"real"* family; as the cliché would have it, being a true *band of brothers*.

Having confessed, the *"brother"* was free to continue his activities as he chose fit, provided he met his other essential responsibility, which was, of course, for each *"brother"* to make regular financial contributions to *"the family"*. Perhaps this mutual trust, benefit and honour amongst a special class of brigand, was what had helped their mysterious organisation remain successful, and elusive. The loosely connected community certainly seemed to be hidden from authorities, whilst their members' individual activities were often in plain sight and may well have been noted out of context.

Each cell, arm, or *tribe*, as they preferred to call themselves, was linked in an unseen mesh; and the leaders, or *tribal chiefs*, were kept aware of what their *"brothers"* were doing. However, this awareness was all hearsay and could not be clarified or evidenced. It was always assumed that somewhere someone oversaw the whole organisation but how that person or persons operated remained hidden by the continued success of this autonomous *"brotherhood."*

The only other unwritten rule in the *"Brotherhood Of Man"* as this *"family"* had become internally referred to, was that despite any appearances to the contrary and unlike the many tribes or fanatical factions that the *"brothers"* had ultimately evolved from, they were not religious or political. They might, at times, find it politic to appear devout but they were definitely not! The *"brothers"* had all witnessed too much horror and mayhem in their past to believe that any God was great! This was why they were truly the *"Brotherhood"* of man!

Sardaar Sarbaah Sar was a *"tribal chief"*, as was his *"brother"*, the *apparent* Londoner in the smart modern business suit. Although both found it hard to talk openly about their actual *"business"* dealings, especially after months of running their own operations, totally alone, and totally in charge, such disclosures took place, for they were a fundamental rule of their organisation. So the *"brothers"* told their stories.

Lord/Sardaar Sarbaah Sar explained his expansion plans. His *tribe* was responsible for the distribution, in his allocated region. His visiting *"brother"* dealt with the supply of the product. Both were tertiary businesses, providing a service that benefited from their connection in their *"Brotherhood"*. Further back, one more link down their chain, another *"brother"* had assumed responsibility for manufacturing and behind him; another *"brother"* would be responsible for developing or producing the primary raw materials.

Reminding his *"brother"* that the risk of distribution was now spread by franchising out new distribution centres, on the edges of his territory, Sardaar Sarbaah Sar boasted that this not only kept overheads down but allowed an admittedly slow but sure expansion into new *"virgin"* territories by exploiting identified local talent. A business model that was obviously based on the *"Brotherhood's"* own successful expansion. Together, the brothers talked the usual gobbledegook of management consultants with equal enthusiasm. Nodding to each other, agreeing and smiling confidently at each jargon filled simplification.

Usually such "talent" (as they enjoyed describing the local crooks they exploited), were small fry who might be ready or willing to attempt bigger things, but if they were not ready or became unwilling, there was always others eager to take over a rivals missed opportunity. Occasional failures were easily replaced and this kept both the authorities and customers happy. The customers thought there was competitive pricing amongst independent dealers and the authorities were pleased to show the public they were doing their civic duty, by winning battles in the war on drugs, not just doing the jobs that Lord or his other *"brothers"* paid them to do!

Both men laughed out loud. Instead of having to compete with local dealers, most of these dealers, even those affiliated to other criminal organisations, were now actually working for an unknown organisation; *The Brotherhood of Man*!

Sardaar Sarbaah Sar finished his "story" by complimenting his younger *"brother"*. He pointed out that because of the quality of product; the Demand was now greater than Supply. His *"brother"* shrugged, sensing not a compliment but an implied criticism. He began to explain that with the international focus switched away from their homeland, at the present time, due to other global political pressures, production of the raw materials was exceeding all expectations. Amadid was also excited by the opportunity generated through the increasingly legitimate demand due to the current trend for Vapours. Flavoursome liquids inhaled through a wide range of electronic devises, such as e-cigarettes, was proving to be a growing legitimate market, and providing an excellent cover for their less lawful activities. He could now import many natural "flavours" legally and he hoped this might help meet the increasing demand for such "legal" highs. Of course, the chemical make up of such products was adaptable, and thanks to modern technology, the skills of eager young scientists and the short sightedness of corrupt officials, this continued to be the perfect cover for more traditional illegal highs.

Amadid also reflected that the migrant problem was both a real blessing and a curse. Initially, transportation issues were affected, partly by increased borderland security, but mostly the tendency for the *'Brotherhood's'* regular "sub-contractors" (the organised crime and gangland smugglers) to abandon once firm arrangements to seek more lucrative short-term work with the human traffickers. However, he was relieved to report that recently the political will to focus on stopping the migrants was beginning to result in greater opportunities as the overstretched authorities began ignoring the more traditional contraband routes!

Lord Sardaar Sarbaah Sar agreed. His distribution network had been based on a chain of kebab takeaway outlets scattered around the Valleys but now expansions were taking advantage of the new trend in legal e-cigarette vapour retailers. The kebab shops were still important as one of the few cash businesses remaining on the high street; they gave a brilliant opportunity for money laundering. Yet vapour stands and market stalls could pop up without the delay and costs incurred in meeting food hygiene regulations. More profitable and transient, they were out performing his origin model, and if investigated, they could simply, he giggled, vaporise! He still maintained the less profitable kebab empire because, like the snooker club, it gave substance to the important illusion that he was a legitimate businessman.

The men were happy to share the good news. Inevitably, they had left the bad news to last. For Sardaar Sarbaah Sar, the bad news was not so bad. He had to confess to losing his temper and killing someone. Death always attracts unwanted attention. His *brother* nodded sagely and listened to the story. The summary he was given was simple. Lord had set up a sweet deal to expand into a new region, using his tradition business plan of taking over a failing food outlet, in this case a sad little English tearoom or cafe', only for the vendor to attempt to pull out. Partly because of a historic issue, bad blood between the vendor and Lord's new local business partner, and partly because the man was a racist! What helped fuel Lord's rage was also the coincidence that this man had been a soldier! An infidel! A member of an occupying force! A killer! Someone who had no doubt done harm in his homeland. The shorter man lent forward at this stage.

'Was his death slow and painful?' He asked in his own language, with a sudden, unnatural glee.

'Yes brother, at my hands!' Lord replied.

Both men broke into a satisfied smiled. Then the younger man casually asked about the cover up.

'I strung him up so it looked like suicide.' Lord laughed out loud.

'Nice!' The younger man smirked.

'Not really!' The elder man winked knowingly. 'There was a lot of hanging around!' Both men laughed again.

'It was really my new business partner's idea. He may yet prove useful to us in more ways than just being our "patsy"! This is where local knowledge pays off eh! Apparently, the man had family problems, he had been depressed!'

'Awe bless 'im!' The young man in the suit broke into mock English before adding bitterly: 'Well 'e ain't fucking got vem no more!'

Both men laughed again, before continuing to speak in their own dialect, which had oddly adopted not only English expressions, but included common slang. Such words might have even confused their brothers back in their homeland. However, as both men had lived in the UK for a number of years such verbal leakage was perfectly natural to them.

'Well the local cops bought it! I didn't even have to pay my man in blue to muddy the waters!'

'Hmm. Funny you should mention that. I've heard a story that our boys in blue might be in for a bit of trouble.'

Sardaar Sarbaah Sar listened carefully. He eventually shrugged when he heard that the police were investigating their own. Nothing new there he thought! It was inevitable that every now and then a new broom swept clean. The casual acceptance of his drug related activities, at least at a local level, had always seemed too good to be true to him. Of course, it was not really a mystery to him, given that a few influential and senior officers were on his payroll.

In addition to such explicit corruption, he had built up a pretty good relationship with many of the "honest" community Bobbies. All through his legitimate business connections, such as the snooker club and his numerous "Kebab Lord" takeaways, now dotted throughout the Taff Valley. Goodwill had been naturally cultivated courtesy of his "apparent" willingness to support their career enhancing neighbourhood schemes, as well as giving them more than a few choice tip off's, which he allegedly heard from his more dubious customers, not to mention the regular free frames of snooker or under the counter kebabs, these "decent" officers enjoyed here and there. Goodwill

141

was a necessary expense in his type of business. However, blind-sided the local plod were, they had been moaning an awful lot about "accountability" and "scrutiny" of head office recently, so perhaps he should have seen an internal investigation coming. Nevertheless, the word, according to his *"little brother"*, was that the local boys had been infiltrated by more than the usual undercover internal affairs spooks. Special Agents! Experts at encouraging nefarious activities, who sought to ensnare not only the simple front line troops, who were the usual expendable targets of such investigations, but also seeking to tease out the bigger fish, those higher up the police hierarchy. In such a climate of fear, his *"little brother"* warned Sardaar Sarbaah Sar, to beware of a sudden return to zero tolerance, or active entrapment. As usual, informers would be everywhere!

Worse still, the *"little brother"* cautioned, part of the investigation into his own "transportation" side of their business, seemed to have arisen from some despatch difficulties experienced back in their homeland. There the unofficial authoritarian policy had not been simply to gather legitimate evidence and apprehend transgressors but to completely break the chain by using covert Special Forces to not only exterminate links in the chain but also attempt to destroy the source of our product through a slash and burn policy! All this he exclaimed was disguised as part of the so called "war on terror" and a very public crack down on *religious* extremists! Luckily for our business, he concluded, the powers that be at home need our contribution to their revenue or we may have been in serious trouble.

Picturing the death and devastation hidden between the polite descriptions of, albeit temporary, mayhem in the "brotherhood" at home, Lord found himself truly shocked and stunned with what suddenly turned into a stern warning, and a final firm instruction. Should Sardaar Sarbaah Sar suspect the start of any similar "destructive" measures affecting his own "chain", he must simply cut and run!

'Cut and run!?!' He repeated slowly in disbelief.

Sipping back the last of his coffee, Amadid the *"little brother"* nodded. His smile was gone.

'Take care Bruver!' He said standing up. 'As always vees are fuckin' bad times!'

Lord got to his feet and they embraced.

Speaking again in their own dialect they wished each other well. Lord then escorted Amadid back down to the club's door, where a damp Mohammed still stood resolutely on guard, having politely but firmly declined all the hospitality Kim and her *two bulky boys* had offered him.

When the visitors had left, Lord merely shrugged to Kim.

'Time to close up.' He then silently turned and headed back to his office. She nervously obeyed, concerned by the unusual frown on his face.

Chapter 15: Breakfast in Bed

Rolling right out of his bed, Mykee Kane dropped straight down onto the bedroom floor and landed with an almighty thud. He had put both hands out to support his fall but his weight surprised him and the flat palms of his hands merely slapped down hard against the polished pine floorboards. His size ten feet kicked into the bare wood less than a second or so later, just before he crumpled flat onto the uncomfortable timber flooring.

Kane did find the strength to prop himself up again, groaning theatrically with the effort, and for a few minutes, his body hung limply beside the bed, whilst he paused, mentally testing his resolve. He did not want to do it but he did, and with an even louder groan, he rather unsteadily began his first press up for perhaps five years. There was a time, many years ago, when he would start and end, each day by doing one hundred press ups, followed by one hundred sit ups. That was back when he was fit and several stones lighter. However, after five awkward movements up and down, he hung in mid air again, neither up nor down, feeling the increasing strain on his arms and legs. How had he allowed himself to get into this shameful physical state? He asked silently and then almost excused himself, when the discomfort in his muscles grew too great, making him think that he should respect his age more. Nevertheless, he remembered his shoddy reflection in the cafe window only the day before, and groaning once more, Kane strained, bravely attempting to push up again.

'Oh my Gawd!' A familiar female voice mocked him from somewhere way above him. Jill Kane, his wife of ten years had just arrived at the open bedroom door. She was now sniggering so much that she struggled to balance the small white plastic tray, which she held out in front of her. The milky brown tea swashed around in the two large mugs, threatening to splash over the china rims, and down onto the white side plate that was stacked recklessly high with lightly buttered wholemeal toast. Jill was dressed in her tight fitting, Lycra active-wear, sky blue leggings and a bright peach coloured light weight, long sleeved, running top. Her usually straight, collar length straw blonde hair, was pulled back into a short stubby excuse for a pony tail and her cheeks were still rose tinted, from the effort of her morning run. Jill Kane's blue eyes sparkled as she added in her soft and jolly West Country accent: 'If you'd said that you wanted to get fit you could've come for a jog with me!' She smiled down at him.

Kane groaned, unenthusiastically, before once again slowly hauling himself up off the floor and flopping dejectedly back down onto the mattress, so that he sat, body sagging on the edge of the bed.

'No way! I don't want you to come into my life insurance just yet! If I went running with you in this condition, you'd have to use your first aid skills! God help me! I'm only fit to drop!' Kane moaned. 'But I accept I have to do something!' He sighed. 'Now before it's too late.'

'Hmm! I think that ship may have sailed me dear!' The blue eyes continued to tease him affectionately.

'It's not easy once you're over forty!' He continued pitifully. 'You'll find out soon enough Miss Fit!'

'Well it won't catch me by surprise like it did you! All that snacking in school doesn't help!'

'Stress relief!' He shrugged, matter of factly, then turned and snatched a piece of toast from the tray, so quick that she blinked. Putting the bread straight into his mouth, he crunched down, briefly savouring the warmth before munching away, whilst reaching back, in a much more leisurely fashion, for one of the matching white china mugs. He grimaced as he realised that he had picked up the one marked "The Boss".

'Watch the crumbs!' She scolded him as she carefully placed the tray down on the bedside cabinet. Picking up the remaining almost identical mug, the one marked "The Real Boss" and a piece of toast. Jill paused for a second, obviously thinking about what she was going to say and then she began talking quickly, whilst pointing the toast at him accusingly.

'So yesterday must have really got to you, if you're now starting to think about your health!?!'

She studied him carefully, her face suddenly all serious for a moment, as he digested her words. Then just as quickly her face lit up and she began to giggle again. She liked him cuddly.

'Oh what is it now!?!' He exaggerated his irritation.

'Brawling at your age! Tut tut tut!' She rolled her bright blue eyes.

'Hmm, well as I told you before, it wasn't really a fight! The idiot just swung at me and hit the wall and then fell over his mate into a load of Frank's tables and chairs!'

She sighed and the light in her eyes went dim.

'Sadly they're not Frank's tables any more, are they My-Key!'

'No, you're right!' He said before taking a long consoling swig of his tea. She sat down on the bed next to him and silently finished eating her toast.

When Kane had arrived home, much later than expected, yesterday night, she knew as soon as she saw his face that something was up. She had anticipated that he would be down. He usually was, after a visit to his old home town, but this was something else, even something more than she had expected, given the reason for his visit. His arrival had actually surprised her because she was half listening for the car, and she had even looked out at the empty drive in disbelief when she had heard the back door open. She was also alerted to the fact that something was up when she heard him lock the door behind him. However security conscious they were, they rarely locked the back door before bedtime!

Concerned, she had sat with him in the kitchen, on the opposite side of their breakfast bar, listening as he talked about his visit to Aberfoist. Watching him carefully as he slowly picked at his share of the supermarket ready meal that she had bought for them. It had been left far too long in the oven, awaiting his return, so of course the Lasagne had dried out, and the slice of garlic bread was rock hard. Well, that was his fault for being late or so she told herself, but she felt a little guilty that she had compromised and bought the "basics" pack. It was cheaper! She had told herself, and these days even a joint income family had to budget carefully. Anyway, she had reassured herself, everyone said they came from the same factory. At least the small plastic tub of ready made green salad was still fresh, not that he paid much attention to the healthy part of his meal. Kane compensated for the dryness, by washing each mouthful down, with a swig of red wine. By the time he had finished eating, the bottle was empty, and he was even eyeing up her half drunken glass!

She had not said much that night. She had not needed to, for he had fairly quickly fallen asleep, on the settee in front of the late night TV. The wine or a tiring day or the usual stresses of the end of term!?! She had wondered to herself. Jill had watched him sleeping and thought about all that he had said. She knew her husband and realised that he would not be able to let his doubts and concerns rest as easily as he had fallen asleep. Back, when they had first decided to get married, she had been truly thankful that he had not wanted to settle in Aberfoist. It might even have been a deal breaker if he had! Now, after so long, she feared that it was going to drag him back. Back into a world that she had

147

thought they had truly escaped from. Nonetheless, Jill was wise enough to realise that there was very little she could do about it, and although she hadn't slept much that night, she had eventually reconciled herself to that fact. Her husband would do what he had to do, and she would have to be there to pick up the pieces at the end of it!

Decision made, she had rolled out of bed in the early hours, after that fitful night, and taken her frustrations out by pounding the roads around their estate. At least the heavy rain that had started just after he got in, had stopped, and whilst damp, the run had certainly freshened her up. So much so, that she was able to banish her worries and easily put on a bold, if false, front.

'Right!' She announced having scoffed the last piece of toast. 'I need to shower!' She leapt up and started to strip off. 'I've got to pop into work for a bit, so you are responsible for picking your son up from his sleep over.' She told Kane emphatically. 'Are you listening?' She added, when he failed to acknowledge her instruction.

'Yes!' Kane grunted back.

'He's going to ring when he's ready, but you know what they're like! I doubt you'll hear from him until midday! But don't laze around until then, and for heavens sake, go and get your car or the people in that street will think some joy rider has dumped a load of junk on them and they'll get the council to tow it away to a scrap yard or something!'

Jill suddenly stopped undressing. She froze and stood there thinking for a moment, quite still, naked apart from the briefest of white knickers and her unhooked sports bra. It was as if something truly important had occurred to her. She then turned back to look at him. He was watching her, with a smug expression on his face, lazily stretched out on his side of the bed.

'On second thoughts! She added in a serious tone. 'Leave it there! They will be doing us a favour! Let it get scrapped!' She

148

finally smirked at him.

'What! My beautiful car!' He roared, leaping off the bed. He was up and at her in an instant, making an exaggerated grab for her! No moan at the effort this time. Perhaps his roar disguised it! She allowed herself to be caught. Laughing and shaking her head, she rolled her eyes as she added:

'You know what My-Key Kane! I think you love that old car more than me!'

'Never!' He exclaimed and then he kissed her. After a minute or so, as their mouths separated, she let out a loud and mocking groan of disgust.

'Yuck! You need to clean your teeth! Your breath stinks of tea and toast!'

'So does yours!' He laughed.

Suddenly she twisted and seconds later she had shoved him in the chest, whilst neatly sweeping his standing foot away, so that unbalanced, he fell backwards onto the bed. She stood above him laughing.

'Think you're hard!' She tutted, mocking him in a put on, deep voice, and then she dived onto him. There was a bit of a struggle but he was laughing too much to fight her off and she quickly had him pinned down to the bed. Slowly, she lowered her face to his and kissed him, open mouthed again.

After making love, he lay on the bed, listening to her humming away to herself in the nearby shower room. The tune was unrecognisable, distorted by the sound of the electric pump powering the water against the hard frosted thick plastic walls of the shower cubicle. He cursed himself. He knew he was mad to risk his current happiness, the safe and secure family lifestyle that they had laboured so hard to create for themselves, and yet he equally knew that he had to go back and find out exactly what had happened to Frank. He just wished he was fitter! With a groan, Mykee Kane rolled out of bed and began another attempt at press ups. This time he controlled his fall and got up to ten before collapsing on the floor beside his bed. It was going to be tough, tougher than he had expected.

Chapter 16: Any Time Any Where

Martini Pace did not love her husband. She loved what their relationship had bought her. So she tolerated him. At the age of twenty six, she still thought Ellis Pace was a good deal for her. Especially when compared to the fate of even the cleverest girls she had known in school. The most successful of whom were living with the debt of their student loans, and either working all the hours just to survive in their chosen professions, or having given up their dreams, settled for the boredom of being a yummy mummy anaesthetised on Prosecco, when not driving their brood of infants around in their impressive but leased SUV's, attending one dreary playgroup function after another. She on the other hand drank champagne, dressed in ludicrously expensive designer clothes and wore matching Jimmy Choo shoes. She didn't have children and pretty much pleased herself; well most of the time, or so she told herself.

Today she had worn her pink Chanel trouser suit, with its raspberry velvet collar, a pure silk, thin white, cut off vest, which exposed enough of her skin to show off the natural tan from her recent winter sun break to Dubai. Her long wavy black hair flowed over her shoulders and way down her back, just like her personal stylist had arranged it earlier that morning. She sat at an antique writing desk, wafting expensive perfume around her pastel coloured office, whilst casually using a top of the range iMac desktop computer to browse through the latest photos of all the talent that was available to the media clients of her modelling agency.

Admittedly, her office window only overlooked the central square of the dilapidated town centre that was Aberfoist, rather than London, Paris, or Milan, but then this was her home town, and as such, exactly where she wanted to be. Aberfoist maximised the opportunities of impressing those people who had only thought of her as that "thick slag" or "ugly CHAV" from the *special needs* class in school. So what if she still did not read or write particularly well, she enjoyed watching the little people scurry passed, imagining that they were on their way to cash in their benefit giro at the nearby post office, or rushing to their poorly paid jobs, or whatever else they "had" to do! All such hum drum activities, which were clearly below her now, literary!

Such paltry activities were only visible if she swung her chair left and glanced down from her aloof position, sat comfortably behind the first floor plate glass window of her three storeys, beautifully refurbished, Georgian Town House. Even more comfortable than the upholstered leather of her swish executive chair, was the knowledge that on the brass plaque to the right of the grand double door entrance was her name. Well the plaque actually read "Martini Enterprises (Wales) Ltd" but it was more than enough for a girl who was once considered to be most likely to amount to nothing by the other kids at school.

In truth, her business only occupied the second floor. An office, a store room, a studio and a salon style bathroom, for the talent, as she insisted on calling the models, stylists, and photographers. The ones she contracted in, as and when required. This was the extent of her empire. The ground floor was given over to her husband's security business and the slightly smaller brass plate on the left side of the door read "Aberfoist Security Services, Proprietor Ellis Pace." The third floor was private. A luxury flat, well luxurious for Aberfoist, now mostly occupied by her husband, since her grandmother, who Ellis could not abide, had moved into the marital home, a farmhouse, located just a few miles out of town, on the small holding they also owned. The arrangement suited them both, as despite her school days reputation of being obsessed with boys, she now preferred horses to men, and the farm, really only a few acres of grazing land on the hillside, allowed her to keep three ponies, fashionably (or so she thought,) called London, Paris, and Milan, of course.

Martini was even prouder of the large canvas black and white "artistic" photograph of her, and only her that filled most of the wall immediately behind her desk. It had been taken at the peak of her own brief modelling career, shortly before she had met Ellis Pace, and it showed her reclining naked on a chaise long, the leather padding of which was cleverly *Photoshopped* scarlet. She was pouting and had tactfully positioned her hair, limbs and hands to cover or block out her most private parts, just enough, to still tease and captivate even the least voyeuristic viewer. She loved the picture. Not because it had been taken when she was still young, possibly ten years ago now, but the lighting and make up hid what she considered to be her worst features, the large brown freckles that had made her desperate to prove herself attractive to men, and set her on an eager, promiscuous pathway, at an even earlier age.

Of course, the kids had been cruel to her at school. "Spotty Dog" had been one of her earliest nicknames! And then, when they had become jealous at the way boys flocked to her, in response to her more physical encouragements, they had started to sing at her, "Anytime, any place, anywhere, that's Martini!" Although their knowledge of that once famous 1970's advertising tag-line, probably said more about the inherent cruelty and small town mentality of certain parents rather than the ignorant spite of her classmates. Yet she chose to own it! Not caring about an already damaged reputation, she quickly began to appreciate the benefits of attracting increasingly older boys and then men, who could afford to not only give her the attention she craved but take her to places other girls of her age could not (and most would not) go!

By the time Martini was fifteen, school had become, like her absent parents, a vague memory. Her widowed grandmother, who was allegedly her main carer, was so obsessed with day-time TV that she was happy enough to wave her ward off in the mornings and never noticed when or if she returned. Spending so much time out of class, in *special* "reading" or "sums" lessons, meant that her teachers never questioned her absence from their lessons. The over worked Educational Welfare Officer never found the time to chase up the unread parental/carer statutory letters, sent systemically in response to the poor attendance alerts, and with no real friends to worry about her, she simply fell through the institutional gaps, especially as her school's Head Teacher did not want her limited academic ability damaging the school's performance statistics. When one of her older *"regular"* boyfriends told her of some work as a life model, for a local photography "club" she jumped at the chance, even though she had no idea what it involved! Uninhibited at taking her clothes off, she had just got on with it and was thrilled to earn some money to buy her own, more fashionable, and truly adult gear.

After a brief fling, with a "professional" photographer, whom she had met at the club, Martini had an informal offer of some proper "fashion" modelling work in London. Whilst this was short lived, a girl she had met at a high street store photo shoot had told her about "casual work" modelling for these new adult web-sites. She did not feel abused, when sat semi-naked in front of a web-cam, talking to *"saddos"* on the telephone, especially when it suddenly began to earn her some real money. Then another "out of work" model, one she met at *"the studio"* had suggested escort work to her. Paid dates with a bit of fun thrown in after, only if she liked the client of course! Martini had had a whale of a time. She had even used a slightly altered tagline to promote herself in that business, stressing the availability of her "modelling" services, "Have Martini, anytime, any place, any*way*!" She was young and busy.

Then she got lucky. She had been hired by Ellis Pace, when he was in London on business. For some reason the rich businessman from her home town was smitten with her and made her a proposal she could not refuse. Now, as Mrs Martini Pace, she could use her "experience" to help him set up the slightly more respectable "MP Modelling Agency" and bring a bit of big city class to South Wales and the West Country. She was not surprised by the demand for her services, just amazed at how many allegedly respectable local women and girls were eager to sign up to earn a bit of extra money!

Those years away from Aberfoist had taught her how to use beauty creams and tanning lotions to disguise her freckles and she used this knowledge to set up another popular business, MP Beauty Therapy. This together with her online fashion business had made her, like her husband, a successful entrepreneur in the local area. She was still young and at first glance beautiful, but perhaps there was something ugly, if not in her freckled skin, definitely in her dark brown eyes, a look which could still alarm those who got too close to her.

Those dark eyes narrowed now on the young man, the one dressed all in black, with a hint of colourful tattoo sleeves showing at the cuffs of his tight fitting black shirt. He had just burst into her office, without knocking. Her eyes stopped him dead in the middle of the room. He fidgeted nervously unable to meet her stare. Eventually he blurted out, in a strong Welsh, and equally camp, accent: 'I'm sorry Mrs Pace, but Mr Pace sent me, he wants the fee, you know, to pay the new model!'

155

'Is she any good?' Martini asked. Her voice sounded cold and disinterested.

Unseen by his employer, who was now bending to her left and opening the lower cabinet door of her desk, the young man pulled a face that said she was not. He struggled to find the right words to accurately describe the poor hopeful, a far too young girl, whom he had been photographing in the nearby studio.

'Well?' The slightly irritated voice moaned from somewhere down behind the desk.

'Hmm, well, she's very young and er, Mr Pace thinks she has potential!' The not-as-young man said rather pointedly.

Reaching into the large space Martini Pace had to use her two hands to grab the medium sized metal cash box. She struggled to pull it out before twisting back up with a sigh, for it was heavy, and dumping it soundly on the leather padding of the desktop in front of her, she muttered, more to herself than in reply to her photographer.

'He would!'

The box had a small sensor pad on its side and she carefully placed her thumb on the pad. Instantly the box responded with an electronic whirl and the young man could hear a metallic clicking as the lid unlocked and popped open. Raising the lid slowly, she looked inside and cautiously removed a wad of twenty pound notes, all bound together with a thick red rubber band. Slowly Martini began pulling single notes off the top of the wad, and hesitantly counting out loud, placed them one at a time in a new pile on her right hand side.

'One, two, three, four, five. That's £100 yes!' She looked to the young man for confirmation.

Once again he failed to meet her eyes, but he acknowledged that yes she was right by nodding his head vigorously, before almost tearfully adding:

'Er, um, Mr Pace asked that we give her a bonus of £50 as he is, er, um!?!' The trendily tattooed young man in black paused and gulped before continuing: 'Going to give her an extra screen test!'

'Really!?!' She responded, almost bemused. The young man said nothing but his right cheek twitched nervously. Martini laughed as she began the slow counting process once more.

'One, two, three!'

The young man squirmed awkwardly as he opened his mouth and was just about to correct the count when Martini Pace spoke up: 'That's £60 yes?'

'Yes Mrs Pace!'

'Let's give her £60 David! If Mr Pace is giving her a screen test then she will have earned it right!?!'

David gave a relieved, knowing smirk, and quickly scampered over to the desk. He was very polite and as he picked up the £160 he said: 'Thank you Mrs Pace.' He turned to go and by the time that he had reached the door, he could hear the whirl and metallic clunk as she shut and locked the money box.

'Oh David!' She called as he had his hand on the door knob about to pull it shut. He turned and stepped back into the room.

'Make sure that you bring me the memory card, the one with the photos on, as soon as you are finished, okay!'

'Yes Mrs Pace!' He said. 'Right away!' David turned to go, but she called out once more, stopping him before he left the room again.

'Tell Mr Pace that he can keep the video of the screen test, okay! That's his business right!'

David let out an awkward high pitched laugh, before saying: 'Okay Mrs Pace!'

David had no intention of saying any such thing to Mr Pace. After all, he was meant to be their fashion photographer. Screen

Tests and the movies, he knew they made, had nothing to do with him. That was their business and they were welcome to it!

Chapter 17: A Potent Cocktail

Automatic screen savers can be both a blessing and a curse, depending on whether you are a hesitant or thoughtful computer user. They can hide your confidential work in progress from prying eyes as effectively as they can obscure your embarrassing dalliances. Yet they can also reveal something of the user's personality. Sometimes they are a happy distraction and at other times an irritation; starting up just as the thoughtful user was about to complete that key note or phrase and thus blocking the creative process through a beguiling display. The customised screen saver had automatically kicked on Martini Pace's computer screen, whilst she had been dealing with David. Her young and talented photographer had finally escaped her office, but when she had turned her attention back to the computer screen, determined to pursue her original purpose, she found her mind seduced by the alluring nostalgia of an animated slide show display, featuring her all time favourite photographs. They were, of course, all of her.

Every few seconds a new image replaced the old. The tacky trail exposing the highlights of Martini's short lived modelling career. She had appeared in a series of colourful snapshots, pulling a variety of what she (and presumably the "professional" photographers) considered to be provocative and artistic poses. In each image, she was almost dressed, in a range of impractical lingerie outfits. Martini smiled, and sat back in her executive style, pink leather chair, very pleased with herself, or at least pleased with the edited way she looked. Watching the screen, she began to wonder whether she was really too old, at twenty-six, for this type of glamour work. Maybe she should get back in front of the camera again. Then, she blinked, and dramatically pulled a face, winching, as the next picture of her (still half dressed in lacy lingerie) appeared, but this time, she was not alone on screen. She was posing, perhaps a little too enthusiastically, with her husband. He was squeezed into an unforgiving black silk, Japanese style, mini dressing gown, which exposed his thin pale legs and sly facial expression. The "happy" couple were toasting each other with pink champagne. Martini quickly reached out and placed her hand on the computer's mouse, moving it ever so slightly to make the image vanish, a trick she wished that she could do to the obviously unpleasant memory. Instantly, the computer returned to the live screen window, which was displaying a page from her modelling agency web site.

Martini breathed in and out deeply, successfully suppressing the anxiety, just like she had been taught by her expensive, but oh so worthwhile, life coach. With her aura now suitably rebalanced, she began, once more, to study the gallery of small thumbnail images. There displayed on one screen, were all of her contracted models. Every now and then she would click on a thumbnail to enlarge it, and either tut loudly with displeasure, or nod her head in silent approval. Eventually, she sighed with despair. The demand for new girls was insatiable and she knew that she needed to find new talent. An increasingly important (legitimate) income stream for her business was the advertising her websites attracted and that varied depending on the number of hits or visitors to the site. Without new girls, the online traffic would reduce, and as the numbers fell, so would the advertising income. She was not short of money, but she was greedy.

Just as she was wondering how she could best use this new girl, David reappeared in her room. He was clutching a small silver memory stick. She forgot all about his failure to yet again knock on her door and without a word or look of reprimand,

160

silently summoned him over with her outstretched hand. He placed the silver device in her beckoning hand and moved silently to stand behind her as she quickly slotted it into the side of her iMac. Her mouth tightened in a frown as she clicked through the new digital images. David was a good photographer and he was using state of the art equipment to do a professional job but even he was limited by the quality of his subject and in this case, she thought, he could have spent his time more productively if he had been photographing a bowl of fruit.

'How old is she?' Martini asked.

'She says eighteen!' He sceptically replied.

'Hmm, we'd be lucky if she is sixteen! More like fifteen I'd guess!' Martini accurately assessed. The boy dressed in black nodded his agreement.

'Did you see any ID?'

'No!' David acknowledged.

'And Mr Pace is actually screen testing her, eh!?!'

'Er yes, um I did try to...' He said weakly but she knew he did not really.

'Well perhaps there is more of a market for this type of girl in his, er, movies, eh!' She said flatly. The boy nodded his agreement silently once more.

'Hmm, he ought to be careful! This one's real jail bait!' Martini continued. 'But then my husband can always produce some convincing ID for her! He's done that in the past hasn't he ...' her voice trailed off as she thought of something else. The boy stared at the screen blankly, neither nodding nor shaking his head. He did swallow nervously, as his throat had suddenly become very dry. He worried that he was at fault for just doing his job. A job he hoped that he still would be paid for! Had he refused to photograph the child, when she had first arrived all shy and nervous, without the allegedly always required but rarely looked at documentation, he would have earned nothing.

161

'Is she local?' Martini asked.

'No, I don't think so!?!' David began. 'She says she came up on the train from Cardiff.'

'On her own? No boyfriend or mother, or big sister or best-friend-forever in tow?'

'Apparently not!' He bit his lip. He was sure that no one had arrived with the young hopeful.

'No uncle? Or agent?'

'No!' He tried to sound confident.

'Hmm! She seems to be all alone then?'

'Yes! She had made the appointment through our online "New Talent" agency advert. She's just young and desperate! That's all!'

'Ah weren't we all once upon a time!' Martini smiled and manoeuvred the mouse to the top of the screen. Clicking to minimise the photo viewer window she deftly moved the on-screen pointer over the graphic icon for her contacts file and clicked twice. She then lent forward and having first clicked once in the search field, pressed the C key with the index finger of her well manicured left hand. A drop down list of contacts, beginning with the letter C, miraculously appeared and she clicked on "Communication Wales" and a new contacts window file opened up.

'Be a darling David and ring Aled for me, he might like this one, he has similar tastes to Mr Pace!'

'Yes Mrs Pace.' The photographer reached over and picked up the hand set of the ornate 1920's antique style telephone, which sat on the far left of Martini's desk. Whilst it was more than a little impractical as a modern communications device, it certainly looked impressive and for someone who had already made so many compromises in her short life, surrounding herself with attractive objects, was perhaps all she could hope for, and insist upon, to justify her questionable choices.

162

David bent over and began to press the numbers on the telephone's dial pad, which was an amusing mock up of an old fashioned roller dial. He twisted back every now and then to check the number on the computer screen. Finally he straightened up and put the handset firmly against his ear, and as he heard the ring tone, adjusted his grip so that the mouth piece was just in front of his.

'Good afternoon, I have Mrs Pace of MP Modelling Services on the line to speak to Mr Aled Harris, Senior Fashion Editor of Communication Wales, please!' He said this all rather formally, but he could not hide the slight nervous hesitation in his voice. Martini reached over and pressed the hands-free button on the base of the phone, just in time to hear a rather priggish young man's voice say, with a slight hint of an Irish accent, that they were sorry but Mr Harris was at lunch and could they ring back later.

'Gerry!' Martini barked at the speaker in her own most uncompromising tone, as she pictured the self important nobody that she had met a number of times on trips to the big city offices of the modest Fashion Department of the media conglomerate that was Communication Wales. She knew that he was merely going through the motions to create an illusion of working for an important, hectically busy trend setter, and she also knew that he was hopeless at making coffee, which was really his main function, when not toadying up to his boss.

'Yes!' Came a firm acknowledgement from the fiercely proud, only male PA, employed because of his mother's family connections to a director of the organisation, which was now the leading, or should that be only, independent media group still operating in Wales.

'This is Martini here and you know very well that Aled will always speak to me! Anytime, anywhere, any Pace! Remember! Anyway, he doesn't do lunch so get a fucking wiggly on and put

163

me through!' She knew Aled of old, from a variety of fashion jobs, and more usefully the odd marketing function, and whilst their relationship was now "mostly" professional, she had almost enough dirt on him to make life tricky, especially in the new politically correct era that seemed to be worryingly dawning, even in the public relations world! He knew exactly who Martini was, and he also knew that her bark was not worse than her bite.

'Er, I'll try but ...'Gerry started, appreciating the sudden transfer of power in this phone call.

'No buts just do it lovely!'

'I'll try!' He repeated, with a slight panic in his voice.

'Thank you!' Her voice had become all sweetness and light. A few moments later she heard a familiar guttural west Walian accent on the phone.

'Martini darling, what the fuck do you want now?'

'Well, well, Aled play nice now, eh! I have a treat, especially for you!'

'Oh my good Gawd!' Aled jokingly responded. 'I've tried to give up treats for lent!'

'Not successfully I bet! Anyway, Aled you're an atheist!' Martini retorted with a chuckle.

'Ah you know me so well!' Aled rolled his eyes and began to pace up and down his office, with his cordless receiver now pressed hard to his right ear.

'Never mind the nonsense, this is business!' Martini continued. 'And you can't have given that up for lent, eh!' She paused briefly for effect.

'Come on you old tart! Don't be a tease, I'm a busy man, what is it?' Aled added as lightly as his gruff accent allowed, but she knew that on the other end of the line his face was probably still red with suppressed rage that he had had to take her call.

'Less of the old!' She laughed.

164

'Ah sorry Marti, I meant that you are wise beyond your years!'

'Maybe!' She doubted that but was easily flattered by the slightest praise. 'Look we have a lovely new "young" girl on our books. Just your type! I think you'd like to meet her!'

'Really!?! What for?'

'Well, for a start, I think she'd be perfect for one of your poor waif victim news library pics! And maybe, when scrubbed up, she could even do one of your "sweet" young teen or family fashion shoots!'

'Really?' He was relieved that all she seemed to want was actually work related, and business with an opportunity for personal pleasure in it, which was really the only way he operated these days. Maybe there was something to his advantage in this and then after what he hoped seemed like a thoughtful pause, he allowed himself to be honest, feeling his stomach twinge with a familiar pang of excitement. 'I'm intrigued,' he said, 'but our budgets are so tight at the moment I don't think I can.'

There was almost a hint of disappointment seeping through the thick blunt tones. She admired his art, albeit an unsubtle attempt at negotiation.

'Well I came to you first because I know your ... er ... particular tastes, don't I!' Martini paused to let the implications of her statement set in. She felt she knew men, particularly men like Aled Harris, well. She didn't like them, for they were all self obsessed hypocrites and when he actually listened to what she was saying between the lines, she knew it would be too easy to manipulate him. She could imagine him cursing her and perhaps panicking slightly but also drooling a little at the opportunity she was presenting to him. She knew he ran on fear and lust. Then just as she could hear him start to clear his throat and knew that he was building up to say something appropriately pompous befitting an important multimedia fashion editor, she added:

'She's very fresh if you know what I mean and would be grateful for the benefit of your experience, you know in getting her started in this modelling lark!' Martini could sense the doubt, desire, and anxiety that Aled Harris was fighting to control at the other end of the line.

'I'd hate to take her elsewhere, when I know you could make the very best use of her, but then ...' she paused again and in the silence she turned to smile at David, who could not hide his own unease. David was beginning to actually go pale, not just because of the implied subject matter, but also from holding his breath. She enjoyed his unease. It was a shame he was gay, she often thought, because she found him quite cute in his naivety.

'You are a bloody witch Marti! You are casting a spell over me and you are going to get me in such trouble with my directors!'

'Ah that's exactly what I don't want to do!' She stopped and listened to the sudden silence at the other end of the line. Had she over played it? She wondered and quickly added: 'That's why I always give you these little opportunities to keep ahead of the game and one step in front of your rivals!' She thought that she heard an actual sigh. 'When shall I bring her down to you?' She asked confidently.

'Tomorrow?' He said quietly but rather too quickly.

'No!' She said firmly and then she tried to sound disappointed. 'I'm afraid I can't make it tomorrow and before you ask no! I'm not letting you loose on her without me getting the contracts sorted out first! We could do Thursday afternoon if you like?'

'Okay Marti!' There was a brief pause whilst he checked his diary. 'About 4 okay with you?'

'Yes that'll be fine! Your offices at 4pm!' She replied.

'Er no!' He interrupted her. 'Bring her straight to the studio; you know the one, down the Bay, yes!'

'Oh yes! That's the one behind the Marina. That will be nice for her!'

Yes, clever boy, nice and private she thought.

'Yes, it's much better than our intimidating "busy" central office!' He agreed.

Yes, much better for her to "audition" without all those other people around! Martini almost added but instead she said: 'Wonderful, look forward to seeing you at 4 pm on Thursday then!' They gushed their fake goodbyes for a few moments more before eventually hanging up.

After firmly pressing the button on his cordless receiver, Aled Harris strode to the open door of his glass walled office and made an angry face to Gerry, who had been sat half listening to his boss and fielding a number of other less influential business related calls at his desk, a desk that was meant to guard the doorway. Shaking his head in disbelief Aled Harris acted out the scenario of being the hard done by, self sacrificing fool, and told his PA to cancel all his appointments for Thursday from 3pm. He tried to hide the smile when he also said: 'You can have my tickets for the opera on Thursday evening. I think I'm going to be stuck doing Marti a favour well into the night!'

He turned to walk back to his desk but before he got there the phone buzzed in his hand again. This time the rhythm alerted him to the fact that it was his wife calling. He twitched guiltily before answering it with a false: 'Hello Dear!'

After pressing the button to close off the call, Martini had held her finger to her lips, warning David not to say anything. She then opened her upper side draw, the one immediately below the antique style telephone and reached in to flick the red switch on the softly purring black box to off. It was a device that was connected to her phone by a cable that ran through the back of the draw and had been set up to automatically record all of her phone calls. Smiling she turned to David and said: 'You never

167

know when that conversation might be useful! Now! I want you to take some more pictures of our new girl. What's her name?'

'Tia Maria!' He said, wisely resisting the desire to roll his eyes. His boss was definitely not the person to share any clever sarcasm about the tasteless trend to call girls after popular drinks, which may or may not have aided their conception.

'Oh that's sweet!' Martini said without a hint of irony, as she maximised the photo viewer, and began to flick through the standard model poses that David had taken of the young Tia Maria. 'Do you suppose it's her real name then?' She asked.

He shrugged. He wanted to say that having spoken to the girl he doubted she had the wit to make it up but when your boss was called "Martini" you were careful not to judge people by their given names, well at least out loud.

'Well we will have to change it probably. We don't want any silly copyright or branding issues! I know we've got our fair share of Maria's but perhaps Tia will do! We haven't got another Tia on the books have we?

David shook his head. 'No Mrs Pace!'

'Right!' She said as if her mind was finally made up. 'I want you to take some more "natural" shots! We'll have to give her another bonus to keep her sweet.' Martini spun around on her rotating chair to look her photographer directly in the eye.

'No unnecessary make up! No need for any nudes this time, okay! I want her to look her age. She should be looking all sad and vulnerable after her screen test!' Martini almost sniggered. 'You can get all arty if you like – a few black and white yes! Get her in jeans and a tight jumper maybe. But natural okay! You get the idea!'

'Yes Mrs Pace.' He gave an almost robotic reply.

'Thank you David.' She said dismissing him.

Just as he got to the door she stopped him once more, as was her habit. 'David?'

168

'Yes Mrs Pace.' He stopped. He was used to her ways, so waited patiently.

'Do we still have that school girl outfit?' She said slowly, her mind obviously calculating all her options.

'Yes, of course, Mrs Pace.'

'Take a few of her in that as well!'

'Yes Mrs Pace.' He turned to go and as he was about to cross the threshold she called again.

'David!'

'Yes Mrs Pace.'

'Take some tidy and some dishevelled! You understand!'

'Yes Mrs Pace.'

'You'll have to feed her! But not before the vulnerable shots understand!'

'Yes Mrs Pace.'

Send out for some sandwiches, okay?

'Yes Mrs Pace.'

Good boy.' Martini smiled. 'Oh we haven't got any other bookings today, have we?'

'No Mrs Pace.'

'Well that's good for a change!'

David left the room and Martini turned back to concentrate on the computer screen.

'Tia Maria and Martini!' She muttered to herself. 'That is a potently lethal cocktail'. And she began to laugh out loud to herself in the empty room.

Chapter 18: Mr and Mrs Pace

Martini did not do lunch. After all she had her figure to think of! However, she was considering giving in to temptation, and escaping the tedium of her office work, for maybe a coffee, one made using the trendy pod machine, which she had recently acquired to impress visitors to her studio, when her husband wandered in. It was probably half an hour after her conversation with David, and she smiled knowingly at the sight of him.

Ellis Pace's face was flushed and his smart casual clothes looked slightly dishevelled, but then, Martini sighed, they always did on him! She doubted that the fashion designers had had men like her husband in mind, when they had began sketching their expensive wears, on the technical drawing boards, in their big city attic studios. The red pin stripped Ralph Lauren shirt had a few too many buttons undone. It was not tucked in properly to the wine coloured chinos, and the trousers themselves were creased, as if they had been dumped in a pile, on the floor somewhere, before being snatched up and hastily put on; no doubt in a guilty rush.

'Tiring audition? Martini asked.

'Oh yes!' Pace smirked, sounding tired. 'But ultimately worth it, you know I think this one could be a real star for us!' He added insincerely.

'Good!' She smiled happily back at him and waited, almost anticipating what he was about to say.

'David tells me you may have got her some work already!?! Some modelling work! With Communication Wales! Thanks to that big headed twat Aled Harris!' Pace looked towards Martini, disbelief written all over his face. Pace did not know much about the fashion industry but even he knew that Tia Maria was not really suitable for "real" modelling work. 'That might affect my plans!' He added in a controlled but slightly irritated tone.

'Only in the short term! Darling!' Martini smiled back at him.

Pace allowed himself a puzzled look by way of reply.

'It would be really useful to us, and potentially very embarrassing for Aled, if he featured one of our er "glamour" models, especially one who was, well shall we say, one of our younger, er, models, in a high profile advertising campaign. You know, only for her to become perhaps better known for her, hmm, how should I put it?' Martini widened her eyes before adding with a smug smile: 'more graphic online performances!'

Ellis Pace had always been quick when it came to devious schemes. Perhaps his greatest advantage in life was always recognising the bad in people and exploiting it. Now he positively beamed back at his young wife.

'Well that's why I love you! Always thinking of the bigger picture! Well done!'

He turned to go and then stopped.

'Oh I almost forgot!' He turned back and grinned at her. 'Talking of the bigger picture, make sure that you are available a week Friday! Late afternoon and evening! I'm meeting our new Security Client. You know the Paki, who bought "The Kettle!" You know the crap old cafe' down the bottom end of town. And I thought we could perhaps mix a bit of business with pleasure, like, afterwards. You know, get to know him a bit better. Put on a bit of a show! Take him for a meal; make a bit of an effort. You'll like him! Yes he's a Paki, but he's a good looking, big boy!'

'Hmm, they're not usually very comfortable with going out in mixed company!' She cautioned.

'Oh, not this guy! He's very er, now um, what's the word?' Martini looked her husband in the face and shrugged as if to say you really asking me!?!

'Westernised, yeah that's it! He even has an English name, Ed Lord! And he loves the movies too. None of this Bollywood singing and dancing shit but the classics! You know,' he paused briefly, 'cowboys and gangster stuff!'

'What you mean is the rubbish you like watching!' She said dismissively.

'Yeah! He's always quoting them. According to his accountant, this Lord has a British Mrs too! Bit of an old "cougar" by all accounts. Anyway, I'd like to show you off and get really close to him. I've a few deals in the pipeline with him! Not just security! Anyway if they takes off, well, we will really make the big time Babe!' He grinned sheepishly at her. 'You've got my permission to push the boat out okay! No holds barred!' He gave her a wink.

She wondered what exactly he meant by that. She surely did not really need to buy a new outfit for a night out in Aberfoist! And then she thought, why not! A girl like her did not need an excuse to spend money on clothes, especially expensive clothes, especially when it was her husband's money.

'Okay then, a week Friday!' She agreed, putting on a genuine cheery smile as she thought about taking the company credit card to Cardiff with her on Thursday.

Ellis gave her one last appreciative glance. 'You're looking the business!' He grinned.

'Yes, I'm very busy Ellis!' She said by way of warning. 'I'm working on the big picture!'

He got the message, no chance of any more "afternoon delights!" He turned once more and began to slink off towards the door. Before he reached it, she called out to him.

'Ellis!'

He slowly turned around with a hopeful look on his face. 'Yes Babe!?!'

'Your flies are undone!'

He frowned and reached down to adjust himself but found that the zip was firmly in place. For a second he looked puzzled and then he started to laugh.

'Love you!' He called out to her as he flicked two fingers in a "V" sign at her.

'Love you too!' She said back without looking up. Yet blindly gesturing back at him, giving him the finger!

When he had gone, Martini reached for her iPhone and began entering the date on the calendar App whilst muttering under her breath: 'a week Friday, more bloody tarting about! Oh well, it's better than working for a living!'

Chapter 19: Being a Bad ASS!

Ellis Pace was living the dream, or so he thought. Even though to others, his dream was probably their nightmare. Quietly humming to himself, Pace paused on the landing just outside Martini's office and took the time to carefully tuck his shirt into his trousers. Then slowly making his way down the stairs to the ground floor of his business HQ, he began whistling. It was a tuneless pitchy sound, which was meant to be cheery. At the bottom of the stairs he checked himself once again, making sure all zips were up. They were! Pace never meant to look dishevelled but he often did. In recent years, as what he liked to call his business empire, continued to grow, Pace had made a regular and conscious effort to try to improve his appearance. Little things became important to him. He would make discrete appointments at posh city hairdressing salons, instead of popping along to the local barbershop. He even wasted money, buying ever more expensive clothes, or rather his wife did. All in vain! Nevertheless, together they made every effort to make him look more like the successful businessman that he had become. However, just below the surface, not too deep within this middle aged man, there still lurked the awkward, gawky, teenage tearaway and typical Welsh boyo, who thought little about the way he looked.

Of course, it did not really matter, because now that both his parents had passed away, only his wife was brave enough to correct him; and even she had to pick her time carefully. Today was fine. He was buzzing with excitement about his big plans, and he had just enjoyed a real bonus, when he had discovered they were auditioning a new model. A young model! A very young model! Pace could tell straight-away, the very first moment that he had spotted her in reception. He knew that she was desperate and really needed the work. So she was just his type. Someone who would do anything to pass her audition and bless her, he chuckled to himself, she did!

Today was a quiet work day really. Mondays usually were and he liked Mondays. The weekly midday meeting, attended by his trusted lieutenants, to review all the weekend's security activities, and then to plan the week ahead. So there was no need to really think about what to wear until much later that evening, when he always went for a "good drink" and gossip at the local Lions Club's weekly get together, held down at The Aberfoist Hotel. For that type of thing, Pace wore what he considered to be the standard "relaxed businessman's" uniform of beige trousers with a check shirt, a rugby club tie and one of the two tweed sports jackets he owned. He knew that the other, more respectable, members of the local businessman's social club, whom he had simply modelled himself on, only tolerated him. Most of them still wore the key to their success, a variety of old school or regimental ties. Even in the alleged meritocracy of the twenty-first century, who you were and your family connections was what ensured most people's success. Pace's connections were unfortunate. Yet all the local "Lions of Commerce" were astute enough to put on a good show of accepting him as one of their own. They realised, not only how healthy it was to keep on the right side of the colourful "Flicker" or rather "Ell" as they now carefully and chummily called him to his face, but also they appreciated how useful he really was, especially when tasked with the loathsome job of collecting debts owed to their businesses. Not surprisingly, he also proved pretty useful at teasing out contributions for their various charities. Fund raising was definitely up since good old Ell had joined their club.

Some members of the club even realised the benefit of employing the upstart to advise on how best to secure their premises. The ugly black and white sticker displayed in their shop window, warning all passers-by that their premises were "Protected by Aberfoist Security Services", seemed more effective at preventing break-ins or vandalism, than any of the expensive state-of-the-art alarms, dead-locks and shutters, fitted by less fortunate neighbouring businesses. Those without a sticker seemed to suffer all the town's break-ins and fires, the odd few that had occurred since Pace had established his firm.

"Are the boys in?" Ellis Pace cheerfully asked the young but fierce looking female receptionist, when he stepped through the open doorway on the left side of the plain white painted and black slate tiled floor from his building's simple entrance hall. The woman instantly put down the typescript that she had been holding up right in front of her face and stopped mouthing the words slowly as was her way when she proof read her typing. Her dark brown eyes stared angrily at him, like a startled animals, out of a pale white face, which was made to look harsher by her flat broad nose and square jaw line. A thick quiff of gelled black hair rose up above her high forehead, and the rest of her hair was close shaved, reminiscent of a late 1970's female punk rocker. The thin dark, purple painted lips, opened and her thick gruff voice unemotionally confirmed they were, with a simple gruff: "Yes Boss."

Pace smiled back at her. He was never offended by her rough off hand manner. His wife, on the other hand, had often said that he should have a more presentable and articulate receptionist to front his business. He knew that his receptionist obviously scared some of her own clients, when they inevitably wandered into the ground floor reception area and had to sit on the simple plastic chairs of his cheap waiting room, a room that still served both businesses. However, he had pointed out to

Martini that he ran a security firm and as such he needed a Rottweiler not a pampered Poodle as his *guard dog*.

Pace also knew that in spite of appearances *his girl* was a good worker, who took no nonsense from anyone. Even his tough lads knew that her "bite" was the "equal to her deep "bark!" Pace had actually seen her win a number of female boxing matches (at local business charity events) and she had even flattened one of his tougher male operatives, who had foolishly made the drunken mistake of trying to get fresh with her at a Christmas staff do, much to the delight of the rest of his team. She even had a boy's name. The only thing that surprised him about Les was that she was not gay. He knew that she lived quite happily with a much older male stylist from his wife's favourite local hair salon, and at the age of twenty–one, Les and the equally confusing Lyn (short for Lyndon) already had three young children. A fact that made her grateful for the above average wages he paid her and ensured her loyalty to him and him alone.

'Hold all my calls for an hour please Les!' Pace instructed his pet Rottweiler.

'Okay Boss.' She grunted back at him.

By the time he had finished walking through the small reception area and opened the black painted door to the firm's meeting room, Les was already staring aggressively at the next piece of paper, holding it up only a few inches in front of her eyes and reading it out loud, to herself, in her scary monotone voice. Pace often wondered if he should suggest she get an eye test but he always thought better of it. He knew that unlike him, some people were far too vain to wear glasses!

Sat around the one end of the long rectangular wooden table, which almost filled the dull and dreary meeting room, were Pace's three lieutenants. Compared to him they all looked thoroughly miserable in their matching black uniforms and their

177

nervous expressions instantly concerned him. Normally on a Monday, he found them irritatingly full of fun and banter, happily recalling all the weekend's wild drunken antics, which they and their team members had had to deal with when "bouncing" the local "nutters" from the various "protected" in-town venues.

"What's up then?" Pace asked curtly as he took his seat at the top of the table.

Initially there was a lot of moaning about how wild things had got on both Friday and Saturday night. Yet they all seemed eager to reassure Pace that it was nothing they could not handle. In fact, when they had actually tackled the usual suspects, who were inevitably at the centre of things, they found them so far out of it, that they were somehow easier to deal with. Pace was pleased with this information, for he knew that he had indirectly been responsible for the madness by distributing free samples of Lord's new drug or rather "legal high" to the local dealers. He allowed himself the briefest of smirks as he anticipated a positive feedback session from those dealers at another pre-arranged gathering at the "Kettle" later in the week.

However, his boys were still looking gloomy and eventually it fell to Liam, a tall and broad mixed race man, with a boxer's flat nose, cauliflower ears only partly hidden by tight compacted dreadlocks and a little goatee beard, to tell his "Boss" the real problem the A.S.S. had experienced that weekend, when Pace had asked if there was anything else?

'Er yes Mister Pace.' Liam began matter of factly. 'You sees I dunno why, now after all this time with nah trouble, but Johnson's Plant was hit last night, and a lot of equipment was shipped out Boss!' Liam stared down at the table as he spoke and the other two shifted uncomfortably on their seats. As he finished talking, Liam looked up and glowered across the table towards the diminutive Dylan Francis, who was sat opposite him.

Pace's cheeks were flushed. He was thinking ahead. He would be seeing Mr Johnson that night, at The Lions Club, and he needed answers. The type of answers that the police would not be able to give old man Johnson, or Pace's credibility would be in question. Pace thought for a moment, his eyes following those of Big Liam.

'Why is Liam telling me about this Dylan?' Pace's eyes narrowed behind the thick lenses he wore. 'Johnson's is your primary responsibility isn't it?' Pace added calmly but coldly.

'Er, Liam took the call for me Mr Pace, because I was, er, trying to get me hand sorted.' The little man held his bandaged arm up as if to prove his point. Pace blinked and noticed for the first time that Dylan Francis was nursing a tightly bandaged right hand.

'Have you had that checked out properly?' Pace asked his voice icy.

'Yes Mr Pace, Tall Dai took me to the hospital on Friday evening, before the rush. They think it might be broken but they couldn't do anything much, until the swelling goes down like! I gotta go back for an ex-ray, like, later in the week.'

Pace shook his head in disgust, before turning to face the other men.

'You two heard what this idiot done!?!' He said rolling his eyes, his voice full of contempt.

The shaven headed lieutenant sat beside Big Liam let out a snigger before sneering: 'Punched the wall trying to look a big man in front of a room full of our dealers, didn't you Dill!'

The little man bristled, his previously pale face going red, his features fired by his quick temper. Through gritted teeth he ground out his angry reply:

'I'd like to see you do better Danny boy! That fat bastard moved quicker than he had any right to!'

'I know that "fat bastard" as you call him of old!' Pace

179

interrupted suddenly losing his own temper. 'He may be fat now but I can assure you he was a right hard bastard when we were younger and you were bloody lucky he moved out of the way or you wouldn't be waiting to go back to the hospital! You'd be in intensive bloody care! And I've a good mind to put you there myself for embarrassing me in front of our new client! What the hell happened at Johnson's?'

Dylan Francis pulled a face and his voice was full of disbelief when he foolishly ignored the question, determined to have his say: 'He might've been hard once upon a time but you've seen him Mr Pace, believe me he's gonna regret crossing me and Tall Dai!'

The little man turned and stared angrily at the shaven headed man he had called Danny Boy, who was beaming back at him. Danny Boy could sense an opportunity for his own promotion in his smaller colleague's disadvantage.

'You can take that smile off of your fuckin' face! We almost had him on Friday night but we lost his car when he got to Cardiff! Still we know roughly where the fat fuck lives!' Francis spat vehemently across the table.

A loud groan caused Francis to stop talking and the three men turned their attention back to the top of the table, where Ellis Pace was sitting with his head in his hands. Slowly Pace lowered his hands. Pace's eyes were closed as if in prayer. Then they blinked open and stared at Dylan Francis with a look of pure evil that sent a chill through the little man, as he realised, too late, that in his arrogance he had said too much.

After what seemed like ages, Pace opened his fingers and finally spoke. His voice was quiet, really no more than a whisper. Just as if he was talking to himself.

'You didn't lose him, he lost you! You really are an ass just like My-Key Kane bloody well said! And maybe, just maybe, I am an ass too for giving you such an important role in my

180

organisation!' Pace shook his head slowly before continuing. His tone was deadly serious. 'I thought I had resolved my problem over Frank John, but thanks to you Dull-one and your mate Dai Bloody Oaf, there is a chance, just a chance, that things are about to get a whole lot worse!'

Dylan Francis was confused, very confused. John was dead. Dai and him had found Frank John hanging from that beam in the back room of "The Kettle". Francis wanted to say something, something back. Something in his defence, but he could not think of what to say. Instead he fidgeted in his seat, as Pace continued to give him the evil eye. Then in a small little lost boy voice, he began to mutter: 'I'm sorry Mr Pace.'

'Yes, I'm sorry too Dull-one but ...' Pace paused mid sentence. Then he suddenly smiled. He knew what to do. Instantly! Clearly! And without hesitation! He knew that he had found a way forward and he congratulated himself as he thought "this is why I earn the big bucks!" Pace's humour changed so quickly that it truly unsettled the other men in the room. They nervously looked at each other before two, not Francis of course, smiled hopefully back at their boss.

'First things first!' Pace laughed out loud. 'We have to sort out this Johnson's mess!' He allowed himself a dramatic frown. 'Liam is your car round the back?' Pace asked urgently. His loud question made the dreadlocked man jump. Behind Pace's building there was a small car park, which had once been the garden of the house, a house which only had pedestrian access to the front.

'Yeah Mr Pace.' The combined reply came. Both Big Liam and Danny Boy were keen to show their eagerness to please. Dylan Francis was somewhat more reserved.

'Good! Come along then gentlemen! First things first!' Pace repeated. We need to have a chat with our old friend Bernie Russell!'

Chapter 20: Slum Clearance

New Town Aberfoist had been built in the 1880's to accommodate an influx of factory workers. Until then these pioneers of the industrial revolution had had to live (and mainly die) in a shanty town, which had been knocked up from the "old" town's cast off's and whatever other rubbish was found in the swamp that was the Foist river meadows.

The new build was not born out of charity or concern for the sturdy families who eked out a living in Aberfoist's two agricultural processing plants, nor to save the town from typhoid and cholera, which inevitably occurred in the rancid "dying conditions" usually tolerated by so called Victorian values. It was built out of the necessity to ensure that sufficient people could survive, albeit in the simplest of dwellings, and be actually fit enough to perform the hard labour required by the factories. Nevertheless, the developer, who became Lord Aberfoist, was considered a saint by those lucky survivors, who endured and paid his extortionate rents. They ultimately erected a statute of their "saviour" at the centre of a lush triangular grassland park, bordered by a brick and stone triangle of terraces, each made up of three linked and comparatively grand, two up, two down, cottages. The residents no doubt took great pride in wiping the pigeon shit from their benefactor's edifice, until the metal was needed for a war effort. Now, only an empty hard stone plinth stood as a, perhaps more fitting, memorial to an aristocrat, who made a lot of money from a town he was named after, but never ever visited.

In the small dark stone fronted dwelling, tightly squeezed

into the middle of the terrace immediately opposite the empty plinth, lived Bernard Russell; or perhaps more aptly, that was where Bernie existed when he was not in prison. How he had paid for the house nobody knew. Yet one day his unfortunate neighbours found that he had moved in, at first, with a wife and several young children. She left him within a few weeks and shortly after that the children were taken into care, but somehow Bernie stayed on. The neighbours on both sides of the house fled within the first year, initially boarding up their property before finally abandoning it after squatters, who were apparently invited in at Russell's behest, used the whole terrace as a 24/7 party venue. Russell would even rent all three properties out, to even more dubious tenants than himself, whilst he enjoyed his little holidays at Her Majesty's pleasure.

A few more years later, all the other houses, in the terraced triangle, were empty and boarded up. Russell's council rates were certainly paid in housing benefits and there were no longer any neighbours to overlook or complain about his comings and goings. Even the cottages in the street directly behind his property, gradually emptied and should a naive estate agent dare auction the properties today, they probably would not fix a reserve on what they would no doubt describe as an unique opportunity for an experienced developer.

Ellis Pace was such a developer. Standing outside the only house in the area, which he did not already own, Pace viewed the property with disdain. He wondered whether he should just send his men in to drag Bernie out, rather than risk his own health by entering what to all extensive purposes remained an almost timeless example of a Victorian slum.

Pace's man Big Liam, was made of sterner stuff. Kicking in the front door, smashing the basic latch lock and splitting the wooden door frame, Liam bravely charged inside. He was quickly followed by an eager Danny Boy, and then the slightly more hesitant Dylan Francis. When the screaming and swearing had stopped, and the muffled thuds of leather covered fists on skin and bone ceased, so that only a women's snivelling could be heard through the broken doorway, Pace methodically pulled on his tight fitting black leather gloves, a standard Aberfoist Security Services issue, and took a long last deep breath of fresh air, ahead of confidently strolling in.

There was no hallway. Pace simply stepped straight into the open plan living room. Dark and dingy, faintly lit by only the last of that late spring afternoon's dull grey white daylight, which had bravely struggled through the greasy, dust covered, cracked glass panes of what was probably the original single sash windows, punched in the centre of the property's thick brick and stone front wall, with it's mould encrusted, crumbling internal plaster and peeling floral patterned wallpaper. The smell hit Pace right away, and despite his mental precautions, he wanted to gag.

Inside the air was a toxic mix of tobacco, pot smoke, stale piss, rotting food and untreated damp. Pace could see plates of all shapes and sizes, untidily stacked beside an equally unsteady collection of half empty, silver foil, takeaway cartons, all abandoned on a small grubby, yellow Formica topped table, which stood in what must have been the kitchen area, at the back of the ground floor. In the shadows behind the table there may well have been kitchen cupboards and work tops, but the only thing that caught Pace's eye, was the fact that there were two free standing refrigerators and a stack of three microwave ovens. The fumes that hung stagnating in the air, were all locked in a desperate aromatic battle, and may have been about to lose out to a sweeter, sicklier, more chemical smell, which Pace could not quite place. All offended his senses. His Dr. Marten soled, Ox Blood coloured brogues, were already sticking to a grimy, well worn, once yellow carpet.

Pace could see clearly to his immediate right, Big Liam and

184

Danny Boy, both standing aggressively over a shirtless Bernard Russell, who was slumped, across an oddly modern, silver grey, crushed velvet covered, two seat sofa, which had been carelessly positioned in the middle of the lounge area. Russell had a newly split lip and there was a fresh trickle of blood running from his left nostril. These injuries complimented the fading bruises under his eyes and cheek scabs, wounds that remained visible from an earlier beating. There were now multiple red punch marks over Russell's bare ribs, angrily standing out on both sides of his emaciated and otherwise pale torso. The blue ink amateur tattoos, decorating his skinny arms were all faded and wrinkled with age and far too blurred to read. A small amount of silver grey, short and curly hair was stuck, matted with sweat, to Russell's chest. Pace's nausea increased as he scanned down and saw Russell's bare feet. He failed to avert his eyes quickly enough from the jagged edged, uncared for, fungi covered, black and blue toenails, which curled awkwardly, back on themselves at the end of long spindly toes. The washed out and torn, once sky blue jeans, which had obviously been pulled up at the last moment, for they were undone at the waist, were a small mercy and the only relief from a neglected and totally abused body; a body that was certainly not a pretty sight.

To his left, Pace was surprised to see a completely naked and equally emaciated woman. She was sat on a worn beige fabric covered arm chair, subconsciously cradling a grey crushed velvet pillow, (probably from the sofa) tightly across her stomach with her own, unnaturally thin, right arm. She had a red slap mark across the right cheek of her tearful face, clearly showing the imprint of the back of the small hand that had probably hit her. Her face looked much older than her pale and scrawny body. A body that was almost girlish, apart from her large, droopy, lopsided, breasts. She had long wavy hair, dyed an unnatural jet black. The hair hung loose, well down below her shoulders,

185

almost covering her pink nipples. This all gave the false impression, mainly due to her slight build, that she was too young for such a drawn and creased face, a face, which had seen far too much of the wrong side of life. She reminded Pace of a witch! One he had seen once in a teenage horror movie. Dark blood and lumps of green snot still flowed repulsively down from her slightly bent nose, in a trail of slimy mucus, running unheeded, into her gaping open mouth, as she sniffed and sobbed, and blew bubbles quietly to herself. The woman was still clutching in her shaky left hand, a long white plastic or possibly clay pipe, and Pace could see a variety of drug taking paraphernalia scattered about the floor next to an over turned teak coloured table that now lay just beyond the chair. Her puffy red eyes looked up, terrified, staring straight at Dylan Francis, who stood on guard beside her. The little man had a look of utter contempt on his face.

'Well done boys!' Pace began and turning his attention back to Russell, he noticed for the first time the long bladed, Samurai sword that lay, where it had been dropped, on the carpet in front of the sofa.

'Nice blade!' Pace exclaimed and with a slight grimace, he freed his feet from the sticky carpet and moved over to where the curved blade lay. Stooping down, Pace delicately picked it up.

'I hope you didn't try to use this against my boys!?! They wouldn't like that, and, well they could get all unnecessary, couldn't you boys!'

On cue both Big Liam and Danny Boy chirped up. 'That's right Mr Pace!'

With that Russell let out a growl and tried to adjust himself where he lay on the sofa. Big Liam snarled back at him like an angry dog. Danny Boy sharply raised his left arm and pushed his hand out in front of him, palm first, with its fingers stretched up, flat, as a visual warning to Russell not to move any further. Just in case, the thug's right hand formed into a fist and was pulled back ready to punch forward, warning the beaten man not to attempt to rise off the sofa.

Pace began casually examining the blade held lightly in his gloved hand. Turning it over slowly at first, he then started swishing it quickly back and fore, right to left. Russell's eyes widened and followed the movement, as if the blade was a hypnotist's watch.

'Bernie, don't you know the police warn people not to carry knives, especially for their own defence. It's just in case they find them taken off them and then used against them! Yep! Did you know that statistically, most reported stabbings are of people stabbed with their own knives?' Pace laughed lightly.

'Fuck you Flicker!' Russell grunted, in a low gasping tone, just loud enough for all to hear.

Pace shrugged casually before teasingly adding: 'I wonder if the statistics are right?' Suddenly, he swished the blade in an anti-clockwise arc, turning it over, so that the tip pointed down. Pace then licked his lips, before stabbing the razor sharp metal straight down into Russell's left thigh, piercing right through the fleshy part of the denim clad leg and on through into the cushion below until he hit wood in the frame somewhere deep within the sofa. With the blade effectively pinning his leg firmly in place, a shocked Bernie Russell let out a high pitched yelp.

'Yes they are!' Pace chuckled to himself.

The woman on the chair began to scream as Russell continued to groan.

'Shut her up Dull-one!' Pace said quietly and coldly below the noise.

The little man slapped the woman hard. This time with his open left hand, causing a sickening smack sound, and she rolled off the chair. Still wailing, she raised herself slightly into a crawling position on the floor until Francis swung his right boot into her jaw. The contact resulted in an audible crack and she collapsed sideways, in what seemed like slow motion, with a splash of blood washing a fractured pair of dentures out of her mouth, onto the carpet. She let out a deep throaty moan, broke wind and then lay still.

Sounding more than a little irritated, Pace also groaned out a reprimand: 'I told you to shut her up! Not fucking kill her!'

The little man shrugged a half-hearted apology back at his boss and then turned angrily to look at Russell, whose groaning had changed slightly into what could have been a moaned curse of "bastards" as he lay bleeding, trapped on the sofa.

'Now, now, there's no need for all this Bernie!' Pace regained his composure, focusing on why they were in this filthy hovel once more. 'I'm sorry for interrupting your little, er, "party"! You celebrating something or what? Anyway, I just wanted to pick your brain about the Johnson's job!' Pace ignored Russell's muttered denials and continued. 'You and I know that no one local would want to embarrass me by stealing from a business under my protection or would they?'

Russell mouthed something. It was indecipherable from pain and frustration. Pace responded by casually resting his right hand on the top of the sword's handle and in a mocking tone said: 'I can't quite make that out Bernie?'

Russell screamed and Pace exerted the slightest bit more pressure, which resulted in an even louder scream.

'Ah that's a bit better!' Pace joked. 'I like the volume!' He smirked. 'But once again, I can't quite make out what you are trying to tell me!'

'I don't know anything!' Russell spat out. He then gasped again. 'Aaaaagh!' Russell screamed as Pace pressed gently on the blade once more and the pressure reverberated into Russell's leg again.

Turning to look at Danny Boy, Pace said. 'I don't like the

look of that leg do you!?! Why don't you see if you can find something we can make a tourniquet out of! I'd hate him to bleed out on us before we finish our little chat!' Then looking down at the even paler than usual Russell, Pace added: 'Look Bernie I really haven't got all afternoon. And to be honest I'm sick of the stink in here! So if you have any ambition to walk again, I suggest you tell me what you did!'

With a flick of his fingers Pace pinged the sword's handle and Russell screamed again as the blade vibrated down into his leg and more blood gushed out of the wound, soaking into the already sticky wet sofa.

'Liam! You and Dull-one have a look around and see what you can find in here. But be careful! I don't want you catching anything infectious!' Pace chuckled to himself at his own joke.

Danny Boy reappeared with a shabby looking tartan scarf and what looked like a foot of cut off metal piping. Pace raised his eye brows quizzically at the pipe before agreeing that that would have to do. The light was starting to fade outside, so it was getting even darker inside. Pace called out to Francis and told the little man to turn the lights on. They then discovered that there was no power in the house. Through groans and moans Russell told them there was a coin operated meter but he did not have any change.

The three men pathetically searched their pockets and eventually produced three £1 coins. Francis was sent to feed the meter, whilst Danny Boy managed to tie the makeshift tourniquet around Russell's upper thigh, about two inches above the wound. Pace left the blade in the leg. He suspected that to remove it now would make the bleeding worse and anyway he was beginning to enjoy the power it gave him over the injured man.

Rather disappointingly for Pace, Russell's befuddled brain realised that he had no option other than to die or tell the truth.

However, he chose neither and instead slowly began to spin a half fantasy, where in he owed money to a drugs gang from Newport, so he had unwillingly been forced to exchanged information with them about local businesses, and Johnson's equipment was on their wish-list. They had done the job and the plant and equipment was now hidden in a barn, on a derelict farm just over the border in Herefordshire, waiting for collection by a gang from Birmingham, in exchange for more drugs.

Pace did not believe the story. He knew that Russell's dubious reputation and existing debts, had probably closed off any previous connections Newport way, and anyway Pace's own immodest reputation had created a kind of truce, preventing unwanted incursions into Aberfoist from that particular nearby city. It was more likely that Russell's hunger for drugs had sent him across the border to some wannabe gangsters in Hereford. There he would find the type of amateurs, who would simply be looking to off load the Plant and Equipment on the nearby West Midlands black market. Pace ordered his men to search the house again, whilst he carried on questioning Russell.

The search produced a plastic shopping bag, stuffed full with about two thousand pounds, in wads of used twenty pound notes. The men also found a map of the border counties, torn off from an ordinance survey booklet, which had a convenient red circle drawn around a field, down the bottom of a remote lane. This Pace felt justified him in amusing himself further, by pinging the sword in Russell's leg every now and then, until he had the full details of the raid. Details he truly believed. Pace then felt confident enough to ring his contact in the local CID.

Little Dylan Francis had not actually killed the woman and when she came around, she went into shock. Pace showed his practical side and ordered her wrapped in a blanket, which Big Liam found upstairs. Following this apparent kindness, Pace briefly tried to get her to confirm the story Russell had told him.

However, her jaw was broken and she could not talk. She did make mournful noises, nodding and shaking her head, until Pace was satisfied with her own sad story. Quite simply, it seemed that the unfortunate woman had met Russell, in a local pub, late Monday night and she had merely come back to "party" with Russell, following his promise of "good" drugs. Pace almost felt sorry for her. He allowed Big Liam to relieve her pain, by injecting her with an unhealthy amount of the drug, which she still craved, and she tripped out, coma like, beside them.

Russell himself was now in a bad way. Well, much worse than the bad way that he was normally in! Whether it was the torture or the loss of blood, or his need for another drug fix, which was causing him to lapse in and out of consciousness, it was difficult for Pace to tell. Yet Bernie Russell was undoubtedly a broken man. The regular first aid, release and tightening of the tourniquet, was excruciating torture in itself, and he still had the sword stuck in his leg. Pace began to show a little compassion in his speech to the now compliant Russell. He listened as his victim confessed, this time sincerely, to selling the information on Johnson's to a Herefordshire gang. Russell even confirmed that he intended to use his proceeds to buy and sell more drugs locally. Good old Bernie, seemed to have forgotten that he was talking to the very man he would be undercutting, in the local market place, had his get rich scheme worked.

Pace cynically weighed up his options. He was not threatened by Russell's scheme. After all, he told himself, the idiot would probably overdose as soon as he had hold of a large quantity of drugs all to himself. Just look at what he had done as soon as he had a little bit of money, no doubt acquired, Pace reckoned, from his share in the Johnson's job. Maybe, Pace concluded, it would be sensible to just speed things along! Of course, the woman's presence was an added complication. She needed the hospital and that would inevitably result in a report

191

of her condition to the police. The Dull-one's heavy handedness, or rather heavy *"booted-ness"* was going to cost him, unless, Pace suddenly realised, he could use her to his advantage. Yes, Pace thought to himself, licking his lips subconsciously, now might be the perfect time to cash in another of his long term money making schemes.

At that moment, Pace's mobile phone began to vibrate. Turning towards his man, Big Liam, Pace sternly told him to "keep an eye on them!" He nodded in the directions of Russell and the woman. Then, slowly removing the still softly buzzing mobile phone, from where it throbbed deep inside his fleece's zipped pocket, Pace stepped outside, breathed in the mercifully fresh air and answered the call. It was good news. For him at least!

Pace's contact in South Wales CID had managed to achieve the almost impossible! He had utilized a neighbouring police force's helicopter. One that just so happened to be on a meaningless motorway observation duty, less than ten minutes cross country flying time from the location marked on Russell's map. The "chopper boys" had quickly managed to confirm, using their expensive night vision cameras, that there was a lot of Plant & Equipment stored in the open fields, near a seemingly deserted farmhouse. Their initial report had come in, coincidentally, as West Mercia's brand new Chief Constable just happened to be touring the Operations Room. He was more than eager to roll up his sleeves and get stuck in, to what was going to be an impressive PR coup, boosting the crimes solved statistics in his very first week in office!

Pace was ecstatic. At this very moment, a cross-border, multi-police force "shout" was being called. Armed police teams were rushing to stake out a farm, less than twenty miles away, in the hope of collaring not one, but two criminal gangs! Oh and hopefully, recovering a valuable quantity of stolen goods. If the

192

police actually managed not to cock it up, Pace would be a hero at tonight's business club. Or so he thought. Pace was now really looking forward to speaking to Mr Johnson. In any event he could distract the members from the fact that his security team had been compromised. Pace suddenly frowned as he realised the damage to his reputation that Russell might have done. He would have to send out a strong message to all the ambitious local boyos, but how? He wondered. Then something caught his eye from across the street.

A white laminated notice was fixed firmly to the first floor window of the heavily boarded up, derelict, terraced house, directly ahead of him. Another broad grin spread across his ferret like features. The notice on the house opposite proudly read: "Protected by Aberfoist Security Services". His eyes continued to scan the two adjacent terraces and his chest swelled with pride. He knew what to do. Pace allowed his gaze to linger on what in the twilight was an unreadable notice board, erected across one of the doorways of the abandoned houses. He did not need to read it. He knew that it said: "Properties now acquired for redevelopment by MP Housing Ltd".

Scum like Russell had their uses but now it was time to begin distancing himself from such unfortunate connections. He glanced at his watch. Hmm! Pace thought, he had better be making a move, but, he also thought that he still had time for a little bit of pleasure before all that business. He deserved his treat! After all pleasure before business could be his motto.

Pace smartly turned around, positively beaming, and after another essential deep breath of fresh evening air, he walked back into Russell's hovel. He had decided that it was now time for a bit of slum clearance and it would all be to his advantage. He really did like Mondays!

Chapter 21: The Morning News

Blinking the early morning fatigue from his eyes, Kane hunched over the charcoal coloured breakfast bar. He was sat on a tall stool in what his wife considered to be the smart modern kitchen of his suburban Cardiff home. He had risen early. Too early, but then he had had difficulty sleeping last night and for a change it was not because of worrying about how long he would be paying off the loan for this smart modern kitchen. The green digits on the nearby microwave's electronic clock silently blinked at him as they changed to display 07:00. This told him that he still had two long hours spare before he needed to leave home and make the relatively short drive back to Aberfoist for Frank John's funeral. The ceremonial goodbye was meant to be held at 11 a.m. later that morning. So Kane tried once again to distract himself and focus on the digital newsfeed that was brightly displayed on the screen of the notebook computer, propped open on the granite worktop in front of him.

In spite of his best intentions, Kane had not returned to his old home town during the thirteen days that had passed since his last visit; the oddly eventful one after receiving the awful news of his friend's death. He had sent Wendy a card. Or rather Jill, his wife, had. She was better at that type of thing and had selected an appropriate one. She had also written a suitable message of condolence. He had signed it, of course!

Jill had wanted to cancel her pre-arranged business trip, so that she could support him at his friend's funeral, but Kane would not hear of it. He felt, especially after his last trip to Aberfoist, that he should not involve her in any of the misery and chaos that seemed to ooze out of his old home town. She, of course had wanted to go, if only to make sure that he kept out of trouble; but then typical of her, she did not want to let her boss down either and Kane suspected that if the conference went well there might be a promotion in the offing for her!

Luckily for Kane, his son was ending the school holidays with a long weekend stay at Jill's parents in Bristol. No doubt the grandparents would be visiting the zoo again. Kane's boy was fascinated by animals. Kane allowed himself a wry smile when he thought that maybe one day he should take Francis to see the wildlife of Aberfoist, but not now, the boy was far too young. Anyway, the release from child care duties was convenient as Kane planned to have a good drink at Frank's Wake and catch up with some of his and Frank's old companions.

Kane expected there would be a good turn out for Frank. Although, in truth, Kane had not contacted any of the old gang, he just assumed they would all be going. And on that basis he had booked an overnight stay in a local guesthouse, one that had been highly recommended on Tripadvisor. It was certainly much cheaper than the Aberfoist Hotel, where mourners had been invited to join the family after the funeral.

Already dressed in his best black suit, which was actually his only suit, Kane had diligently wrapped a large tea towel around his neck. It was a souvenir of a recent staycation and featured various cartoon images of the castles of Wales on its brightly coloured cotton. Kane hoped that it would protect him from any accidental tipage as he occasionally scooped spoonfuls of creamy porridge from the large bowl to his right and kidded himself that he was certainly not missing the two spoonfuls of sugar, which he would normally have enjoyed on this or any other cereal before he his recent keep fit regime. Kane was already sure that the trousers were looser around his waist, as a result of almost a fortnight's exercise, and diet! However, his freshly ironed white

195

shirt was still open at the neck. Well, the collar had always been too tight for him, and open collars were now trendy or so he reassured himself. In spite of this delusion or perhaps because of it, when Kane began idly scrapping the bowl, he wondered if he could get away with a piece of toast.

"No!" He told himself firmly, in an inner voice that sounded a lot like his wife's jolly West Country accent. So instead Kane attempted to distract himself once again by browsing the local news. Fortunately for his diet plans, Kane's attention was caught by a relatively sensational headline, certainly one that might be considered extraordinary for any Local Newspaper website but especially for the once conservative Aberfoist Gazette. It read *"Armed police in incident at border counties farm."* Kane clicked on the link and was disappointed by the limited information available. He read the story twice.

"Armed response teams and a police force helicopter are believed to have attended an incident in the Crossway area of the Border Counties, between Aberfoist and Hereford, in the early hours of Wednesday morning. Reports from the area say that shots had been heard in the vicinity. West Mercia Police confirm that a number of arrests were made at or near the derelict Crossway farmhouse and that a large quantity of suspected stolen Plant & Equipment had been found at the location. No-one from Gwent Police was available for comment as to whether the items recovered were those stolen over the previous weekend from local business Johnson's Plant Hire. Chief Constable Goode of West Mercia

Police is expected to make a full statement on the incident in due course."

Several clicks later, Kane was feeling frustrated and gave up on his search for more up to date information from other sites and he returned to the Gazette's home page.

Kane had been in school with a Jeremy Johnson and wondered if there was any connection. However, the story was merely a minor distraction to him, a sign of the times perhaps, in that serious crime could afflict those who thought they had escaped to the country, just as much as those who still lived in the city. He was really looking to see if there was any mention of today's main event. There wasn't! Kane began to wonder if avoiding the news altogether, and not yoga or meditation, was the real answer to gaining peace of mind in the modern world. Nevertheless, he continued to scroll down and discovered another intriguing story.

The headline read: *"Gwent Police appeal for information following fire at Newtown Terrace."* Kane clicked on the link and read that "police were appealing for information following Monday night's tragic fire at Lord Aberfoist Gardens, in the Newtown area, on the outskirts of Aberfoist town centre." Kane focused on the key part of the story. He read through it carefully, twice:

Officers had attended the scene, alongside colleagues from South Wales Fire and Rescue Service, following reports of smoke and flames billowing from the only residential property known to be occupied in the vicinity. The blaze is believed to have been underway for sometime and had spread from the central two bedrooms home

to the adjoining derelict houses. The charred remains of a man and a woman were subsequently recovered from this terraced house. Local sources named well known Aberfoist eccentric, Mr. Bernard Russell, as the property's owner. Police are unwilling to comment on the identities of the dead man and woman at present, until DNA checks have been completed and family members notified. It is understood, however, that Mr. Russell has not been seen in and around Aberfoist since the night before the fire. Relatives have also reported local woman, Gaynor Powell, as missing since the weekend and witnesses report that Ms. Powell was seen leaving the Old Station Public House in the company of Mr Russell late Sunday night. The cause of the fire is still under investigation and officers would ask anyone with information, no matter how small, to please call 101 quoting Log 2 LAG or ring Crimestoppers anonymously on 0800 555 111.

It was a sobering thought for Kane that two of his childhood contemporaries had died within weeks of each other. For reading between the lines and based on what he had seen of him during his last visit to Aberfoist, Kane had no doubt that Bernie was one of the victims of the reported fire. He wondered where Russell's family were and how long it would be before an official confirmation was announced. He was sad for Bernie's fate but not surprised. Perhaps, given the state of the man, it was for the best. He pictured him passing out after another heavy session down the pub, or worse, "shooting up" as he believed was the appropriate phrase for taking hard drugs, and he imagined the fire starting accidentally, maybe a chip pan carelessly left on the stove or hob. Kane vividly remembered the warning films that used to play on the TV and in cinemas like The Coliseum. The oil or fat would be getting hotter and hotter before bursting into flames, and then the fire would quickly spread. What a horrible way to go but then, Kane sighed silently to himself, in his experience there never was a good way to die. All you could hope for was that it would be sudden and unexpected. Well at least Bernie was probably asleep or more likely out of it and the end would have certainly been unexpected.

Kane wondered about the woman. What was she like? She had been missed so she must have had a family. He pictured the dishevelled, slurring, toothless, wreck of a man that Bernie had become. What type of woman would willingly leave the pub with a man like Bernie? What could he have promised her? What did she want from Bernie Russell? He sighed silently to himself again. Another wasted life, someone looking for one more good time, reality distorted out of proportion by alcohol. Those flattering "beer goggles" perhaps or maybe Bernie had even drugged her and then instead of pleasure, finding the pain of a pathetically wretched end. His mind pictured them asleep in bed, after, hopefully, a drunken last hurrah! Living the nightmare or so Kane thought, with a frown. And then he imagined the two of them, needles in veins, spaced out on a sofa or lying on the floor, overcome by smoke, as the flames crept from the cooker, closer and closer to them. Kane actually shook his head to try and shake off the horrible images.

Something else was beginning to bother Kane, rather than just his overactive imagination. It was a distant memory, flickering in the flames so graphically visualised in his early morning day dream. He closed his eyes and tried to recall it better. Kane pictured the flames bursting out of the chip pan. He saw them spread quickly across the cooker top and then engulf the whole kitchen. This vision was not from a cinematic advert or a TV public information film. A man stood back from the cooker, his features blurred by the black smoke, only a skull on a chain, hanging from his one ear, was visible. It was swinging back and fore, as a blurred head shook left and right, as if saying no! He could almost hear Bernie's voice laughing. 'What me cook!?! No way!' The words were repeated again and again. 'What me COOK!?!' They seemed louder each time. The word "cook" took on a greater importance each time he heard it repeated in his head. And then another face slowly came in to focus. Kane recognised the pale, ferret like, features, grinning at him from deep within his own imagination. The beads of perspiration on the upper lip that drew his attention were so familiar. It was all from another time, another place.

***

'Look at the flames!' The other voice from Kane's past repeatedly hissed. 'Look at the flames! I likes the flames, don't you? The flames! They are so beautiful! Look at the way they *flicker*!'

The schoolboy Kane was frozen, staring at the flames rising from a rapidly blackening chip pan. It was on an electric hob, in a school's classroom kitchen. A young Frank John pushed passed Kane. He had a damp tea towel. Plain patterned in red and white stripes. Frank dropped it over the pan, smothering the flames. A third boy standing by the cooker let out a howl of displeasure and then in a low long growl exclaimed.

'Why did you do that Frankie? I likes the flames!

200

Don't you? The flames! They are so beautiful! I like the way that they flicker!'

'Well done Frank!' The teacher, a tall fair haired woman, with long elegant limbs and a calm relaxed voice, which suited her pleasant face, was suddenly standing behind them. She held a small fire extinguisher confidently in her raised right hand. She was dressed in a long white and spotlessly clean apron, which protected her smart navy blue, maxi length dress.

'You have saved the day!' The lady announced in a happy sing song voice. 'Yes, well done Frank! Da iawn! My good boy!' She gushed, before turning her bewitching green eyes on Kane. They scolded him, even before she spoke. 'Mickey Kane, I told you to keep an eye on this young man!' She now glared disapprovingly at the third boy, who stood twitching and agitated to her left. 'I am very disappointed in you! Both of you!'

The teacher then turned her attention solely on to the third boy and frowned. Her pretty face becoming quite ugly as she began to rant: 'You! How many times do I have to tell you! You do not play with fire in my lessons!' With that she placed her left hand on her hip and waved the fire extinguisher held in her other hand, at the third boy in an aggressive manner. 'You can't be trusted at all! Can you? You will never ever cook again in any of MY lessons!' Her eyes narrowed. 'Do you understand Master Ellis Pace? You will never be a cook because you like to burn everything! And you will never cook again in my lessons, as long as I am at this school!'

Kane could not remember whether it was when they packed away or on their way to the next lesson that Frankie had first called Ellis Pace by the name "Flicker" but by the end of the next lesson the whole class had learnt Pace's new nickname, and by the end of the day, the whole school seemed to be calling Ellis Pace "Flicker"!

Kane also remembered that it was only about two weeks later, when the school's Home Economics' Department had caught fire, one evening, long after school had finished for that day. The subsequent investigation by the South Wales Fire and Rescue Service found that someone had left a chip pan, full of oil on the hob. Ms Rudd, the Head of Home Economics was blamed and duly sacked by the Local Authority. Even though the poor teacher swore that she had checked everything carefully and switched the power off before locking up that evening. She had left her keys in the staffroom, which although common practice was it turned out, a disciplinary offence. The National Education Authority also banned cooking potato chips, and using deep fat fryers, from the Home Economics curriculum, as a consequence of this one incident.

The alarm that the school was on fire on that dark winter's evening had been amazingly raised by a pupil of the school. Oddly enough, the pupil concerned had coincidentally been taking a short cut through the school grounds that evening, on his way home from his Karate class at the nearby Youth Club. The pupil became a bit of a hero to the Local Authority and thereafter could do no wrong in the eyes of the Head Master. The boy had been presented with a Good Citizenship Award by the Mayor of Aberfoist, and Kane remembered the feted pupil, Ellis Pace, being quoted in the congratulatory article, published that week, in the Aberfoist Gazette as saying: 'I saw the flames! The flames! They were flickering, I knew it was bad but they were so beautiful!'

**

An alarm, a mobile phone alarm buzzed, in Kane's suit's jacket pocket, calling him back to the here and now. He knew that it was time for him to get ready for his journey, back to Aberfoist.

Chapter 22: Capel Heddwch

Capel Heddwch was a small church-like rubble stoned building, located at the heart of Aberfoist's main cemetery. With a pyramidic slate roof and an impressively tall octagon shaped bell tower, complete with late Victorian mock Gothic style turret, the chapel had stood for well over one hundred years as a constant, if somewhat grim, reminder to the townsfolk of their imminent mortality. However, its proud profile was now lost amongst the new millennium's urban sprawl. A variety of flimsy new builds, mostly starter homes, constructed out of plasterboard and breeze block, stretched up from the river meadows to the graveyard's ancient stone boundary walls. Even the once imposing tower, in its elevated position, on a rise of green, was now blocked from view by the recently erected, imposingly high, temporary roadside signage; which promised an out of town supermarket and (a vigorously argued over) new retail park development.

This controversial bland modernisation successfully offered expedient commercial distractions from the traditional caution of death on the horizon. When the bell tolled, or rather electronically chimed, which it did at Capel Heddwch following a council approved cost saving modification, the municipality were not alerted to another resident's passing, because the increased traffic noise from the town's by-pass conveniently drowned it out. Nevertheless, the chapel still stood ready to welcome all those who did not want to be there, as they gathered mournfully to say their final farewells.

The historic building's recently re-branded Welsh name, meaning *chapel of peace*, was now etched on the large wooden plaque that had been proudly fixed beside the arc shaped, metal embossed, heavy planked, Gothic double doors. In fairness, the cryptic name created a much grander and mystical status for the

203

building. Well at least in the minds of its majority English language speaking users, who constantly sought a convenient connection to imagined traditions of the past, if not necessary their past. Inevitably this desire for phoneyism made Capel Heddwch the preferred venue over and above other less conventional, duller named, non-denominational, civic ceremonial options, which were perhaps more appropriately generally available for non-religious funerals in and around the area. Not that the dead ever had much to say about whether their final choice of location lived up to expectations. Obviously there was no access to *Tripadvisor* in the afterlife!

In reality a moat-like, one car wide, tarmac track, flowed around the building, before meandering down the hillock in gentle twists and turns, running around the main burial plots, with their weathered marble or stone markers, until it reached a similarly rubble stoned and slate roofed, single storey gatehouse. There, a suitably miserable looking, grey haired caretaker, lent against the gatehouse wall. His younger, long haired, apprentice, dressed in dirty camouflaged combat trousers and black earth stained donkey jacket, sat on a nearby ledge of a small arc shaped, lead lined, frosted glass window. Both men were casually finishing off cigarettes, muddied shovels propped beside them. They respectfully nodded at each car that entered the cemetery and watched them carefully as they began the slow drive up the hill.

Mykee Kane did not like the way the older man had looked at him when his Mazda pulled in through the open cast iron gates. It was as if the old man was sizing him up and calculating how big a hole he would have to dig. The caretaker frowned. Then spat unpleasantly on the ground, before turning to speak to the younger man, who grinned nervously back in Kane's general direction, before also spitting on the ground. Bad habits or were they cursing him for the extra work such a lump of a man might one day cause them.

The Mazda was only the third car to arrive at the chapel. An old silver Ford had parked half on and half off the tarmac track at the back of the building, and there was an even more battered looking beige Renault parked directly in front of it, so that Kane was left with the awkward necessity of parking on the bend. Eventually, after a few painstaking manoeuvres, he was satisfied that there was just enough space should a hearse wish to pass by, and he turned off the engine.

Kane had not thought to check with Wendy if anyone needed a lift to the funeral. In fact, he had not spoken to her since his miserable visit, almost a fortnight ago. Just as he began to fret, foolishly imagining that in her reduced circumstances she might have to take the bus to her own husband's funeral, he spied a convoy of cars led by a hearse, come through the gates at the bottom of the cemetery. They each received in turn, their individual salute from the "guardians" at the gatehouse, before beginning their own slow ascent. On seeing the convoy, five people, three women and two men, all older and much greyer than Kane, got out of the Renault and headed towards the chapel's gothic doors. Kane did not know or at least recognise them. Nevertheless, after an uncomfortable glance or two back towards him, he felt obliged to get out of his car, and almost bolt to the chapel in order to reach it before the convoy pulled up. Embarrassingly for him, the five were now engaged in hushed conversation with an equally aged couple, who had been stood just inside and were now blocking the doorway. Kane did not recognise them either. He faked clearing his throat to alert them to his presence, before striding quickly passed them all.

Inside Capel Heddwch, spring sunshine shafted through the large east facing stained glass window, creating a hazy multi coloured spectrum of light that illuminated dancing specks of dust in the otherwise dimly lit interior. Plain wooden benches had been arranged in three sections on the dark grey flag stoned floor. Five tight rows filled the back of the chapel. They were directly facing a slightly raised chancel, which stood immediately below the large window. A small gap had been left on the chapel's north side for access to these rows. At the front, four much more generously spaced bench rows were arranged parallel to each other, two North and two South, all neatly lined up side on to the chancel. There was a wide gap between them, which

205

had been obviously left for those entering or exiting from the middle main doorway on the south side. Across from the door, a plain wooden table stood guard. It was almost empty, apart from three items. There was a small Wi-Fi router, blinking a green LED greeting to all. Then next to it there was a large round, wooden collection plate. On it's green felt centre someone had placed one shiny Euro coin. To the plate's left a small number of leaflets were fanned out. On entering Kane had instinctively reached for one until he spotted the title, "Friends of Capel Heddwch." This had caused him to leave them well alone.

Kane also noticed that a simple lectern, matching the plain wood of the benches, stood on the otherwise bare chancel. Pairs of narrow lead lined windows were set deep into the stone walls behind each seating area, but they obviously struggled to let in sufficient daylight for fluorescent tubes had been fixed in a dozen open white plastic rectangular boxes, and were hung at regular intervals, high up on the stone walls, to obviously boost the light on darker days. These were connected by a thin white snake of plastic coated wire, which no doubt also provided power to the small white square speaker boxes that were positioned on the circuit between each electric light fitting.

All signs of traditional religion had been removed to make the building not only truly non-denominational but also unlikely to cause offence to any secularist or rival religious group users. Kane wondered how many of the younger visitors today would have been totally unaware of the building's original Christian intentions. He still instinctively nodded towards where once an altar must have stood as he chose his place, hopefully well out of the way, on the far right of the first rear row facing the lectern. He had assumed that the side rows, ahead of him, although unmarked, must be reserved for family.

Briefly alone for a moment in the peaceful quiet, Kane said a silent prayer for his friend. Then he heard the sound of cars pulling up outside. There followed the brash noise of car doors opening and closing, followed by a low murmur of voices, which drifted in as the chapel doors opened slightly. The hushed discussion seemed to die away, occasionally interrupted by the odd short lived nervous laugh, before returning slightly louder each time as more people arrived. Relatives, family and friends, were all clumsily greeting each other in the saddest of circumstances. Kane felt well out of it all in the isolation of his quiet refuge.

A smartly dressed middle aged woman walked in. She was using both hands to carry a large brown leather bound silver zipped portfolio.

She smiled dutifully at Kane, before striding towards the lectern and once there, she placed the case on the sloping shelf. He watched her closely as she methodically unzipped and opened the case up, ultimately arranging it in front of her, like an open book. After carefully removing an iPad, she appeared to switch the computerised tablet on, before raising it above her head and slowly waving it in the air. He tried not to smile. Oblivious to her audience of one, she seemed to count, her lips moving silently. He joined in under his breath and had reached twenty when she lowered the tablet to look at it again. She frowned, then began stomping her way back up towards the doorway, holding the device out in front of her. Halfway up the corridor, between the side rows she stopped. She smiled and retraced her steps, carefully studying the screen as she went. He assumed that the Wi-Fi network had successfully connected to her device.

Back at the lectern she seemed to touch the screen with her index finger and a few seconds later, soothing classical harp music began to play through the speakers. Kane did not recognise the old Celtic tune but he considered it suitably peaceful. It certainly set the right tone as the first of the mourners, on hearing the music, began to enter the chapel.

The woman ignored the new arrivals and busied herself at the lectern, organising papers, presumably her notes. Seemingly satisfied, she removed her silver grey scarf and bending down, placed it on a hidden shelf, somewhere behind the lectern's wooden frontage. She undid the buttons but did not remove her pale green raincoat, merely opening it slightly to reveal a plain black knee length dress. She also wore calf length, black leather, flat heeled boots and thick black woollen tights. Although the spring day outside was bright, and quite warm for the time of year, her choice of outfit was wise, given the chill air inside the stone building.

Maybe a dozen or so mourners had taken their places, mostly in the rows behind him, when Kane first began to worry that he might be at the wrong funeral. He still did not know or recognise anyone. He twitched nervously and then almost sighed with relief, when at last he spotted his first contemporary.

Every friendship group has a member like "Ginge" amongst them, especially in Wales. Kane and Frank John's childhood gang were no different. Now in his forties, Ginge had long ago lost his trade mark mop of red ginger hair. What little was left he kept close shaved to the side of his head, in the futile hope of avoiding emphasising the bald, shiny dome, on top of his round soccer ball shaped head. He looked remarkable cheerful for someone at a funeral and Kane was almost sure that his old friend had been whistling as he came through the doors.

Ginge glanced around casually. Kane could clearly see him thinking whether he should sit on the left or right of the front side-on benches. Then Ginge turned and looked straight at Kane. For a moment his face froze and then contorted into a rather puzzled expression. Still sat on his own, for not surprisingly very few people like to join a stranger sat in a row when there are alternatives available, Kane could almost hear the cogs whirling inside Ginge's brain until finally it identified this particular stranger as friend not foe. Ginge broke into a broad smile and instantly moved to join Kane. They shook hands.

'How the hell are you? You fat bastard!' Ginge enquired affectionately but far too loudly. Kane felt all eyes on them. Even the woman at the lectern looked up from her preparations.

'Good! All things considered!' Kane lied in a more respectful whisper. Just then a short dumpy woman, with a heavily highlighted shiny bob of a hair style and far too much make up plastered over her face, rushed in. She was dressed in a smart black overcoat, black skirt, nylon tights and black high heeled shoes, which clicked loudly with each step over the flagstone floor.

'Sharon!' Ginge called out and the woman clicked quickly over to take her place next to him, whilst doing her best to outwardly ignore him.

'This is my Mrs! Sharon!' Ginge told Kane, and the rest of the congregation.

The woman smiled politely as Kane leant across Ginge to awkwardly shake her hand. He was aware from the puzzled eyes above her instant smile that she probably had no idea who he was, so Kane said as quietly as possible: 'Hello Mrs Thompson, I'm My-key Kane.' Sharon Thompson continued to smile back, obviously none-the-wiser, whilst Ginge equally obviously frustrated at her lack of recognition insisted in an even louder voice than before: 'C'mon luv! You must've heard me talk of My-Key! He's a bloody legend! When we were ... oh I'll tell you later!' Finally Ginge had realised that the music in the chapel had stopped.

A family of seven had walked in, just as the music died and Ginge's voice echoed around the hushed chapel. The woman who obviously led the family was looking at Ginge with undisguised contempt. Kane instantly recognised her. She was Janice, Frank John's elder sister. The family likeness was remarkable, regardless of the fact that she, like Kane, now looked so much older, older than Kane could ever have imagined her. Yet Kane was more shocked by the appearance of the man who stood beside her. An old man, looking uncomfortable in a pin stripped suit, his black tie worn too tight. His frizzy hair was tied back into an untidy long pony tail, like an aged 1970's rocker collecting an OBE. There was a white streak down the middle of the grey crown, which reminded Kane of a cartoon artist's attempt to sketch an elderly badger. Kane suddenly remembered then and there that Rawlins, (nobody had ever called Janice's husband by his first name), for that was who the man must be, was a good ten years older than Janice, and she had been at least ten years older than her brother Frank. It had been quite a scandal when they first got together. One of the two adults in the party must have been the "love child" who ensured this relationship became fixed. Unfortunately, this recollection caused Kane to smile as he could hear Frank's childhood voice, full of awe, as he boasted about this Hell's Angel guy, who was knocking off his stuck up sister. Janice certainly noticed the smile on Kane's face and glowered back at him, proving instantly to Kane that Janice was still as stuck up as she had been in her youth. Kane did try his best to make his smile seem sympathetic but it was an unsuccessful attempt at showing real empathy. Janice blanked him and turned sharply away. Ushering her doddery husband and surprisingly young children or were they grandchildren, into the front row of the benches on the right hand side of the chapel. They all sat down directly ahead of the lectern, a variety of pompous frowns and or bewilderment on their faces.

A man, obviously the undertaker, for he was dressed in the most formal suit Kane had seen in a long long while, had followed Janice's family in, and now he nodded, solemnly to the woman at the lectern. She had stopped the harp music by a quick flick of a finger on the iPad screen and now that Ginge was also silent, she spoke out. Her voice was surprisingly loud.

'All please stand!'

The gathering stood up. A few coughed as suddenly they found their throats dry and then there was a stunning silence.

'As the deceased is brought in we shall listen and reflect on a recording of the 23rd Psalm, as requested by the widow, Mrs John. The Lord Is My Shepherd.' The woman touched the iPad screen and the sound of a Welsh Male Voice Choir erupted from the speakers. The undertaker turned and nodded back to the open doorway and two tall and broad, snowy white haired, well groomed men, dressed in the same formal suits as their boss,

210

slowly steered a four wheeled stainless steel trolley into view. A simple, satin varnished, teak coffin rested on the trolley.

Kane was momentarily impressed at the art of the undertaker and how well he managed to walk backwards, not putting a foot wrong, and more importantly not looking ridiculous, whilst calmly directing the men, in perfect practical formality, to the front of the chapel.

Behind the coffin came Wendy John, dressed all in black. She wore an expensive looking satin or silk blouse, a knee length skirt, sheer nylon tights, and flat court shoes. Her hair had been cut even shorter than she had worn it when Kane had last seen her, and it was jet black, as if it had been freshly dyed. She also wore an open, long black, woollen cardigan, which hung down just below her knees. This, together with the flatness of her shoes, served to emphasise how short and fragile she looked. Wendy John was supported by a much taller teenage girl, who must be her daughter Jan or so Kane naturally assumed. He had not seen Jan since she was seven or eight years old and he was amazed at how grown up she now looked. Jan was dressed identically to her mother but there the similarities ended. She was tall for a girl, almost six-foot, and there was something about the way she wore her cardigan, fully buttoned up and dragged down at the front, which somehow troubled Kane. Her hair was longer than her mother's, falling down past her shoulders to the small of her back, straight and russet brown, a combination, he concluded, of her mother's natural red and her fathers brown hair. Both faces were pale and blank, cheeks sucked in tight to fiercely hold in their emotions. They had linked arms in mutual support of each other. Hovering just to their right, looking slightly embarrassed at being part of the procession, was Frank's son Kevin. His unruly jet black dyed hair as untidy as ever. He wore black shoes, trousers and shirt. No tie or jacket. Kane frowned initially at the informality and then slightly envied Kevin

211

as he remembered that his own top button was undone, hopefully disguised by the large knot of his black tie, which nevertheless, felt as if it was slowly choking him. Kane vowed to buy a new formal shirt, with a much larger collar size, as soon as he could.

Whilst Kane worried about clothing, the family had taken their places along the front row on the left hand, north side, of the chapel, so that they could turn slightly to their left and diagonally face the lectern. A fourth undertaker, a woman, in similar dark formal attire, excepting that she wore a skirt instead of trousers, had followed the cortège, slightly behind the family, carrying two small wreaths. She now stepped forward and placed the red, white, and green flowers on top of the coffin. Kane could make out the word "DAD" at the heart of each wreath. It was then and only then, that it truly occurred to him that the wooden box, resting on the now stationary trolley, right in front of the lectern, contained the mortal remains of his once best friend. Kane sighed, instantly regretting that he had not made the time to visit the casket at the funeral home and say a proper personal goodbye to Frank John. His stomach turned and his mind drifted away as the sad music continued to fill the air.

Chapter 23: The Valley of Death

A thin line of light split the darkness to the east. Slowly it grew fatter and fatter, gradually thickening into a wide and irregular golden band, whose brightness highlighted huge jagged edged lumps of impenetrable black, occasionally stabbing up and piercing its bottom rim. The space above began to change from pitch black to navy to blue and the sharp shaped giants were soon revealed to be no more than rocky outcrops. Too bright for the naked eye, the sunlight continued to prise the land and sky apart, causing long sinister shadows to be cast out towards the west just as the view shimmered into focus revealing a stone and sand covered desert.

Four smaller shadows now danced out across the rough floor. They seemed to move in an unsteady zigzag, stretching then narrowing before transforming into thick set lower case t shapes. The hunched soldiers, who made the shadows, had moved silently out of the dry dusty river bed at dawn's first light and were now quickly crossing the desolate open ground towards a dark mass huddled in the shadows of a north western hillside. Within minutes the early morning sun revealed a ruined village and began to bake the shattered remains of the flat roofed, clay brick dwellings. The brighter the light the more gaps appeared in the crumbling mud wall, which had once surrounded the ancient settlement. Inside the fractured perimeter only a few buildings still stood without a hole or two in their bomb shattered roofs. Broken timbers fell out or hung across most of the holes and dust seemed to cover everything.

All was quiet in the valley, apart from the soft crunching of thick leather soles on dry earth. No dogs barked. No babies cried. No bodies were strewn across the street. In the cold light of day the houses looked abandoned or maybe each dark recess hid an enemy, a silent sniper, waiting patiently for the soldiers to

213

come into range. With the sun becoming warmer on their backs, the soldiers darted through one of the largest gaps in the village wall. They then spread out and began searching each building, pointing their rifles into each hole in the wall and letting the bright flashlights, fixed firmly to their gun barrels, shine into the dark interiors. It was a simple task, for the houses tended to be open plan and without furniture. Oddly, no rugs, pillows or mattresses, common to such dwellings, had been left behind when the former occupants had fled.

Each new step brought danger and each man's heart beat faster as they anticipated an imminent attack and the resulting fire fight, or worse the explosion, the screaming of another and the smell of burning flesh. They even anticipated their own shock, surprise, and pain. Yet all bravely pushed on, disregarding the mounting dread of something, which they had already witnessed too many times before, happening again in this deadly country, where so many equally brave but less fortunate comrades had triggered the cowardly improvised explosive devices and paid the price of heroism.

By the time the soldiers were halfway through the village, moving up the hard mud of what passed as the main street, morning had truly broken, and the sun, which had been providing welcome warmth on their backs, after a bitterly cold night, was now becoming oppressively hot. The lead man stopped suddenly, turned and whispered back, slowly shaking his head.

'I don't like this Sarg!' He hissed and then pointed with his gun to his left, towards a wooden door, that had been left slightly ajar, at the next house up, on what passed for a street in the rural Middle East. The window, no more than a hole in the wall, next to the doorway, was also uncovered, exposing a gaping black chasm, so unlike all the other houses, which the soldiers had cautiously visited already that morning. Each house had had remnants of wooden shutters or torn blanket blinds, still across them. This did not! The next house, diagonally opposite, on the right side of the street, was similarly open.

Sergeant Frank John nodded and held his hand up as a warning to the other men who were still moving in a zigzag formation to his left. Mykee Kane squatted down against the wall just before the first open door, a knowing smirk spread across his face as he raised his rifle to cover the doorway, the one that was wide open, diagonally opposite him. Almost immediately he heard the explosion and blinked as a second flash and subsequent explosion came from within the darkness across the street, as an unseen automatic rifle discharged. Kane returned fire instantly and at the same time felt warm dry mud dust shower him, after his hidden adversary's bullets hit the wall, just above his head. A single shot was fired again from the open window and as Kane adjusted his position, to return fire, he felt the heat as hot lead flew just past his cheek and sliced into the wall beside him.

Sergeant John was already moving right, running quickly across the street directly at the house. He had thrown the first of his grenades into the doorway, just as a burst of fire spat out of both the opposite door and window, on the other side of the street. Somehow the bullets did not hit him. John managed to hurl a second grenade through the right window as he dived onto the floor and twisted to get into position to shoot left. The lead soldier was now returning firing in quick bursts towards the house on the left but he had a circle of red rapidly expanding on his sand coloured camouflaged jacket.

The fourth soldier had bolted to the right and a gas pumped thud sounded, when he fired a grenade from his AG36 rifle, straight into the doorway. It was on target. Nothing seemed to happen and time stood still. Then the first explosion sent dark grey smoke out of the holes in the house to the right. Only a few seconds later, after a gap of time that seemed to be like a lifetime, there was another explosion on the right, and briefly an agonised screaming accompanied the dust out onto the street. The third explosion then occurred on the left drowning out the screaming. Another thud sounded as the fourth soldier, having reloaded his grenade launcher sent another 40 mm shell towards the house on the left. This time it flew directly through the open window cavity. Another few seconds or was it hours later, a man, dressed from head to toe in black native loose fitting trousers and shirt, with a turban wrapped around his face, ran screaming from the house, blindly firing his rifle into the street. Kane fired twice from his squat position to the insurgent's right. The first bullet hit the side of the head and the second tore into the man's back as the first had spun him violently around, and down he went, into the ground, just as the grenade exploded with a flash, deep in the house behind. Dirt, heat and smoke billowed out. All was suddenly calm. There was no more screaming to the right or the left.

Then a man's voice could be heard bellowing out: 'Though we walk through the valley of death fear no evil, for I am the biggest bastard you will ever meet!' When he finished shouting Frank John roared with laughter, as did the fourth soldier.

Kane did not laugh. He was not amused. Ever since Frank had seen that bloody awful Vietnam War movie he had repeated that line again and again. Whether he was intimidating someone in a bar or following a fire fight like this one. Each time he got the words wrong, which usually made Kane laugh, but it did not that day. From his squat position, leaning back against the mud wall, Kane could see the lead soldier, a man called Joe Davies, was slumped against the wall. Blood was soaking into the sand beside him and Kane knew from the pale face, that Joe was dead.

Inside Capel Heddwch the music had stopped. Those present were all invited to sit down. The lady at the lectern then announced in her loud, firm, but polite voice:

'My name is Trudy Morgan.'

Kane abandoned his thoughts of the past and began to listen to her. She had a voice with only the slightest hint of a local accent. Yet her local routes came through strongly when she said names. Otherwise, it became obvious that she was working really hard to refine her general speech, and whilst not exactly achieving pure "Received Pronunciation," the way she addressed the room was pretend posh enough to irritate Kane. He hated people trying to be something they obviously were not! It was not that he objected to ambition or self-improvement but he resented delusion; particularly if it resulted from a desire to create the pretence of superiority. Kane simply believed that if she was an Aberfoist girl, then she should sound like one! Especially on home ground! That said, he did not expect her to swear, like most locals did, and he certainly hoped that she could avoid punctuating her words with the usual local vernacular of "er" or "um"! He need not have worried. Trudy Morgan had been coached well. Her voice calm clear, still emoted the right level of sympathy and support, whilst pretty much staying on the impartial and rational humanist script.

'I would like to welcome you all, on behalf of the family, to this celebration of the life of Frank John. The unexpected death of someone we know and have loved is truly shocking and painful to us all. So it is only natural for us to want to come together to express our sadness at their passing and our loss. Nevertheless, it is perhaps more fitting to focus on the way they lived their life and today we shall show an affectionate appreciation for the time we shared with Frank, by paying tribute, through words and music, to the positive contribution that Frank made to his family, his friends, his community, and his country, during his brief time with us.'

Fine words or so Kane thought. Such fine words were not said over Joe Davies' body. Frank John had grunted a brief

217

apology to the corpse, which ended with a strangely unsatisfactory "but we got the bastards!" No doubt an officer had made a fine speech in front of family and friends at the memorial service back in Blighty but Kane had not been there. Both he and Frank could not be spared. Instead they had been sent out on another equally important (or was that, ultimately pointless) mission.

Immediately after Ms. Morgan had stressed "affectionate appreciation", Kane glanced from Wendy to Janice. Both women looked angry, and he did not doubt that they were playing the blame game against each other over Frank's apparent suicide. Suicide was a word that Kane was sure would be avoided in all of today's eulogies. It had already been smoothed over once by the use of the term "passing". He wondered whether this was right. The general acceptance of Frank's suicide by the authorities had been endorsed by the mere formality of a minimal coroner's report and the convenient lack of open questioning or suggested alternatives had irritated him a lot more than compromised wording. Kane felt he was missing something and his own frustration was making him angry. It was probably this anger and exasperation that had stopped him returning to Aberfoist before the funeral. "What could he do?" He had asked himself, except make matters worse for all involved. Inside his head he heard Frank's voice grunting over Joe Davies' corpse. "We got the bastards!" Kane could only wonder what "bastards" needed to be "got" for Frank's death!?!

Jan John, the daughter no doubt respectfully named after her aunt, Frank's beloved, but stuck up, elder sister, was now moving towards the lectern. She stood nervously in front of a microphone, which had suddenly been propped up from behind the lectern by Ms Morgan. The lead celebrant stood supportively by Jan's side, ready to step in if the youngster became over emotional and stumbled over her words.

Kane wondered if he had missed something. Maybe words had been said whilst he was off in deep thought about the past. He assumed Jan was about to lead the tributes. Perhaps he should be saying something himself. After all, he had been briefly his friend's Commanding Officer. Frank had not liked that, nor had Kane. Kane reminded himself that he had actually thought about saying something. He had actually rung Wendy to suggest he did say something, but she had not taken the call. Instead he had spoken to Kevin, who had insisted it remain a "family-only-thing!" Kane had not been happy with that decision but he had had to accept it. Looking around the chapel now and noting the distinct lack of military comrades, Kane wondered if any others had been put off by young Kevin's insistence that this would be a "family-only" affair!

Nevertheless, the fact that no official representative from the Forces was there, apart from Kane, was odd, especially given Frank's specialist service. Surely someone else from the regiment should be there. Yet no one had contacted Kane. Normally someone got in touch. Kane would have been surprised by that, but he realised that there really was not anyone else left. Well maybe one or two. Even their old regiment had been retired, just like him and Frank, and the type of mission they had undertaken contracted out over the past decade, so there probably was not anyone else back at base, wherever base was these days, to fulfil that role anymore. Even so, Kane looked around him, carefully studying the mourners, just to check one more time.

No one looked like they were representing the Services. No one, apart from Ginge, was in a blazer. No one was there in a Services overcoat. Kane realised once again, that there was by now probably no one left anyway, apart from him, from their old unit. So why should anyone else send someone. He looked around again, whilst Jan continued to read slowly, from the sheet of paper she held up shakily, in front of her face.

'My father liked the hymn we just heard. He was not obviously religious but he did tell me that he had a faith in a God. He told me all soldiers at war believe. He said no one in a fox hole was an atheist. He also used to say that he did not fear the valley death because he was the meanest, er, *worst* person out there. He said it often but it was a joke, a bad joke. My father was not mean or cruel.' She paused, before adding amongst increased sniffles, 'Really!'

Ginge leaned over to Kane at that point and whispered into his ear: 'Thank God she didn't "really" know her father that well then!'

'My father just pretended to be bad.' Jan bravely continued. She allowed herself a final sniff and a tear ran down her cheek as she took a deep breath before starting again. 'He wanted the best for us and tried to be tough for us. I wish he hadn't tried so hard. Then maybe he would be still with us today.'

That was it; she started to really cry then. Trudy Morgan quickly put a comforting arm around Jan and then could not resist giving the girl a hug.

'Well done!' Ms. Morgan said. 'From what I know of your father, I think he would have been very proud of you, being brave enough to come up here, and say that about him!'

Kane cringed at the naff sentimentality of it all and desperately avoided eye contact with Ginge, who had actually sighed, equally exasperated at the last statement. They could both hear Frank John moaning: "Get a bloody grip mun!"

Jan's new "best friend forever" escorted her back to the bench and then strode confidently back to the podium. In her mind, Trudy Morgan felt that things were going well. Genuine emotion! The family would, she thought, today achieve a real sense of closure! Whatever that meant! She took a deep breath and then began her well rehearsed address.

'I am sure we are all moved by that lovely statement from

Jan, Frank's daughter. Although I did not know Frank personally, I have met with his family, and some of his friends, to learn about Frank. And what I have found out has deeply impressed me. He seems to have been a man who tried, for most of his life, to put others first. His commitment to serving his country, often at great personal cost, especially in time, time he could have spent with his wife and family, is evidence of his heroic character. Not only did he serve in the Armed Forces from a young age but he actually fought bravely for his country in a number of conflicts. He is, I suppose, what we used to call a hero!'

Kane bit his tongue to stop him standing up and correcting the "new age" phraseology that was slowly creeping into the modernist tribute. His face was flushed and he wanted to roar that Frank was a hero! A man, who yes, actually killed for his country, and believe it or not, who actually made the world briefly a safer, if not better place.

Yet, Kane knew this caring woman was doing her best to describe someone and something she probably disapproved of, for she was most likely only aware of such horrors through television news and biased newspaper or magazine articles. In her experience, and belief system, she would certainly have felt that there was a better way. A good logical chat, an emotional appeal, these would surely have sorted out the mistaken individuals, who, however misguided, had just as much right to believe in what they did as we did. Kane stopped himself. She had not said any such thing. He was letting his own prejudices run away with his imagination, but it was just the way she looked, so certain and confident in sharing her "truth!"

'When he returned home Frank continued to serve others.' Kane heard the compassionate celebrant say. 'He ran the wonderful Copper Kettle Tearooms in Aberfoist, where he catered willingly to so many older members of our community.'

Kane listened as she went on skimming through Frank's

economic battles and friendly tea making talents, as if they were his real achievements. Maybe she was right. Perhaps they were. She spent very little time on his army career. For some reason his medals were not on display. Kane wondered if Frank had sold them, when times became hard.

Eventually Ms. Morgan's tribute came to an end and there was an awkward moment, when a few of the mourners started to clap. She quickly told the gathering that it was now time for them to spend a few moments in private and "silent" reflection about the Frank John they knew, whilst listening to another one of Frank's favourite pieces of music. Kane froze for a moment, expecting the speakers to blast out what he knew to be Frank's actual favourite song, "Rock The Kasbah" by the punk rock group The Clash. He held his breath in anticipation and then seconds later, as the orchestral theme to the movie "Gladiator" sighed out of the speakers, Kane could not help but retune it into that other, less apt, soundtrack, which began playing as background music to his latest internal vision. He could see clearly his friend dancing to the song, well if truth be told, drunkenly stomping up and down, on a bar room table, during a weekend's leave in Aiya Napa, Cyprus, whilst yelling Frank's own, out of tune version, to his personal favourite, as it played on the jukebox.

"Shaaa-reef don't like it! Fuck the Kaszzz-bah! Fuck the Kaszzz-bah!"

Face red, beer and sweat stained royal blue T-Shirt, white sports shorts, and dirty red suede Adidas trainers, no socks, brown hair shaved close to his head, Frank John's bulk was a daunting sight to the two Greek bouncers, who were trying so very unenthusiastically to get him to come down. Kane sat laughing at their dilemma, with the rest of their strike team, all of them too drunk to stand. All were relieved to be kind of home, safe after another Middle Eastern mission. Kane then remembered that he had also got drunk that night because he had to tell Frank his news. Kane had been offered a promotion. One that he was going to take, despite the stick he knew that he would get from his old school friend; who was a man who had no interest in rising through the ranks.

What a surprise it had been when Frank had eventually told Kane, in return, as they had relieved themselves into the harbour, that he, Sergeant Frank John, the life long serviceman, was going to resign and leave the army to set up of all things, a Tea Room, back in Aberfoist! Kane had laughed at first. Briefly, Kane had thought that it was a ridiculous idea back then, but the look in Frank's eyes told him that his friend was serious. Unfortunately, he had persuaded him to delay his plans for another year or so. Another few years of adventures, enjoyed until the inevitable injury had forced Frank to be invalided out. At least his compensation had helped bolster his savings and this had actually helped him achieve his simple dream.

Life was full of surprises, or so Kane thought, now listening to the real music still playing in the chapel. Recognising the tune, he thought it apt. There was more than a touch of Russell Crowe's Gladiator in Frank John. The music even had echoes of the Middle East in it. Kane watched as the undertakers began a slow march, down the main aisle, towards the coffin. A beam of sunlight must have hit the stained glass window on the wall behind the lectern and a bright yellow haze, from one of the pains, seemed to fill the previously dull space. It made Kane's eyes water. This is what funerals did he told himself. They made you remember. They made you cry. The other thing Kane knew in that instance was that his friend, Frank John, would never have willingly given up on his life. He was a true Gladiator. He would have fought on until the end.

Although the music played on in Capel Heddwch, Kane had stopped listening. The recorded choir had sung the words "though I walk in death's dark vale". Yes Frank had used to spout out his own version of that psalm. Something he had picked up from a movie. Frank was like that. He rarely watched films or listened to music but he had a knack for picking up other people's catch phrases and then getting them wrong. Frank's errors usually made Kane laugh and because he laughed Frank would repeat it again and again. Well maybe Jan had been right after all. Her father was not really the evil one. That dubious honour belonged to someone else. Someone who now needed to get out of Capel Heddwch and get on and find out exactly what happened in "The Kettle", the night when Frank had died.

Chapter 24: Internment

The mourners had gathered around a freshly dug grave, approximately two hundred or so metres away from Capel Heddwch. They all watched in respectful silence whilst the professionals carefully lowered the coffin down between the smooth soil sides of the bleak rectangular hole. Then, as the undertakers withdrew, Trudy Morgan stepped forward. Her coat was neatly buttoned up. She always took great care to stay warm, fearful that anyone watching might mistake a chill shiver for a nervous tremble. Ms. Morgan prided herself on never ever showing her own nerves or real emotions. Instead, she now rewarded those around her with her most sincere smile, before finally beginning the next part of the service.

'Our final words today were written by Margaret Mead.' Trudy Morgan spoke, raising her voice so that all could hear above the constant wind roar of distant traffic, which was annoyingly floating across from the Aberfoist bypass, as normal life ignorantly sped on. Watching her work, Kane raised his eyebrows momentarily surprised that she could actually read the backlit tablet device, which she was constantly glancing down at, in such bright daylight. Maybe she could not and it was merely a prop. He had the sense that she had said all this many times before.

'These words are meant to bring comfort as we say our final farewell.' Trudy Morgan continued. Then raising her voice even higher to ensure she won her battle with the distracting traffic noise, she added a dramatic tone to the simple but highly emotional words, as she read out the chosen poem in her finest "RP".

'Remember Me to the living, I am gone.'

Kane was remembering Frank and he allowed his gaze to lift up to the surrounding mountains. Whilst the poetry truly moved all who heard it, he fought against the calculated sentimental triggers by allowing his eyes to slowly trace a wriggly weaving line along the high ridges. Right on cue, the rolling grey centred clouds began darkening the hill tops, making them look as black as their name, and quickly changing the blossoming shades of spring green into a bleak dreary uniform darkness.

The Black Mountains! An area of outstanding natural beauty, but perhaps an area best viewed by fragile town and city dwellers from behind the warmth of a car window. Both he and Frank knew these infamous wild and lonely sandstone uplands to the north west of Aberfoist well. Ranging from the south east borders with England, right up into the heartland of Mid Wales, the raised knuckles, formed so long ago by the great prehistoric ice cap, still peeked out above the managed remains of the original dark medieval forest. They were an area that had given foolish invaders nightmares. A bleak and usually treeless plateau of high scrub-grass-lands, which would regularly change colour under the shadows of low lying clouds, but mainly preferred lurking dark and menacing, brooding up on the skyline. They were never intended for the faint hearted but they remained an adventurer's playground.

'To the sorrowful, I will never return.
To the angry, I was cheated.'

Kane kept his face rigid, trying not to show the anger he felt raging within him. He really was "the angry" that Tracey Morgan referred to in her oft quoted verse. Angry! Because he felt his friend was "the cheated!" Kane could not say how or why but he just sensed it. His instincts were telling him that Frank John had been "cheated!" Cheated of sharing this fine spring day! Cheated of the privilege to stand in this beautiful landscape! Cheated of the time needed to fix his broken family! Cheated of a proper investigation into his death! Cheated of the support and respect that he was due! Cheated of a proper acknowledgement of his true value!

226

Trudy Morgan was coming to the end of her performance. She was certainly pleased to note a few tears in the eyes of those closest to the grave. She was never ever embarrassed by an outpouring of grief. It made her feel that she had done her job properly. She believed that tears spilt now would surely unburden the mourner. However, today she hoped for a little restraint and a bit more of the British stiff upper lip. After all she had another funeral to celebrate in just under an hour's time. She took a deep breath and carried on.

'The times we fought, the times we laughed.
For if you always think of me, I will never be gone.'

For a moment Kane was almost overwhelmed. A few women around him were actually crying now. Snivelling into hastily produced white cotton handkerchiefs or dabbing their eyes with cheap paper tissues. However, his own eyes remained dry. Some how he managed to control the raw emotions that he felt. He wished Jill was here, for he knew, that without her calming influence, someone, somewhere, sometime soon, would suffer from all the bitterness bubbling away like bad gas inside his gut.

Lowering his gaze away from the highlands, Kane now watched Frank's family lining up. They were getting ready to take part in the rather odd but traditional ceremony of individually throwing soil into the open grave. Kane always found this custom odd but particularly so today, when unlike many of the funerals that he had previously attended, there was no priest, no vicar, no sad military chaplain, uttering the immortal words: "dust to dust" and such like. Kane did wonder what on earth the point of it all was! Why borrow one popular tradition without the other, abandoning its religious significance for a purely physical act. To him it was truly something and nothing! Yet it was popular and he calmed himself, simply concluding that that was what most organised religions did anyway. They all borrowed popular sentimental traditions, and attempted to make them their own. Well, if it made people feel better, why the hell not!

When the family had finished with this simple ceremony, the gathering just stood still, silently waiting around the grave, actively avoiding all eye contact with each other. Some were probably wondering whether they should grab their own handful of soil. There was plenty left on the conveniently placed pile of earth. Should they just join in or did they need permission to form a new line. Others wavered, eagerly waiting for some formal permission to begin edging away from this most final acknowledgement of death. Just as the silence and inaction was becoming truly awkward, Trudy Morgan put on another of her trademark brave smiles and spoke the final, rather informal, but very human words, in a slightly less dramatic accent, which at least concluded the proceedings.

'Well I'm afraid that's it! I would just like to take this opportunity to thank everyone, once again on behalf of the family, for their attendance, and to remind you, that you are all very welcome to share a few drinks and snacks with the family at The Aberfoist Hotel, in town!'

Relieved people nodded silently to nobody in particular and then began to drift quietly away. Kane watched Wendy approach Trudy, who had stood her ground after the dismissal and was boldly nodding approvingly back at anyone who dared to make eye contact with her, as if to say: "Yes! You can go now!" Wendy, no doubt, began to thank the celebrant, who gave her a sisterly hug in response to the sudden but inevitable teary breakdown. Jan stood awkwardly beside her mother, whilst Kevin shuffled his feet.

Feeling awkward, by this additional open show of emotion from someone he should know better, Kane decided to beat his own hasty retreat back to his car. He had nothing to say to anyone anyway. No hugs or perhaps more appropriately, no words of comfort were poised on his tongue. No wisdom to share with the fatherless children. No promises of retribution for the widow, just an impotent awkwardness. So stepping back towards the gravel path, he carefully avoided treading on another freshly laid grave. Someone else's story had ended with this plot, on which only a simple wooden cross was planted. It was a cross that resembled something that Kane might have made as a child, with two used ice lollipop sticks stuck together. Seeing it near his polished black shoes, Kane could not help but wonder if a grand headstone had been commissioned or whether this was all that could be afforded. Dying was an expensive business these days or so the constant stream of day-time TV adverts had told him each time he had escaped the pile of marking in his home study and turned the television on during the school holidays. He doubted that Wendy would be able to afford an impressive stone for Frank. Maybe that was something he could do for his once best friend!

Behind Kane, someone had started whistling. It was an almost jolly yet ultimately tuneless sound, carelessly punctuated by the occasional muttered curse. The briefest glance back, in the direction of the attempted melody maker, confirmed that the whistler was Ginge. He was trying to make his way back to the main path but stumbling over the uneven ground, seemingly unaware that each grassy swell was a recently filled-in-grave. Sharon, Ginge's wife, was dutifully following her man across the low level obstacle course, but blushing profusely as she too, constantly stumbled, and every firm step seemed to result in her high heels sinking into the freshly laid turf.

'Steady on old girl!' Ginge broadcast insensitively, when she almost fell, after losing her balance after prising one foot free. 'We don't want to lose you too eh!'

Kane quickly turned away and left them to it and was soon standing back on the firm tarmac path. A few moments later he was hovering alone by the chapel's open doorway, and whilst waiting for Wendy to return, finally having thought of something appropriate to say to her, he decided to take one more look up towards the dark and distant mountains. Romantically, he imagined Frank John's spirit soaring over the ranges. If such a thing was possible that was where he felt Frank would choose to go. Up to a place where they had had so many adventures. That might be heaven! Or so Kane silently told himself. "Yeah, as long as you couldn't feel the cold eh!" A deep voice teased him. It only spoke to him, far inside his fanciful imagination and actually sounded an awful lot like Frank John's distinctive tone! Kane suddenly remembered their last dark night, spent together, up on those bitterly cold black mountains and he shivered slightly, even though the spring sunshine, now shining down on his face, was perhaps at its warmest.

***

Bright amber sparks spat out from the small camp fire, whilst twigs crackled foolishly on the hearth. Glowing wisps danced free, rising up into the thick dark night air, like tiny orange imps intent on causing mischief after being magically released from deep within enchanted wood. Separated from his men, Kane had sought refuge in a rare hollow worn into the bleak hillside by old winds. He had been just as surprised to find dry fuel this high up on the snow covered slopes of the Black Mountains. Yet somehow he had salvaged two fallen branches from a nearby dead or dying tree and perhaps rashly made the fire. Maybe the wizened old trunk had once thrived here after its seeds had fallen from the wind and grown in the extra shelter provided by a rough stone walled enclosure, built long ago into the steep south facing hillside by some forgotten shepherd or hill farmer, who had sought to protect their flock from such a cruel night as tonight. Now neglected and abandoned to nature, the wall had mostly tumbled down under years of intense physical pressure from the harsh weather typical to such a high hillside. Without its protector, the tree had become no more than a bitter and twisted remnant of its former modest glory. Yet it made a perfect image for any passing rambler to dream they had found evidence of an old Celtic legend. Proof that some cursed Welsh prince had paid for an evil deed or perhaps a simple lovelorn countryman had been tricked out of humanity by some wicked mountain witch. Whatever! The princely tree or wretched victim had royally redeemed itself that night, proving it's usefulness by making the ultimate sacrifice, to thaw out the not so young soldier, who now sat carelessly close to the warm glow and making up stories to pass the time on a bitterly cold night.

Kane was certainly looking for any escape from reality. He had been getting increasingly feed up with spending his time in constant war gaming, high in those winter mountains. Especially so when he knew that just a few miles down the hillside, in so called civilisation, people were laughing and drinking, apparently wasting their night time away in trivial social activities, squeezed into the pubs or restaurants of the local villages and towns or even simply sat in front of a TV screen, watching nonsensical variety, in a cosy centrally heated home. Kane remembered years ago, laughing at his old school friend, Frank John, sat at the bus stop on the edge of town, dressed in his Territorial Army Cadet uniform, waiting for a Friday evening army truck pick up and excitedly cradling his large backpack, ready to spend a weekend on exercise up on the stark hills.

'You must be mad!' Kane had said. 'It's bloody freezing and it'll be even colder up in the Beacons! I'm off on the pull!' Yes, those were the days when he had boasted. 'It's Nurses Pay Day! They'll all be out on the town tonight.' Before winking cheerfully and proclaiming. 'Yep! A belly full of beer and a smooch or two at the rugby club disco and who knows eh!'

231

Frank John had laughed back at him. 'I knows!' He had said cynically. 'You'll waste all your money, look foolish, and then get knocked back! All you'll end up with is a hangover and gut ache after a dodgy takeaway! I've seen it all before mate!'

Frank was not wrong about the outcome of Kane's night out. Frank had even gone on to brag about how much money he was earning, just by having a laugh with his fellow TA cadets; and he had told Kane about all the smart girls in the unit. Somehow, over time, he had persuaded his friend to give it a go! One thing led to another, and so now here Kane was, too many years later, huddled over a small fire on a mountainside in mid-winter. No girls! No fun! Just mind numbing duty!

Outside the scant shelter of the deep rut that nature had furrowed into the steep hillside, snow flakes whirled around on the sudden gusts of wind. Mother Nature's icy breath, mercilessly added to the expected chill and shifted the white dusting up into the air before releasing it down into deep and dangerous drifts. The pretty dance was only occasionally illuminated, each time the moonlight burst through the dark, fast moving clouds. Kane had miraculously still managed to hear the noise. The sound he had been waiting for, beneath the wild air's groan. It told him in a hissed whisper that his cold vigil was nearly at an end.

Somewhere out in the darkness, frosty snow hidden beneath the fresh fall, gave another faint crack under the weight of regulation army boots. Kane did nothing, other than to continue to rub his hands over the fire. Any observer would have seen by the firelight, a shadow of a man, lost and beaten by the weather, only concerned in seeking comfort to help him survive the conditions for a few precious moments more.

'Freeze!' A young American voice commanded him. It was accompanied by the instantly recognisable cocking of a gun. Then, as Kane did nothing but sit still, a dozen camouflage uniformed figures emerged from the black night. Dark shadows threatening him from just beyond the edge of the fire light.

'You gotta be kidding!' Kane grimaced, attempting what he hoped might sound like an over the top mock American accent. 'Of course, I'm bloody freezing!' He leant forward, even closer to the fire, as one of the shadowy figures, on his left, stifled a snigger.

'Don't move!' The urgent almost panicky bleat came from the lead shadow, which was soon revealed by the firelight to be a young officer pointing an ugly looking black automatic pistol directly at Kane's chest.

Ignoring the advice, Kane sat back, straightening up and smiled, but only after slipping a small silver cylinder, which had been concealed up his left sleeve, onto the fire. Kane felt the thud on the centre of his chest about the same time as he realised that he had heard a gun shot ring out. Paint burst out of the plastic pellet that had struck him, creating a yellow, thankfully not red, stain across his chest. Kane lent further back and began sarcastically tutting out loud before closing his eyes.

'Uh! You got me!' He over-dramatically mocked the young officer, before adding, 'or rather, you would've got me, if I wasn't wearing the latest in Russian body armour!'

The young American Officer did not believe Kane. He quickly countered with a loud and proud bark back, which at any other volume may have passed for a smug statement, instead of a childish rant. 'In reality that would've been a head shot! Sir!'

As the sound of the youthful and earnest gloat floated away on the wind, the young man heard, for the first time, the strange sizzling sound and realised that it was coming from the fire. He opened his mouth to exclaim. 'What the fu ...' but he did not get to finish. There was a loud pop and instantly the whole area was illuminated with a shockingly bright flash of fluorescent white light! Startled, some of his men actually yelled out! Temporarily blinded, a few discharged their weapons in a panic, mainly plastering the rough stones in the wall behind Kane with yellow paint but one pellet stung Kane on the back of his hand. Kane had fortunately raised that hand to protect his face. Another pellet clipped his shoulder.

'Well! Well! Lieutenant!' Kane addressed the officer's rank, using the American, rather than the British pronunciation. 'We are all dead men now!' He added wistfully.

'So are you!' The younger man spat back. Although his voice betrayed an obvious frustration in his almost infantile, snivelling, tone.

'Yes but perhaps that was the point! I'm not just sitting here in these black robes for warmth!' Kane gestured to the traditional Afghan clothes that he was wearing over his British Army officer's uniform. 'If you'd read the script.'

'I did!' The young officer of US Marines insisted, projecting so much irritation and intensity into the two words of his interruption, that Kane felt more bruised by them than the original pellet punch to his chest.

'Or rather, paid attention to it!' Kane continued, correcting tersely. He was cold and tired. The pellet that had hit him on the back of his hand had drawn blood and a thin line of dark scarlet was beginning to bubble up amongst the yellow paint. His hand was also stinging because it was bitterly cold. Not surprisingly this was all making Kane unusually grumpy.

'You might have remembered what these clothes mean!' Kane continued, gesturing angrily this time at the black robes. 'They are meant to suggest that I might be part of a suicidal Jihardi group! The one you were sent out to track down! And I might have been quite happy to die, if my death teased you and your men into my trap!'

The young American may have been blushing or it could have been the reflection of the fire, which had died down again, following the dazzling explosion, into a chemical orange glow rather than the previously bright and constantly flickering yellow white flames.

'Maybe you didn't get all of us with that blast!' The Lieutenant suggested hopefully, if rather unconvincingly. His face twitched and his right eye blinked twice, as he spoke out, in an involuntary nervous reaction. He then stuttered, perhaps in recognition of the frailty of his next statement: 'Bbbb-but we got you!'

Kane shrugged. 'No matter.' He murmured softly to himself, whilst looking directly into the remains of his fire. Then raising his eyes and staring straight at the darkness behind the young officer, he raised his voice slightly. He said: 'Go on Frank! Prove my point! Educate the young man!'

Seconds later, a series of pinging noises erupted in the clearing, as pink paint pellets exploded on the back of the American Marines camouflage covered metal helmets.

Frank John barged his way through the stunned crowd of soldiers, nudging the young officer, disrespectfully, as he passed by and finally stepped into the fading firelight. As usual, he had a big smirk on his face. He winked as he whispered:

'Thanks for the head shot tip! Sir!' The last word was disrespectfully delayed. The Lieutenant blinked or twitched again and his body sagged in resignation. His errors of judgement were obvious to all, especially his own men.

Frank, now chuckling out loud, squatted down by the fire.

'Any spare virgins in paradise then Captain?' He asked nonchalantly.

'You know I'd rather a hot whore in hell!' Kane joked back. 'At least she'd be warmer! Sitting here waiting for these guys to show up, well, I'm bloody freezing!'

'Ah, then this must really be the day that hell freezes over then!' Frank said shaking his head slowly as he looked into the

235

dying fire.

'Any more wood?' He asked doubtfully.

Kane simply shrugged by way of reply to his friend.

'You know I'm getting too old for all this shit!' He said, more to himself than anyone else. Frank frowned and turning his head to the left, he yelled out in his loud sergeant's voice: 'Alex, make yerself bloody useful then! Go get us some more firewood off that dead tree! The skipper's gonna catch his death otherwise! Oh!' He turned around to look at the impotent figure of the American Lieutenant still hunched as he stood directly behind him.

'Hang on a moment, I forgot!' He continued sarcastically. 'These dead Yanks have already done for him!' Frank John chuckled to himself, before finally raising his voice, so that it was loud enough to wake the dead. 'But I'm bloody freezing! So let's be 'Aving yer! Right!'

'No worries, Sergeant!' A cocky Australian accent rang out and a tall soldier stepped in from the darkness behind the Americans left flank. The marines jumped again at this man's sudden appearance and their officer twitched nervously once more. The Aussie's rifle was casually hanging ready for action from a strap tied tight across his chest and in his right hand he held a large black bladed commando knife. He was soon hacking away at the last dead branch, which had been lonely, poking out from the dead tree stump.

'We've got a good hour before it starts getting light and we can walk off this God forsaken hill. We might as well make ourselves comfortable.' Captain Kane announced to everyone in the vicinity. Then turning towards the American he added: 'Lieutenant!?! Have you guys got any coffee?'

The young American was embarrassed to admit they did not.

'Any Coke-a-Cola?' Sergeant Frank John teased.

236

'Don't you be worried about dat!' The final member of Kane's crew spoke up and startled the careless Yankees all over again. Stepping from the darkness on their right flank the young man was waving his army regulation flask with his left hand but still held his rifle grip in his right. His warm smirk almost glowed out from behind the scarf, which was pulled high up over his face.

'A little bit of Jameson's for the officer!' He added in a thick mock Irish brogue.

Kane grinned back. Yet, in spite of all this Boys Own "fun and games" he had made up his mind. It was time for him to resign his commission. Training allies was fine but being paid a pittance whilst your specialist skills were being sold at a premium, at the same time as your own units were being cut back to the bone, was getting on his nerves. He really did not want to sign on for another five or ten years of grief and at the end of it finding himself on the scrap heap or worse. At twenty-nine he was convinced professional soldiering, these days, was an even younger man's game, or even a woman's, as he had been pointedly told on his last "Command Course" by a stunning young nursing officer, named Jill Hope. She, of course, was another reason why he wanted to move on! You could say he had high hopes for his own future but they did not involve the army anymore!

Chapter 25: A Brief Briefing

'A little bit of Jameson's for the officer!' An overtly thick mock Irish brogue sounded just behind Kane as he stood beside Capel Heddwch. 'My God it looks cold up there!' The voice added but this time it had settled back into a mellower tone, yet one with a distinctive twang of a real Northern Irish accent.

'It always is!' Kane replied turning away from the mountain vista with an astounded smile on his face, truly shocked that his daydream had become real. Kane knew the face, as he had done the voice, but not the name. It took him a few more seconds to recall that, even though the broad shouldered, bi-racial, thirty-something man, looked different to the image that had immediately popped up in Kane's mind. Quite simply the man who now stood beside him looked much older. No doubt Kane had also changed and not for the better. Nevertheless, the cheerful brown eyes greeted Kane with genuine affection. Although smartly dressed, and wearing an appropriately plain black tie, the Irishman's light grey Farah trousers, blue and white check patterned shirt, and unbuttoned three quarter length, old fashioned, fawn coloured mackintosh raincoat, certainly contrasted with the more sober suits worn by all the other men present at the funeral. In fact, Kane could not remember seeing the man in the chapel. He would have stood out. There was a warm whiff of fresh tobacco smoke coming off the stranger. Glancing down Kane spotted a discarded, partially smoked, cigarette, still burning faintly where it had been dropped, near the wall of the chapel, to the right of the doorway. Kane also noticed that one of the scruffy tan suede Desert boots that the man was wearing had its lace undone. Raising his eyes he saw the plain and

238

simple, brown leather strapped, wristwatch, worn tightly to the man's right wrist. Its face was protected by a well weathered, firmly clipped down, matching leather cover identical to Kane's own timepiece.

'Yes, I remember it well!' The man laughingly acknowledged, his brown eyes widening in exaggeration as he began to make a jokey teeth chattering sound. Kane smiled back at the light brown face, with it's rough grey chin stubble, which rose up the side of the man's puffed out cheeks, and right up passed his flat oval ears to join the matching grey stubble across the top of his close shaved head. At first glance the thick covering had disguised a wide but faded scar, which ran down in a straight cut from the left ear to the end of the broad jawbone.

'You don't recognise me do you, Sir?' The man sounded disappointed but his broad grin remained fixed on the aged face, seeming to indicate that he was proud of this confusion as if he had intended some deception.

'Yes I do!' Kane paused for effect before adding with a laugh: 'Calamity!'

'Blast! I thought I had you, for a moment!' With that Kane's apparent old acquaintance roared with laughter. Banishing the slight shrug of disappointment he had made when first correctly identified. It was a roar nonetheless that caused an immediate sharp look of disapproval from those mourners who were by now passing the chapel on their way back towards their parked cars. Kane nervously twisted his head around to glance back towards the grave. Wendy was still there deep in conversation with a slightly twitchy Trudy Morgan, who seemed to be unprofessionally checking her watch. Kane was relieved that she had or so it seemed, not heard the men's laughter. Turning his full attention back to Calamity, Kane spoke softly.

'So you still carry that flask of Jameson's on you!' The Irishman gave a sly grin by way of reply. 'Then, I think once

239

everyone has gone we should perform the old unit toast for Sergeant John over there, eh!'

***

It took a good half an hour for all of Frank's mourners to leave the cemetery. Wendy only gave Kane the briefest of nods as she walked passed on her way back to the hired black limousine and with Tracey Morgan back inside the chapel; Kane and Calamity strolled over to the open grave. Once by the edge they looked down at the dirt splattered coffin, before they each took a long swig of Irish whisky. Calamity, drank from his silver hip flask and Kane, gulped a mouthful from the quarter pint bottle of Jameson's; a bottle that he had bought especially for this very purpose just a few days ago. Having swallowed their swigs, they tipped the remaining contents of their containers into the grave. Then, in unison, they stood to attention, performed a military salute, stepped back, saluted the grave one last time and turning away, formally quick marched back towards the chapel in mutual silence.

It was only then that Kane noticed the old caretaker was lurking on the nearby tarmac path. The old man had a strange smile on his face, which Kane took to be confirmation that he was an old soldier or at least that he had seen similar scenes here, many times before. The caretaker began to shuffle down towards the grave, using two shovels as if they were Nordic walking sticks. When he reached the grave, the old man bent over and pulled the discrete green throw of fake grass off the large mound of earth. Kane half expected him to start shovelling the earth into the grave but the caretaker let out a single sharp and indecipherable cry, whilst waving his hand casually over his head. Glancing in the direction that the caretaker was waving, Kane could see that he was signalling towards his apprentice. The

240

younger man was at the far end of the cemetery, proudly sat aboard a bright orange miniature digger. The engine coughed twice before bursting into noisy action and the caterpillar tread crept forward, moving the small but heavy duty plant vehicle up the pathway towards the open grave and the previously hidden pile of earth.

'Where to now?' Calamity had asked, his voice almost drowned out by the din of the digger. Kane shrugged and asked if Calamity was coming back to the wake. The Irishman shook his head sadly, and said something that Kane could not hear but he managed to lip read that Calamity had to go back to work. Seeing the disappointment on Kane's face, Calamity mouthed something else. Kane translated it as a rather confusing statement that Calamity was actually working now! Kane allowed the natural puzzlement he felt show on his face. Fortunately at this stage the apprentice switched the digger's engine off, dismounted and began helping his boss level the earth neatly with the shovels.

'I shouldn't really be telling you this but I know "we" can trust you, Sir!' Calamity had begun whispering rather formally. Kane had in turn began to protest that the only people who called him "Sir" these days were the kids at school, and that most of them did not even bother doing that! However, Calamity had quickly retorted that Kane would always be "Sir to him!" Then Calamity quickly glanced around to make sure that they were still standing alone before he continued his story.

'It's like this, Sir. I'm still part of *The Pack!*' Kane was surprised. He could never really forget about Major Paul Packwood and his dirty tricks Special Forces unit that had acquired the dubious nickname of *"The Pack!"* Both he and Frank John had served under Packwood but the last thing that Kane had heard about his former CO was that the man had retired to study a PHD in History at Cambridge University. Now Kane, (who had spent the last decade trying hard to block out his past dalliance in that dark world) simply wanted to say how sorry he was for Calamity but he stopped himself and just listened instead.

Calamity was now working as a police officer! Detective Sergeant O' Neil transferred into Gwent Police from The Met. Or so his cover went. He was involved in a "secret" multi-agency investigation into police corruption. Kane had sighed at that. In his limited previous experience, multi-agency and secret were not compatible, but he merely said flippantly that: 'It's a dirty job but someone's got to do it!' However, he then could not help himself but observe that such work was a little bit provincial for the "Pack" to be involved in!

'Ah! There's an international dimension to the corruption!' Calamity let slip, trying to sound all mysterious! And of course, Kane could not resist asking if Calamity, being in the police, knew the truth about, as he put it, "this business" with Frank? It was then, at that stage, when Calamity looked his most uncomfortable, that Kane knew, instinctively, Frank John had not committed suicide. Sucking air in through his teeth as he spoke, Calamity immediately confirmed all of Kane's worst fears.

'We knew you'd turn up sooner or later and quite frankly we are worried about what you plan to do!'

'Was Frank working with you?' Kane asked slowly.

'No! It's all an unhappy coincidence!' Calamity stated, perhaps too casually, as was his way, before suddenly realising what he had said and forcing himself to look straight into his former officer's eyes, cold eyes that had narrowed intently as if blindly focusing on some invisible target.

'Look we will deal with it! Sir! I will deal with it!' He tried to sound convincing but Kane was only half listening. 'Sir!' Calamity deepened his voice, attempting to add gravitas to his next words but hesitated slightly, not used to giving orders to someone, who ten years or so ago, had been giving him orders! 'The, er,

Brigadier, er, Dr. Packwood, er, wants me to get your assurance, um, that you will not, repeat not, get involved in what's going on here. He said you can go to the wake by all means but then you must go home.'

'That's nice of him!' Kane's irritation was obvious now. He spoke through gritted teeth.

'Look you leave this mess to us. We are the professionals now Sir! There's a lot more at stake than you could possibly be aware of! Honestly! You're lucky Sir! I'm told that you have a normal "happy" life, away from all the madness!' Calamity was trying hard, too hard. It was a style that did not truly suit the former easy going Corporal. Kane was certainly not convinced but he still had enough of his old wits about him to realise that the sensible thing was to give Calamity exactly what he wanted.

'Well! I haven't a clue what you are on about but it sounds like you are letting me off the hook a bit here!' Kane began slowly, sounding like he was talking to one of the young Assistant Heads back at school. 'I certainly wasn't happy with this story of Frank topping himself, but I didn't have a clue what to do about it!'

Calamity's eyes bore into Kane's new slightly bewildered look, as the undercover man tried to tell if Kane was being sincere. He had not expected such a soft reaction.

'Look Sir! We don't know that Frank didn't commit suicide, for sure. All I can say is that I promise to get you an answer, and er, however, er, against the regulations it is, um, I'll properly debrief you once I've finished my, er, assignment. Can you assure me that you won't go poking the nest so to speak!?!'

'What nest?' Kane said looking Calamity in the eye and feigning relief. 'You can tell the Major that My-key Kane won't do anything unnecessary! Okay!'

Calamity breathed an exaggerated sigh of relief. Then sounding every bit like the policeman he was meant to be,

243

Calamity added: 'Thank you Sir!' Well if that's sorted, I'd better get back to the station, before I'm missed!' He winked knowingly, with his right eye, as if he was sharing some great secret with Kane. 'Now you make sure that you have a good drink at that wake and knock back an extra one or two for me, why don't yer!' This last sentence was said jovially, in Calamity's best mock "Oirish" accent. The undercover agent then nodded and with a one last glance back towards where both council employees were busy finishing off their levelling, Calamity turned away from the chapel and strode off down the path to where presumably he had parked his car. As he went he called out, without looking back, using his serious voice one last time: 'I will be in touch! Sir!' And then he was gone.

Kane needed a drink!

Chapter 26: A Sleepy Wake

'Coffee?' The teenage girl in the short white server's apron asked in her politest put-on-posh tone as Kane entered the not-so-Grand Function Room of the Aberfoist Hotel.

'No thank you, Zara.' He replied, equally politely, having quickly scanned the staff name badge that she had rather awkwardly pinned just above the swell of her ample left breast, on the tight fitting nylon blouse of the hotel's otherwise suitably mournful, black uniform. Kane had also noted the outline of her nipple, which was pushing out against the tight no doubt statically charged material and he quickly diverted his eyes, glancing down perhaps too quickly, at the two dozen white china cups she had neatly laid out on the table to the left of the doorway. The girl seemed slightly taken aback, surprised even, that he knew her name. 'I need something stronger Zara! Is there a bar?' He added with a hopeful smile and risking a glance up, he met her eyes and performed what he considered to be his most innocent, nice chap, wink.

'Yes Sir.' She replied, slightly hesitantly. She wondered how she knew this man. Maybe he was a friend of her father's, he looked about the right age or was he one of the old blokes who tried to chat her up in The Coliseum. Maybe she had let him buy her a drink or two! Anyway, she thought that she must know him because he knew her by name, so she smiled nervously, and in a suddenly over familiar, but slightly hushed and confidential manner, because he obviously knew her, she whispered an informal warning, almost an apology, that it was "only" a cash bar today. His new friend then began gesturing with her chubby right hand, the one with a circle of tiny blue ink stars crudely tattooed on the back of it, towards the green carpeted stairs on the far left hand side of the function room. Kane could see that they rose up through a wide arch in the smooth plastered, apple white painted wall. Nodding his thanks Kane strode off towards the stairs. He felt pleased with himself that somehow he had managed to stop his eyes from glancing back down to the girl's chest. She seemed a nice young girl and he really did not want her to think of him as a dirty old man.

There were half a dozen or so people already gathered in the room. Most were quietly sipping their free coffee whilst listening to what was probably polite small talk from the few brave enough to indulge in meaningless reminiscences. A few glanced up in his direction only to flash a rather sad smile, before quickly averting their eyes. Like him, they had immediately realised in that brief moment of mutual contact that they were not acquainted with each other and probably feared, whoever he was, would latch on to them and demand more than idle chatter. All present wished to avoid awkward questions about how well they knew the deceased and whether they had suspected he might be suicidal. In truth no one there had suspected how bad things were for the nice chap who owned "The Kettle" and just like Kane, those who considered that they had known Frank well, were still struggling with the shock of his untimely death. Kane was also wrestling with a mixture of sadness about the number of people who had attended the funeral, even fewer of whom had actually made it back to the hotel, and the personal disappointment that those who had were obviously strangers to him. He had been away from Aberfoist for too long and certainly lost touch. Part of him hoped that he was still one of the first to arrive at the wake. Surely others must be on their way. The family were not here yet! Like him, they may have been delayed in the struggle to find a parking space.

Rather than attempting to find a secure, long stay car parking space in the town centre, or pay to use what he had expected to be the busy (and well known to be inadequately small) hotel car park, Kane had chosen to drop his car off at the relatively nearby guest house, where he had booked into for the night, in what now seemed like the rather rash expectation of a boozy send off for his old friend. Times had changed. Where were the people they had known growing up!?!

Anyway the frantic dash across town from the "Mountain View Lodge" had taken him twenty minutes! Perhaps the others were taking longer or maybe word of the lack of a free bar had got around and put people off.

'Tight bastards!' Kane bitterly muttered under his breath. He was beginning to realise how foolish he had been to expect a big "traditional" send off for a bankrupt suicide. Nevertheless, having made the effort, Kane was determined to start as he meant to go on and if no one else was going to, well he would toast his former friend, comrade, and *"butty"* in the style that they had once been used too!

Fortunately, Kane was not totally alone in expecting to have the traditional booze up. On reaching the top stair to the bar area, he was relieved, if not truly surprised, to find Ginge was already there, pint glass in hand.

'Poor show!' His indiscreet friend blurted out as soon as he saw Kane, in the otherwise empty alcove.

'Well, at least we're here!' Kane shrugged back at Ginge, adding a thin pensive smile in an effort to show respect for the occasion.

'Do you want another?' Kane nodded at the half full pint, which Ginge was nursing protectively in front of him.

'Thought you'd never ask!' The mock reprimand was belched out, just as Kane reached the bar. On the other side of the teak laminated counter, a bored looking barman, immediately roused himself from his day dream and stepped forward with a quick, professional smile. Nodding clearly to the Guinness pump, Kane deftly raised two fingers, the polite way, to confirm his order.

'Where's yer misses?' Kane asked Ginge and had to wait patiently for a reply whilst Ginge gulped down, in one long swig, all the black liquid that had been left in his glass. Ginge burped again and then began bemoaning the fact that she had had to go back to work. Ginge then smiled, as his eyes focused on the barman filling a fresh glass, and he licked his lips in anticipation before adding: 'but she's picking me up later!' He slapped the empty pint glass down on the bar and actually began tapping his fingers in impatience.

'It's the way of the world I'm afraid!' Kane sighed. 'No time for anything these days! It's lucky I'm on Easter break really! In my place, they had the nerve to announce recently that they were changing our employment conditions and only going to allow paid leave for funerals of direct family members! I ask you! Bloody ridiculous! Insensitive penny pinching!' He merely mouthed a last swear word to avoid giving further offence to any of the old dears, who may have been listening from their seats near the foot of the stairs.

'Twelve pounds, please.' The barman asked in his strong Eastern European accent, as he allowed the half-poured drinks to rest on the bar in front of him. Kane forced a smile back at him, as he reached into his jacket pocket for his wallet. He was trying not to show the shock in his eyes at the expensive prices, but perhaps failed, for Ginge lent in towards him and tried to whisper some sympathetic words in his ear but merely splattered it with what Kane hoped was the wet remnants of the Guinness just consumed. Kane fought the instinct to wipe his ear and said: 'Sorry?'

'I think we'd better adjourn to The Coliseum pretty quickly or we'll be topping ourselves too!' His friend repeated, raising his voice so that the barman and the old dears, as well as Kane could hear him. And then realising what he'd said, Ginge added, rolling his eyes skyward: 'No offence Frank!'

Kane tried not to laugh. Ginge always had been a complete idiot but Kane liked him. He knew there was no harm in him. He was "just a bit Twp!" or so Frank had told him on so many occasions in the past.

'Absent friends!' Ginge loudly toasted the air with his now full and settled pint, before taking a long swig. Kane felt obliged to do the same and made his second "air" toast that hour in salute to his absent friend.

The Grand Function Room's bar was still disappointingly empty by the time Kane had finished slowly supping the rest of his pint, and although there was still a low murmur of conversation coming from the main part of the room, it all sounded far too quiet for the celebration of Frank John's life that Kane had been anticipating when he had made his plans to stay and drink rather than drive home that night.

'He was a good bloke! A top man!' Ginge announced suddenly, before taking another swig from his almost empty glass. Kane nodded in quiet agreement. His mind was wondering where Wendy and the rest of Frank John's family were.

'I can't believe it!' Ginge continued.

'What?' Kane asked and then attempted to answer his own question. 'You can't believe that Frank killed himself?'

'Well that too, but I mean!' Ginge rolled his eyes dramatically. 'I can't believe that so few people are here!'

'Why do you think that is? Apart from the prices of course!' Kane added, quickly anticipating Ginge's most obvious answer.

'Well you see My-key! Old Frank, he fell out with a lot of people, like, before the end!'

'What over? Money!?!'

'Well yes, in a way, but in another, it was over Ellis Pace!'

249

'What Flicker!?!' Kane exclaimed not hiding his contempt for their common acquaintance. 'You know, I half expected him to be here!' Kane added, sounding irritated.

'Hmm!' Ginge took another swig, draining the last of his drink. 'See now Ell ... er ... Flicker has changed quite a bit, like, since the old days. He has a lot of, like, influence in this town now, if you know what I mean, especially with the new people! Those who, like, settled here after you and Frank had joined up. Ell has a lot of plans, a lot of fingers in a lot of pies, like! He's quite enthusiastic for Lower Town and he talks a good talk, like, these days. Got a lot of people excited! He did!'

'He always did talk the talk!' Kane muttered into his nearly empty beer glass.

'Well anyway, Frank, like, took against Flicker. Frank was always, you know, like, the same. He wanted to keep things, er, traditional, like, and well, Flicker, er, Ell, er, well, he was all, like, for, err um, change. And I guess Frank became a bit of a pain, like!'

'How's that!?!'

'Well! Not selling his business for one, and er, like, pointing out that Ell, er Flicker, ain't done much for the town really, apart from, like, look after his own businesses!' Ginge glanced around nervously before carrying on. 'But, you know, like, in these difficult times people listen to the money, don't they? And the town council, and the business club, like, they all wanted to share in the redevelopment profits! So not only was Frankie, like, struggling to pay his way, but he was also, like, stubbornly getting in everybody else's way, by not selling up, like, and Ell, well! He blamed Frankie for the lack of investment in the town, like! And then bugger me, things got so bad, with his family and all, Frankie, he just gave up, like, and sold out. I guess that's why he topped 'imself in the end! I mean, a man like Frank, like, he just couldn't bear to sell up, like! Maybe he realised then, like, when he sold, like, that he'd lost everything!'

Kane did not like what he was hearing and shook his head. He looked at the empty pint glass in his hand. He was wondering what exactly Calamity really knew about Frank's death. Ginge for once, stayed silent, and looked into his own empty glass thoughtfully.

'I hear what you say!' Kane finally started to speak again. 'But it still doesn't make any sense to me! This is Frank we are talking about! He just wasn't like that! He would go down fighting not just skulk away and hang himself.'

'How the fuck do you know?' An aggravated young voice caused both men to look up and over towards the entrance to the bar area. There stood Kevin John. His face was for once sharp and attentive under his unruly mop of dyed black hair. His eyes were red and angry. For a moment Kane could see something of his father in the youth, and then as his mother's tears started to well up in the soft lad's eyes, the similarity was gone.

'How do any of you know!?!' The boy repeated despairingly. 'You weren't there!' He added accusingly. 'I was! He was my father!' Kevin snivelled slightly and Ginge attempted to speak soothingly.

'All I was saying was that Frank was a good bloke, like! The best!

The boy ignored him, choosing instead to spit out the message that he had been sent to tell. 'Look, I only came here to let you know that my mother isn't coming. Not surprisingly, she's too upset!' He snarled the last bit at them, his eyes wet and seemingly glazed over, began staring blankly passed the two men. 'She's gone home with Jan! So there won't be any free drinks today, we haven't got the money!' He hissed and then turned on his heel. As he walked away, both men could hear another unmistakable snivel from the big lad.

'Wait son!' Ginge, blushing called after Kevin. 'Wait a

minute!' He began to get up.

'Let him go!' Kane said flatly. 'He's just upset.'

'He has every right to be! I suppose!' Ginge acknowledged, with a shrug of his broad shoulders, and he sat back down and began looking longingly at his empty glass. 'Well, we'd better, like, be going then!' Ginge suggested his mouth turning down as he watched an irritated Zara appear and stomp over to the barman, presumably to tell him to close up the bar.

'No wait a minute!' Kane was riled. 'I came here today to mark my friend's passing, in the way he would have wanted. It might just be us two, for a whole number of reasons, but I'm having another drink! What about you?'

'At these prices!?!' Ginge looked worried.

'Yes at these prices!' Kane insisted. 'But don't you worry!' He continued quickly. 'I'm buying!'

'Good for you, like!' Ginge smiled encouragingly. 'Then I'm bloody staying, like, too!' His eyes suddenly twinkled. 'I'll have a Guinness thank you!' Ginge raised his empty glass in eager anticipation.

Kane got up and went to the bar, with the two empty glasses in his hands. However, the barman pulled a disapproving face and said unemotionally in his thick accent that he was sorry but "I closing the bar."

'It's okay Pavel we can serve these two gentlemen a little while longer!' The surprisingly young yet obviously more financial astute girl quickly interrupted. Pavel shrugged back at Zara and silently turned to pick up a clean glass from the almost full rack behind him.

'Two Guinness?' He asked casually over his shoulder, without turning his head.

Kane nodded, and said a strangely relieved thank you to them both. He resisted the temptation to offer the staff "a drink!" That would have been too flash, at these prices! Kane

252

had other ideas. He wanted to find out a lot more about Ellis Pace's plans and that so called redevelopment scheme from his sole drinking buddy!

Chapter 27: The Early Birds

After a long leisurely afternoon, filled with the coarsest catch up chat that Ginge's inconsistently memory was able to share, Kane was none the wiser about Ellis "Flicker" Pace or his grand design for Lower Aberfoist. Nevertheless, Kane had become very familiar with Ginge's long run of bad luck and he had acquired an almost encyclopaedic knowledge of the various ailments that had combined to force his long lost chum out of work and onto disability benefits. Kane had also parted with an extortionate amount of money, all of which had been unwisely invested on smooth black alcohol, the one with the trademark white head. At least the high prices paid had guaranteed them a certain unsought after exclusivity in what quickly became their own "private" bar, at rear of the Aberfoist Hotel's so-called Grand Function room. However, all good things must come to an end, thankfully, and as Ginge's digital wristwatch bleeped a faint confirmation that it was 5 pm, Pavel the casual Eastern European barman, finally announced in his most miserable tone, that he "really must close" the bar.

Ginge quickly put on a brave show by insisting that he was just about to "get a round in" and he seemed genuinely indignant when Pavel flatly refused the slurred pleas for just one more. On the other hand, Kane was a lot more accepting of the bar's closure and quickly won Ginge around by suggesting that, as it was just gone "tea time" and he was "starving", perhaps it might be a good idea if they "grabbed a bite to eat" and of course, it would be his treat!

Much "um-ing" and "ahh-ing" followed this proposal, whilst

Ginge considered the limited options available to them, given that 5pm was a rather awkward time to eat in Aberfoist. The numerous takeaways, found on this southern side of town, did not open until much later and, of course, the "Kettle" was closed down. It was also, apparently, far too early for pub meals. Not that Aberfoist had many pubs left according to Ginge, who shook his head sadly as he explained that it was also far too late for the only other café, which was right over on the west side of town, to be open.

Pavel happily informed them that the hotel's restaurant did not open until 6 pm. He then let out an over exaggerated sigh, before pulling down the metal shutter in an unsettlingly loud way to ensure that they knew his bar was truly closed. He wished them both a "gudnight" as he skulked away to whatever other duties awaited him elsewhere in the hotel. It was just then that Ginge's eyes sparkled with a sudden eureka moment. Face beaming; he proudly announced that they should go to no less an excellent eatery than "The Himalayas Indian Restaurant" which, thankfully, was just across the road. 'They', Ginge added enthusiastically, 'have been open since lunch time! And they should now be offering "early bird" specials until six thirty!' He winked joyously, as he finally recalled: 'They also serve draft Guinness!'

***

In spite of the grubby appearance on the outside of the uninspiring whitewashed brick fronted building, "The Himalayas Indian Restaurant" was on the inside surprising quite presentable. So what if it looked like any other typical Indian Restaurant that one could find up and down the valleys of South Wales, and probably in most other post industrial towns throughout the UK. Here, the walls were plastered by large, plastic coated, blown up

255

picture posters of snow covered peaks, which Kane assumed were different views of Himalayan summits, at least one of which had to be Mount Everest. Kane had been more impressed (and certainly relieved) to spot the green food agency sticker, stuck boldly to the glass window of the inner front door. It happily proclaimed a high 5 out of 5 hygiene rating for the restaurant.

The ground floor dining area had been divided into two halves. The front was a traditional open plan eating arena, with a traditional variety of four or two seater rectangular tables, which were all covered in heavy, shiny satin, cream coloured, tablecloths. These were a fair colour match for the faux leather style vinyl padded upholstery, on the otherwise simple, cream painted, wooden chairs. This area was separated from a slightly more private rear dining area by an impressive large dark wood and ivory screen. The ornate divider rose from the coffee coloured carpeted floor to the cream (or more likely off white) coloured artex contoured ceiling. The two-tone screen was slightly let down by the fact that it featured crude stereotype silhouette style carvings of women, in what your average local would have assumed was traditional Indian garb. These "exotic" dancing girls appeared to be entertaining the occasional turban wearing male figure, who sat cross-legged in the middle of each cluster. The freeze was also punctuated by the inevitable elephant or tiger silhouette. Kane wondered if the ivory was as false as the conventional images of India displayed. His imagination, no doubt fuelled by alcohol, briefly indulged in a fantasy of enraged politically correct environmentalists storming the restaurant, only for their protest to be side-tracked by ardent feminist activists and racial equality campaigners vigorously debating with each other about who should be the most offended by the decor.

Shadowy shapes hunched around a large circular table that had been set up just behind the screen. There were maybe ten or perhaps as many as a dozen customers back there, already eating and drinking, almost hidden by the atmospheric lighting or should that be a dark and dingy ambience, purely designed to disguise the lack of cleaning between environmental health inspections. Kane hoped it was the former. Whatever! The party seemed to be mainly men but the occasional shrill out burst of over excited laughter, could be clearly heard amongst the otherwise general hubbub of deep conversation, from at least two women. At first glance Kane presumed they were a works outing, and from the merry constant chatter, they were no doubt celebrating a significant event, a retirement, the bosses birthday, a new contract or more likely in these austere times, imminent redundancy.

By contrast the front area was quiet, empty even, except for one table, located at the far end of the room. This table seemed to be set aside from the others, as if it were guarding the gap between the front and rear eating areas. At the table sat two, very large Eurasian looking men. They were informally dressed in matching grey tracksuits. They were not eating but sat silently playing with their own individual, oversized, smart phones. Occasionally they took a dainty sip from the gold and white china tea cups, placed on ornate matching saucers on the table in front of them. One man glanced up and stared blankly back at Kane for all of two seconds before looking back down at his phone. Kane presumed they were waiters, on a break, or more likely kitchen staff, who had arrived early for their evening shift. Behind them, in the back room, the group of people were still making quite merry.

On arrival, Kane and Ginge had taken no more than two steps through the door, before they were intercepted by an eager young male waiter, who obviously knew Ginge well. The young Indian broke into a full, brilliant white, toothy smile and quickly ushered them to one of the vacant, two seater tables that ran

257

neatly along the right hand wall. Kane noticed admiringly that the waiter, who was particularly smartly dressed, in stiffly starched white shirt, black waistcoat and trousers, seemed to be perfectly comfortable, wearing his black tie and collar tightly done up.

Ginge immediately ordered another two Guinness and the waiter, who from his dark complexion, impeccable diction and authentic sing-song accent, may actually have hailed from the Indian sub-continent, beat a hasty retreat towards one of the two parallel doors, neatly set in the wall adjacent to the screened divider. A sign above the door, which the waiter actually pushed through, read "IN". The sign above the other door, read "OUT". Kane presumed the kitchen was behind them and he smiled in his semi inebriated state, imagining the chaos that might result on a busy evening should someone go in through the "OUT" door by mistake. He could almost hear the clatter of plates and see the general spillage of red brown curry sauce that using the wrong door at the wrong time might produce. Kane was slightly disappointed when he could not see any old stains on the floor near either door to evidence such a collision. Nonetheless, he consoled the devil in his merry mind by hoping that maybe tonight was the night!

'So what do you recommend?' He asked, turning his full attention back to his friend. Ginge's face twitched and ran through a range of puzzled expressions as he thought for a moment before resetting to his normal look of good cheer. He then began extolling the virtues of the "House Special" Biriyani. Well it had a bit of "everything" in it! Kane nodded by way of reply, happy to go along with his friend's choice and avoid the confusion of reading a strange menu in the dim light. He was also resolved not to think too closely about what Ginge actually meant about "everything" being in the meal. In fairness, Kane was pretty much sure that he had eaten "a bit of everything" in the native cuisine he had been obliged to scoff, when back in the

258

day, he had been on tours of duty in the real Himalayas. Kane consoled himself that a hygiene rated restaurant in darkest Aberfoist should not dish up the worst meal he had suffered on his travels. Then again he would not bet on it!

A different waiter appeared from the "OUT" door. He was dressed identically to the first. This one was carrying two large laminated cards, which were presumably the early bird menus. Ginge greeted him by name and told Sanjev bluntly that they already knew what they wanted. The young man flashed a warm smile back at his regular customer before announcing in a slightly high pitch voice: 'Ah the usual Mr. Thompson, eh!'

'If by "the usual" you mean the House Special Biriyani, like, you're damn right! And my friend will have the same, okay!' Ginge chirped back.

'Poppadoms?' The young man asked his tone still pleasant and jolly.

'Is the Pope Catholic?' Came the rather out of context answer.

The waiter nodded and turned back towards the kitchen, laughing out loud, as if Ginge had just told him the funniest joke. He disappeared through the "IN" door just as the first waiter reappeared through the "OUT" door, theatrically carrying a stainless steel tray with two empty straight pint glasses and two tall black cans of Guinness Draught proudly set out on it. Kane tried not to laugh as the waiter continued to present the tray as if the cans were an exclusive sample of fine wines brought especially for them from the cellar of a château, and not the kitchen fridge. He continued watching, perhaps a little too closely, as the man carefully placed the tray on the table in front of them, and then, extending a long brown finger, purposely tapped each tin, three times on the top, before pulling the tab and releasing the gas trapped inside. Whilst waiting patiently for the hiss of escaping gas to subside and the plastic widget to cease

259

clunking within the can, the waiter asked them if today was "a special celebration?" He also declared his surprised to see "Sir" as he referred to Ginge, in so early on a Friday evening. Kane was finding the old-fashioned style service all a bit too surreal and way over the top for a twenty-first century curry house in Aberfoist. However, Ginge was obviously at ease with it all and was carefully and most sincerely explaining in what his drunken mind must have thought was a polite and posh manner that they were celebrating the life of a "dear friend" whose funeral they had attended earlier that afternoon. Ginge went on to suggest that Ravi, as he now was calling the waiter, may have known the poor man himself, "Mr. John" who used to own and run "The Kettle" café, just up the street! Yes! Kane reflected to himself, Ginge really did seem to know all the staff by first name.

'Ah yes, Mr John. How sad.' Ravi acknowledged, rather flatly. 'I am sure he was a good man.' He continued and then rather oddly, and slightly out of character for the subservient role that he seemed to be playing so eagerly, Ravi added: 'You know he never ate here and he never made any of "us" feel welcome when we tried to take our breaks there!'

'I'm not surprised Ravi!' Ginge rather bluntly replied. 'He was a racist bastard at the best of times!' Ginge began laughing uncontrollably, as if being racist was hilarious. Ravi nodded sadly in straight faced agreement as he finished steadily pouring the contents of the second can into the tall glass. Somehow the mass produced can simulated centuries of tradition, in the same way as the first can had and once poured, the creamy brown storm quickly settled in the glass, emerging as a pure looking, black liquid in almost the same way as the real draught would have settled had they been in a Dublin bar. Yet, Kane noticed this glass had the "Cobra Beer" logo etched in white lettering on it, instead of the more appropriate Celtic harp. So it was a curry house after all, thought Kane.

Having achieved two perfect frothy white heads in the two matching Cobra beer glasses, Ravi smiled and withdrew, seemingly very pleased with his work. He was immediately replaced at their table by his colleague, Sanjev, who was carrying in one hand a plate stacked with four large poppadom crisps and in the other a stainless steel chutney and relish server, complete with four bowls and four teaspoons all balanced on a shiny steel serving tray.

'I love this shit!' Ginge exclaimed as he snatched up the top poppadom the instant Sanjev had placed the tray onto the table in front of them. Brutally snapping the deep fried crisp into pieces that fell fortunately onto his side dish, Ginge immediately helped himself to several heaped spoonfuls of chutney and relish from each bowl, to create a rather off putting multi-coloured mess on top of the thin fragments. Kane averted his eyes as Ginge began to devour the delicacy and instead watched Sanjev disappear into the kitchen, once again disappointingly gliding through the correct door.

'Are they always this efficient and polite?' Kane asked. Ginge, with his mouth now full, grunted something back between the crunches, which Kane took to mean yes! Remembering that he was hungry, Kane grabbed a crisp and after adding a restrained splatter of onions and herbs from one of the silver bowls, he began snacking.

A flicker of movement to his right caught Kane's attention and he looked over just in time to see two women, a blonde and a brunette, emerge from the rear dining area. They were almost floating through the gap in the wood and ivory screen. He also noticed that both of the track-suited men immediately looked up from their phones and began staring at the women as they made their way across the restaurant towards the front door. The men's eyes seemed to linger on the younger of the two women. She was a brunette and was wearing the tiniest pair of black Lycra

261

short shorts, which revealed two of the most sensationally smooth and perfectly tanned legs that Kane had noticed in a long time. The way she walked demanded attention and she knew it. He struggled to raise his eyes above her toned thighs but when he did his natural blush increased on his cheeks as his eyes met hers and she seemed to smile, knowingly, right back at him. He could not hold her gaze and lowered his eyes, immediately realising that he was now appearing to stare at her fulsome cleavage, exposed provocatively, and purposefully, by the design of her open fronted, figure hugging, black cotton halter-neck top. Kane's eyes darted guiltily away but only as far as her blonde companion, who although more mature by a fair number of years, perhaps even a decade or two, and slightly more modestly dressed, in a white lacy top and tight fighting, burgundy, designer jogging trousers, with shiny puce-pink double stripes running down the side of each tailored leg. In any other company her physical presence would have gained a man's sole attention. However, Kane could not resist looking back briefly at the brunette.

Both women looked tanned and fit but the blonde looked physically stronger. Scarily so! As Kane's eyes darted from one to the other as they moved towards the restaurant's front door, the blonde's biceps rippled as she moved across the room and her legs bulged in all the right places under the tight fitting trousers, pumping up and down, almost like a body building champion's showcase performance. She continued to display her physic with each carefully pronounced step, as if she were the inspiration for a biologist's anatomy chart, so much so that she actually reminded Kane of one of the female American wrestlers that he sometimes watched, with his son, on Saturday morning TV. Although he sensed there was nothing fake about this woman. She was also much taller than her darker companion, even though the brunette wore dangerously high, stiletto heeled, black snakeskin shoes. Kane wondered if the shoes were an attempt to gain the height her petite build lacked.

Miss Fit, or whatever her real name was, by contrast wore flat, low top, tennis shoes, with pink leopard skin fabric sides. There was a glint of an expensively thick gold chain around her otherwise bare ankle. Kane resisted the temptation to snobbishly dismiss her as a bit of rough or a "CHAV" in a track suit, because he was automatically recalling his wife's recent scolding, when he had expressed surprise at the return of the eighties "shell suit" fashion, after returning home from a recent non-uniform day at his school. Mrs Kane had insisted, most indignantly, that "sportswear chic" was back and not some five minute high street fad but a real high fashion proposition, with crazy prices to go with it. Kane did not doubt her opinion anymore, as he watched fit-style being smartly modelled, in of all places, an Aberfoist curry house!

Form is temporary but class is permanent! Or so the old sports cliché goes. However, just as Kane paid an internal mental tribute to the two "classy" ladies before him, he noticed that each carried in their hands, flashy examples of what he understood to be new trendy electronic Vape pipes. So much for class! He instinctively thought, almost dismissively, and perhaps unfairly, but in his mind these substitute smoking devices made the two women just like the youngsters he had seen at The Coliseum, on his last home-town outing, the other evening. So these two contrasting models were in reality being true to *Aberfoist form*. Their distracting catwalk was merely a typically common trip outside for a "fag" break! Something that was very much to be expected at an Aberfoist curry house!

Despite his time in the forces, Kane had never taken up the tobacco habit. The more that he had been encouraged to do so by his happily puffing contemporaries, the more he had resisted, what he had always considered was a filthy habit. Now,

263

disappointed at the dream girls crass failings, he returned his attention to his table and was not in the slightest bit surprised to see, that through his distraction, he had lost the poppadom battle to Ginge. Three one! His companion burped as he washed the last relish coated crispy crumb down, with a well timed swig of Guinness.

'Marvellous!' Ginge broadcast at the top of his voice across the table.

Much to Kane's surprise, Ginge continued in a much lower tone just as the restaurant's front door shut behind the exiting two women.

"Yep! Those women are bloody marvellous eh! Mate! But do you know who that brunette is? I bet yer don't!?!' Ginge paused for effect, looking so proud he could burst! 'That was Mrs Ellis "Flicker" Pace! What do you bloody well say to that eh!?! The old boy done good, eh!'

Kane was truly lost for words.

***

From his position, hidden behind the teak and ivory screen, Ellis Pace was smiling at what he had just witnessed. He always got a kick out of watching jaws drop when "his wife" passed men for the first time. His voyeuristic glee was only exceeded by the joy he took from the respect people showed him, once they knew who she was, or rather who "owned" her! They would try hard to hide their attraction to Martini. He habitually encouraged her to flirt with them, which the little tart enjoyed way too much, but he loved to see their panic knowing that she was his! And although he told himself their stress was born out of a desire not to offend him, he knew it was really fear. For him it was a constant reminder that however small the Aberfoist pond was, he was truly now a big fish.

Watching Kane's sly observations had given him an idea for a bit of what he called fun. An idea, which might help resolve a few of his recent worries. He turned and smiled at his guests. Slipping his hand inside his trouser pocket, he checked that his mobile phone was there and not in the jacket on the back of his chair. It was! Then quickly making his excuses and he headed out to the toilet at the back of the restaurant. He had laughed graciously as Mr Lord, who was sat next to Pace's temporarily empty chair, looked up, interrupting his enthusiastic conversation with his neighbour on the other side, Mr Khan, the accountant come lawyer, and cheerfully called after him words of encouragement, in what was an awful impersonation of John Wayne: 'A man's gotta do what a man's gotta do!'

Lord then lent across the table towards the two other men, who were uncomfortably still wearing their suit jackets and had been sat there, silently sipping on their post meal coffee. Lord's easy smile was suddenly gone, as he began talking in a hushed, solemn and very deliberate tone.

'Now that the ladies are out of the way and Mr Pace is on his, er, comfort break, let us talk some serious business!'

'Sure thing!' Detective Sergeant John Joe "Calamity" O' Neil replied earnestly. His partner, a slim, nervous looking, young man, with a blue Police Federation tie, worn loosely around his neck, lent in closer, intending to listen carefully to the proposition they had been waiting all afternoon to hear.

Chapter 28: Two Birds One Stoned

From the relative privacy of a single toilet cubicle, located at the back of The Himalayas Indian Restaurant, Ellis Pace made two quick phones calls. The first was to his man Dylan "The Dull One" Francis. Pace simply told him that Mykee Kane was back in town and that he could be found "stuffing his face at the Himalayas!" Pace had thought that that was all he would need to say, but he was soon reminded yet again that people just did not think like him. Francis had seemed so eager for revenge (on account of his broken hand). However, Pace could almost hear Francis over thinking things. The hesitation gave Pace time to come up with what he suddenly thought was an even better idea. The kind of twisted idea Pace liked. An economical one, which could kill two birds with one stone!

'I thought you told me to lay off of him!?!' The strangely cautious employee eventually responded.

'I've changed my mind!' Pace said curtly, and even though he should not have had to say anything more to his man, he did. Pace felt obliged given Francis' obvious hesitation, to outline his new plan of action, slowly, so that even someone as apparently dim-witted as "Dull-one" Francis, could actually understand. Pace certainly did not want things to fizzle out, as could easily happen with such a squib as "Dull-one". So he relit the blue touch paper and began gleefully dreaming of fireworks. 'Look I want to impress my guests!' Pace muttered in an attempt to justify his sudden change of mind. 'Now listen carefully!' Pace waited a few seconds until he heard his man acknowledge that he was in fact listening carefully with a simple grunt of "Yes Boss!"

Pace cunningly, or so he thought, insisted that all Aberfoist Security employees never used staff or client names on open lines. He called it "complete deniability" but his boys often called it "bloody stupid" as they often wondered who or what he was talking about! Attempting to keep to this protocol, Pace began his explanation.

'Now you turn up pretending you want to see me, okay?'

'Yeah, okay!?' Francis made another slightly baffled grunt down the line.

'But when you see him, I want you to try and pick a fight with him. Okay?'

'Who?' Francis asked dully.

'Kane, of course!' An irritated Pace almost screamed down the phone, breaking his own rule again.

"I'll do more than that! I'll bloody murder him. I'll break his arms and legs! I'll ..."Listen to me!' Pace impatiently interrupted his minion's rant. 'I don't want you to actually fight him!' He could almost hear the other man's jaw drop open. 'It'll damage the Himalayas!' Pace quickly continued. 'Just scare him a bit!' Pace could sense the "Dull-one's" confusion in the continuing dead silence of his ear piece. In truth he doubted that Francis could actually scare Kane. Certainly not the Mykee Kane that Pace had known growing up, and on the evidence of their last encounter, in the "Kettle" Francis stood next to no chance of actually winning any fight, even against the current well out of condition Kane; but then that was not part of Pace's scheme. 'Are you still there?' Pace asked when the silence had become too much.

'Yeah!?' Francis sounded uncertain.

'Listen carefully now!' Pace began again. 'I want to step in and rescue him from you! Can you understand why?'

Francis obviously did not, so Pace tried his best to make him realise that by saving Kane, he, Pace, would gain his trust and he could then find out if he suspected anything.

267

'About what?' Francis blurted out sounding truly perplexed and making Pace cringe. The schemer wondered for a few seconds whether his man was really up to the job or could he even be trying to entrap Pace into saying something compromising about Frank John's murder on an open phone line! However, Pace then realised that "Dull-one" did not know that the death that he had discovered down the "Kettle" was not a suicide! Also, given his man's general slowness, Pace concluded that Francis was unlikely to have worked out what really happened to Frank John! So Pace pressed on with his instructions in the simplest way possible.

'I want to make it crystal clear to all my guests, that not only am I in charge, but that I can keep control of the wild and dangerous men in my team! Okay?'

Pace could sense the small man's continued confusion. So he tried again. 'Look, I want my guests to see what a wild and dangerous guy you really are! Okay?' Pace almost heard the gasp from the other end of the line. Now he imagined Francis' instant and foolish pride at being considered "wild and dangerous". He could visualise him nodding in agreement as he heard the begrudging response in a slightly deeper, almost complacent, tone.

'Okay boss! I get it!'

'Now listen carefully to the next bit. Okay?'

'Okay.' The bewildered voice still sounded far from okay but Pace could picture the stupid smirk on "Dull-one's" face.

'After I've had a good chat with your man, I'm going to send him out the back way and you will be there and you can do whatever! Got it?'

'Yeah! Thanks Boss!' A suddenly gleeful Francis replied.

'But listen; make sure you have "company" with you! You know who! Understand?'

Dylan Francis had had no intention of going up against

268

Kane on his own. He never did anything violent on his own and had already made the mental note to get Tall Dai to go with him. Yet he still felt obliged to tell Pace that he did not need any help to do the "fat old bastard" in. His boss was not listening. Against his better judgement Pace sought reassurance by insisting that Francis repeat the plan, "slowly" back to him, even though it was over an open line. Then finally satisfied, that his moronic minion had just about grasped it and that "company" would be there, Pace told Francis to be there within the next half an hour. His final words of warning were to make sure that the "company" waits outside so that he (Kane) does not see him. 'And remember, he is a tricky bastard, so come tooled up!' Pace listened impatiently for yet another unsure "okay" to come through his phone's speaker before he moved the phone from his ear and pressed the on-screen, red disconnect icon.

That call had taken much longer than Pace had hoped and he was a little bit nervous that he might have missed an opportunity to set up the second part of his plan. Nevertheless, Pace carried on and quickly rang his wife. He heard the ring tone as he raised the speaker back to his ear and nervously waited for an answer, all the while hoping that she had not inhaled too much vapour off the silly juice, she was supposed to be "discreetly" testing that afternoon. He was just in time by the sound of it. He could hear both women struggling to control their giggles as she eventually answered his call. He wondered who would understand his instructions better, a doped up wife or dopey employee. Nonetheless, Ellis Pace continued to implement his scheme.

***

On the street just outside the Himalayas Indian Restaurant, Martini Pace breathed out a thick cloud of white, sweetly scented vapour and watched it float up into the rapidly darkening, navy

269

blue sky. She then smiled blissfully across to her older, equally intoxicated companion, who after the briefest of meetings was well on her way to becoming her new "best friend forever!" After all they had a lot in common, not least the drug they had been inhaling during regular girlie breaks whilst the men back in the restaurant discussed business. Kimberly Jones smiled back at her and let out a surprisingly girlish giggle, blushing slightly, before sucking once more on her own silver plated Vape device. Kim, as she preferred to be called, felt an immediate buzz as the vapour filtered through her lungs and the chemicals released into her system surged around her body in her tainted blood stream. Wow! She really liked this new stuff. It was sweet! Not only did it make her feel instantly "epic" but unlike the weed she used to smoke, there was no bitterness or after effects. Or so she believed. Her clothes did not stink of tobacco smoke nor did she have to use mints to freshen her breath afterwards. Her lover, Lord, had described it as the new Alcopops! Yet, he had insisted that unlike alcohol, there would be no hangover, when she came down from it. Kim also appreciated that this mix was going to make them a lot of money and what's more, she had laughed to herself, it was a totally legal high. Well at least for now!

Her Lord had been right about the first blend that she had tried. She loved the way it made her feel. Strong empowered and it seemed to help her train harder when using it. She would feel no pain as she pumped her body up to the next extreme in the weights room back at The Potting Shed. Yes, she told herself, she could still function effectively on this stuff. Or so she thought! However, she did wonder about this new batch. It was starting to make her feel giddy, but in oh such a nice warm way.

Kim giggled again, looking across at Martini Pace. Maybe it was not the drug that was making her feel giddy. She gazed at the younger woman's pretty face. Wow! Kim suddenly thought that Martini was really beautiful, so gorgeous, sophisticated, and

270

exciting. Well, she had lived in London and worked as a real model! Kim was so looking forward to getting to know Martini better. Such a glamorous name too! Unlike Kim, a name which her parents had chosen long before she was born, when they were hoping for a boy! Kim laughed out loud, recalling their frustrations. And yet she knew that to a certain extent her parents had got a boy. For most of her life Kim had been nothing more than everyone's idea of a real tomboy. What else could she have been with her rough upbringing and the fact that her parents gave her boy's clothes to wear. A single child lost in an uncaring adult world. She had had no time for girly things. Perhaps that was why, when she reached her teens, she had become fascinated, even obsessed, by the pretty "girly" girls she knew in school, but only from a distance. She had been too rough for them to entertain playing with her. Yes, she had amazingly got married! Married young! Quite unexpectedly, she had become Mrs Rahman. A name that she had dropped, almost as quickly as her husband had disappeared after their wedding. Kim (and everyone else) had been very surprised when "he" had been attracted to her. The neighbour's lodger! She was quickly infatuated, even though the friendship had ruffled a few feathers at home, what with him being foreign and all that! Inevitably, in her small minded Valleys' community, she had still had to marry him, when she fell pregnant, even though he was a foreigner. Yet the marriage had worked, well sort of! He got his British citizenship confirmed and she got her two boys. Funny really, she thought, after her man had left her, just over a year later, disappearing God knows where, she had not really been bothered by men, or a lack of them, until much much later that is, when Lord took over the club where she was doing casual bar work. She took a real shine to her new boss as he did to her, despite the age difference. Perhaps it was him being foreign too!

Now for the first time in her life, under Lord's influence,

271

Kim liked to appear to be more feminine. Her hair colouring, her nails, even her boobs, were all false! Unlike her physic, that was definitely real.

She had not always been so well defined. It was only after her boys discovered the weight's room at the local Leisure Centre that she took an active interest. Soon she was working out with them and for the first time in her life, taking a real pride in her appearance. It gave her the confidence that many of the local single mums lacked. Okay, she thought, maybe some of her physicality benefited from drugs, but then everyone down the gym took them, steroids was only like taking medicine, or so she told herself. Anyway, Lord seemed to like strong women, which was rare for men of his race in her limited experience. However, making an effort was worthwhile. Kim believed the glamorous Mrs Pace was evidence of that! She was certainly high maintenance. And yes! Kim had been thrilled when Martini had praised her appearance. She had even suggested that Kim, now an actual grandmother, could do some modelling for her agency. Apparently there was a big demand for sexy mature women. Kim was truly made up when Martini had said that. It made her feel special too. She secretly hoped that Lord would let her have a go.

Then suddenly Kim was distracted by the street lamps. Somewhere, somehow, a built-in micro chip, a timer switch or perhaps a light sensor, kicked in and automatically began the lighting up process along the street. Kim stared upwards as the reinforced plastic covered bulbs flickered on, one after the other, and, in her bedazzled eyes, they began projecting a weird and wonderful spectrum of colours against the twilight of the quickly fading early evening sky.

'Look!' She told Martini Pace and pointed upwards. 'The lights are as brilliant and beautiful as you!' Kim did not realise what she had said but Martini did and she smiled back. She appreciated being attractive and she always enjoyed compliments, even when they came from an old rough looking dyke, like Kimberly Jones.

'Come on!' Martini started sweetly, offering her new best friend her hand and when it was taken, she squeezed gently. Her husband had wanted her to get close to his mysterious new business partner, Mr. Lord, and that of course, meant befriending his Mrs! But surely, even the old pervert would not have expected her to do it this way. She giggled as Kim returned the squeeze. Martini was used to being regularly exhibited as Pace's "trophy" wife and she loved a good tease, whether the victim was male or female. Well, she liked games, so she did not mind! In fact, Pace had just asked her over the phone to perform another dubious favour for him! Maybe, just maybe, her new friend would join in. Yes! Martini decided, in her chemically enhanced merriness, Kim and her would have a real laugh!

'Ell wants me to wind up those two old blokes inside!' Martini began telling Kim with a laugh. 'You know! The ones who gave us an ogle, when we on the way out!' Kim didn't! She had only had eyes for Martini as they left the restaurant. 'He says they're old school friends of his and he wants them to er, "appreciate" what a lucky man he is!' Martini continued unashamedly.

'Well he is! A lucky man I mean!' Kim uninhibitedly shouted back.

'Do you fancy,' Martini paused, before adding tartly, 'helping me put on a bit of a show then?'

Still dazed by the street lamps seemingly psychedelic light show, Kim did not really understand what Martini meant but she was enjoying holding the younger woman's soft hand. She watched slightly agog as Martini pulled down her tight fitting T-shirt to expose more of her open cleavage. Unable to resist, Kim, compromised by sadly letting go of the soft hand and then eagerly and slightly unsteadily, used both her hands to adjust the

273

fabric even lower.

'Maybe just a little bit more!' She winked.

Equally emboldened by the chemicals in her own blood stream, Martini Pace reached over and slowly undid another three buttons on Kim's lacy blouse; so that it could fall open almost down to her bejewelled navel. Martini watched closely as the enhanced bra-free bosom that stretched and held the lacy fabric in place, rose and fell as Kim's breathing suddenly deepened. This was too easy, Martini thought. She affected a nervous laugh, whilst letting her hands rub gently across the top of the impressive surgically enhanced breasts whilst she pulled the blouse ridiculously open, in the style of a red carpet Hollywood starlet. Leaning in towards the older woman, she let her palms rest on the brown tanned skin. Martini whispered ever so sweetly and softly into Kim's ear that she was so glad to have met her.

'Me too!' Came the over excited reply, in the deep breathless Valleys' voice.

Across the road, an old man, on his way to collect his regular evening newspaper, walked into a lamppost.

Chapter 29: A Flirting Disaster

Inside "The Himalayas" Indian Restaurant the two old friends were enjoying their main course. The "Special" Biriyani was "special" because it came with egg! A thin omelette was spread delicately over the top of a sizzling risotto, which consisted of spicy rice, fried onions, chicken, lamb, and King Prawns. Ginge had already tipped the whole bowl of his accompanying vegetable curry sauce over the mountain of rice in one happy *splosh!* Having vigorously mixed it all together, he was now shovelling mouthfuls of dark brown mess into his mouth, whilst simultaneously smacking gravy smothered lips together and making self-satisfying purrs of appreciation.

By contrast, Kane having peeled back the egg covering was individually targeting the darker meat with his fork and cautiously tasting it, initially to check whether it was actually lamb. In fairness, it did seem to have the appropriate consistency for the menu declared meat. However, all he could really taste were the spices it had been marinated in. The chunks of chicken were not too dissimilar in flavour, especially if eaten with his eyes closed. This was a wise tactic given his companion's table manners. Kane also carefully tested a small spoonful of his curry sauce and only then, once satisfied by the smooth creamy taste, did he decided that it was actually safe enough to add liberally to his meal, in order to alleviate the dryness of the rice.

Eventually Kane, having finished exploring the dish in front of him, dared to look up and in between modest mouthfuls he attempted to distract Ginge from his rather off putting mewing, by restarting their conversation.

'So what's the story behind our old mucker snagging such a looker then?'

Ginge tried to speak, suddenly desperate to share his knowledge. Yet with his mouth full, he ended up making only a strange and unpleasant gurgling sound. He rolled his eyes dramatically pleading for more time to reply and then he tried to swallow too much at once. Struggling not to choke, Ginge urgently reached for his drink. He repeatedly gulped most of the remaining beer down. When he finally spoke, his words were accompanied by the inevitable hiccup or two.

'She's a local girl. Hiccup! Hiccup! I used to know her mum! Hiccup! Hiccup!' Ginge gave Kane one of those suspiciously knowing winks. The type of wink that Kane never took seriously because it was the type of wink he always understood meant that the winker was bullshitting him.

'Bit of a tart! But I liked her! Hiccup!' Ginge continued. 'The mum! That is! Like! Hiccup!' Ginge quickly added. 'And the girl's a bit like her! You know! Or so I'm told! Hiccup! Hiccup!' Ginge smirked and gave Kane another knowing wink. 'Brought up by her Nan, like! After her mum went off with some bloke! Hiccup! A travelling salesman or something! Like!' Ginge then burped loudly.

'Do you want some water?' Kane helpfully suggested. Ginge looked at his almost empty glass and shook his head.

'God forbid! Hiccup!' He began scanning the restaurant for a waiter and seeing one adjusting cutlery on the far side of the room, called out. 'Oy! Hiccup! Another two Guinness over here ta!'

Kane seeing that his glass was half full, quickly placed his hand over the top of it. Slowly shaking his head he called across to the waiter: 'Only one thanks!'

The waiter unintentionally frowned at the interruption to his artwork but then realising his discourtesy began eagerly nodding and immediately abandoning his current masterpiece, moved gracefully towards the kitchen doors. Ginge satisfied that the man was on task, looked back at Kane, his face showing signs of genuine concern.

'You feeling okay?' Ginge asked.

'I'm fine.' Kane shrugged. 'Anyway, you were telling me about thing-a-me!' He gestured with a turn of the head towards the front door.

'Oh yes!' Ginge paused for a moment, gathering his thoughts before hiccupping twice and then carrying on with his gossip.

'Martini Morris! Class name eh! Hiccup!'

'What Morris?'

'No! Hiccup! Martini! Like! Remember the drink? Hiccup!'

Kane did. Although he suspected Ginge was referring to the warm red liquid that Kane's mother had drunk occasionally at Christmas, poured out of the dusty bottle, which she kept for years in the back of the sideboard, rather than the suave vodka based cocktail, like the one that Roger Moore insisted was "shaken not stirred" in almost all of those cheesy but must-watch-movies that had, like the alcohol in the sideboard, become a secular "British Christmas" tradition!

'I loved those adverts! Hiccup! Funny as fuck! You know the ones with the bloke from, hiccup! Oh what's it called!?! And the actress from that American soap opera!?! You know! The British one! With the dark hair! Like! Hiccup! Hiccup! Remember!?! He was always tipping the drink over her!'

Kane laughed, resisting the temptation to correct his friend's confusion and instead simply said: 'Ah innocent childhood memories eh!'

'Well "innocent!" That's not a word often mentioned in the same breath as, hiccup! Martini Morris! Like! Now Mrs Martini Pace! Hiccup!'

Sadly Kane could not resist commenting: 'what you mean, anytime, anywhere, any *pace*!?!'

Ginge nodded, his face beaming. 'So I heard!' He winked again. Then he hiccupped loudly.

'Thank God!' Kane was referring to the arrival of the new can of Guinness. Both Sanjev and Ravi must have been on a break, for this new waiter just left the can on the table for Ginge to do the business. Maybe he had been put off any pretence at culture by the appalling state of the food on his customer's plate or perhaps he was overcome by a fear of catching the hiccups. Whatever, the waiter beat a hasty retreat back to the other side of the restaurant, where he immediately began busying himself, by once again readjusting the cutlery on the already laid tables.

When the ring was pulled and the gas had hissed, Ginge quickly refreshed his glass and gulped a mouthful before the drink was settled. So it was no surprise that when he started to tell his tale again, the words were punctuated by even more hiccups. As intrigued as he was, to find out all the hearsay about the current Mrs Pace, whom Ginge was trying to tell him had left school and Aberfoist early to be a model in London, "if you know what I mean! Like!" Kane felt obliged to stop the story in a last ditch attempt to cure his friend's unpleasant hiccupping.

Keeping eye contact, Kane began to slowly talk his friend through an ancient method that he himself used, whenever he needed to calm things down.

'Open up the palm of your hand. Yes any hand! Now stare at the flat palm. Breathe in, deeply, through your nose only. Put your tongue on the roof of your mouth and keep that airway closed. Fill up your stomach with the air breathed in through your nose. That's right! Push your stomach out. Hold it. Now squeeze your guts in to push the air out through your mouth not your nose. Do it slowly, again! Perhaps at least six times! Go on! In through the nose, fill your stomach, then out through you mouth. Ahh! That's right! Six times! You can close your eyes to concentrate if you like. Come on! You can do it!'

Kane watched his friend struggle for a few minutes. The hiccups did disrupt the technique during the first two attempts. However, eventually, Ginge got it and after perhaps a dozen more cycles, he had regulated his breathing and could talk without hiccupping, if not punctuating every other phrase with the word "Like!"

'Bloody 'ell!' Ginge exclaimed. 'That's a neat trick! Like!'

Nodding in modest agreement, Kane asked Ginge if the palm of his hand was warm.

'Too right!' Ginge acknowledged, staring down at the upturned palm of his hand.

'That's your chi energy!' Kane confirmed.

'You're what?'

'Chi! It's what the Chinese call your life force energy.'

'Fuck off!' Was the unsurprising reaction from Ginge. 'You always were into that Chinese mystical shit, like, weren't you!?!'

'It works!' Kane shrugged.

'Well it's sorted my hiccups! I'll give you that! Bugger me! Chi energy eh! Now where was I?'

Kane shook his head and quickly lent forward to whisper a warning to Ginge. From his seat, with his back to the wall, he could see the whole restaurant and more importantly, he could see the front door. It had opened and the two women were coming back in. As usual, Ginge ignored the warning and carried on talking. 'All I was going to say was she went off to London "modelling" and the next thing we knew she was back! Like! And married to Flick-er-Ell! I mean! The word was they met at a business event in the City, he was buying and she was selling!' Ginge winked again. 'And it was "love" at first payment! Like!' He added sarcastically. 'All a bit of a whirlwind romance, well according to her Nan. Like! Ouch!' Kane had managed to kick

279

Ginge in the shin, under the table.

'Hello Mr Thompson, I thought it was you!' Martini Pace was now standing directly behind Ginge, so close that when, in his inebriated state, he spun around to see who it was, he almost put his face into her breasts, for despite her high heeled shoes, Kane could see now, close up, that she was not very tall at all. Martini ignored the nearly comic collision, in very much the same way that she had pretended not to hear the conversation about her that Ginge was previous broadcasting out whilst she had approached them. Of course, she loved the fact that they were talking about her! And unknown to Kane, Martini had had her orders, so she could not afford to be offended.

'My Nan will want to know what brings you out, so smartly dressed, this early on a Friday.' It may have been the alcohol but Kane could not help reflect on how weird her voice seemed. She talked like an over excited school girl, gushing, trying to be sexy, putting on an occasionally husky tone in an accent that was at times nasal London and others deep throaty Aberfoist. Whilst she spoke, Martini Pace stared directly at Mykee Kane. She was all big eyes and each pause was accompanied by a put on, grotesquely unnatural, *trout-pout* of her lips. The statuesque blonde stood beside her merely giggled. Kane could see that her hazel eyes were unfocused as she leaned in, unsteadily against her shorter friend, seemingly for support. This casual posture seemed at odds with her strong impressive physique and comparative maturity. Kane noticed, once again, the silver Vape pipe clutched in her hand. He remembered his recent evening at The Coliseum. She looked, and he concluded probably was, higher than a kite. He also could not help but notice that the blonde's blouse buttons were almost all undone, seemingly right down to just below her belly button. She was almost giving him an eyeful in a very different way to the young Mrs Pace.

280

Not surprisingly Kane was totally distracted by the attractive women in front of him, and whilst he may have heard what Ginge was saying to them, the words certainly did not register with him, until alerted by Ginge's suddenly sad face, he heard Martini Pace's dismissive coo of "that's sad!" Before realising that she had gone on to ask Ginge who his "cute friend" was!?! Kane had been called a lot of things recently but never cute! Not even by his loving wife!

'This ladies, is the legend that is My-key Kane!' Ginge was proudly announcing. His sad expression was gone in an instant.

'Mickey?' The blonde giggled.

'No! My – Key! Ginge insisted. 'Believe it or not he was in school, like, with me and your husband. Mrs Pace!'

'Ohh! He doesn't look old enough!' She lied, obviously. 'And what do you do 'May-Key?' Martini asked Kane directly.

He felt his cheeks redden slightly and his heart sink. Telling people that he was a teacher never ended well. If you were lucky it produced admiration, if not contempt. Whatever reaction was short lived, before people inevitably drew on their own experience of being in school, and volunteered soul destroying advice on what was wrong with education these days!

Luckily Ginge spared his blushes. Well, at least some of them, by quickly proclaiming: 'He's a clever bastard this one! He's a teacher now! Aren't you! But when I knew him, like, back in the day, he was a right boyo! Like!' Ginge grinned up at the women.

'Oh I bet he could teach us a thing or two! Don't you Kim!?!' Martini teased.

In response, Kim giggled again and fluttered her false eye lashes at Kane. Unfortunately the effort unbalanced her and she stumbled into Ginge, so that her blouse opened wider and her firm breasts provided a pillow for the back of Ginge's close shaved head.

'Sorry my lovely!' Kim said softening her deep valleys' accent before both girls fell into a fit of giggles.

'Phew! My pleasure! Like! Entirely! Like!' Ginge attempted to humorously answer, smirking across at Kane, allowing his eyes to almost pop out his jolly face.

In the corner of his own eye Kane noticed one of the two track-suited lads rocking with laughter. The other was shaking his head and looked embarrassed. A dark shadow then appeared just beyond the gap in the screen.

'What's going on here then?' A familiar sounding voice boomed out in a forced mock serious tone! Kane turned to see Ellis "Flicker" Pace emerging from the back room. He tried not to frown but failed. It was now Ginge's turn to blush. Suddenly he sounded all sheepish as he said in an uncharacteristically quiet tone: 'Oh! Hello Ell!'

'Well, well, well! Mr Thompson! I do declare! You are moving up in the world! Mixing with all the best people I see eh!' Then, once again, in less than a fortnight, Pace greeted his old school friend with what appeared, this time, to be genuine glee. 'Mr Kane! How nice to see you again so soon! I do hope you are not going to start smashing up the furniture or breaking anybody's hand in this establishment!?!'

Kane studied the man stood in front of him. Pace had his hands palm up in a mock plea, as if begging for restraint. Although labels and motif's meant little to Kane these days, he still recognised that the clothes worn by his old school friend were not the cheap supermarket brands that could be found in his own wardrobe. They were also certainly not market stall copies, like the counterfeit ones that he and his mates would have worn back in their youth, when smart casual was the in-thing. So Kane concluded there was something genuinely upmarket about the new Flicker, if only in the way he dressed. Then Kane noticed the huge, rather expensive looking watch, which was strapped to Pace's left wrist. It sparkled each time it caught a beam from one of the restaurant's many spot lights, adding a real razzle dazzle to the unnecessarily over the top hand gestures Pace was now making to illustrate his sarcasm. The fact that the real diamonds set in a watch-face were probably worth more than Kane earned in a year certainly irritated Kane, a lot more than Pace's ostentation. Turning his head slightly, Kane looked at Martini Pace. She also wore diamonds but her bright eyes glistened more than the flashy gems around her neck. Her clothes, what little she had on, were also expensively cut. Kane recognised that this girl was far too high maintenance for your average "honest" local businessman.

'Let me guess! You handle the security for this place as well as "The Kettle" or should I be actually thanking you for cooking this truly excellent meal!?!' Kane kept eye contact with Martini whilst he spoke. 'I remember you were always a keen cook! Weren't you Flicker!?! Although I also remember you like things well done, almost burnt eh!'

Martini's eyes had widened. She had seemed surprised at first, and then they almost burst out of their sockets as she made sense of Kane's rant. Momentarily horrified they suddenly darted away from Kane's, as if to check out her husband's reaction, but on seeing Pace dumbfounded, her gaze quickly returned back to Kane, who winked confidently at her as he added: 'Anyway, I think, if you remember rightly, Flicker it was your guys who were responsible for all the damage done down "The Kettle!". I hope you docked their wages!?!'

Martini's eyes narrowed as she studied the man sat still seemingly relaxed beside her. Then they beamed brightly at him once again and her red lips parted in a half gasp, half giggle, before widening into a broad smile. Kane guessed that she was not used to hearing people challenge her husband in such a confident tone, but she had obviously liked it.

Pace's checks burnt red. This was not how he had imagined things going. Although it only lasted for a few seconds, it seemed as if the room had lapsed into a long and awkward silence, which was only broken when Ginge nervously and extremely loudly, began to hiccup again. Kane glanced back at his friend, and noticed his face was suddenly worryingly pale.

'Ginge, try a glass of water now!' Kane suggested. Then turning back to Ellis Pace he continued to maintain the initiative by saying: 'I expected to see you at Frank's funeral today! What with you being old school mates and business associates, etc.'

'Was that today?' Pace finally said softly, after what could have been a very telling pause, and then unable to resist the bait, Pace snapped in a less controlled and slightly harsher tone: 'We were never business associates!'

'Oh you didn't do security for "The Kettle" then?'

'No! Frank reckoned he didn't need it!' Pace let slip.

'No short-term loans for an old mate either!' Kane quickly added.

'Certainly not!' Pace retorted, once again perhaps rather too quickly. 'Old Frankie was known to be a bad risk! Who said, I lent him money?' The tone had grown cold and Pace looked directly at Ginge Thompson, who began wildly shaking his head in a silent but obviously vigorous denial.

'Oh I just wondered myself, you know, because it's just the sort of thing a successful businessman might do! You know, helping out an old mate!' Kane kept his tone light.

'My-key! Didn't I tell you last time? Frank really didn't like me! I'd 'ave been the last person he turned to!'

'Oh! And why is that?'

Pace thought for a moment. This really was not the way he had seen things play out. That was the problem with people like Mykee Kane and Frank John! They always did things their way and that always made things so awkward! So unnecessary! Pace sighed and then he shrugged.

'We fell out over his daughter! Didn't we babe!' Pace looked at his wife, who in turn looked confused. Perhaps not as confused as the blonde, she was now half leaning on the shorter woman and half resting her hands on Ginge's shoulder for support, whilst blinking her eyes, as she wondered in her dizzy state, what on earth was going on!

'Remember Jan John!?! Babe!' Pace hinted heavily at Martini.

'No' was the flat reply.

'Well that was the problem! Really! She wanted to be a model! We tried her out but she just wasn't memorable enough! And Frankie boy got all resentful about it!' Pace concluded, all very pleased with his pocket summary of a lost dream and a failed modelling career.

Kane had been studying Pace as he spoke. Now Kane allowed his eyes to narrow, intentionally displaying his contempt and disbelief at Pace's story. Kane knew that Frank had his faults but Frank was never one not to be grateful if anybody had tried to do him a favour.

'Talking about Frank!' Kane started again. 'Your boys found him, yes!'

'Yes!?!'

'They must've called you in pretty quick! Yes!'

'Yes!'

'Well what exactly happened?' Kane asked belligerently.

'Look I don't want to talk about it now.' Pace suddenly sounded all defensive.

'Why?'

'Because there are ladies present!' Pace gestured almost apologetically towards the two women. 'And it's just not nice, especially given that you just said it was his funeral today! I mean, I don't want to speak ill of the dead but he killed himself My-key!'

285

Both Martini and Kim were intrigued by the way the conversation was going, in spite of the fact that the men were suddenly ignoring their charms. Martini was particularly enjoying watching her husband flustered. She, like Kane, had noticed that he had lost his polished, confident tone of voice and that he was starting to let his accent slip back into pure adolescent Aberfoist! Her mind was racing, perhaps it was the drugs or the wine she had been drinking earlier but she kept looking at Kane. She had begun to wonder if he was the opportunity she had been waiting for. She looked back at her husband. His upper lip was wet. His grey blue eyes seemed to be shrinking behind the thick glass lenses of his spectacles. She had not seen him this upset in a long time.

Then Dylan Francis burst through the restaurant's front door. Ellis Pace's pink tongue slipped out of the corner of his mouth and its tip completed a slow clockwise rotation, licking his lips, before disappearing as he broke into a thin smile.

Chapter 30: Bitter Banter

Dylan Francis had not anticipated a crowd. He suddenly froze on entering the restaurant and simply stood still, staring across at the people who were gathered around his intended victim. A victim who looked much bigger and bolder than Francis remembered. In that moment Francis questioned his plan of attack. The one, in which he just strolled confidently into the restaurant, poked the fat guy in the back, abused him, and challenged him to come outside. In truth he had been nervous about having to confront Kane alone. He rarely acted without Tall Dai being right there beside him. If the bigger man was not actually holding their victim down, his oafish presence was usually distracting them or even terrifying them into inaction. This always gave Francis the advantage. However, this time Francis had left the big man outside, as instructed by Pace, and the half bottle of whisky, which he had swigged down in the car on the way to the restaurant, was not nearly strong enough to anesthetise his fears.

"Do you remember me? You fat bastard!" That was Francis's intended opening line. Although in reality his theatrical entrance really demanded rather more dramatic dialogue, and the staging now seemed very different to the set anticipated in the little man's mind's eye, what with Kane sat comfortably facing him, his back protected by the restaurant wall. Unfortunately Francis had never been great at improvisation, so he spat out the rehearsed words; their hostility weakened somewhat by an inevitable nervous stutter.

The reaction they provoked was also not anticipated. It was clearly obvious that Kane remembered him from the look on his face, but it was not the look of fear that Francis had expected. Kane simply stared straight back at Francis with an amused smile. Then the "fat bastard" spoke, in a deep confident voice, which reminded Francis of almost every sarcastic teacher he had ever had during his limited schooling.

'Well! Hello!?! It's the very man!' Kane announced calmly to the room. 'Dull-one! Isn't it?' Kane continued with a wicked glint in his eyes. 'Why don't you tell us all about that night you found my friend's body? What exactly happened?'

The little man had certainly not expected that challenge. He was beginning to wonder if the script had been changed since his recent solo, post phone call, mental rehearsal, and he allowed his eyes to drift towards Pace, seeking further direction or encouragement. His boss said nothing. The cold eyes just stared back, widening slightly, their irritation magnified by the lenses of the almost comically oversized spectacles. The two well dressed women, who had had their backs to Francis, now turned to look at him. They had been laughing and their faces remained cheery as they focused on him. He blushed slightly. He was never confident with women, especially attractive ones. The little man recognised the beautiful one immediately as Mrs Pace and averted his eyes. However, the other lady, the older one, a fit looking blonde, he did not know but he instantly wanted to!

Dylan Francis had a thing for older women. He began ogling her like a child in a sweet shop, unable to take his eyes off her even in these circumstances, but then the drink always affected him like that, and the whiskey made her firm dark tanned torso, which was clearly visible through the gaping blouse, an obvious distraction. She kind of reminded him of someone he knew. There really was something familiar about her. Then Francis remembered with a shock. She had to be about the same age and she certainly had the same hair colouring. Perhaps that was it. But this woman was gorgeous by comparison. Not as gorgeous

288

as Martini Pace but wow! Or so his simple mind thought. Yes! Francis liked a bit of rough but only if he had power over them. That other old blonde had needed him. She was an addict and as such she had been a good customer to him. One who was more than willing, and able, to satisfy Francis' needs in exchange for what she thought was discount on the drugs he sold her. That was why Francis had been so cross to find her with Bernard *bloody* Russell. Too cross. He knew he had lost it! Pace had warned him about it, but Francis did not care, he had enjoyed hurting her. She deserved it for betraying him. Yet seeing her burnt body, afterwards, had sickened him. These brief memory flashes confused him. Yet he quickly reassured himself that bad things always happen to people who cross him, and what happened to that old dog of a junkie was nothing compared to what he was going to do to this fat bastard in front of him today! Of course, Francis conveniently forgot that he actually did very little. Then all of a sudden, he realised that everyone was staring at him. Waiting for him to do something, or at least speak.

'Don't ask Flicker! He wasn't there! Or was he?' Kane spoke quickly, allowing an angry sneer to appear on his face as he sought to put more pressure on the seemingly dumbstruck interloper, who still appeared to be looking to Pace as if for some further instruction.

'It, it was the fire ...' Francis began muttering, remembering what he had been asked and picturing the burnt bodies inside the gutted New Town terrace once again. His words were said almost in a whisper. Yet because of the hushed anticipation in the room, they were loud enough for all those around Kane's table to hear. For a moment Kane did not understand.

'What did you say?' He asked.

'When you mess with us you get burned!' Francis snarled back at him.

Kane immediately noted the use of the words "us" and

"burned" but Francis did not realise his mistake and was only slightly confused by the sudden fury in Pace's eyes. Again the angry reaction was clearly magnified by Pace's bottle-bottom-like lenses, so that Kane also noticed the look, and he realised instantly that the "dull-one" had thought Kane was asking about finding Bernard Russell. Kane also saw the quizzical look that was beginning to appear on Martini Pace's face. It was a look that she was attempting to share with her husband.

'Good God!' Kane exclaimed before punching the next question home as he attempted to seize the initiative. 'How many bodies do your guys find working for Aber Security Services then Flicker?' Kane allowed himself another amused smile as he saw Pace struggling to contain his obvious rage at the repeated use of his childhood nickname in the present company. Pace started to say something in an indistinct growl. Kane thought it might have been along the lines of "I've told you before nobody calls me *that* anymore!" But Kane was not concentrating on Pace. Kane had turned his attention back to the little man, who whilst still standing by the front door, appeared to be taking short deep breaths, as if pumping himself up and readying for action.

'I'm talking about you finding my friend at The Copper Kettle! Dull-one! Now tell me what happened there!'

Francis heard the question as he inhaled. He did not like the tone or the subject. He felt a fool. He was being belittled again in front of his boss, his boss's wife and the sexy blonde tart! Everyone in the restaurant now seemed to be looking at him that is apart from the old guy sat by Kane. Even with his back to him, Francis recognised the old man as Ginger Thompson. He knew Ginge was a harmless prat! A two faced coward, who had once had a reputation for being a bit of a rogue about town, and the fact that Kane was with someone like Ginge gave Francis a misguided confidence boost. Ginge had not turned around. He was nervously studying his half empty plate, genuinely concerned

290

that it was going cold on the table in front of him but also more than a little fearful of the deteriorating atmosphere around him. If he had been an ostrich, Ginge would have buried his head in the remains of his curry and convinced himself that nothing bad would happen. He wasn't, so instead he began imagining his wife's voice, scolding him that there was no such thing as a free lunch! Indeed, Ginge was more than a little worried that he was going to pay for accepting his old friend's hospitality. And that payment would be made to Ellis "Flicker" Pace and it was going to be an unpleasant experience.

The hesitant body language of Kane's friend and the very mention of The Copper Kettle triggered the irrational anger building up within Francis. He felt the weight of the plaster cast on his broken hand and this managed to get him back on script. He stepped forward, waving his plastered hand in the air! 'Look at what u made me do! U fat baa-stard! I'd like to string u up! Jus like that twat of a mate of yours! Ha! U should of seen him! Dangling there, trousers wet through, with his own fucking mess! He thought he was a big man too! Just like u! But he was past it! Just like u! U fat fuck! I'm gonna break yer arms and yer legs! Yer fat baa-stard!'

'Whoa! No you're not Francis!' According to the script those words or something similar should have come from Ellis Pace. However, the deep voice that rang out from the back of the room had a hint of Irish about it. In spite of the apparent frenzy released by the alcohol and those competing bitter memory flashes, burning through Francis's sub conscious, the unexpected but familiar voice had the intended effect of freezing the little man in his tracks. He was no more than half way towards Kane's table.

The voice also had the unexpected effect of startling Kane. He tried not to show any sign of recognition on his face but the amused smile had vanished. Kane had not been expecting to see

Calamity again. The surprise was worse because Kane realised that Calamity had been dining with Ellis Pace, and that get together had sounded exceedingly friendly. Kane now took a closer look at the other men in Pace's party, who were now standing around the gap in the restaurant's partition screen. They were watching on in a mixture of bemused curiosity. Kane immediately recognised the large figure of Mr. Lord. Even though the previously gaudy green wearing motorcyclist was now dressed in smarter if perhaps still surprisingly casual clothes for what Kane had assumed was a business lunch. The big man had an amused smirk on his face. He was flanked by the two men in tracksuits. Kane had not noticed them get up from their table, which worried him slightly. For big men they must have moved quickly and quietly. He also realised that those two were not, as he had originally assumed, restaurant staff. They obviously worked for Lord. Calamity's face remained fixed in a serious frown.

Francis had immediately recognised the voice. He knew Detective Sergeant O' Neil and what he knew was that O' Neil was not a man to cross. Over the past three months, since being posted into the area, the policeman's London connections had proved useful to Ellis Pace, which was a relief to Francis but the bent copper had always made the little man nervous. Francis also spotted another familiar face in the crowd gathering behind O' Neil. The younger police officer, DC Haymer, was easier to get along with. Francis had found him a lot more appreciative of the bribes he had handed over on behalf of his boss. Behind the corrupt law men stood the "big Paki" whom Francis knew was Mr Pace's new VIP client, Mr. Lord. Behind Lord was the accountant Kahn. Kahn looked the most worried man in the room. He was even more nervous than Ginger Thompson. Then there were the other two, the professional body builders, who were squeezed into their grey tracksuits. They were on their feet but they did not look worried. Francis had never spoken to them but he knew that they were Lord's minders and to a small man like him they looked like serious trouble. Pace had told him that if they were with Lord they would be really useful, so Francis had given them a wide berth.

'What in hell do you think you're playing at Dill!?!' Pace suddenly took the initiative back. He started forward as if to intercept his man. 'You're a bloody idiot! I've told you before!' Pace sounded exasperated. Given the growing audience and the unexpected police presence, Francis really hoped that they were back on script. Turning his head slightly to look at his boss, Francis could see that both the "IN" and "OUT" kitchen doors were open behind Pace, and a number of concerned restaurant staff were huddled together, heads bobbing about, trying to see what was actually going on.

'This man is an old friend of mine!' Pace continued, turning slightly, and shrugging apologetically at Kane. Pace also took the opportunity to glance reassuringly towards his guests, and rolling his eyes he added: 'Please go back to the table. I'll deal with this!' He nodded reassuringly to them, before turning back around, and quickly moving forward the short distance required to block Francis' path to Kane, muttering profusely as he went: 'I really don't know what gets into you! You're embarrassing me! Have you been drinking?' Pace made sure his calming voice was loud enough for all to hear. On reaching his man, he could smell the whisky on his breath. He glared at Francis for a second and then remembering his audience, lightened up!

'Come on; go home, we'll talk about this tomorrow! Did you come for a takeaway? I'll get one sent over! Go on! Get out now before you make things worse for yourself!'

Francis stood his ground and just looked at Kane. For a moment Pace wondered if his man had forgotten his role in this little play. The red glow on Francis's face reflected a real method actor or more likely a man who had almost lost the plot. Francis had not expected so many witnesses when he had agreed to play the part of a fool and in playing to the audience he had gotten himself really worked up. The alcohol had helped him give what he now hoped had been a realistic performance and he was more than a little confused, feeling a mixture of irritation and relief. He badly wanted to hurt Kane. He wanted to show the watchers, especially that blonde tart that he really was the wild and dangerous man Pace had suggested he was on the phone. Unearthing his half buried resentment that his own pet blonde had gone off with a man like Russell, a man who had openly laughed at him because of Kane, had truly unhinged him. Then slowly Francis remembered that this was only the first act. Kane was going to be his anyway. Yes! Francis told himself, he was going to get the drop on the "fat fuck" soon enough and Tall Dai would be there to back him up. Francis confidently believed they would all hear about what he did to people who crossed him. Kane, who was watching everyone intently, noticed the sly glances that Francis was giving everyone in the room, as the little man eventually began to talk to Pace in a surprisingly cowed tone.

'Sorry Mr Pace!' Francis said. His insincerity was obvious in spite of the attempted conciliatory tone of voice. The little man was not a good actor and he allowed himself to be ushered out a little too quickly for so recent a mad dog. When Pace finally closed the door behind Francis, the staff members gave an audible sigh of relief and quickly sought the safety of the kitchen. Kane kept one eye on the front door and his other on Pace. Even though he had smelt the ham, Kane thought that old Flicker was actually looking genuinely sheepish as he slowly made his way back towards them; but then he knew Pace of old and never trusted him.

294

'What the ... was that all about?' Martini Pace started to ask her husband. Pace shrugged and was about to say something, when both he and Kane were distracted by DS "Calamity" O' Neil.

'That is a first class question Mrs Pace.' The deep voice with the hint of Irish in it boomed out, as the policeman approached Kane's table.

Chapter 31: No Such Thing as a Free Lunch

Opening out his wallet, Calamity showed Kane his police identity card, then putting on his most serious and official "PC Plod" accent said: 'Excuse me Sir! I am a policeman and wondered if you,' he emphasised the "you" in what he thought was his best Plod, 'have any idea what that was about?'

Before Kane could answer the restaurant's front door opened. All heads turned nervously in its direction and all breathed a collective sigh of relief when they saw that it was not Dylan Francis returning but instead a smartly dressed young man. Even so there was something unsettlingly familiar to Kane about the young man who strode in. However, he could not place him and so quickly turned his attention back to Calamity, who was still holding out his wallet.

Kane made a big show of looking at the identity card. It was displayed behind a clear see-through plastic window in the worn black leather wallet. Then looking up directly at Calamity, Kane performed an inquisitive face check against the picture in the wallet, before speaking in what he hoped did not sound too sarcastic a tone.

'No! I have no idea why that man acted like that officer!?! Maybe he was drunk!?!' Somehow Kane managed to avoid smirking after saying that last word. If anyone was drunk that evening it had to be him, given the amount of Guinness he had already consumed. A waiter swerved passed them and rushed towards the potential new customer, who not surprisingly had stopped nervously hesitating by the door, after all heads had turned to him as if he had stepped into a Wild West saloon and not Aberfoist's finest curry house.

'Alright Sandi?' The young man called out cheerfully. 'I've come for me takeaway! I rang about twenty minutes ago! Okay?'

Kane heard the waiter giggle with what must have been the relief of resuming to normal business and then chirp: 'Ah yes!' Sanjev added courteously: 'Follow me!' From the corner of his eye Kane watched as the waiter led his new customer up the far side of the room to a table at the back of the restaurant and ushered him to sit down at a two seater table quite close to the one that had been occupied by the two track-suited men. Sanjev then disappeared through the "In" door, presumably to fetch the ordered meal. Kane then gave Calamity his full attention.

'But you were talking to him like you knew him? Asking him questions about something or other?' Calamity allowed his voice to sound irritated. 'Didn't I hear you mention bodies?'

'Oh no! Why ever should I?' Kane knew his voice was now sounding sarcastic, which was not particularly helpful given his promise to protect his former comrade in arms' cover earlier in the day. Although, he himself had already been playing a sarcastic git from the moment Pace had approached his table so he hoped nobody would notice. 'You must have misheard the banter I was having with our mutual friend Flick-er, Ellis!' Kane now tried harder to sound innocent and sincere. He had decided to calm things down. Well at least try to! He had actually heard all he needed to, for now, and until he had a chance to speak directly with "Flicker" Pace on their own, there really was not any point in provoking the situation further. Indeed from the look on Calamity's face, Kane suspected that he might be in danger of being arrested by his former soldier, whom Kane felt was probably trying just a little bit too hard to avoid having his cover blown, and should not have got involved at all. Then again, if he was pretending to be a policeman, maybe Calamity was doing

297

exactly what policemen were meant to do; keeping the peace!

'Isn't that right, Ellis?' Kane gestured towards Pace, who was now standing silently with his obviously confused but gorgeous looking wife beside Kane's table, apparently listening carefully to the police enquiries.

'Um, yes, that's right John Joe!' Pace began cautiously using the informality of Calamity's real Christian names. 'Just a bit of banter that got out of hand! I don't think Dull-One was in on the joke' Pace confirmed uncertainly gesturing with a backward nod of his head towards the front door, before running his tongue, once again, nervously across his top lip. 'Look!' Pace raised his voice as he began to address everyone still standing around. 'Come on let's all go back to our table and have another drink on me. There's absolutely no need to involve the police in this nonsense, eh My-key!'

'Yes, I totally agree Ellis!' Kane stared coldly back at Pace. 'Maybe we can have a chat on our own later, eh!'

'Yes, splendid idea!' Pace nodded enthusiastically, sounding more like the *pucker* businessman he pretended to be. 'Come on everybody!' Pace turned from Kane's table and began walking away, gesturing with his hands as he went, in an effort to usher everyone in his party back through the gap in the partition.

Just through the gap, Kane spotted an elderly white haired Indian, nervously playing with his large but elegant moustache. The gentleman was dressed immaculately in a formal white dinner jacket and white bow tie. Looking like someone from a bygone era, he began politely helping Pace's guests take their seats, whilst sharply calling the individuals drinks orders to a nearby waiter. Kane thought that the gentleman must be the owner of The Himalayas Indian Restaurant. He even looked like a much older version of the waiter who had taken Ginge's order. This gave Kane the idea that "The Himalayas" must be a proper family business. However, Kane could also see that the presumed

298

owner's face lapsed into a weary and troubled look every time a guest looked away. When Pace reached him, the gentleman allowed an over familiar arm to be wrapped around his shoulder. Pace then appeared to whisper something, possibly words of encouragement, into the owner's ear. The old man smiled but to Kane, even at that distance the eyes did not seem truly pleased by whatever Pace had said. Nevertheless, the restaurateur nodded in obvious agreement, turned and still smiling bravely, he rushed over towards Kane's table.

'I am so sorry for the disturbance!' He began on reaching the table. Ginge still kept his head down. Kane had noticed how his normally merry friend had remained uncharacteristically quiet throughout the whole "Francis" incident. 'Mr Pace is most insistent that he ...' the smartly dressed owner paused, as if he was trying to find the right words, and then almost in a sigh he said: 'pay your bill.' He quickly added as if he needed to justify this statement: 'Er, by way of apology, Sirs!'

Ginge's head darted up, suddenly all smiles. 'Result!' He crowed towards Kane. Then all of a sudden his complexion darkened, as if he was actually embarrassed by his over eager response before adding: 'Well that's very, like, generous of him! Isn't it My-key?' Ginge even glanced bravely towards the back of the room and waving both hands, tried to catch Pace's attention before mouthing his thanks the moment Pace looked up. Pace kept looking, silently waiting for Kane's acknowledgement. Kane only frowned. Ignoring Pace, Kane looked the owner in the eye.

'Please tell Mr Pace that there is no need. This is my treat not his!' The owner visibly twitched and ran his right hand over his thick white moustache.

'Please Sir! Accept this offer for me as I really do not want anymore trouble this evening.'

'Trouble!?!' Kane asked feigning confusion. Then looking at the owner's weary face, he thought better of his refusal. If he wanted Pace on his own, perhaps he had best play along.

'Okay, if that makes you happy, you may tell Mr Pace we accept his kind offer!' Kane announced. Ginge let out a loud sigh of relief, followed by an immediate request for more Guinness. Kane looked down at the remains of the meal on his plate and shook his head slowly. 'Not for me! Thank you! But I would like some water, ta!'

'Thank you Sir!' The owner or manager, whoever he was, said very pointedly to Kane, before turning back to attend to the larger party. On his way he intercepted one of his waiters and quickly conveyed the additional order for drinks.

As soon as he had moved away, Ginge had smiled slyly at Kane. 'I forgot how dramatic like, things can be around you! My-Key! Are you going to use that knife or what?' Ginge asked nodding towards Kane's right had, which had slipped down, and out of sight, below the table. Kane grinned back at Ginge. Slowly raising his hand and letting the unused and surprisingly clean, stainless steel table knife slide out from beneath his shirt cuff.

'Old habits die hard!' Kane said whilst watching the two track-suited men lumber back to their table. They took a brief interest in the new arrival, the smartly dressed young man, who was still sat waiting for his takeaway on a nearby table but they soon returned to the fascination of the glowing screens of their smart phones. Kane began to study the young man carefully whilst pretending to listen to a reanimated Ginge, who was prattling on about Ellis Pace being actually quite a tidy bloke, being as he was "like, paying for their food!" Kane suspected from the sad expression on the restaurant owners face that Pace did not pay for anything in The Himalayas Indian Restaurant. At best the restaurateur managed to offset such expenses against the money Pace probably demanded for his security firm "protecting" the premises.

Kane was also noticing that the young customer's eyes went

everywhere, exploring the restaurant, whilst he waited for his takeaway meal. They briefly made contact with Kane's and both men had indulged in a bit of an awkward, blank faced stare off, with both not acknowledging the other but refusing to look away, until after what seemed like ages, the younger man had nodded in recognition. It had been almost as if he was trying hard to remember where he had seen Kane before. Kane, himself, was intrigued at the arrogance of the young man, for he seemed unperturbed about trying to stare out an older man. Oddly the youngster seemed to possess a casual, could not care less attitude to being stared back at, rather different to the usual, often aggressive, response by local young men to a stranger's stare. Then Kane realised where he had seen him before. He was the gravedigger's scruffy apprentice.

'That Dylan Francis really doesn't know you like I know you!' Ginge allowed himself a small, slightly nervous laugh.

'Let's hope he never finds out eh!' Kane winked back at his friend.

'For his sake, like, and not yours!' Ginge replied as he began to flick his fork through the little pile of food that remained on his plate. 'Damn shame those girls put me right off my grub! But they were hot stuff eh!'

'Spicier than my curry!' Kane acknowledged with a smile.

'Yeah and likely to cause more, like, trouble the next day if you know what I mean!' Ginge laughed, a little bit more confidently. He was relaxing. Things were going to be okay now or so he told himself.

The waiter arrived carrying a jug of water, a can of Guinness and two clean glasses, all neatly arranged on his silver tray. Then the restaurant's front door opened. All three men's heads turned nervously in its direction and all three were relieved to see that it was not Dylan Francis returning to the restaurant but new customers were arriving, a middle aged man with a

301

much younger woman. They were smartly dressed and looked as if they had come straight from work. Ginge turned and stared. He chuckled and then turned back to face Kane.

'Well, I can tell you for nothing, like, that's not his wife!' Ginge winked at Kane.

'Nor his daughter either!' Kane suggested.

'Some people have all the luck, like, eh!' Ginge sighed, before he began reminiscing about the two gorgeous women once again. They had obviously brightened up his evening, before all that unpleasantness. Ginge even seemed to think that they fancied him! Somehow Kane was not surprised by his friend's delusion. Same old Ginge! He thought glancing back over towards where the surprising smart young gravedigger was patiently sitting, still waiting for his food. Kane noticed that the young man now seemed to be performing a similar staring routine with some unseen person hidden from Kane view behind the partition. That particular stare-off ended suddenly, when the young man gestured with a backward nod of the head, seeming to invite his unseen staring rival to come and join him. A few moments later, Ellis Pace casually wandered through the gap in the partition, a glass of white wine in his hand.

Pace jovially sat down at the gravedigger's table. His back was to Kane but Kane could tell that Pace appeared to be listening intently to what the young man was saying. Annoyingly, the back of Pace's head blocked out the younger man's face, so much so that Kane could not even tell the mood of the conversation, let alone lip read. The only movement Kane could see was Pace constantly sipping his drink, so that when Sanjev arrived with the carrier bag full of cartons, Pace made another dramatic gesture, with his hands, which seemed to indicate that he would pay for the meal. Kane did see the young man casually put his money away. Sanjev did not smile at this generosity and actually disappeared behind the partition and returned a few

302

moments later with the now very weary looking owner, who nodded his seemingly reluctant approval of the extra transaction being added to Pace's account.

The gravedigger made a big show of thanking Pace and took his time to firmly shake all three men's hands. He then got up and was led to the front door by Sanjev. On passing Kane, he graced him with another brief overly familiar nod. Kane could have sworn the man was smirking. At the door Sanjev held it open and then seemed to watch after his customer for an unnaturally long time, before closing the door firmly and rushing back to the table, where Pace and the owner were engaged in a long conversation. Kane could not see Pace's face but from the look on the owner's face, they were not sharing a joke. The owner's countenance worsened once Sanjev arrived back, and relayed what seemed to be devastating news. Kane interrupted Ginge's rambling nonsense by saying: 'Something's up!' His friend suddenly fell quiet and started to glance nervously around as Kane watched the owner and Sanjev quickly disappear into the kitchen. Pace took his time to finish his drink and then slowly got up, leaving the glass on the table, he stiffly moved back behind the partition.

Kane carried on watching. Trying hard to hear what was being said. A few seconds later a hush fell amongst the party at the back of the restaurant. A low voice, a man's, probably Pace, was speaking to them. Kane strained his ears again, trying to understand but to no avail. He could only make out a muffled chorus of voices sounding off following Pace's address, as if the group were discussing something of vital importance. The owner reappeared from his kitchen and joined the party out back.

'Well Ginge! I wonder what's spoilt the party.' Kane grinned across the table. His friend pulled a face, as if to say: "Don't be a clever dick!"

A woman's nervous laugh rose above the distant murmuring

303

and then a deeper man's voice said something and a woman's voice said loudly enough for Kane to hear: 'Well alright then!'

'Interesting!' Kane grinned mischievously again at Ginge, who began to pale. Lowering his eyes to the table once again, Ginge nudged his head to the left. 'It looks like we're going to find out what it's all about now!' He said quietly. Kane looked left and saw a procession heading towards them. It was led by Sergeant O' Neil and the restaurant owner. Mr and Mrs Pace were bringing up the rear. O' Neil was blushing. The owner was grim faced. Pace was trying to appear serious and all business like. He was let down badly by his wife. She was positively beaming.

When they arrived at Kane's table it was O' Neil who spoke first. 'Mr Kane, we have a bit of a problem.' Although the voice was formal, Kane could see the glow of a blush under the light brown cheeks and O' Neil's eyes were raging. Kane did not have to guess that this was the last thing the undercover agent had expected to be involved in tonight. Nevertheless, he kept his patience and proceeded to explain, all formal like, that Sanjev had informed them that Dylan Francis was still waiting outside. He apparently did not look happy.

Kane laughed. Ginge nervously shook his head. He was thinking that when all was said and done he had to live in Aberfoist. He knew that even if the legend that was Mykee Kane could see off the little thug, his association with Kane would mean trouble for Ginge in the future.

'That attitude isn't helpful Mr Kane!' O' Neil's eyes were almost pleading with Kane now. 'We all want to avoid trouble.' Beside him, the Indian Restaurant owner was nodding his head and vigorously pulling on his moustache in agreement.

'Mr Pace has suggested a solution to our, er, your immediate problem. Mrs Pace will take you out the back way and you could wait safely at his office whilst he and I sought out young Mr

304

Francis once and for all! I would be really grateful if you would do that! Mr. Kane!' O' Neil gave Kane the eyes again. 'Ellis tells me you both wanted to have a chat together about old times! After we've sorted this unnecessary nonsense out, perhaps you two can have that catch up over a coffee or even something stronger, back at Ellis' place eh!'

Kane smiled directly at Martini Pace. 'How could I refuse such a lovely escort? Thank you Ell-is. What a helpful suggestion. I was hoping we could have a quiet get together and reminisce about old times and mutual acquaintances!' Kane turned his head slightly and looked Pace directly in the eyes. They seemed to be smiling behind the reinforced magnifying glass.

'That would be great, wouldn't it?' Pace confirmed, breaking into his most charming smile. A smile that sent shivers down Kane's spine.

'But what about your other guests?' Kane asked affecting the sincerest concern.

'No, they were just about to go anyway. Mr Lord's PA is a little bit too merry and needs to have a rest.'

'Oh dear and your Missus isn't, er, too weary to look after me while your "sorting out" the Dull-one!?!' Kane could not help himself, having another dig at Francis but he did not intend to start Martini Pace off. Nonetheless, she laughed out loud as if he had said the wittiest put down about the little man.

'Come on, I'll show you my modelling studio, while we're waiting for Ell, you should like that!' She added, rather enticingly between girlish giggles.

Kane smiled politely and turned to Ginge. 'Well mate, it looks as if I'm in demand and I'd better be off eh! You gonna to be okay without me?'

Ginge actually looked uncertain. He turned his head slightly, braving a glance towards Ellis Pace. Pace blanked him and said nothing. However, the restaurant owner quickly spoke up.

305

'Mr Thompson is welcome to stay with us, whilst Sergeant O' Neil and Mr Pace resolve the, er, local difficulties, yes! Another beer yes Mr Thompson?'

Ginge put on a brave face. 'One of your whisky coffees may be better for me now!' He winked.

'Of course, Mr Thompson!' The owner forced a smile.

'Well I'll see you soon then!' Kane said, slowly getting to his feet. Ginge was not too sure about that and although he did not say it and his face did not show it, he hoped Kane, knew what he was getting himself into. Then again, Ginge thought this was "My-Key" he was worrying about and he knew the old My-Key could certainly take care of himself.

'Oh the back way, please!' The owner said quickly whilst gesturing towards the kitchens.

Kane smiled politely. 'Of course!' He then agreed.

Chapter 32: The Alley Shuffle

'This way!' Martini Pace grabbed Kane's hand and giggled. He felt a tingle of excitement at the touch of her warm hand. Her skin felt smooth and so soft against his, like the expensive kid leather gloves his mother once wore. Martini stretched her childlike fingers to reach between his and squeezed tight. Her grip was surprisingly strong for someone so petite. Suddenly Kane could smell her perfume. It smelt expensive and provided an exotic relief from the otherwise overwhelming aroma of curry, which was being pumped out into the yard ahead of them via a large ventilation grid, somewhere high up to their left or so he guessed based on the whirling noise of the industrial sized unit's extractor fan.

She tugged on his arm and he allowed her to lead him out of the brightly lit kitchen into the cool night air. Two steps into the restaurant's unevenly paved backyard and the heavy door slammed shut on its strong springs. It made an unsettlingly loud bang behind them and they were instantly plunged into darkness, just as if someone had flicked off a switch. The noise and the sudden darkness did not faze her and she continued to pull him blindly towards a slightly less dense space of blackness, which as his eyes quickly adjusted, Kane realised was a gap in the tall stone wall that bordered the alleyway. Beyond this boundary were other grim shadows. All menacingly cast by the terraced row of old grey stone buildings. They had been built so close to the restaurant's wall that they combined with the pitch black of the night sky above to create an illusion that they now were entering a tunnel.

Just as he began to see his way forward again, Kane was blinded as brilliant white burst down at him from a security light fixed high up on a wall ahead of them. It must have been triggered by a hidden sensor. Dazzled, Kane staggered forward and almost tripped as his toe connected with the raised edge of an uneven flagstone. Making the adjustment to regain his balance caused him to pull back slightly and lose contact with his bold guide, who on feeling his resistance had released her grip. He could still hear her stiletto heels clicking on without him, as their metal tips struck sharply against the stone floor. Squinting, Kane saw her blurred outline making strange darting movements along the pathway ahead. It was almost as if she was playing some children's game and avoiding the cracks in the pavement. Slowly he followed this weaving shape out of the shaft of blinding bright light and up the dimmer then dark lane that was meant to be their escape route. Back down the lane behind him, the security lighting switched off and all was dark again.

A dozen paces or so ahead the lane forked, twisting right into even deeper darkness or left into an inviting half light cast by some distant lamppost. Martini had stopped at this junction, her dark outline turning back to face him. Her pretty face leaned forward out of the shadows into the faint light. Then behind him, something or someone triggered the security lighting back on. The light made her eyes unnaturally glint back at him. They looked like a wild animal's, one that had suddenly been caught in the headlights of a car. They were alert, as if excited by an approaching danger. Kane also noticed from her dark profile that her breathing had changed. She was almost panting and the outline of her prominent breasts were rising and falling, in and out of the half light. Her lips parted and she seemed to whisper something. He thought he heard: "come on" but he held back, aware that her face had assumed an ugly expression. Then quietly Martini Pace was stepping back, disappearing deeper into the

308

shadows, out of harm's way, as Dylan Francis strode confidently around the left bend.

'I thought u might try to escape me this way!' The little man chirped joyfully before adding in an over-dramatic and possibly manic tone, 'but there ain't no escaping my revenge!' Then he almost chanted. 'U fat baaa-sss-stard!'

Francis's right hand was still heavily plastered and as such should not have been a threat, but in his left he held a small six inch thick black cylinder. With a casual flick of the left wrist, a dark extension tube whipped out and a metallic clunk could be heard as it clicked into place. The little man swished it around again and with another firm click, a slightly thinner tube extended the device even further, so that it was now perhaps a good twenty inches long. Francis began to move closer, swinging the pole left and right so that it arced in front of him. Even in the poor light or maybe because of it, Kane could see the bold smile had gone and Francis' features had twisted into a look of pure hate.

The little man began spouting off, rapidly goading himself rather than attempting to communicate with Kane and then after roaring like a wild beast, possibly intending to intimidate his victim, he began constantly swearing how he was going to break "yer" arms and legs. He was certainly promising to make the "fat baaa-sss-tard" regret crossing Dylan "Fucking" Francis.

Kane was more focused on the side to side movement of the baton than the worthless words being spoken. The metal wand continued to swish left and right, coming closer to him with each swing. His assailant was acting wild but he was not completely out of control. The advance was steady almost purposeful. Kane remained frozen to the spot. He first thought of flight. The little man had moved subtly to block off escape up the lane. The door to the restaurant might only be a quick dash behind him but Kane knew that it had been firmly closed and he

309

might trip again on the uneven floor. If he remembered rightly the alleyway lead back down to the main street where there might be people and cars passing by. There might even be help, perhaps, in the form of Calamity. The undercover agent might be standing outside the restaurant, wondering where Francis had disappeared to! Pace could be there too! Then again things may have changed since his youth and the alley might be blocked off! It could be a dead end.

Kane's eyes flashed passed Francis to the darkness of the right fork where the girl should still be standing. She must be watching him. He then heard her giggle with glee and he knew that he had been set up. He also began to realise that the little man had not rushed him and had actually, despite the increased threats, been gradually slowing down the closer he came. Instinctively, Kane knew that there was a greater threat coming from behind him. His adversary was expecting back up and Kane's instincts told him that it was now or never.

The steel baton swished to right, less than a foot ahead of Kane, who rushed forward, just before the little man could swing it back to his left. Kane's aggression was a surprise. Francis simply panicked and immediately swung the baton back with all his force trying to hit Kane but his target was already passed the dangerous arc of the in-swinging metal. Only the biceps of the little man's left arm collided with the back of Kane's broad shoulder. The blow unbalanced Francis. Kane hopped further forward, raising his left knee up as he did so. The hard kneecap thumped into Francis' unprotected groin. The little man's roar of effort, which he had made during that last desperate swing, now turned into an almost comic, high pitched yelp. Francis' head bent forward, an involuntarily reaction and as Kane's left foot found firm ground, Kane braced himself and pushed both his hands up, forming them into closed fists, before smashing them firmly into the defenceless face. This resulted in a sickening smack, forcing Francis' head back. The blow also sent shock waves of pain from Kane's knuckles, back down his hands into his wrists but he gritted his teeth and immediately swung both hands out wide to ward off any incoming blows. There were none. Instantly recognising his advantage and opening up his hands flat, Kane immediately swung them down in a double chopping motion cutting into each side of the unshielded neck, completely exposed in front of him.

Kane did not hear the gurgling noise that Francis made as the little man staggered backwards, for he was too busy, dropping down into a forward crouch position, on his own haunches. He was just in time. The air whooshed above his head and a deep grunt sounded behind him. There may even have been an expletive, spat out almost six foot up above him. There certainly was as Kane rolled forward right and his shoulder connected with the hard stone path, just as another violent whoosh of air ended up with a metallic clunk ringing out and actual sparks flying up from the sudden impact with the floor. An impact at the spot exactly where Kane had crouched just seconds before.

Completing his rather ungraceful roll, Kane somehow landed on his feet and they had the unsteady strength and somewhat awkward gymnastic technique to allow the momentum to push him up, so that he was suddenly standing. He turned quickly, his back now to the far wall, so that he was facing what seemed, in the darkness, to be a monstrous black mass that was almost too tall to be human. This dark shape was clutching something long and cylindrical that tapered up into a thick and dark symmetrical barrel tip that looked like an oversized American baseball bat. In his shocked and confused state, the nightmare in front of Kane reminded him of a fairy tale cartoon ogre! One armed with the type of club only seen in pantomime productions of Jack the Giant Killer. The dark outline that was the club had been raised up in the air again and the giant or ogre

311

lurched forward towards Kane. Perhaps it was the effort or maybe the unsteady paving stones but the tall man seemed to slip as he swung the club down at Kane. The weapon was aiming for Kane's head but the slight slip allowed Kane to step quickly to his left, just out of the way and an ominous clang sounded as metal hit stone once again. The vibrations from the strike must have shocked the ogre and Kane took full advantage, counter-attacking with a high snap kick connecting to the giant's left knee. Kane knew that it only takes five pounds of pressure to shatter a knee cap and the ball of Kane's foot, curled in his leather soled shoes, may not have been as heavy as a standard supermarket bag of sugar but the force with which it connected to the knee bent the knee unnaturally backwards, and Tall Dai or perhaps the more aptly named Dai Oaf, for even in the darkness of the lane, Kane knew who his second attacker must be, let out a mournful wail as he collapsed in agony and dropped the bat, which made a final metal clang as it hit the flagstone and rolled harmlessly away.

In the wilder days of his youth Kane may have called out "Timber!" He certainly thought about mocking his assailant as the tall man wobbled, taking what seemed like forever, but in reality was mere seconds, before he fell heavily to the floor with a dull thud and sad groan. However, the more mature Kane did not have the energy. He merely staggered backwards, sweating profusely from his efforts and gasping in the cool yet strangely curry fume filled evening air, until feeling the relative safety of the stone wall at his back again, Kane raised his hands nervously in a standard but not surprisingly weak self defence ward off stance. He looked around for another attacker. Was there someone else lurking in the darkness? His mind asked desperately but fortunately there were none.

To his right Kane could see the small shadow that was Dylan Francis, crouched on his hand and knees, like a three legged dog. He was still making choking noises, his good hand grasping his throat. To Kane's left, the long body of Dai Oaf lay moaning in agony. Then, slowly stepping out of the shadows, appeared Martini Pace. Her breathing was fast, so fast that she seemed to be almost panting again. Even in the half light her face seemed flushed.

'Quick! Come with me!' She said urgently between deep breaths. She snatched Kane's left hand and squeezed tight once more. Her touch still felt good but this time he could sense a tremor as if her whole body was shaking, shivering perhaps. He wondered whether it was fear or shock. A part of him hoped that she had not known about the ambush. Maybe it was all down to Francis. Pace had seemed genuine in reprimanding his man in the restaurant but deep down Kane knew better. Flicker was not to be trusted, nor was his wife. Nevertheless, when she began to tug, Kane allowed her to drag him away back up the lane towards their original escape route.

They soon came closer to the still gasping Dylan Francis and Kane almost stumbled again. This time because his right foot slipped on the little man's metal baton, which lay discarded on the floor. Having been forced to stop, Martini whispered to Kane in an odd, kind of excited, almost high pitched voice: 'Is he going to be alright?' Kane paused. Finally he allowed his anger to consume him. Maybe it was because of the dull menacing clunk the metal had made as it scrapped along the floor under his foot or his sudden recall of the tirade of threats spouted at him as he tried to avoid conflict weeks ago in the Copper Kettle and then the restaurant earlier and finally in the alley only a few seconds ago; or the fact that Kane had simply had enough of playing the mild mannered victim! Whatever! Kane realised that this little man had meant to do him serious harm and even now would pose a threat if he could. Kane also heard in his head, the callous words that had been said about his friend. The exalted tone in which "The Dull-one" had recalled finding Frank John "swinging

313

there, dirty in his own mess!" Those words, and the pictures they conjured up, fed Kane's anger and it boiled over. The red mist finally enveloped him. He became the old Mykee Kane. The one people needed to fear.

'I doubt it!' Kane said coldly. Then letting go of her hand, he shook her grip off. Kane took one, two, three steps towards the man and swung a right foot kick to his head at almost point blank range. He had deliberately curled his toes up so that the leather sole covered ball of his foot connected just below the jaw, raising the head of his target, extending the neck with an audible snap. The impact lifted the little man a few inches up off the ground before he collapsed to the stone cold floor with a soft thud. After rolling over on its side, the body exhaled one long deep rasp of breath, before lying still and silent.

Kane instantly regretted his action. Not least for the pain he felt in his foot as he returned it to the ground. Nor because of the jarring sensation that had shot up, all the way from his ankle to his knee to his hip but because he had returned to being what he feared most, the brutal blunt instrument that he had successfully repressed for over ten years. The one his wife had feared he would always be. Yet the anger had not subsided and even in that moment of regret, Kane turned back to face the taller man. Dai Oaf was still rolling on the ground, moaning sadly like an Oscar winning footballer, appealing to an unseen referee. It was a pathetic sight and Kane knew from the awkward angle of the leg that this "player" would not be getting up and running that injury off anytime soon. The cruel damage seemed to satisfy something inside of him. An inner voice told him quietly and calmly, that the tall man was just an unthinking heavy. Stupid enough to do others bidding without any enmity towards his victims. Kane remembered the face looking out of "The Kettle's" window, after their first encounter. The look had almost

314

been that of guilty embarrassment. Perhaps this man was not a long term threat.

Then Kane heard an odd noise behind him. It was almost a high pitched snorting. He spun around and realised that it was Martini Pace. She was actually giggling so hard that she had lost control of her breathing. Her silhouette looked like a cartoon outline of a naughty school girl. One found in an old fashioned comic. Her lower lip was pushed up over the upper one, trying to stop herself laughing, and the air escaping down her nose, as her body convulsed uncontrollably, was making the weird snorting sound that he could hear. She was in shock, Kane told himself. However, inside Martini, her mind was racing, almost overwhelming her as she considered the exciting possibilities that this once seemingly innocuous man who was standing near her, could present her. She wondered whether at last, he would present her with the chance of independence from her own "old man" and she was suddenly joyfully working on her own plot.

'Come on!' She grabbed Kane's hand in hers, locking her petite fingers firmly between his broader and longer digits once more. This time he winced as he felt what was meant to be a reassuring squeeze, aggravate his bruising knuckles. She tugged and he followed. Still stunned and confused, and beginning to feel increasingly disgusted with himself, Kane allowed her to lead him away, like a naughty boy, up the right hand fork and on through the maze-like-alleyways. Behind them the bright halogen white shimmer of the infa-red security light clicked off and the lower alley was plunged into darkness.

315

Chapter 33: What a Shower

Kane stood in the brightly lit hallway of the impressive three storey Georgian building, which he had just been informed was not only the headquarters of Flicker's business empire but also apparently the town centre residence of Mr & Mrs Pace. Mrs Pace had been a real chatterbox during their rushed journey through the back alleyways of Aberfoist and he had absorbed a lot more information from her about his old acquaintance in the past ten minutes than he had from an afternoon and evening of drinking with Ginge Thompson.

Why she had chosen to be so candid with him was a little beyond him, particularly at this moment in time, when he had so much else on his alcohol addled mind. Perhaps the most pressing concern of many now suddenly seemed to be: what on earth was that horrible smell!?! Whatever it was, it was certainly not the cold water that was dripping off his rain soaked hair and sodden suit, before pooling onto the pristine black and white mosaic tiles of the smart reception hall floor.

The unlikely couple had just been caught in a particularly vicious cloud burst at the very moment when they had stepped out of the alleyway into the exposed openness of an empty car park. The subsequent dash through the car park and then the breathless scamper across the neat but dangerously slippery brickwork pavement of the town centre's pedestrianised precinct had been fun but not saved them from getting drenched.

'Oh my God!' Martini Pace cheerfully exclaimed whilst shivering beside him. 'I hope that's you and not me!' He could see the goose bumps rising along her naked arms and across the smooth tanned skin of her diamond chained neck. The wet look certainly suited her and he had to avert his eyes quickly to avoid staring at the prominent nipples rising out of her wet T-shirt. He was also beginning to recognise exactly what the stink was. Dog Shit! And Kane knew it was coming from him. Well he had been rolling around on the floor of a backstreet alley. What else could he expect! Kane began dramatically glancing around, slowly for effect, before he joked: 'I rather hoped you had a nervous guard dog in here! But I'm afraid it's me!' It was a poor effort at humour but she laughed and then pretended to be all offended.

'I hope you're not calling me a dog!' The beautiful young woman beside him laughed again. It was not a false laugh. Kane thought it an oddly relaxed reaction given the circumstances that had led them to be alone together. They were two very different people. Strangers in every way and yet she was perfectly carefree, laughing, seemingly unaffected by what had gone on before. Thoughtless behaviour perhaps but Kane found it rather endearing. Maybe the alcohol was still working its magic and releasing him from the cautious conservatism that he had sternly adopted over recent years. He reasoned that she was so young compared to him. Someone used to having fun, regardless of the reality of her situations. He guessed that assuming such an attitude must be a necessary reaction to being married to Ellis "Flicker" Pace. He did not envy her that experience. Especially given what she had been telling him. Then again, he thought, whatever she had been vapping must have also had an effect on her. Maybe she was still on that chemical high and it was making her carelessly over familiar.

Looking down at her afresh he recognised that she was bewitchingly beautiful. Her moist skin was shimmering in the otherwise unforgiving natural white light that was shining down from the multiple LED spots, which had been built into the high whitewashed ceiling above them. The lighting had cleverly

317

popped on as soon as she had stepped through the doorway, probably as a result of some unseen infra-red security sensor or other expensive, artificially intelligent system. The perks of her husband's business or so Kane assumed.

He really could not help himself and was becoming absorbed in his appreciation of her beauty. His eyes subconsciously began to follow a tiny bead of water as it ran down her glistening skin, dropping slowly from the raised ridge of her fine collar bone, working its way across her chest and then disappearing inside the tight gap of her exposed cleavage. He blinked, and tried to look away once he realised that he was again studying the pattern that was the sharp protrusions of her pert nipples. They were pushing further out through the cold wet Lycra of her tightly clinging black top. Try as he might, her lovely body demanded his full attention, with each and every exaggerated breath she took.

Lost in the moment, Kane was naturally aroused. Until, that is, he became abruptly aware that her eyes were staring up at him. He blushed with embarrassment, knowing immediately how much older he was in comparison to her. Not to mention how tired, fat, and ungainly he felt in his heavy, damp, suit. His white shirt was equally wet and clung sticky to his sagging chest. He was a complete contrast to the fit young woman beside him. He quickly looked away. Deep within him an inner voice was repeating those unfair words, from that unruly child, the one in the Isolation Room, back at school. "You Paedo!" His conscience repeated. Now he noticed that his sopping wet black trousers were also stuck comically high to his thickset legs. A centimetre of hairy calf was clearly visible above a damp black sock. He shrugged. "What am I doing here?" He began to wonder to silently himself once again.

Suddenly Martini Pace began retching. Not the most encouraging of responses to being caught ogling a young lady, even one who had just dragged him through the darkness, away from two assailants, and invited him in, out of the rain to the shelter of her home but perhaps an inevitable reaction, or so he thought, sadly, to himself. Hunching his back, Kane began awkwardly checking the soles of his shoes, clumsily hopping from one foot to another.

'Oh my God!' She repeated. This time she did not laugh. He was mortified and about to apologise, when she added, in an exaggerated mock-horrified tone of voice, that "it" was all over the back of his jacket! Then, suddenly, she was laughing again. 'Well I suppose that's what you get for rolling around in back passages!' She scolded, echoing his thoughts on the matter, yet with genuine and totally disarming warmth returning to her voice. Then, sounding to his guilty ears, slightly like his wife, she sternly told him to follow her. She turned away, kicked off her high heeled shoes and began jogging, bare foot, up the wooden staircase. He kept his shoes on and they squelched as he shuffled, awkwardly up the stairs after her.

He could remember when this building had been the offices of Goldsworthy, Brace, & Hutchinson, esteemed local solicitors. Of course, that was a long long time ago, in the days before Legal Aid had been abolished and lawyers could earn a good living from members of the public, so needed a presence on the High Street. Kane had been one of the few fortunate ones back then to have never needed their services. They specialised in representing the local ne'er-do-wells at the Magistrates Court and given his youthful misdemeanours it was a wonder that he had not been one of their regular clients. Then again he had always been a lucky so and so.

"Your Honour, my client saw somebody looking at him aggressively, so acted in self defence. He had drunk eight pints of lager and as a result did not realise it was his own reflection in the shop window when he hit out. He certainly did not intend to smash the glass!" For some reason Kane always remembered reading that particular case in the Aberfoist Gazette, although he could never recall whether the defendant had got off. If he had, Kane thought for a moment, then Goldsworthy, Brace, & Hutchinson were one of the best law firms in the country and maybe he should give them a call at their new location, wherever that was, and see if they would act for him because after his actions earlier he probably needed a good lawyer.

On reaching the first floor landing, Martini turned and directed Kane through a door marked in dark stencil like writing: "The Studio". Switching on the lights as they went in, Martini quickly led him through a small waiting area and into a side room. He found himself standing in a dazzlingly bright, all white, changing room, complete with an impressive walk in shower unit. She looked him up and down, and then rather matter of factly told him to strip off.

'Don't be shy!' She added. 'I'm a big girl now! I promise you I'll have seen it all before!' Her brown eyes flashed with a fierce pride. 'After all, I am a top modelling agent!' She exclaimed without a smirk. 'And I have boys as well as girls on my books!' Her tone of voice made it sound as if she had a first class medical qualification, rather than the simplistic ability to spot good looking people and persuade them to pose for a camera. Nevertheless, seeing a plush set of white bath towels on the shelves next to him, Kane got the idea. He removed his wallet, car keys, and phone, all from his jacket pockets and placing them carefully one at a time on the empty shelf space beside the towels, he began to get undressed, whilst she pushed passed him to turn the shower on.

'I'll get a bag for those things!' She announced, attractively wrinkling up her nose whilst extending a slim, glossy black, acrylic gelled, long nailed, finger towards the growing pile of damp and stinking clothes. When the door of the shower room

320

closed behind her, Kane dropped his trousers and underpants, before stepping into the warm soothing water that sprayed out from the multi headed top of the range device. This was the sort of shower unit that he could only dream of owning on a teacher's pay. Powerful, broad jets of water, shot out diagonally from built in circles of perforated metal, hitting acupressure points all over his upper body with an equally consistent force, whilst a warm mist descended soothingly from the wide rectangular shower head above. Kane was impressed and for a moment closed his eyes, lost in the pleasure the hydro-experience provided. However, seconds later a little voice inside him began teasing him. "They wouldn't have showers like this in prison!" It hissed.

Although he actually felt no real guilt for his actions against the two men who had attacked him, he knew that there must be consequences. For a few seconds, only a few, a part of him felt that his act of kindness in sparing Dai Oaf was a mistake. He had left a witness for the prosecution. Yet here he was, seemingly been under the protection of the thugs employer, and the only other witness was their boss's wife, a woman who had not seemed in the least bit worried about the two seriously injured employees. Why was that? He asked himself.

Kane knew, from his dark past, that Aberfoist had always been a law unto itself. It was a real Jekyll and Hyde town. He had wanted to find out what had really happened to his friend and the only person who had been willing to talk about Frank John's demise would, because of Kane's own unnecessary reactions, not be talking to anyone for a while, if at all! Whatever! He shrugged. His inner voice began telling him that he had poked the nest and he should know what would happen next. One thing was for sure, Kane quickly concluded, standing naked, lazily enjoying the luxury of the shower, this was not what he had expected and he had better get ready quickly, for he was fully exposed at the moment.

Opening his eyes he noticed a soap dispenser fixed on the wall to his right. He quickly helped himself to a handful of gooey green liquid gel and gave it a sniff. Satisfied that it smelt suitably soapy, Kane started to lather up, working from his head down. Just as he closed his eyes to avoid the possible sting of the suds, he was sure that he heard something. Was that the handle on the changing room door? He froze, just for a moment and strained his ears for another noise to confirm his suspicion but all was quiet, apart from the buzz of the power shower and the splashes of the water, as it hit him and bounced against the plastic screen. Although he usually trusted his senses he was too far gone in the process of washing the stink from him to want to stop. So he gave in to the urge to get clean and continued the process, grabbing blindly for more gel, applying it around his bulk, albeit at a more anxious pace. A minute or so later he was done. Cleaning foam now washed clear, he turned blindly but suitably refreshed, to face where he sensed the exit of the cubicle must be and as he stepped out of the spraying water, he opened his eyes.

There she stood, smiling up at him, blocking the exit. Martini Pace was completely naked. Without her heels on, her lovely face was only as high as his chest. Her eyes beamed up at him, for a second they seemed to be wide innocent pools of brown, drawing him to her, then they glinted as she smiled and began wickedly scanning him, up and down, with a knowing hunger that was far from innocent but just as difficult to resist.

Kane had always been good at controlling shock. His martial arts trainers had always joked that this was because he was slow. "Active stillness!" Lao Fu had once said to him, before comparing him to a snake waiting in ambush. Yet, instinctively his body knew that Martini's presence was not threatening him. So there was no need to strike. His only reaction was to breath

322

in, which was really a wasted effort; because she would have seen at first glance that his soft flabby body was way beyond such simple remedies.

Hypnotised by her obvious physical charms, Kane did not react when she reached out and cupped his privates in her right hand. Suddenly trapped by her teasing, gentle but firm grip, he could not pull away from the unwanted but naturally appreciated attention. He did not want to anyway and his body continued to betray his subconscious desire, whilst his mind raced for something credible to say. Instead she spoke first.

'You're a dark horse!' She said, teasing him for a second time in less than an hour but this time giggling girlishly, as she purposely lowered her gaze. She squeezed him gently. Then expertly released her grip and let her fingers run along his growing affection.

'Er, mm, Mrs Pace! I don't think this is a good idea do you!' Kane eventually said in what, apart from his initial stutter, he hoped was a cool and mature voice, rather than an inevitably weak and helpless plea.

'Oh I do!' She responded, in what really was one of the coolest and worryingly most mature tones that he had heard in a long long time. She followed her bold statement by letting her tongue slip out the side of her mouth and slowly, it licked across her upper lip before she broke in to yet another, enticing, girlish smile. Then she began flicking her tongue teasingly off the upper front row of her brilliantly white teeth. She was good. She knew she was. Her years of experience were not wasted when it came to situations like this.

'I'm, er, happily married!' He bleated, far too quickly to maintain the deep tone that he had intended. Risking a step back, he found his attempted escape manoeuvre frustrated, as her hand instantly locked on to him, and then she stepped in, even closer too him.

'Me too!' She whispered to his chest, as the warm water washed over them.

'I don't think Flick, er, I mean Ellis, would understand!' Kane groaned uncomfortably. Mentioning her husband created an image of them together in his mind, which instantly began to undo her skilled work.

'Oh, you'd be surprised at how understanding he can be!' She said, whilst applying another gentle squeeze and trying to look up at him, only to get splashed in both eyes by an inconvenient hydro-therapy jet. This made her momentarily let go of him, so that her right hand could instinctively help her left, rub the stinging water from both eyes. Her disadvantage in being so petite allowed Kane a few vital seconds to escape from her, albeit only a few centimetres away before he felt the tiled wall at his back.

'We have an "open" marriage!' Martini said rather tartly to Kane.

'I don't!' He replied bluntly. And as she tried to grab for him once more, he successfully intercepted her by catching both hands at each wrist.

'Look!' He began to say firmly, as his strength managed to hold her off. 'I find you very attractive! And I will certainly regret this, so please don't be offended, but I just can't! I love my wife!'

She frowned, twisting her mouth briefly in an obvious show of displeasure, before breaking into a wide smile as a new idea dawned on her. 'I suppose being rejected means I should like you more.' She suddenly said. 'You may well be an old fashioned gentleman! You know your wife is a lucky lady!' Martini concluded performing a slight sigh.

Kane considered that Jill would have thought it extremely unlikely that she was a lucky wife, given her husband's actions that night. It also began to dawn on him how unlikely it was that this attractive young woman had suddenly become so

324

passionately infatuated with him. Surely the drug she had taken earlier could not have been that powerful. He knew that he was hardly the type of bloke a girl like her would want. Then again she had married Ellis "Flicker" Pace! Kane felt her relax and in doing so he risked letting go of her wrists. What was her game? He wondered, whilst watching her calmly step into the main spray from the shower, reach for some soap from the dispenser and casually begin to wash her stunning body. Whilst her actions were not obviously provocative, being in such close proximity to such beauty was beginning to produce another awkward natural reaction, one that might obviously betray his good intentions and apparently successful counter argument.

'Excuse me!' He said playing the gentleman once more. 'I'd better get dry!'

'If you're sure?' She sighed again, before slowly moving to one side and allowing him to pass by. She pulled a sad look on her glistening, wet face. 'It would be sooo good!' She promised.

'I'm sure it would! He agreed as he squeezed passed her, feeling more than a little foolish. A part of him knew that there would be cold nights ahead, later in life, when his memory might regret this decision. Nevertheless, he was soon distracting his current consciousness by vigorously rubbing himself down, with one of the large soft white towels from the shelf. Just as he finished the process, Kane allowed himself one furtive glance back at Martini Pace, whilst she finished, uninhibitedly, washing the luxurious and lucky lather from her exciting body. 'You're a bloody idiot!' He muttered to himself, and then he laughed out loud.

Chapter 34: Home Movies

The fluffy white towelling robe may have been marked XL but it had obviously been designed for much slimmer builds than Kane's truly extra large bulk. Nevertheless, he was grateful for small mercies and wore it, just about covering his modesty. Although, he was also well aware that it was probably a pointless exercise, for as Martini had immodestly predicted, she had already "seen it all before!" In marked contrast, the tiny robe selected by his hostess fitted around her comfortably. If anything it was far too long and skirted all the way down to the floor, almost hiding her tiny but perfectly formed feet behind its wide curtain like flaps. However, the old adage that out of sight was out of mind was not really true, for Kane could never forget the currently concealed body, which she had so recent offered to share with him!

Post shower Martini had ushered the almost robed Kane into her "modelling" studio and served him a small but thankfully hot and surprisingly tasty espresso coffee, which she barely made by operating one of those stylish automated pod loading devices. Kane had only seen such machines before on TV but he understood they were beloved by exclusive beauty salons and executive car showrooms. The shiny and expensive looking contraption had greeted them as soon as they had entered the studio. It was boldly displayed on top of a matching white plastic four-wheeled trolley, complete with bijou glass cups, all smartly set out on a glacial white tray, ready for visitors, who would no doubt be expected to marvel at how sophisticated and professional Martini's studio must be.

Kane was just grateful for the caffeine. He knew that he needed to be alert and the excessive alcohol intake enjoyed earlier that day was inevitably beginning to make him drowsy; in spite of the refreshing shower and his heart racing close encounter with Martini. Luckily for Kane, everything on this floor had been brightly decorated in what he considered might be called a shock of Arctic White and as a result this flashy ultra-modern theme was anything but cosy and relaxing. So cool and dazzling in fact that he found it was quite easy to sit upright on another expensive looking accessory, a remarkably pristine but rather uncomfortable, white leather two person sofa. This all combined to make him awake enough to pretend to be eager to enjoy the promised slide-show of glamorous photos, which Martini had claimed were the highlights of her very own modelling career.

Behind the act, Kane was racking his brain, desperately trying to decide what he should do next. His instinct had been to confront Flicker, particularly before anyone found out what had happened in the alley. However, Kane guessed that it was probably too late now and he wondered whether he should stay and wait or simply go and hide. With every minute that passed he half expected the police to knock on the door or Pace to arrive with a gang of heavies. Kane certainly did not fancy his chances if the two well drilled bouncers from the Coliseum turned up with Pace. Having watched them at work only two weeks ago, he knew they were not the clowns Little and Large had fortunately proved to be!

Martini seemed oblivious to his dilemma. She had laughed cheerfully when she saw him awkwardly trying to tie up the ill fitting dressing gown. They had both known that his own clothes were unwearable and she had thoughtfully announced that they were "too wet, too dirty and too smelly" to bother with, before promising to find him something "mm, more suitable" to wear. Clearly satisfied that he was appreciating the automated

327

slideshow of almost life size, no doubt professionally and expensively taken, high fashion snapshots of most of his hostess, which were being lovingly beamed from a ceiling mounted projector (operated by a nearby computer) onto the long bare brilliant white painted wall that substituted for a more traditional home movie screen, she left him alone, after a teasing assurance that she would not be "too long!"

When she had reached the door, Martini had turned back and cheerfully reminded him to enjoy the show; and Kane was a little bit ashamed to admit to himself that he was! Nonetheless, he hoped that whatever she found on her quest would cover him a lot more than the outfits she was almost wearing in the photographs, which still continued to flicker up, one after the other, onto the wall in front of him.

Kane could obviously vouch for the fact that Martini was certainly beautiful to look at in the flesh but the series of photographs had failed to capture the true essence of the younger Martini; and even the fashion ignorant Kane could clearly see that she was probably not the type of beauty who would attract the attention of the top end *fashionistas*. Perhaps, she was just too real! Not extraordinary enough to feature regularly in the glossy magazines that far too often considered unnaturally thin or even ugly and extreme physical features, more attractive to their allegedly sophisticated audience, than the normal good looking people you might meet in everyday life.

As the slide transition continued, the photographs could not hide the desperation in the young girl's eyes. High fashion garments were slowly replaced by the more mundane wear favoured in commercial product advertising. Simple sales shots, turned into family friendly underwear catalogue modelling, then the portfolio on display became increasingly provocative and erotic, with lingerie snaps soon stripped down to naked, full frontal, soft pornography. Kane began to wonder if Martini was aware that the timeline of her slide show evidenced her descent from promising modelling career to gutter press work and finally awfully sad under the counter circulars. Maybe she viewed it differently. Unhindered by morality, the final collection of seedy, indecent, full frontal poses, and graphic hard core images, may well have earned her a lot more cash than those early glossy and artistic pictures. Kane could not help but hope they had, for he saw above the false pout she now pulled constantly, a girl with cold dead eyes. Finally, the show reached its sad conclusion and Kane actually felt guilty for not being turned on by the supposedly incendiary poses, which she had so painfully twisted her youthful body into.

Putting his empty glass cup down, on the possibly antique, inevitably white, coffee table in front of him, Kane was about to get up and see what, if any, useful information about Pace Enterprises might be stored in the computer's file bank, when the computer, which was obviously still linked to the projector, automatically up loaded a new and very different video stream.

Whether by accident or design, it began to beam a moving image against the plan white wall, one that should have remained hidden on the dark side of the Internet. The title read "Casting Couch #221" and Kane immediately recognised an artistically out of focus sofa as the one he was currently sat on. The image quickly pixilated and when it cleared, a young girl was sat cross legged on the middle of the sofa. She wore a short blue denim skirt and tight white blouse, undone to reveal a cleavage more mature than her child like face. She was smiling nervously at the camera. Then the unpleasant guile in Ellis Pace's unmistakable voice boomed out of an unseen stereo speaker. Its distance from the projection on the wall momentarily gave the worrying effect that Pace was actually in the room; possibly standing right behind Kane. Although Kane knew that the sound must have come from a surround-sound speaker, near the computer, he still felt

329

obliged to glance behind him and then around the room, before returning his horrified gaze back to the flickering image as Pace began asking the girl, in his most sickeningly sly tone, why she wanted to be in his movies.

'Because I wanna be, like, famous! An' have all the things I do dream of, like!'

It was an inevitably naïve reply that pained Kane. There was something about her voice that he almost recognised. Maybe it was the accent. Kane studied the projection carefully. His teeth clenched tight and his eyes watered slightly. Finally, he realised why the young girl sounded so familiar.

'Well show me your assets then!' Pace's voice leered out of the speaker again. The girl let out a grunt rather than a truly decipherable word. 'Whaaa?' She appeared to be highly amused at the "weird" words her interviewer had chosen to use, and was now squeezing her face up into a tight expression of incredulity that wrapped her chubby cheeks closer around her button nose. This look seemed to indicate that she wanted to snigger at the stupid man who talked funny, but at the last moment she fought her natural instincts, possibly fearing she might offend this man, whom whilst truly a weirdo, was so important to her career prospects. Instead she released her face into a blank smile, perhaps hoping that he would ask her again but use simple words that she could understand. Obviously impatient at her ignorance, Pace did.

'Get your tits out!' The crude command was grunted out by the unseen director. The girl seemed to understand that command and was not in the least bit offended. Her features morphed into a smug naughty school girl type of grin, which seemed to say confidently that you are going to enjoy this! Her fingers then began to nimbly undo the buttons on her blouse.

Kane may have wanted to look away as her blouse opened up to show small rolls of puppy fat still around her mid rift but he found that he could not close his eyes to the unpleasantness unfolding before him. Worse still, Kane imagined Pace's tongue slowly flickering out as it licked across that sweaty thin upper lip, whilst the video camera's lens zoomed in to catch the moment the girl confidently released the front catch of her lacy pop up bra.

'Very nice!' Pace sighed. 'Now squeeze them for me!'

The girl seemed to hesitate for a moment, her confidence disappearing.

'Oh come on darling!' Pace could not hide the irritation in his blunt demands. 'Show me!'

For a second or two, Kane thought that the girl was going to cry. Water seemed to well up in her big brown eyes, but then she complied.

By the end of the mercifully short video, as Pace's voice could be heard talking to an unseen audience Kane felt sick to his stomach.

'Do let me know if you want to see even "MORE" of our Little Tia in action! I know I do!' Pace sneered out of the hidden speaker, before adding very matter of factly: 'To vote "MORE" or "LESS" visit our Aber's Tarts website and click on the link for Tia.' The website address, www.aberstarts.com/Tia was then superimposed over a frozen black and white still of the topless girl, pouting provocatively at the camera.

'Well, you dirty old man!' Martini Pace chuckled. She had quietly entered the room and naturally mistaken his posture, necessarily sat bolt upright, frozen to the edge of the very sofa used in the flick, as a sign that he had been entranced by the nasty show. She now moved towards him, jokingly tutting out loud with each step. Held out in front of her was a neatly folded pile of clean clothes. 'You should have said you liked "younger" girls! I'm quite upset! My photos not good enough for you eh!' Her mocking tone actually sounded forced for a moment, and as

331

he stared up at her face he thought he saw the jolly mask she wore slip into a look of genuine hurt and disappointment. Kane wanted to explain but could not find the right words quickly enough.

'You know, us older women, have a lot more experience, than those young girls!' Martini added bitterly, thinking to herself that maybe "knowledge" was exactly what scared most men away and made them want the younger, inexperienced girls in the first place. 'You really should see some of the films I've made! They are in a different class!' She suggested brazenly. 'Yes, that might make you appreciate an old girl like me!' Martini seemed to be talking more to herself than Kane and dumping the pile of clothes down on the table in front of him, she moved quickly over to the computer and began fiddling with the mouse. He watched in stunned silence as the projector showed her search through a worryingly thick catalogue of folders, and sub folders until she found the file that she was looking for and said with more than a hint of satisfaction: 'Watch this one and tell me if it's not way better than the crap Ellis produces!'

Kane really did not know what to say or do next, so he sat still and dutifully looked up at the new images moving across the wall. His eyes occasionally dropped down to exam the pile of clothes in front of him. He correctly assumed they were for him to wear. There was what looked like a large black tracksuit, a black round neck T-shirt and a thick pair of black woolly socks. All were labelled with the Aberfoist Security Services logo. They appeared to have been freshly laundered and had been neatly folded underneath two thick rubber soled, black ankle boots. It all looked big enough for him to wear.

Of course he was still appalled and angry. Not just at the video footage that he had been exposed to, but how a part of him was just wanting to go; to run away from this seedy underworld he had suddenly found himself in. A world where a young and pretty woman like Martini thought she was passed it! To him she was still a "young" woman. Too young for him not to feel guilty at fancying, for he had! He knew that she had to be at least a dozen or more years younger than his own wife Jill! Maybe, in her sad world, where the men around her only seemed to be interested in ever younger girls, he was perhaps the first person to have rejected her advances and now she had an urgent point to prove. Unbelievably, after all that she had witnessed already that evening, she only appeared to be concerned with proving that he must find her more attractive than a teenager!

What seemed to make it even worse was that Martini appeared to accept that older men's attraction to younger girls was perfectly legitimate. Even inevitable! She obviously had no care or concern for the young girl, who presumable had come to her modelling agency looking for her big break, only to be given over to Pace to abuse and ultimately make public her humiliation on the World Wide Web as mere click bait. Kane wondered whether Martini was actually aware or even cared about how young the girl was, or was that just part of what she had called their "open" marriage!?! How had she been groomed and brain washed into this existence or was it in her nature to be like this? Did she feel that it had happened to her when she was under-age, so that was just the way it was!?! Or should she be excused because she had married a much older and possibly more devious man. Yet, Kane had seen her name was on most of the businesses listed on the notice board downstairs and she was certainly not behaving like a victim.

'You really don't need to show me this!' Kane began, finally finding his voice.

'Oh we have time! Ellis has texted to say he is going to be delayed.'

Kane immediately thought that Pace had found Francis and Dai Oaf lying in the lane behind the restaurant. He suddenly felt such a fool. Whilst he had been sat here watching pornography, Pace was setting up a more effective ambush or were the police already waiting for him outside! Their entry only delayed by some misguided concern for Martini's safety.

Thinking it over again and again, Kane felt that Calamity was bound to have noticed the dark passageway if had he actually stepped outside to sort Francis out with Pace; and having checked it out, what would he have done. Protect his cover by leaving it up to Pace or insist that they get an ambulance and call in the local boys in blue, before sending them off in pursuit of Kane. They had probably started a murder inquiry! Pace would have certainly pointed them in the right direction with glee. But then maybe Pace would want to avoid an official police investigation into his affairs.

'Don't worry!' Martini smirked. Kane thought that she must have seen the look of concern on his face. 'It's not about Francis! The Dull-one as you called him.' She started to giggle. 'He hasn't a clue about that and if he had I think Ellis would be giving "The Dull-one" the sack and offering you his job! Especially,' she winked, 'if I put in a good word for you!' She strode over and stood next to him. 'But I'll only do that if you're nice to me!' She laughed again. 'You will be nice to me! Won't you?'

Kane wondered if she realised that his last kick at Francis had been intended to be fatal or was this just one big joke to her.

'Oh well a girl can but try!' She suddenly frowned and became all serious. "It's to do with that Mr. Lord! He wants Ell to sort something out with him and that Irish copper, over at the thing-a-me! Oh! What's it called? That café they're developing!?! The Kettle! That's it! Anyway, he's asked me to keep you entertained! Well I am trying! Aren't I!?!' She added the last bit suggestively, immediately pulling another sad little fake pout with her pretty face. Then glancing up at the flickering images on the wall, she broke out into a bright smile and said: 'You should watch this! Don't you think it's clever? I think it's very artistic, even though I'm in it!' She chuckled again. She seemed rather pleased with herself.

Kane knew that he was being set up. It had to be and he wondered what he should do next. A small part of him could still picture him walking away from all this, even now, just leaving and heading back to the safety of that comfy bed waiting for him in the tidy and respectable guest house. Could he forget all about the fight in the alley? His friend's death? And the seedy reality of Aberfoist? Kane shook his head. No! He told himself. He still needed to learn exactly what had happened to Frank John. This was probably just another little test. A delaying tactic, but was it hers or was it all part of Ellis Pace's grand design!?!

Up on the wall a younger Martini was assuming a theatrical pose in the style of a classic silent movie heroine. She was employing all the subtlety of a sledgehammer, suggesting that she had heard a noise. To her character's obvious horror, a giant of a man, dressed like a pantomime villain, in a tight stripy "comic" burglar's jumper, with a black Lone Ranger style face mask wrapped around his eyes, and a Victorian era bowler hat firmly pushed down on his head, had climbed sinisterly through the curtains of the not-so-cheap set's open window. However, whatever the budget for this black and white skin flick was, it had not been enough to prevent the window wobbling or the set wall moving under the male actor's weight. Once in the bedroom, it was now the burglar's turn to feign surprise on discovering that the room was occupied. On seeing the occupant was Martini and that she had already innocently stripped down to her lacy underwear, the burglar soon began leering menacingly at her, and comically licking his lips, leaving nobody in any doubt that he had abandoned all thoughts of robbery and was now intent on attempting another, much more personal crime.

Martini's performance was never going to win her an Oscar but perhaps it was in keeping with the demands of this surprisingly accurate parody of an old fashioned, early twentieth century, silent movie. Her character was now rushing around the room, acting out her panic and fake distress. The man gave chase. All that was missing was a silly tune being belted out on a tinny piano or movie theatre organ but then this, Kane deduced, was meant to be a silent movie, and in a strange way the silence added to the tension in the room. When the man eventually caught up with Martini, she swooned and fainted, conveniently falling, onto the large brass framed bed. Kane looked away.

'Don't you appreciate my acting?' She had been watching him closely and now huffed in frustration, before adding, with a real hint of resentment: 'Maybe you would like me to put on another film featuring a younger girl! We've got plenty!' She added tartly. At that moment the screen wall went dark and Kane glanced back up to see that the scene had faded to a black card, with classical white writing etched over it, in another suitable parody of the storytelling devices used in those old silent movies. Kane could not help himself and he started to read someone's idea of a clever pun. He only got halfway through it before the scene cut to an image of Martini coming round to find that her wrists had been tied, rather mysteriously, by her silk stockings to the brass bed frame. The robber was now ripping his own clothes off, revealing an impressive physic, one which must have taken years of hard work in a gym to develop. The camera curiously lingered on Martini's petite feet. They were daintily kicking out in frustration but oddly still wearing her high heeled ankle boots. Then the camera slowly panned up her shapely legs, before focusing on her slender Basque wearing body, then pausing on her fully made up lips as her mouth teasingly began opening and closing, as if she were calling out for help. It was a silent movie, so no one could possibly hear her screams! In spite

336

of her passion, Kane suddenly found himself distracted from the drama. He was actually wondering of all things about how and why the man had removed her stockings to tie her wrists to the bedposts whilst leaving her kinky boots on!?!

When he looked back, the camera had zoomed in for a close up of her eyes. They were widening in disbelief as on the wall behind her the shadow of man showed that he was removing his trousers. Her reaction made Kane think that maybe Martini could act after all, because her expression changed from one of horror to one of longing, suddenly hinting so unrealistically, that seeing the man naked for the first time had changed her mind and she was now no longer going to protest but would be willing him on with his evil intent!

'This guy was a natural! See!' Martini piped up smugly.

Up on the wall, behind her, the actor was clearly displaying his exceptional star quality. However, Kane was not watching the projection. He had just had one of those eureka moments and was looking passed the real Martini towards the computer. She had not noticed his change of focus. Her mind was elsewhere, recalling the reality of filming porn. She could still see the bored look on the faces of the cameraman and lighting technicians. She could also hear the director's flat matter of fact cockney accent, as he tried patiently to coach an adequate performance out of his "stars!" She even began to follow his directions once again, here and now in her studio, desperately trying to recreate the same smouldering looks of desire that her younger self had so successfully achieved. She turned and tried to slink over to where Kane was sat. When she was close enough for him to touch her, she stopped and dramatically allowed her robe to fall open, revealing that she was wearing what appeared to be exactly the same Basque as she had worn for the film. Kane could not but notice and he actually gulped at her extraordinary performance, but then he ruined it all by blurting out the

337

question, the one that had crossed his mind just a few seconds before, the one he just had to ask her now.

'Did Frank John's daughter do one of those screen tests with your husband?'

It was a simple question but it took her totally by surprise. For a moment she thought that she had misheard him. Then, realising what he had said she became really angry. She wanted to hit out at Kane. Dig her long nails into his skin and tear chunks out of his cheeks. How dare he? He had hurt her pride, offended her vanity. Kane asked her again but she was not listening to him. Her mind was in temporary melt down. How could he actually want to watch footage of such a plain Jane, she asked herself, when she, Martini, a real pro, was actually offering herself to him! Yet deep down, she knew that Jan John was a much younger girl! And she feared youth in others.

'Do you know Jan John?' Kane was puzzled as he watched the pretty face in front of him turn ugly. He spoke quietly, staring straight into Martini's suddenly wild and angry eyes. 'She's my friend Frank's daughter?' Kane repeated the fact slowly in an effort to get through to her. Thinking out loud he sought some form of confirmation from her by slowly talking through his own thought pattern.

'If Jan John had made one of those miserable "Casting Couch" videos and my friend Frank had seen it!' Kane stopped talking and paused for a moment to let his reasoning catch up with his natural instincts, so that he fully understood exactly what he had been attempting to say.

Martini Pace was not totally stupid and even in her sudden rage, the real purpose of his questioning was beginning to hit home; and suddenly it dawned on her that she had been going about this all the wrong way. In that awkward moment Martini realised that she did not have to seduce Kane to entice him into a plot to kill her husband. She felt such a fool as she looked up into Kane's blue eyes. She could see a different kind of anger in them to her own. It was a cold resentment. Finally she understood. Only Kane himself had not fully realised it yet!

'Frank would've killed your husband or died trying!' Kane simply and matter of factly concluded his reasoning and the actress beside him allowed herself to show her natural incredulity and as her face reflected the sudden change from rage to a stunned disbelief, Kane guessed that Martini Pace knew exactly what he was talking about.

'Did your husband kill my friend?' Kane finally asked, trying but failing to hide the real menace in his softly spoken words.

In the time it took her to re-fasten her robe and cross her arms, Martini had decided that honesty might actually be the best policy in this situation. Then again a serial liar like Martini Pace could not tell the whole truth and nothing but the truth.

'Frank John knew that Jan wanted to audition for us but he believed me when I told him we couldn't use her.'

'You knew Frank?' Kane's question surprised her. Surely he knew that everybody knew everyone in Aberfoist.

'Yes! I used to meet my nan for coffee once a week in his museum of a café.' Martini began her version of the truth. 'She liked it! I didn't! But then I never liked my nan much either!' Martini rolled her eyes. 'Anyway, it was there that I suggested Jan try out as a model for us. A proper one, you know, not glamour! And certainly not fashion! She had an ordinary look, you know! I thought it might work for adverts! I know a few people who like using plain young things. But the camera didn't like her!' Martini shrugged dismissively as if Kane should understand exactly what she meant.

'Then Ellis did his usual thing and started sniffing around her. He likes the young girls.' Martini rolled her eyes again and added: 'He likes all the girls. But he got keener on this one when he found out who she was!'

'Really?'

'I think Ellis wanted to provoke Frank, you know get one over on him and tease him about it!'

'That would've been a dangerous game.' Kane said quietly, almost to himself.

Now it was Martini's turn to say: "Really?" It was an apparently surprised and sarcastic response to that implication. Martini had been bitterly disappointed in Frank John. He had been her Plan A. However, in spite of her attempted manipulation, the so called "tough guy" had not reacted in the way she had hoped. Yes, she reflected to herself. It had all started out innocently enough. She had actually warned Frank, in good faith, that her Nan's favourite tea room waitress was not really model material. Then she had even advised Frank, confidentially, to check out the "Aber Tarts" website as Ellis was nagging Jan to audition for it! However, the idiot had actually told her that he trusted his daughter! He expected Jan to do the right thing in such a situation, whatever the right thing was! Idiot! The memory made her flinch as she recalled the conversation. Men, particularly fathers are fools or so she thought; although she had never known her own father. Okay, Frank may have been distracted at the time. How was she meant to know that his business was going bust! Martini subconsciously shook her head, suddenly remembering that Frank had actually been right in a way! When the time came for Jan to audition, secretly, the girl had refused to perform for Pace. That naive young girl had even come running in to Martini's office, sobbing her heart out, telling her "friend" what a sick man her husband was and what he had wanted her to do! Of course it was then that Jan had told Martini about her father being ex-special forces and suggesting that if he ever found out about what Mr Pace had suggested, he would surely kill him. That was the moment when Martini had seen her opportunity. She had been thinking for a while that getting rid of her husband meant that she could keep everything and perhaps she could actually run a legitimate business for the first time in her life. Well Frank John bloody well did not kill Ellis did he! He hung himself! So much for the tough guy, Martini thought angrily. The things she had done! Martini silently shook her head again. She did not do regret but the thought of her perfect scheme unravelling like that certainly irritated the hell out of her.

Kane sat watching Martini's reactions, wondering what was going through her mind. Both were now ignoring the silent grappling being beamed across the wall of the studio above them. Martini seemed deep in her obviously troubled thoughts and Kane was attempting patience, hoping that she was about to tell him everything he needed to know.

However, Martini certainly was not going to tell Kane that she had had to drug Jan, with that subsequent comforting cup of tea, before letting Ellis make his sick video with the dopey spaced out little girl. Martini had then waited and waited but her husband had not up loaded the film up to the site! Well it was a pretty bad movie, sick even by Ellis's standards! So in the end Martini had had to do it herself. Still nothing happened. She had even dropped in to the café, just as Frank was locking up one night. Okay, he had seemed more than a little distracted yet again that night. How was she meant to know that he had just sold the business? She had been so cross with Frank, he had simply fobbed her off. She was furious that Frank John had not even checked out the website! At least she had reminded him. No she was not guilty. She could not believe he would kill himself instead of seeking physical retribution but then that was what her husband told her had happened and that she had better keep a low profile or it would damage their business and be especially damaging for her if local people knew she had told Frank about his daughter making a porno movie!

Martini now looked at the other soft lump of a man sat in

341

front of her. Compared to Frank this man did not look so tough but then she remembered his fight in the alley. She smiled, turned and walked over to the computer and moved the mouse. One click stopped her performance and three clicks later the file called "Casting Couch #219" began to play.

'I think this is what Frank John saw the night he died!' She sang out almost triumphantly, as she sat down beside the deadly silent Kane. The bitter and angry look that began to spread over Kane's face excited Martini.

Chapter 35: An Inevitable Reaction

Taking care to cup his black gloved right hand protectively around the standard issue military watch, which was strapped firmly to his raised left wrist, Kane flicked open the leather cover with his thumb before glancing down at the luminous analogue dial and quickly calculating that it had been just over an hour since Martini had first shown him the recording of Jan John's brutal audition. A lot had happened in that hour and he hoped that a lot more would happen in the next. Kane firmly pressed the weathered cover's loose end back down onto the securing stud, ensuring that the faint green radiation glow would not escape from the watch face and alert anyone to his presence deep in the shadows cast by the old building that rose up behind him. He was standing at the entrance to yet another back alleyway in Lower Town, Aberfoist. This alley was more of a driveway, rather than the grim narrow pathways he had explored earlier that evening on the other side of the town's main dividing road. It was a road that was hidden from view by the ramshackle terrace of dark historic buildings to his right.

His watch was a personal souvenir and worn as a constant reminder of his own military service. However, the only thing he thought of now was catching up with Ellis "Flicker" Pace. Martini had eagerly volunteered the information that her husband would be in a meeting with Lord, down at the "Kettle" for a few hours. She had also happily confided in Kane that her life with "Ell" was not really a happy one and she obviously laid the blame for all her worldly woes on her husband's round shoulders. In spite of all this she had not been so keen on letting

Kane see any further evidence of her complaints when he had wanted to access her agency's computer. His surprisingly bold insistence had upset her, but unlike her alter ego, the scantily dressed skin-flick movie character, Martini did not swoon or faint. In fact, she had put up a pretty convincing struggle, eventually biting and scratching, like a real alley cat, until finally Kane snapped and punched her, only once, but the blow connected squarely on her jaw and sent the instantly unconscious woman sprawling to the floor.

Kane could not remember ever hitting a woman before. He felt bad but then that could have been down to the constant stinging from the three scratches that ran down his right cheek. The deep red impression left by her sharp teeth on his upper left hand surprisingly did not hurt half as much as the long thin red lines. Even so, Kane felt embarrassed by his reaction. He knew she had been playing him all evening, and he had become increasingly irritated about her confused loyalty to a man, whom she seemed to be encouraging Kane to view as being solely responsible for not only the statutory rape of young gullible girls but also Frank John's death. However, he should have dealt with her better.

Luckily the long towelling belts from those fluffy white dressing gowns that they were both wearing had proved useful in restraining her. He had tied her petite wrists and pretty neat ankles securely to the nearby radiator; the large white one that was fixed firmly against the even whiter studio wall. Whilst this would limit her opportunities to attack him again, her response to confinement was very different to the fantasy she portrayed in her mocked-up silent movie; so Kane had also used one of the small towels, conveniently available from the shower room, to gag her, for when she had started to come round she had begun to hollow for help. He hoped that she would not choke but that hope was not out of kindness. However pretty she was and

344

however unfortunate her own circumstances had been, he wanted her to suffer the legal consequences for her part in the exploitation and abuse of minors. But first he had a personal score to settle with her husband.

After dealing with Martini, Kane had quickly dressed in the borrowed all black Aberfoist Security Services uniform, which unlike his Swiss engineered watch, no doubt originated from a sweat shop in the Far East. Nevertheless, Kane was truly grateful for the gift of the dark clothes. He considered himself to be almost invisible in them, as he now sheltered from the persistent drizzle, under a mercifully overhanging slate roof, and kept watch across a stretch of wasteland, peering through the darkness down to where a thin rectangle of yellow light outlined the back door to The Copper Kettle Tea Rooms. Ironically it was behind that door, inside his late friend's former business premises, that Kane knew he would find Ellis "Flicker" Pace. The problem was Pace was unlikely to be alone.

Parked outside the shabby back door of what was once his friend's premise, Kane could see a large Mercedes SUV. He had no idea whether this dark vehicle with it's blacked out windows was Pace's or Lord's. That did not matter to him but its positioning did. With luck, Kane decided, it would block the view should anyone happen to look out from the Kettle as he made his way across the wide open "no man's land" down towards the highlighted back door. Why he worried he did not know, after all, this was Aberfoist! Who would post a look out? Certainly not Ellis "Flicker" Pace! Or so Kane thought. Yet years of experience had taught him to be cautious. So he waited and watched from his hiding place. He was no longer tired nor drunk but running on pure adrenaline. The dry stone wall at his back was that of a converted barn, which thanks to the contractual generosity of the gambling institution that was the National Lottery, had a proper roof and now served as a community centre for the nearby parish church. Kane allowed himself a grim smile as he stared out of his dark sanctuary and considered the harsh community service he intended to do Aberfoist that night.

Yet when he closed his eyes in an attempt to focus on exactly what he considered needed to be done, Kane could only see the pale nakedness of the drugged Jan John. Her body lying limp across the white leather sofa, the one that he had been so uncomfortably sat on as he watched her, eyes blank, seemingly unaware of the camera lens moving slowly above her whilst Pace's sly voice promised sick voyeurs similar sights should they click on his perverted web site. In spite of this haunting vision, Kane remained calm. He was surprised how calm he actually was, given the anger and resentment smouldering away deep within him.

He had been calm enough back in Martini's studio to take action that should ensure whatever happened in the next hour, Pace's mucky enterprises would soon fail. Martini's studio computer had been conveniently unlocked and lacking in password protection, so he had been able to open her insecure business account and send emails to the police. He had also sent electronic copies to both a national and the local newspaper, as well as the Social Services Local Educational Welfare office. Thanks to the wonder of the 'net, Kane had found all the addresses he needed through a quick Google search and simply inserted hyperlinks, which should take the readers directly to the under age sex videos that had already been foolishly uploaded onto the "Aber Tarts" website, or at least the one specific under age, and thereby illegal video that he was only too aware was already freely on view there. His emails merely confirmed the full contact details of all participants and of course, made specific reference to the identity of the pornographic producer, director, and leading man, the noted local businessman, Mr. Ellis "Flicker" Pace. Surely someone would act on the information provided.

However, Kane was not the most trusting person when it came to the authorities and he had taken other precautions. Just in case the official agencies turned out to be technophobes or worse corrupt, Kane had also taken time to burn two copies of the movie file, the one featuring little Tia Maria, onto two handy DVDs, which he had found amongst a pile of blank discs, again so conveniently placed on the shelf, right next to the computer desk. Kane had raided the office, the unlocked one he discovered across the hall, for padded envelopes, note paper and amazingly, two first class stamps. It had amused him at how easy it had all been, for Aberfoist Security Services certainly did not practice what they must surely preach to their clients!

Having scribbled an anonymous note to the Head Teacher at his school, and popped one disc, with the note, inside the padded envelope, Kane had addressed a second similar package to himself. These envelopes had been carefully dropped into different post boxes on his stroll over to the Kettle. There was no going back now. Although, he had also cautiously carried out a black bin bag with him, the one containing his damp and dirty clothes, in the forlorn hope of removing the most obvious evidence of his presence as a whistleblower at Martini or was it Pace Enterprises. Kane had even remembered to collect his damp shoes off the radiator in the changing room, adding them to the bin bag. Ultimately he had hidden the bag carefully, in a bush just the other side of a broken down fence behind the parish church. He could not afford to lose his best suit; it was after all his only suit, and he intended to collect it later, if there was a later.

It was a Friday night and Kane did not expect any of those agencies to respond quickly. So he had also turned the radiator off so that Martini would not burn. With luck, someone, hopefully the authorities, would find her before she dehydrated or caught a chill in her cool Arctic White studio, but he was more than willing for her to take that chance should things not go well for him during the next phase of his reactionary plan and he was unable to return to her.

Opening his eyes, Kane stared up into the dark damp navy blue sky. He was grateful for the unpleasant black rain clouds because they blocked out the starlight and covered the full moon, which must be shining somewhere up above them. He knew that he could not wait any longer. The nearby town hall clock would have struck nine, if only the local council had been able to spare the money required from their limited budget to repair the antique mechanism. Kane was well aware from his regular habit of consulting online news feeds on his once hometown that the Victorian technology had failed. Whilst sadly considered inevitable by some, this break down was apparently the first in over one hundred and twenty years, and allegedly due to the extremely icy weather suffered throughout last winter. Of course, the council had regrettably had to lay off their long serving and once loyal maintenance team, as part of an efficiency drive, just the year before. The concerned councillors were now, according to the local newspaper, eagerly negotiating a sponsorship deal with a renowned Oriental digital watch manufacturer. Nevertheless, in spite of two heavily reported executive committee fact finding trips to the exotic Far East, all at the rate payers expense, a deal was yet to be struck. So the traditional chimes remained silent. Never mind, the good towns folk could always rely on the clever modern technology of their expensive oriental produced smart phones to tell them the time. Kane took a deep breath to counter the petty frustrations he still harboured about the obvious political mismanagement. It amused him that he could feel almost as angry about things like that as he had about Pace's activities. However, there was an obvious difference; he could do something about Pace. He already had! And now it was time for him to confront his old acquaintance.

Pulling the nylon hood of his borrowed black lightweight jacket back over his head, before stepping out of the shadows into the wet night air, Kane began his cautious march down the wide pathway passed the derelict out-buildings on his left. There was little cover away from this broken down boundary and he felt truly exposed as he began crossing the open ground towards the Kettle. It stretched out like no man's land to his right, up to the huddled blackness that was the rear of the closed main street shops. In the past this area had been informally used for staff car parking but in these difficult economic times, the shops were no longer staffed. So tonight, like most other times of the day, it was no surprise to see that the spaces were empty; all that was apart from the space immediately behind the Kettle.

As Kane moved quickly on, he noticed the outline of familiar looking signs fixed to the buildings. It was far too dark to read the signs but he did not need to, he knew they said "Under the protection of Aberfoist Security Services!" It began to dawn on him that Pace had control of a significant amount of real estate and gaining control of the Kettle must have been vitally important to Pace's plans for the area. Whatever those grand designs were!?!

On reaching the large stationary Mercedes Kane paused briefly. Then slowly he crept up to the back door. His eyes traced the yellow electric outline that ran around the door. He was looking for tell-tale dark patches in the light, which might indicate whether bolts and catches were locked in place. There seemed to be none. He tried to remember whether the door opened in or out. He could not. Studying the hinges, at the top and bottom of the door, on his left hand side, Kane decided that the door must open inwards. He then closed his eyes. Breathing in deeply, then out and in again, slowly concentrating as he tried to picture what was happening inside the café. Kane slowed his breathing and listened hard. Thinking who could be in there. He

349

thought about the people he had seen in the restaurant. He counted them in his mind. There would be Pace, Lord, Calamity, the two track-suited men, and another Indian, the one who looked like an accountant. Kane cringed. He knew if someone was describing him then they may have said he looked like a scruffy unsuccessful accountant rather than the man of action he once was and now intended to be again.

For a moment Kane considered the two large men; the ones in the identical tracksuits. They had to be Lord's men. His minders! Who was Lord? Kane wondered. If he was involved with Pace he had to be dodgy. That must have been why Calamity was with them. Then Kane remembered the blonde, Kim, he had heard her called. He did the maths. Eight! Only one of whom might be on his side. That was too many. He knew that he would have to wait and hope to get Pace on his own. Oddly, as he half dreamed about Pace simply stepping out of the back door, for some fresh air or such like, Kane could have sworn he could hear sobbing. It was a strange sound. Child-like but not child-like. Perhaps it was too deep a sob for a child or even a woman. Then his sensitive ears were almost deafened by a high pitched scream of pain. The shriek came from deep inside the Kettle and shattered the silent night like breaking glass. At that very moment, immediately behind him, the car door of the Mercedes swung open. Kane froze.

'Oye! Butty! What U doing?' A deep voice, with an unmistakable heavy Valleys' accent asked. Thanks to the bright interior light from the Mercedes, which had switched on as soon as the door had opened, Kane could see a dark shadow of a big man reflected against the back wall of the Kettle. It seemed remarkable close to his shadow. Kane thought about hitting out at the man, quickly calculating the distance and angles. He even began to stiffen his elbow ready. However, Kane reminded himself of one of his golden rules. "If you have to think about hitting someone, don't!" Luckily for them both, the man spoke again.

'Your boss is inside! He told me that if U comes round like, to tell U there's no need for any security checks 'ere to-nite!'

Kane sighed, relieved. What luck! The clothes he was wearing had obviously made the big man think that Kane was one of Pace's security guards and that he was there just doing his rounds.

'Fair nuff, like!' Kane grunted, trying to emphasise his own (once local) accent. Turning around, as if to go, Kane could now see inside the car, it's internal lighting illuminating everything as if it was day. The big man was one of the two tracksuits, Lord's man from the Himalayas. The man was actually casually turning his back on Kane and was about to climb back into the front passenger seat, probably determined to escape the miserable drizzle and chill night air. Yet with the car's interior light obviously nullifying the darkened privacy glass, Kane could also see, curled up on the back seat, was Lord's blonde. Unfortunately, at that very moment, the woman began to rouse herself from a deep sleep. No doubt irritated by the light coming on and the grunted conversation. She looked hung-over, but her eyes blinked and suddenly she was wide awake and looking straight at Kane's face. Their eyes met and the mutual recognition was instant.

Kane could not hear what she said but no sooner had her mouth opened, the big man was turning around to take a second, suddenly suspicious, look at Kane. In fairness to the big man he went from mild surprise to the full realisation of his mistake in seconds and was leaping towards Kane just as Kane smashed a left hook up under his exposed chin. Kane followed up almost immediately with a second blow, slamming his right fist bang on the big man's nose, flattening it and knocking the big man flying backwards into the car. Amazingly, the big man seemed to regain

351

his senses instantly and bounced back off the passenger seat, roaring forward, spraying snot and blood everywhere whilst snorting like an angry bull. He hurled himself towards Kane, who simply slammed the door shut. The side window shattered on contact with the man's angled head. Kane reached through the remains of the shattering glass and grabbing the back of the man's tracksuit jacket's collar, and hauled him forward through the broken glass until his shoulders and upper arms were firmly wedged, trapping the attacker in the window frame. Perhaps it was unnecessary but nevertheless, Kane then chopped down hard with the flat side of his right hand, connecting across the back of the man's neck. The unconscious head dropped down until the chin rested on the outside door panel.

In the back seat the blonde had miraculously revived. How she had recognised the hooded Kane given her hangover was a mystery. However, her eyes were open wide and staring straight at him in total shock at what she had just witnessed. Her mouth was also wide open and he and probably everyone else in the vicinity could hear her scream.

'My boy! My boy! My poor boy!' She was yelling now, as she kicked open the back driver's side door and began to haul herself out of the car. By the time Kane had stepped back, she was already racing around the front of the car to confront him. Kane had already hit one woman that night and it looked as if he had no alternative but to repeat the misdeed as she rapidly approached him, her arms swinging aggressively in a strange almost comic but quite worryingly menacing pincer movement. She was looking like a demented crab, clawing wildly just out of reach of a fisherman's line, and he was the bait. Then, just behind him the Copper Kettle's back door swung open. Bright light flooded out into the back yard. Kane twisted slightly, standing sideways to take a look, as a different but similarly sounding deep Valley's voice boomed out: 'What the ..'

352

Hesitation is always fatal. Kane knew that much and the unseen owner of the voice's shocked reaction on first viewing the unexpectedly violent drama unfolding outside the back of the Copper Kettle may have given Kane a slight advantage but in the same instant that Kane recognised the man behind him was Lord's second track-suited thug, and he began to spin back around, intending to flee, the blonde slammed into him. She was incredibly strong and she had momentum. In what seemed like slow motion but was in fact the merest ticking motion of the second hand on his covered watch, she drove Kane back through the open doorway, so that their combined bulk collided with the shocked second track-suited man. Having correctly stopped attempting to seek an explanation, the big man had made his second mistake; he had decided to rush and grab Kane. This meant that he was fatally off balance when the collision occurred. She pushed just as the big man was about to pull and Kane became like a rag doll, trapped in dual brut forces of nature. His full weight was lifted off the floor and his body rocked backwards onto the man. The force snapped Kane's head back and the hardest part of his fortunately thick skull crashed into the softer face of the second tracksuit man. Blood spurted forth and nose cartilage snapped. The impact made both men wobble. They saw stars, much brighter than those hidden above the clouds somewhere up in the dark night sky. The blonde continued to push, roaring like some savage beast until the slight ridge across the floor of the door frame caused all three to fall. The track-suited man took the full impact as the huddling mass hit the floor. The whiplash caused the back of the man's skull to thud down first onto the thinly carpeted, cement based, solid floor of the Kettle's back-room. Kane actually felt the man's body beneath him suddenly relax and soften.

Still screaming, the blonde rolled off Kane, spinning to the right. This somehow allowed Kane to roll free to his left.

353

Pushing himself up with a groan he managed to get to his feet. Just as he did, for a brief second he saw her from the corner of his eye. She was hunching over assuming in his imagination, the shape like a spooked cartoon cat. Then she roared in rage and anguish. She was reaching for something. Before he could react, she had grabbed a wooden tea room chair and hurled it towards him. It missed and smashed onto the floor just in front of two other men, who were standing there frozen, seemingly incredulous at the whirlwind that had blown into their room.

The noise of the chair shattering on the floor brought a momentary pause to the blonde's frenzied attack. She stood still for a few seconds, trying to make sense of where she was and what she was doing. Wiping the angry tears from her eyes, the woman stared blankly around the brightly lit room. Then immediately on seeing the track-suited man's unconscious body on the floor, lying lifeless at her feet, she let out a loud wail and dropped to the floor. Instantly forgetting all about Kane, she frantically began attempting to revive her son. Feeling a sudden sense of respite, Kane turned towards the two men, who were standing, in stunned silence to his far right. He recognised them both instantly, as they did him, in spite of the hood still partially covering the back of his head. They were Pace and Lord. However, even more worryingly, behind them there was another man. Hanging from an exposed ceiling beam by a course fibred blue nylon rope that tightly bound his hands, and stretched his arms up above his drooping head, was a tip toed, semi-conscious, Calamity O' Neil.

Chapter 36: Proaction

The back room of the Kettle looked much bigger than Kane remembered. Perhaps it was because the tables had been cleared away and stacked at the far end of the room. All the chairs were still arranged around the perimeter, as they had been when Kane had last intruded on a Pace and Lord gathering, but back then everything had been in the shadows. Tonight, all the lights were on and the atmosphere in the room was clearly more hostile.

Nervously glancing around the room, Kane could see that Calamity's weight had caused the nylon cord to cut another fresh groove in the wooden beam and this mark helped emphasise a much deeper indentation just a few millimetres away, where Kane realised that another rope had been tied and taken an even heavier strain on the beam. Kane felt his cheeks flush and his face reddened with rage. He needed no further proof than the evidence of his own eyes to convict Pace, who now seemed to be cringing away from the hanging man, the terror of discovery now obvious on his pale and pasty face.

However, it was not Pace who demanded Kane's immediate attention. There was another, much taller and broader man blocking Kane's route to dealing out justice. Lord had broken into a manic grin and was striding confidently towards Kane. He was saying something. Kane thought he heard: 'You're a big man but you're in bad shape. With me it's a full time job.' But the words did not make sense. Nevertheless, Kane recognised the immediate threat of the big man and reacted. Somehow Kane managed to avoid the full force of Lord's pile-driver. The blow was aimed accurately towards Kane's solar plexus. Twisting slightly, just as the large fist connected with his body, this slightest of movements proved just enough for the blow to glance away and continue punching hard through the space where Kane's body had been seconds before his deft evasion.

Whilst Kane was shocked by how quickly the big man had covered the short distance between them and struck, Lord for his part was more surprised. His strike had connected but somehow its force had been deflected and his knuckles merely brushed across the black material of Kane's borrowed jacket. This was the first time in all his adult life that Lord's trade mark attack had failed him. He immediately swung a left hook at where the hooded man's chin was, only for that too to be pushed away to Lord's increasing disbelief, by an open hand ward off, that almost unbalanced the attacker. Lord swiftly changed his footing and grunted as he twisted his shoulders to swing a powerful right fist back at his elusive target's head. A left forearm blocked off his blow and then a right forearm powerfully blocked off Lord's instant, lightning fast follow up, of a usually reliable left snap punch. Lord could not understand this latest failure and confused, he instinctively stepped back, with his own arms now raised to protect his own head from the expected counterattack. Lord was surprised again, when the counter attack did not come, and he took full advantage to gasp in some extra oxygen, which immediately helped calm his own rage at Kane's unexpected intrusion and violent interruption of what had been a rather enjoyable after dinner interrogation. The inhalation and brief respite helped Lord begin to reassess the situation he now found himself in.

The hooded man was saying something to him. What was it? Lord had never failed to connect with all four opening blows in any fight ever before and he tried to cast away the nagging doubt that was suddenly and unexpectedly intruding on his normally cool calculating. Ah! He suddenly understood the words spoken but not their context. The statement puzzled him almost as greatly as his failure to hit the target, causing him to pause longer than usual in his protective stance, as his normally quick mind began to decipher what was actually being said to him. He repeated it to himself. "I may be out of shape but you're right I am a big man! You ought to give me more credit! It might not be a full-time job for me but I am a very gifted amateur!" Kane's words equally amused and irritated Lord and he took another step back.

Kane watched the big man, with the borrowed bravado, retreat. He was also taking deep breaths but although there was perspiration on his brow, he was grinning. He was enjoying the success of his desperate defence. From the corner of his eye, Kane could also see that Pace had finally turned back to face him. Still standing sensibly out of range, but now elevated up on the step to the passageway, the one that ran from the back to the front of the Kettle, Pace now had a relieved smirk on his sly face. He was holding something in his right hand. Kane gradually recognised the metal cylinder. He had seen a similar one earlier that evening. It was an extendible baton, just like the one Dylan Francis had tried to use against him. Kane concluded that these weapons were obviously standard issue to all *ASSes!* Worryingly he could actually see the confidence growing on the pale face now that Pace had the comfort of a cosh in his hand.

More worrying, Lord had nothing in his big hands but he still seemed naturally more confident than his partner in crime. He was a big fit looking man. Standing strong and proud, like a championship boxer, eager for the bell to ring again so that he could start his next bout, and prove exactly what he was capable of doing this time.

'Idiot!' Kane muttered to himself, as his inner thoughts continued to silently reprimand him whilst he watched and waited for the next inevitable attack. What was he expecting to do that night!?! Why hadn't he armed himself!?! What exactly had his plan been!?! Kane repeatedly questioned himself, whilst desperately glancing around for some clue as to what he should or could do next. He knew that he certainly was not the professional he had once been and he doubted that he was close to being the gifted amateur his misplaced euphoria at surviving Lord's initial assault had led him to boast. Yet, he was somehow controlling his breathing and seeing Lord step back had filled him with a familiar self-confidence, one that he remembered from his early years spent in church halls and community centres, practising with Lao Fu, fighting without fighting. It was something that he had excelled at but it was something that he had not practised for years. He had missed it!

Kane suddenly sensed a slight movement behind him. The blonde woman it seemed had abandoned trying to revive the man on the floor. She was getting up, awkwardly, then once on her feet, she hunched again, hands curled, with her fingers hooked like claws. He was aware that she had stopped snivelling and was now giving Kane a look of pure hatred, whilst slowly edging sideways ever closer to blocking him off from the open doorway and his obvious escape route back out into the dark and damp night air.

Any escape towards the front exit would be effectively blocked by Lord and Pace. Also, Calamity was hanging from the beam, providing another significant obstacle in the path to the front way out. Calamity was not unconscious. He seemed to be muttering to himself senselessly in what must have been shock. Kane spotted that Calamity's trousers were wet and they appeared to be unnaturally stuck, almost melted, to his lower legs. There were faint wisps of steam still rising from them. On the floor, one step ahead of Kane stood a large metal saucepan. Catering size. It still had a few centimetres of what looked like water floating around in it. Kane quickly deduced that it must have been put down there by Lord's large track-suited man. The (fortunately for Kane) unconscious one, who was still lying silently on the floor to Kane's left. No doubt he had been sent to see what was happening outside and had been surprised. Very surprised. Kane took an instant pleasure in the fact that one of his friend's torturers seemed badly injured.

Just then Lord chanced a step forward and Kane aware of the slight movement broke the silence, nodding towards Calamity with a subtle movement of his head to ask: 'So what have you lot been doing to him?'

'Torturing him, obviously!' Lord jeered back.

'Why?' Kane asked not expecting an honest answer, he was just desperately buying time in the hope that he could work something out. It was Pace who answered:

'Well, believe it or not My-Key, we wanted to know why he was with you this morning! At the cemetery! What a wasted effort! If only we'd known that you were coming we could have waited and simply asked you!' Pace sneered back at him.

'And what did he tell you?' Kane asked, watching helplessly as Pace slowly moved around a little further to the left, so that they had Kane at the centre of a semi-circle, with his back to the wall.

'What do you think he would have told us?' Lord spoke with almost a hint of hope in his voice.

'No such thing as a free curry!' Kane surprised himself at his coolness.

'Very droll!' Lord smiled back sounding like a character in a movie but Kane was not sure which one. 'But seriously, I am not an unreasonable man.' Lord continued. 'However, I suspect Sergeant O' Neil here, might disagree!' Lord gestured with a slight backwards tilt of his head towards the semi-conscious man hanging behind him. 'But then he has betrayed me! Doing business with us under false pretences and it is very important to me that I find out why that is! If you could help us in this matter we would certainly make it worth your while!'

Kane heard the words but was concentrating on Lord's breathing. It had calmed right down and was as steady as his voice. The big man had also, ever so subtly, moved a little closer again and was oddly taking his time to remove the rather theatrical red cowboy style kerchief from around his neck as he talked.

'Ah, but I don't think your lady friend over there is in the mood to be reasonable!' Kane gestured, with the slightest movement of his head, towards the angriest looking woman that he had seen for years. Lord followed the nod with his dark eyes. They narrowed slightly.

'Kim will do as I tell her! Won't you Kim?' His voice had become as deep and dark as his stare, which briefly met her eyes.

'Ah but good old Flicker there!' Kane continued and Lord could not help but follow Kane's eyes as he now nodded his head and glanced towards Pace. 'He knows me of old! And he'll tell you that I'm an unreasonable type of guy, won't you mate!?!'

Lord's sideways glance was not much of a distraction but it was enough for Kane to surprise the most dangerous of his three adversaries. Stepping forward, Kane kicked out and somehow managed to connect with the handle and flick the saucepan off the floor, so that it flew up towards Lord's groin. The big man quickly bent back, just in time, successfully ensuring that the metal did not strike him with any significant force. However, the remaining water sprayed out into a small arc and splashed on Lord's right leg. The water was warm rather than hot and had lost its sting, having been off the boil for sometime now. Yet, Lord surprisingly anticipated a scald, pulling a pained expression on his face, before actually beginning to shake his leg instead of striking back at Kane. When the big man realised that he had not been horribly burnt, like his latest torture victim, it

360

was too late. The saucepan clattered harmlessly down to the floor but it made a loud enough noise to startle the nervous Pace, who jumped back as he also expected the worst. In the confusion, Kane had started for the open back door. Kim was alert and had angrily leapt over to block his path. She was snarling at him, her brilliant white teeth bared like the wild lioness she really was! Yet, her movement had left a gap to her left and at the last minute, Kane swerved away from her reach and in a zigzag darting movement, he completely changed tack and made for the kitchen. His sway away from the back door confused Pace, who in his panic, had flicked out his baton to its full length and tried clumsily to swat Kane. Pace missed but caught the advancing Lord instead. The blow was shrugged off by the big man, even though it had stung a lot more than the warm water. Nevertheless, it all gave Kane vital seconds, which proved to be just enough time for him to reach the narrow gap in the serving hatch partition to the tearoom's open plan kitchen.

Once in the kitchen, Kane stretched and snatched up a second saucepan. This, he had noticed, had been boiling away on the kitchen's commercial gas hob, forgotten by the others. Kane hurled the almost full pan of bubbling water blindly behind him and almost immediately heard the howls of pain as it splashed into the faces of his two pursuers. He did not look back but pressed on, into the small rectangular side room, which had been his friend's kitchen and once the hub of his business. Kane could hardly believe his luck. There, still laid out with military precision, hanging from open hooks, and unbelievably ignored by the new, non-catering owners, were a full set of professional kitchen knives.

Kane grabbed the lowest first, a small thin bladed boning knife. He turned and threw it expertly towards his target. Spinning through the air its rotations ended when the blade caught Pace hard in the gut. Just as he let out a winded gasp, a

361

second blade was flying through the air. Lord, the back of his hands and his right cheek, turning red from the scalding water, saw it coming and ducked down behind Pace. This time, the balance of the slightly longer bladed fillet knife was slightly off and it was the hand grip which hit Pace in his left shoulder, which although painfully bruised, merely deflected the knife off and away down to the floor. By the time Lord's head had popped up, Kane had grabbed the largest knife from the top of the rack. It was a long thick bladed chef's knife. He held on to this in his right hand and waved it menacingly, making short cutting motions in the air. Lord got the message and began to back away. In his own mind, the big man vowed never to go anywhere again without a proper weapon, and not just the simple kerchief he enjoyed using to strangle the unexpected. He now held this uselessly redundant in his hand when what he needed was a sword or a gun!

Pace backed away also, or rather staggered backwards, allowing Kane to advance, knife first, towards the wide open server worktop. Pace's face and neck had red blotches over them, where the boiling water had splashed him. The collar and chest of his shirt were wet and were sticking to the scalded skin below. However, Pace's hands tightly gripped around the knife's hilt as it protruded from his stomach. A small sticky red patch was growing bigger around his hands by the second. Finally, Pace plonked himself down on one of the wooden chairs that stood at the side of the room. The effort made him groan with pain as his body sagged and he felt the knife metal deep in him.

Kane dipped his head down cautiously to look through the open hatch. He was slightly confused by the big man's slow retreat towards the open back door. Lord was silently gesturing to Kim and together they squatted down to grab their tracksuit wearing man, who although still on the floor, was slowly beginning to move as he started, at last, to hesitantly come

362

around. Yet he was obviously concussed and unable to get up by himself. It took both Lord and Kim to unceremoniously drag him backwards, each holding an arm.

Lord looked back at Kane with a puzzled gaze on his face. Kane assumed that he was probably wondering why Kane did not pursue them but Kane had other objectives and he did not want to risk them by fighting with strangers. Lord and the woman would be a force to be reckoned with, even though Kane was now armed with the large long bladed kitchen knife. It was wise to let Lord go because glancing over to where Calamity was still hanging, body now limp Kane knew his old comrade badly needed hospital treatment.

'Don't go! Don't leave me!' Pace suddenly realising that he was being abandoned by Lord, began crying out in a pathetically mournful repeated bleat from his seat. He tried to get up but stopped as the slightest movement added to his pain. Hunching over, head down, Pace whispered weakly. 'We're partners! We've got big plans!'

'This is your mess! You sort it out!' Lord spat out as he disappeared through the open doorway out into the backyard.

'Noooo! I need you!' Pace was in a panic and almost crying now. He tried to get up again and failed again.

'Sit!' Kane growled, pointing the big knife's steel point at his apparent prisoner. Pace sat.

Using his left hand, Kane produced his mobile phone after an awkward battle unzipping his borrowed jacket's left hand pocket. He glanced towards the empty doorway, half expecting to see Lord and Kim rushing back in with some kind of weapon, before taking the risk of looking down to dial the emergency services number, relieved that he did not have the added palaver of entering the usual security protocol of his pin number. There was no ring tone or at least he did not hear one, only the young woman's calm and business like voice bursting out, almost

363

instantly, from the hands-free loudspeaker. 'Hello, you've dialled 999, which emergency service do you need?'

'Ambulance please!'

'Are you ringing from your own phone?' The woman asked.

'Yes this is my own phone. We need an ambulance here immediately! A man has been badly burned or rather scalded at The Copper Kettle Tea Rooms in Lower High Street, Aberfoist Town Centre.'

'And stabbed!' Pace added pitifully in the background. Kane hoped the sad little voice had been too faint to be heard at the call centre down the other end of the phone line. He took a deep breath and thumbed the hands free speaker off, whilst starring menacingly back at Pace, giving what he hoped was a clear indication that he had better shut up! At the same time Kane also tried to sound calm and patient, like the voice on the other end of the line, which had begun reading through a check list of questions, all part of the process designed to identify if this was a genuine call or one of the many hoaxes that constantly plagued the emergency services.

'No I don't know the number or the post code!' Kane answered the woman's next question, having raised the phone to his left ear. 'Yes, it was an accident. No, I don't know how it happened. I wasn't here at the time. I have just arrived and found a badly injured man. I think he is in shock. My name!?! Yes, it is Ellis Pace. I am the security guard for the premises.

'I am putting you through to the emergency service now, Mr Pace. Please stay calm.' The woman sounded calm at her end of the line. She had been well trained. Kane just about remained calm at his end of the phone. He was wondering how he was going to explain his actions that night to the paramedics. They were bound to report the incident to the police and because he had used his own mobile to ring 999 there was no denying that he was there! Using Pace's name had been a mistake but Kane had enjoyed provoking the scum-bag currently whimpering in the chair just across from him, who less than five minutes before was eager to hit him with a metal cosh.

Pace had heard Kane use his name and he had actually forgot his woes to bristle at being described as only a "security guard" but then he had quickly returned to his muttering and moaning when another sharp pain throbbed across his stomach. The only real distraction from the fact that he had a steel blade in his gut was the hot sting from his own burns. Yet resentment was at times acting like a mild anaesthetic and like a child, Pace had started to constantly repeat to himself: 'It's not fair! I don't deserve this! I had big plans!'

***

Kane need not have worried about his excuses or the woman on the other end of the phone hearing the muttered moans of the real Ellis Pace. Technology was such these days that when it worked properly, it was a truly an amazing aid to the emergency services. The operator already knew the identity allocated to the phone number because it was displayed on her screen and it was not the name given by the caller. She could also see on her screen that name identified as the phone's owner was the same name as that which had been posted just minutes before on a special location request that the system had received from Gwent Police. The system had matched the incoming call to the request and was now alerting Police Headquarters. Within minutes, Kane's location would be transmitted to a young blonde CID officer, who was conveniently standing in a newly discovered crime scene less than five minutes walk away. The detective had been off duty in Aberfoist but after staff at The Himalayas Indian Restaurant in the town had reported finding two men lying in the alley behind their premises, he had been alerted and in the absence of any more senior officers, instructed to lead a serious assault investigation. Apparently the report call had been slightly delayed because the owner of the restaurant had first tried to get hold the men's employer. Unfortunately, the employer had turned his phone off, so he could not be called or subsequently located, until that is Ellis Pace had allegedly called the Emergency Services, using the phone of another *person of interest* currently being sought by the police, all thanks to information suggested by the young blonde CID officer.

With the mobile phone pressed hard against his one ear, Kane listened intently with the other to the sounds coming from outside. He thought he could here the woman wailing and certainly there was a deep man's voice cursing in a foreign language. A car door slammed shut. Another one opened. Then the sound of a large diesel engine spluttering into life was followed by a loud ticking, like a tractor was idling out in the backyard. Eventually wheels spun and gravel crunched under the weight of the car reversing away. Then a smoother engine sound could be heard as the drive gear took over and the car sped away.

Kane could not believe his ears. For a brief moment, he still expected Lord to reappear. Kane then wasted time wondering to himself, why Lord or Pace did not have a gun! Why would a person capable of torturing someone, especially someone whom they thought was a policeman, not carry a gun these days!?! The only possible answer Kane could come up with was arrogance. Lord was a big and useful man; a man with two large minders and a powerful woman beside him. Perhaps he sought to avoid the unnecessary complications carrying a firearm could bring if he was stopped by the police, just like he had been the other day, on his motorbike, when Kane had first seen him. Only one other fool had gone into this situation without a weapon and that was an idiot called Mykee Kane! That idiot suddenly found himself smiling to himself as a childishly stupid thought crossed his mind. Not carrying a weapon had got them all into hot water!

Stooping down with the thin smile still creasing his otherwise stern face, Kane quickly gathered up the fillet knife from the floor using the hand that still held his mobile phone. He swapped the knife clumsily into his right hand just as a different woman, with an equally calm and professionally polite voice could be heard faintly calling out of the phone's speaker:

'Gwent Ambulance Service!'

Chapter 37: A Night on the Tiles

There were eight tiles in each line across. Ten tiles in each line along. That probably made nine or eleven, if you were generous when adjusting the figures to allow for those split tiles that fitted into the corners or made up the top and bottom rows of the slightly uneven walls. Kane continued counting the white rectangular tiles, intent on checking the figures now stored in his head. Each tile was about the size of his hand span, when his hand was spread as wide as he could make it. He was eventually satisfied that there were twelve parallel lines, each running over the long wall beside him and they appeared to join up neatly to the lines on each of the neighbouring walls. So, according to his mental arithmetic, Kane had calculated around forty tiles in each of the lines that wrapped around him, as he had sat nonchalantly waiting all night long, perched on the tiny bunk bed, which was fixed flush to the back wall of the small cell. Yes four hundred and eighty tiles in total, he concluded again. He was proud not so much of his mathematical prowess but his ability to distract himself from the stress of his uncomfortable incarceration.

If the strong smell of disinfectant was anything to go by, then the cell must have been cleaned fairly recently. Nonetheless, the tiles still looked extremely grimy to Kane. They were definitely not as soiled as the stainless steel toilet, which was fixed squat against the left hand side wall, a little less than two foot from the pillow that had been fastened at the head of the hard bunk bed. Nor were they as grungy as the mini steel sink, just a short stretch further along and two rows up from the tarnished steel bowl, with its worn smooth, yet dark stained, wooden blocks, screwed down tight onto the rim, as a poor substitute for a civilised toilet seat. Yes, Kane decided, all the tiles were tainted, covered in the kind of dried on dirt, that no doubt had begun to congregate almost immediately on the intended to be shiny surface of the new tiles, when they had been first fixed to the cell walls. All ruined probably because the original tiler had considered it beneath him to actually wash the surplus adhesive off properly, and his apprentice, if he had one, had happily skipped that job too.

Nevertheless, the tiles were definitely white. Which was more than Kane could say about the colour of the unevenly spread grouting? Perhaps it was always meant to have been greeny brown. Then again maybe it had been white too, once upon a time, then cream, and at some stage even plain brown, but now it was most definitely neither brown nor green. Kane hoped that it had been corrupted over time by the gallons of disinfectant used. In his optimistic imagination he saw whoever was responsible for cleaning the cell, generously slapping on the cleansing agent in an anxious effort to rid themselves, rather than a prisoner, from the risk of infection, knowing that they would be required to breath in the same air more often than the individual members of society's low life that temporary resided here. If only the cleaner realised, Kane thought, that the real criminal contagion that infected society was usually bred in less obvious places than local police station cells.

Just as he was beginning to count the larger, blue grey floor tiles one more time, Kane heard footsteps stomping down the corridor outside. They strode towards him in a quick purposeful march. Heavy footsteps and their makers sounded as if they were in a rush. When they eventually came to a halt outside his cell, he could hear someone, still moving around, unable to stand still. A pair of soft soled shoes was pacing about nervously, whilst the noisier boots remained stationary. Kane had heard those heavier

369

boots marching up and down the corridor at least once an hour during the night, probably to check the cells or more likely their owner was enjoying disturbing the sleep of his guests. Their owner was most likely to be the one responsible for was using the clunky metal key that excitingly sounded like it was unlocking the reinforced steel door to Kane's cell.

Kane had been left isolated for perhaps eight noisy checks, or was it nine; he had only started counting them after the first few, when he realised that they were going to be regular events, punctuating his stay. Anyway, Kane had almost lost track of time. He must have been there all night. Eight or nine checks were probably four or five hours or longer. All he really knew was that he had been there for what seemed like a long long time, but now they obviously needed to talk to him. And from the clamour their feet had made along the corridor, they wanted to talk to him urgently. He did not need to talk to them, for he still had the floor to count if he was to complete his mental audit of the cell's building materials.

When the key finished turning, the metal plated viewer, positioned three quarters of the way up, in the middle of the door, clanked open. A pair of cold grey blue eyes stared in blankly, just as they had regularly throughout the night and then, unlike the previous checks, a deep mature voice suggested in a polite but firm and slightly sardonic Welsh accented tone: 'Now stay sat on your bed. There's a good gentleman. Thank you, Sir!'

Kane recognised the tone of an old-fashioned soldier. An NCO, who expected to be obeyed but was prepared to deal with any disobedience in the same matter of fact way as he spoke. Kane was happy to comply with the command, for now.

Seemingly satisfied that Kane was going to be "a good gentleman", the handle turned and the door opened in to its left. Kane's right. The bald, barrel-chested, Custody Sergeant, who had actually brought Kane a plastic cup of weak, heavily sugared and thus for him undrinkable tea, an absolute age ago, gave the prisoner a curt nod before stepping speedily aside. He was replaced by a tall, grey haired man, who looked, because of the worry lines creasing his face, to be at least ten years Kane's senior. Stepping nervously into the middle of the cell, this man was dressed in an immaculate dark blue police officer's uniform. On the jacket his epaulettes bore one pip below a crown. Kane was not aware of exactly what rank that made the man but the fact that he still wore his peaked cap inside the building, seemed to indicate to Kane, that whatever rank he was, the officer felt it was essential to keep up appearances if he was to maintain authority and respect. Therefore Kane deduced that he must be a high ranking officer, who was useless at his job. He was obviously agitated and fidgeted uncomfortably, rocking back and fore, as he stood in front of the prisoner. Kane sat perfectly still, on his bunk, keeping his eyes down as he continued to pretend to count the tiles on the cell floor.

The over-excited officer was followed in, rather casually, by the tall blonde, plain clothed officer, who had been with Calamity in The Himalayas Restaurant. The younger man had already changed his clothes from those he had worn when he had arrested Kane at The Copper Kettle Tea Rooms, during what must have been last night. He appeared to be very clean and well rested in his smart light blue, bespoke lounge suit. Yet he still wore the same Police Federation tie, which somehow looked cheap and out of place against the very dapper tailoring. Even though Kane appeared to keep his eyes down, he also noticed that the young man wore a large, expensive looking, wristwatch, which must have absorbed most of the policeman's annual salary.

'Thank you Sergeant. That will be all for now.' The older, agitated man dismissed the jailer, with more than a snap of impatience in his voice. The Sergeant, for his part, looked slightly concerned at the command but after the smallest of shrugs, he

371

disappeared from the doorway and Kane could hear the heavy boots retreating up the corridor away from the open cell. Of course, just before he moved, the sergeant had given one regulation stare, deliberately at Kane. It was the simplest of looks from those cold grey blue eyes but it conveyed an uncomplicated message, with real authority. Behave or else!

'So Kane!' The Commander began, his blood shot eyes bearing down angrily at his prisoner's forehead, for Kane's eyes were still scanning the flooring. 'Why do you think you are here?'

Kane said nothing in response but he did slightly raise his right hand and slowly opened it out flat and wide, in a gesture that seemed to say: "Hang on a minute!" Or even "Can't you see I'm in the middle of something!" The blood shot eyes darted furiously to the left and briefly bore into the younger man's brighter brown eyes. The Commander seemed to be equally offended and bewildered by Kane's casual response. What on earth is this man doing? The question was silently communicated between the policemen before the red eyes darted back to bore into Kane's face. Then ultimately they looked down, glancing, puzzled and utterly perplexed, in the general direction that the prisoner was looking but they saw absolutely nothing, only the floor of the cell.

'Twenty-five!' Kane suddenly spoke up, casually nodding as if to confirm how pleased he was with himself. Looking up he added: 'That makes it five hundred and five in total!' Kane then allowed a genuine smile of satisfaction to brighten up his face and his clear blue eyes finally met the pulsing, blood shot eyes, full on for the first time.

The smartly uniformed man was starting to redden in the face. The relaxed nature of the meaningless exchange was more than enough of a challenge to his authority to almost produce a violent heart attack in the Commander. Finally he exploded in a rage and spat out a torrent of angry questions. 'Have you gone

372

mad? What are you actually saying to me?'

'Five hundred and five in total!' Kane interrupted the rant rather matter of factly and turned his benevolent smile towards the young officer.

The Commander's hands flopped awkwardly by his waist and began curling in and out of fists, as he struggled to avoid totally losing his composure. 'I asked you a question and I want an answer!' The words were now spoken through gritted teeth and then the officer hissed a repeat of his original question at Kane. 'Why do you think you are here?'

'Oh I was rather hoping you gentlemen were going to tell me that!' Kane shrugged quietly.

The Commander's right hand began to visibly shake. The younger man frowned for the first time and he stepped forward, almost protectively blocking Kane from what, for a few seconds at least, seemed likely to be an inevitable physical assault.

'Perhaps I should, Sir!'

'Yes Haymer, please do!' It was almost a groan and the uniformed man stepped back two paces, almost ending up out across the threshold of the cell, before swaying left and right, his hands now clasped behind his back but still nervously pumping the fingers of his right hand in and out of a grip around his left.

'You will be charged with a serious assault on a police officer and the suspected murder of Mr Ellis Pace.' The young man calmly but sternly announced. 'Why do you think that is?'

'Good question!' Kane nodded his approval.

Haymer rolled his eyes but kept his patience and tried again. 'What Superintendent Charles here would really like to know, Mr Kane, is exactly what happened at The Copper Kettle last night?'

It was a good question in fairness to the young detective and in truth Kane was not really sure. Yes, he could if he chose to, actually recall the events that he had witnessed and participated in, but so much had happened before his brief and rather

373

dynamic intrusion that he was still struggling to put the whole evening into context. Kane had also been trained not to dwell on such events, until a formal debriefing, in order not to betray his true purpose or role in them, and the fact that this current interrogation was not what he would call formal and his interrogators obviously had their own agenda made him disinclined to co-operate. So instead he distracted himself by returning to his counting, this time attempting to calculate how many tiles were blocked out by the open cell door.

The young plain clothed policeman was prepared to wait patiently for an answer. He had read in a book during his time at university, where he studied Criminology of course, that the ability to wait was strength and that waiting was a positive tactic. Unfortunately, his superior had not been to university. He had risen up the ranks because he was a man of action and luck. Now fearing he was out of luck, his limited supply of patience was exhausted by the silence and the blank looks, he was sure that Kane was purposely giving them. Pushing passed the younger man; Superintendent Charles grabbed Kane by the collar of his borrowed black Aberfoist Security Services T-shirt and began to shake him violently as he tried to drag him up from the bunk.

'What did O' Neil say? Tell me you bastard?' Charles shouted into Kane's face, spraying him with spit as he did so.

Outside in the corridor, the custody sergeant bit his lip. He did not hold with this "old school" treatment anymore, especially as the prisoner was technically his responsibility. However, he had known, and liked, Sergeant O' Neil. He knew that the Irishman was in the local hospital's Intensive Care Unit and might not pull through. So he thought that if this prisoner was responsible for that, let along being responsible for the brutal death of a prominent local businessman, then who was he to get in the way of a senior officer and a bit of "old school" interrogation. Maybe just maybe, this time, he should turn a blind eye, even though the Sergeant knew from past experience that these methods rarely worked, unless they were part of some dodgy fiction.

At first, Kane did not seem to resist the uniformed officer's strength. He merely pushed himself up adding to the force that was dragging him off the bunk. At the optimum moment, just as the younger officer was apathetically calling out (for the record), "Sir! Please!" Kane slipped his left arm straight up in the gap between the extended forearms above the gripping hands, flattening his hand, so that his thumb pointed out to the left, slightly distracting the aggressor. Kane then twisted it, led by the thumb, turning his palm in, back towards his own face. At exactly the same time his right hand locked on to the officer's left wrist and with the gentlest of pushes or was it a pull, Kane had broken out of the grip and somehow, perhaps the highly polished soft leather black shoes had slipped on the heavily disinfected floor tiles, or maybe it was the pressure of Kane's left arm, arcing down and pushing the angry man's right arm away by knocking into his forearm, whatever, the uniformed officer began sliding down to the left and he ultimately landed on the tiled floor with a thump, and his smart peaked hat flew off.

The Custody Sergeant's "blind eye" saw the whole incident. He had his regulation truncheon out in seconds and had leapt into the cell, swinging at Kane, who sensing the attack, merely sat back down and watched the wood narrowly miss his chin by millimetres and carry on down to collide with the top of the senior officer's head. Downward momentum had met the upward energy exerted by the senior uniformed man as he had pushed upwards, whilst foolishly struggling to get straight back up off the floor. The blow drew blood.

Enraged at his own clumsiness the Sergeant swung his right fist, still gripping firmly onto the truncheon, back at Kane's face. Kane reacted late but still managed to move his head away at the very last moment, leaving the blow to initially hit thin air before swinging on until the knuckles inevitably connected with the tilled wall behind the bunk. In that instant, Kane was sliding his body across to the far end of the bunk. However, he could not resist the opportunity to hook the Sergeant's left foot away from under him, causing the suddenly unbalanced body to fall straight down onto the empty side of the bunk.

Looking up into the younger officer's horrified brown eyes, Kane tried not to smile and simply said: 'Really!' He then added: 'I hope the CCTV footage will be made available for my solicitor, when she arrives.'

Slowly shaking his own head, in obvious disbelief at what he had just witnessed, the younger man began to pull the Sergeant back up off the bunk. Disorientated as he was, the Sergeant obviously wanted to hit out again but he found his arms were held back by his wiser helper and through the red mist he heard Haymer say: 'I don't think this is a good idea, Sarg!'

Kane now watched, with his arms folded passively, from his new place to the left of the men, as together they helped the Superintendent up off the floor. A thin trickle of scarlet was dribbling from behind the Super's hairline. Seeing the damage he had done to the superior office, the sergeant blanched and instantly forgot his own stinging knuckles.

'Sorry Sir! We'd better get this seeing to!' The Sergeant said trying but failing to regain his composure. On finding his feet, the embarrassed Superintendent tried to brush him off, gruffly saying that he was alright and as both the uniformed men began backing out of the cell, the not so "Super" Superintendent barked a final command to the plain clothed officer: 'Haymer, I want the prisoner charged with assault!'

The young man blinked at the stupidity of it all. He quietly stooped down and collected the Super's hat from where it lay on the floor. Then straightening up he looked over at Kane and said rather too calmly: 'We will talk again, soon!'

'What about my solicitor and phone call?' Kane cheekily asked as the cell door shut on him once again.

Chapter 38: Fifteen Minutes of Infamy

Sat all alone again in his cell, Kane stopped counting the tiles and finally allowed himself to be tortured by the memory of Pace's sad voice, bleating pathetically like a little boy lost in his self pity. 'I don't deserve this! I had big plans!' Yet the recollection that really hurt Kane was of Pace crying and pleading: 'I didn't kill Frank! Honest My-key! I didn't!'

***

Having completed his 999 call to the Emergency Services and believing the ambulance service would be on their way, Kane expected to have no more than fifteen minutes alone with the wounded Pace. However, he could not concentrate on this longed for interrogation, until he had helped Calamity.

Using the big kitchen knife to saw through the nylon chord, Kane struggled to free and lower the now seemingly unconscious O' Neil to the floor. After checking for and thankfully finding a pulse, Kane ensured that the airways were clear. A quick glance down confirmed that the trousers looked to be stuck fast to Calamity's lower legs. Whatever remained beneath the material would surely be badly burned. Kane knew that normally clothing should be removed and the burn cooled but the ghost of repeated military first aid courses haunted him with good advice, so he decided not to attempt to remove the clothing.

Instead Kane asked the phantom medic hovering in his mind; about how long it was before cooling the burnt area would be pointless. Not surprisingly he received no answer. Kane tried to work out how long ago the scalding had happened. He remembered hearing the scream as he stood outside. Was that less than five minutes ago!?! Maybe! It seemed like hours, a lifetime ago possibly, for some certainly! Kane glanced over to where Pace sat clutching his red stomach. He felt no sympathy for Pace as he could still feel heat emitting from Calamity's wet legs. Kane wondered whether that was the first time the boiling water had been used. From the state of Calamity Kane guessed it was not.

Then hearing Pace moan out loud and sensing that time was passing, Kane made a decision. He leapt up and snatching the saucepan from where it lay on the floor, he ran back to the kitchen. Placing the pan into the big double sized commercial kitchen sink, Kane turned on the cold water tap and began to fill it up.

On hearing the noise of the water Pace looked up from the misery of his chair and seeing what Kane was doing, began to bleat in panic. 'No! No! My-key! No!' His once sly voice was pitiful to hear. Kane grasped what Pace was thinking and smiled. Beside him the gas hob was still burning away, flames brightly flickering up, a good two centimetres off the metal burners. Kane made another decision. Quickly, retrieving the second pan from where it had fallen when he had thrown it at his attackers, Kane swapped it, with the now overflowing first pan. Leaving it to fill with water, he enjoyed hearing Pace's continued pleas but said nothing in response to them. Instead Kane dashed back over to where Calamity lay.

In one sense Kane was relieved when his former comrade began to moan. The volume suddenly increased, as Kane had expected it to, but as Calamity cried out Kane continued to pour the cool water carefully over the scalded legs. Kane had given first aid to burns victims before. It was never easy. It certainly was not pleasant. The victim always struggles against the

379

treatment yet Kane knew that he had to be cruel to be kind. The whole thing was nothing if not painful and shocking to both the victim and the aider. At least no one was shooting at him here and now. Yet strangely Kane realised that he was crouching, just like on a battlefield. Unlike a battlefield, Kane had no morphine to administer. Nevertheless, he tried to reassure Calamity. 'Hold on mate! The medics will be here anytime now!' And then finding the strength to make his voice sound firmer, he added: 'Hold on soldier! That's an order!'

The moans Calamity made were hushed compared to the self pitying groans coming from Pace. Between sobs, he had continued to mutter to himself. 'I don't deserve this! I had plans! Big Plans! It was going to be so good! I had everything under control. Fuck you My-Key bloody Kane! Every bloody time! You turn up, you spoil my plans!' Pace, in his increasing delirium, was getting angry. Oddly, he was remembering, when as a child, or rather a young teenager, he had tried to set fire to the old football stand in the derelict Aberfoist Park Rangers ground. The Gatekeepers, as the team had once been called, had had a proud history. They once played in the English Southern League and the historic wooden grandstand was still the envy of much bigger clubs. It would be filled, with hundreds of paying spectators, most Saturdays, but that was back in the Sixties and Seventies, according to Pace's father. With the gradual closure of the local factories and subsequent financial ruin of the club's benefactors in the infamous recession of the late Seventies and early Eighties, the club had shared in everyone else's hard times and eventually folded. The land was obviously wanted by developers and only a few nostalgic supporters were still trying to raise funds to out bid the builders. A refurbished grandstand was an essential part of the fan's rescue plan so Pace had seen an opportunity for pleasure and profit. His enterprising scheme had been frustrated because that evening Kane, with Frank John and a few other pals had decided to have a sneaky kick about on the old pitch. Like Pace, they had ignored the "Keep Out" signs and barbed wire. The boys were not best pleased to discover young "Flicker" trying to set fire to their beloved stand. This time it was Kane who had beaten the flames out, while Frank, in particular, had beaten Pace out! It was yet another reason why the young arsonist had borne a grudge against his so-called schoolboy chums; a grudge that had survived well into adulthood.

All the time that Kane dealt out first aid, he really could not believe that Lord and his lady had gone. Although Kane understood that he had done serious damage to their men and in any event, keeping your distance from a knife wielding manic was definitely a sensible thing to do, if you could, he was half listening for the sound of the returning car.

The coolness of the water, the shock of the burns or the general chill of the night air, entering through the still open back door, was now making Calamity shiver. Kane looked around the café and fortunately found a stack of cotton table cloths in a deep kitchen draw. He covered his injured friend in them. Kane did wonder whether he should use the roll of cling film that he had noticed, hanging from an open roller device next to the now almost empty knife rack, to bind Calamity's wounds. However, it looked dusty and so he decided the dirt might spread rather than prevent infection. Surely the ambulance crew would be here soon and they must have something better in their kit. Kane knew that he did not have long left and with nothing more practical to do for his friend, he turned his full attention back to the bleeding Ellis 'Flicker' Pace.

'Why? Ellis! Why?' Kane had asked, sounding almost sorry for the man he had despised so much, less than two hours ago. 'Why?' It was the one question that had troubled him for the past two weeks. Pace did not answer. He simply sobbed, consumed by pain, sorrow, and fear for his plight. Kane walked into the kitchen and purposely moved the second saucepan from the sink to the burning hob. He then moved closer to Pace and standing over him asked again: 'Why?'

Both men knew why the saucepan was beginning to boil. Pace shook at the thought of what he had witnessed earlier now being done to him and in spite of the pain of the knife, which was still stuck in his stomach, he found the strength to answer angrily. 'Why what?' Pace sneered back.

In truth Kane was not sure what he was asking Pace. Why did he abuse young girls? Why had he helped torture Calamity? Why had he killed Frank John? Kane might just as well have asked Pace why he liked flickering flames. He knew that it was just something evil in him! However, when Kane finally asked again he was more specific and he was surprised at the reaction to his question: 'Why did you kill Frank John?'

'I thought I wanted to kill him once!' Pace had started to say; surprisingly lucid given the blood loss he was suffering. 'He always got in my way! You both always get in my way!' Pace twisted his mouth into a snarl and then grimaced in pain. 'You two always tried to stop my fun! And you've done it again, tonight! Haven't you! My-key Bloody Kane!' Pace tried to snarl again but another wave of pain washed over him and he merely whimpered instead. 'I should never of trusted Dylan Francis to do you! You were right about him. He really is a Dull-One!' Kane ignored the distraction of the poor grammar, although he did register the fact that Pace seemed not to know about Francis and Dai Oaf. Patiently he asked Pace again about Frank John.

'Honestly, I wanted Frankie alive!' Pace began to insist, as sincerely as his sly nature would allow him to be. He carried on swearing that he wanted Frank John alive before craftily adding that he wanted good old Frankie alive enough to witness Pace's own success in business. Alive enough to know how dodgy that business was and alive enough to realise that there was nothing he could do about it. Pace paused for a moment, but just as Kane thought Pace had finished his bitter rant the injured man began again, this time boasting that he particularly enjoyed parading his sexy young wife in front of "Frankie" knowing that the man was alone, divorced and estranged from his own wife and kids. Pace surprisingly did not ask after Martini. Instead he continued to punctuate each spiteful statement with the phrase "alive enough to know" and he freely admitted corrupting Frank's daughter, Jan. Pace seemed proud to have tricked into her into making the video and laughed that it would always be out there, online for all to see, especially as it was a pathetically poor performance from the wannabe model.

Kane listened and with each bitter statement that was spat out by the miserable excuse for a man in front of him, his own anger grew. Somehow he kept himself under control, as his own outrage burnt not hot like a fire but cold like the sting of ice, freezing him from any natural compassion for a dying man. A man he had grown up with, a man whom he should have stopped a long time ago.

Finally, Pace told Kane that he was only disappointed that Frank had not worked out that it was he who had destroyed the Tea Rooms business by buying up the other struggling shops in the area and closing them down or worse, renting them out to less salubrious competitors.

'Did you know that it was my men who kept Frankie's boy supplied with the wacky baccy?' Pace added, almost rejoicing now.

'So if not you, who killed Frank then?' Kane asked coolly, refusing to show his growing frustration. 'You don't expect me to believe he really hung himself do you!?!'

'Got you worried though! Didn't it!?! Your bloody hero! Big Frankie eh! No, the suicide was all my idea! Clever, eh!' Pace began to laugh and carried on laughing, in spite of the pain it

383

obviously caused him. Kane took a deep breath and tried hard not to strike the vile man. Pace did not notice the clenched fist. He had his eyes closed, as if concentrating hard, to remember exactly what had happened, instead of the many lies that he had already told. Eventually he got his story straight in his mind and with a deep breath he began his sad confessional once again.

'No! No! It wasn't me who killed Frankie John. It was your recent dancing partner, the Paki! Bloody Lord Almighty himself!' Pace frowned. He paused for a moment, gathering his thoughts. 'Old Frankie was right about one thing! You can't trust 'em eh! He bloody well ran away! Bloody foreigner!'

Kane could not stop himself from staring towards the open doorway. The man he had let go was the man who had killed his friend. His impulse was to go after him right now but how? And where? Instead Kane stood still and listened to the whole story as Pace began to brag once more.

Pace was proud at how he had set up a sweet deal with Lord, his new drug supplier. Kane heard how they were going to invest their profits in the regeneration of Aberfoist, pretending the cash earned from the drugs trade were genuine loans from members of a fictitious consortium. Kane just had to interrupt. He did not believe that in these times of austerity the local drugs trade could really make that kind of money. Pace had just laughed back at him, then grimaced again and cried out in pain, all before trying to put Kane straight. 'You have no idea how much money people can find to get high!' Pace's breathing deepened but he carried on talking. 'They can't feed their kids but boy can they score!' He crowed excitedly. 'But the best thing now is this vaping lark! It's going to revolutionise everything! A totally legitimate cover! They reckon it's even going to be funded by the NHS! Safer than smoking tobacco see! No risk of cancer! Well maybe! Yep mix in a few "special" flavours, these so-called legal highs!' He chortled. 'Over the counter sales are actually encouraged by the

Government. Bingo! They will disguise all our under the counter deals and boost super profits!' Pace, as always, was in love with the sound of his voice. He kept on talking regardless of the pain, rambling on and on.

With time slipping away Kane had to refocus Pace and remind him. 'So Flicker, what about Frank?'

'Of course, Big Frankie wouldn't sell me his dead duck of a business! Blocking my plans he was. It bloody cost me! I used my influence to get the council to put up the rates. Priced a lot of the old boys out of the market eh! Well everybody shops online now anyway and if you don't go out shopping you don't need to stop off somewhere for a coffee eh! Soon had his business on its uppers! Mind you, I had to put pressure on the local bank manager to call in his loans! Lucky really that the old boy down at the bank liked my videos! Ha ha! Always visiting my web site, even on the bank's time! What you might call a proper banker eh! Isn't technology wonderful! You can track everybody, well if you have friends in the police that is!' Pace was enjoying himself now. He seemed to have forgotten the pain and the blood loss. Kane could not tell how bad he was, well Pace always had looked pretty pale and pasty.

'Anyway,' the injured man continued. 'So I got the Paki Valley Boys to front the deal to buy him out! Frankie had no other option! But then he bloody well changed his mind. Your mate Lord tried to change it back but you know Frankie, stubborn bastard!'

Of course Kane did. He could imagine his old friend was not one for friendly or any other kind of persuasion.

'Do you know your mate Lord' Pace continued suddenly full of his old sly sarcasm, 'has this thing about sharing a nice cup of tea with people. He drinks the tea and pours the boiling water over them. He reckoned it scares the shit out of them. Hurts like hell too! But he obviously didn't know Frankie eh! Old Frankie likes a bit of pain and he can't stand foreigners can he! Frankie had a right go at Lord! Telling him all about Afghanistan and Pakistan and wherever else bloody-Stan. Told him all that stuff you two got into over there! And what he was going to do to Lord. Stupid really! Lord seems to have a bit of a thing against our brave soldiers. He reckons we caused the war that killed his family. He completely lost it! Throttled poor old Frankie using that scarf he always wears! Told me it was like some Thuggee thing! Remember those villains in that Indiana Jones movie!?!'

Pace's eyes closed, and the pink tongue slide out like a snake, slowly slithering over his upper lip as he paused thinking about it all. 'Have you ever seen someone strangled My-key?' Pace hissed. 'Yes you probably have eh! Their eyes bulge out don't they! Weird eh! Bit of a mess really! But I kinda liked it! I get why Lord enjoyed it so much! I do! Anyway! I sorted it all out! Even the luscious Wendy believed her darling topped himself! Ha! You did too! Go on! Admit it! Didn't you!?!'

Pace's eyes half opened and slyly peered across to Kane. When Kane said nothing in reply, Pace simply carried on. 'Anyway, everything was going to be great, even when that tool, Russell, you remember him My-key!?! Old Bernie Russell, from school eh! A real nutter but a real bloody waster too, eh! He did have contacts mind you! Ha ha! Good contacts amongst all the local druggies! I used him but he almost spoilt things for us! You wouldn't believe it! He reckoned our new "legal" mix was too weak! Suppose it was for a crack head like him! So he had to add his own stuff to the juice we gave him to sell! Well we had our weekend users going off their bloody heads! Chaos! Well over the top! Mind you they were all eager for more! So I guess he did us a favour!'

'So you killed him too eh!' Kane interrupted and almost instantly regretted it because it had the effect of shutting Pace up as he realised what he had been saying.

386

'No, er no! He had a fire! I've never killed anyone My-Key!' Pace said defensively and then unable to resist, he added with a sneer: 'Off his head he was! Lucky for me though! I can develop the estate he lived in now. Nobody wanted him as a neighbour! Now he's gone there's money to be made!'

Kane could imagine the smug glint in Pace's eyes. Even behind the closed eyelids. 'A fire, hmm!' How unlike you Flicker! Is there any of my old associates that you haven't burnt?'

Pace smiled, even though it hurt him to do so! Then suddenly he seemed to remember the pain, and he groaned: 'How long are these bloody paramedics going to be?'

'Maybe Lord has gone to get them!' Kane suggested, happy to unhelpfully remind Pace that he had been abandoned by his partner in crime.

'No he's bloody legged it back to Ponty, I bet! Fucking coward!' Pace groaned and then he sneered: 'He bashed old Frankie but he couldn't touch you!' Pace's comments were not intended to sound like a tribute and his bitterness became more evident as he carried on. 'What happened to my boys? I didn't think Dylan could touch you but I thought Dai Oaf would've done you! He's a big wiry bastard but thick as shit!' Pace tried not to laugh as he said: "Dull-one" quietly to himself and then he groaned out loud again as the muscle contraction sent another savage ripple of pain through his weakened body.

'Oh I don't think Dai Oaf will be playing baseball again soon!' Kane tried not to smirk. 'Ponty? Which Ponty? Pool or pridd?' He did not mean to sound curious but he did and he was!

Pace ignored the question. Gritting his teeth he too was suddenly curious about how Kane had outwitted his ambush.

'Did the Dull-one run?' Pace bravely opened his eyes and seeing Kane dressed in one of his firm's uniforms, he began to wonder why?

'What about Martini?' He suddenly asked whilst gritting his teeth once again.

'Oh she was very helpful!' It was Kane's time to sneer. 'You know something Flick, er, Ell?' He added without hiding the sarcasm in his tone. 'I don't think she has your best interests at heart!'

'Huh!' Pace grunted, almost as if he could not care less. 'She knows what's good for her!' He spat out before groaning out loud when his stomach suffered yet another involuntary twitch. 'Where the hell are they!?!' He said urgently, meaning the paramedics. 'I'm going to bleed to death if that ambulance don't get here soon! I pay my fucking stamp!' His voice drifted down into a low grumpy mutter.

'Oh they're not coming for you!' Kane said quietly, with a real chill in his voice. He knew they could not be much longer and he was running out of time. Stepping forward, Kane placed his left arm around Pace's shoulder, then with his right hand he pulled the knife out of Pace's guts. There was a gasp of shock from the wounded man, followed by a loud cry of pain. Then Kane thumped the knife back in, once, twice, thrice, again and again until the high pitched screaming had turned into deeper winded grunts. With each stab, Kane had shouted: 'This is for Tia! This is for Jan! This is for Bernie! This is for Calamity! And this is for Frank!' Kane stepped back, leaving Pace hunched over in the chair, making a hushed gurgling noise. When it stopped Kane watched as the lifeless body rolled off the chair onto the floor.

It was probably less than five minutes later when the first of the emergency services arrived. They were not the paramedics. They were the police. The blonde plain clothed officer, with the police federation tie, nervously led four other uniformed officers, in through the back door. He looked distraught to see Pace lying on the floor in a pool of blood. Oddly the young officer seemed

388

to be even unhappier when one of the uniformed officers called out to him that Sergeant O' Neil was still breathing!

'Sir!' Another uniformed policeman yelled out a warning from where he was stood frozen, in front of the kitchen hatch, baton drawn and held up in a defensive stance. The fair haired man looked around, to see Kane, watching him, nonchalantly standing at the kitchen sink, where he had just finished calmly washing the blood off his hands. At that moment, the paramedics rushed in.

'Over there!' Kane called out, pointing towards Calamity. 'He's still alive!' Then turning to look at Pace Kane muttered. 'This one's dead! I really couldn't save him.' Kane paused and then almost in a whisper, he added: 'This time!'

***

Sat all alone in his cell, Kane allowed himself to be tortured by the memory of an argument with his old friend. Frank was all wound up. He was swearing that he was going to kill "Fucking Flicker!" That was a long long time ago. Kane had been horrified. He considered it beneath his friend. It was such a childishly and stupid reaction. He could not believe it, wanting to kill someone just because the town's old football stand had burnt down. At the time Kane had thought it was an accident waiting to happen. After all it was only a week or so after Frank had given Flicker one hell of a hiding for playing with fire. The little weed could not have been stupid enough to actually burn the stand down. Not after that warning!

"He's killed the spirit of the town!" Frank had raged. For Pace had returned to the old ground even after Frank and Mykee had thought they had warned him off!

A few months later a building company had bought the land and ended any chance of resurrecting the much loved local team.

The old football ground became "Gatekeeper's Park", an exclusive housing development, where large executive homes were built and sold to commuters mostly from the cities of Bristol, Hereford, and Gloucester.

The young Ellis Pace suddenly seemed to have come into money. A lot of money! He bought a brand new sports car. Alone in his cell Kane thought that perhaps he should have let Frank do it. Kill Pace! It could have prevented a lot of people's subsequent suffering.

Chapter 39: Regret in a Fast Car

Lord wrestled with his conscience much more than the steering wheel of his big black car, as the four by four had roared along the dark wet country road. He cursed his "Brotherhood" for their so-called code of discipline. A part of him wanted to breach the strict protocols and go back to confront Kane. His pride was hurt but he also knew instinctively that he had made the right decision. Amadid had warned him of an investigation and reminded him of his duty to the organisation, but this chaos was not the exit strategy they had had in mind. Lord had begun to recognise that even though the Irishman had admitted nothing, the very fact that he could so courageously withstand the torture surely meant that he was not your run of the mill bent copper. So Lord had really known deep down that the game was up long before Kane had arrived. The fact that Lord had also failed to best that fat man in their fight should have been proof enough that whatever Pace said, they were not up against a nosey ex-soldier but special law enforcement agents and it was definitely time to abandon his operations. However, being right did not make him feel better or less of a coward or hide his shame from Kim.

The woman was now sat in the middle of the back seat of the car, attempting to nurse the semi-conscious lumps of useless muscle that were her sons. Lord could see that they were in a bad way, and the fine spray of rain that blew constantly in through the smashed passenger window, soaking everyone was not helping matters. Lord did not care about them. He resented the fact that the boys had let him down. He had thought that he had trained them well, but they had proved themselves to be no more than just stupid thugs. No better than Pace and his men.

Lord felt no guilt for abandoning Pace that was always his plan. He doubted that the ambitious back street gangster would die from the knife wound, not these days what with all the advantages of this country's National Health Service; or at least not before Pace had talked to the authorities in a feeble attempt to get some kind of a deal, and in doing so tell them all the lies Lord had fed him. Lord allowed himself a thin smile of consolation. Pace's stories should cause maximum confusion and ultimately shield his secret organisation. With that thought in mind, Lord finally abandoned his mental search for some more palatable solution to his current dilemma. He sighed and allowed his big left hand to release its firm grip on the thick leather rim of the silver star embossed steering wheel. Slowly moving it down, he extended his long index figure towards the telephone up symbol, highlighted on the left stem of the three spoked circle. He pressed hard on the black button and a matching symbol lit up on the dashboard in front of him. Lord barked out the gruff instruction: 'Call Number One!' The device responded instantly and automatic dial up tones could be heard loudly tapping out an embedded code. Without turning his head Lord snarled into the back of the car: 'You lot stay quiet now!'

A few seconds later a loud ring tone sang out from the car's expensive six speaker sound system. After only five rings had been heard the call was answered and Lord immediately recognised the cheeky London accent of Amadid, in spite of his one word answer: 'Watcha!'

'Hello is that the Kabuli Kebab!' Lord began his deep voice sounding strangely nervous.

'For sure,' was the instant nonplussed response.

'Good! I need to order a special Kabuli takeaway!' Lord was unable to hide the resentment in his voice as he spat the coded words out through his gritted teeth.

'Home delivery or collection?' The Londoner spoke simply and unemotionally.

'It'll have to be a collection! I am not at home tonight!' Lord tried to make the statement sound matter of fact in spite of the unsettling background noise of the air gusting through the broken window. Realising that his speed was not helping, Lord eased his right foot's pressure on the accelerator pedal.

'Okay, what's your order please?' The voice at the other end of the line asked politely.

'Four house specials please!' Lord sighed.

'No problem Bro! About half an hour, okay?'

'Yes.'

'I can see your number on my device and know vat you are a regular customer so I'll text you vee collection point on your number as soon as we are ready, okay?'

'Yes!' Lord then added an almost sincere: 'Thank you!' But the phone line had gone dead.

So the deed was done. Lord would now have to learn to live with the humiliation of his first failure for The Brotherhood. He knew it had happened to others and it was the strength of The Brotherhood to accept and support each other in failure. Actively encouraging *"brothers"* to accept the inevitable and pull out of such compromised "situations" had been proven to be a successful strategy, which had so far ensured the existence of their organisation had remained a secret from the authorities.

Nevertheless, failure was hugely frustrating for someone as proud as Lord. Let alone costly. Everything had been going so well. Too well! Lord silently cursed Ellis Pace again. That man had tried to be too clever too soon but deep down; Lord knew that it was his mistake. He had encouraged the local villain and after all, killing that café owner was no one's fault but his own

393

and it had been that mistake that had led to all this. He increased the pressure on the accelerator pedal and drove on.

Ten minutes and ten miles further along that road, Lord noticed a luminous sign reflecting back from his car's headlights beam, indicating that he was approaching a lay-by one mile ahead on the left. He began to slow down. The reckless speed had never been about getting away from Kane or Aberfoist. It had been all about his personal rage. He knew it was reckless, foolishly tearing down the dark country roads, blind to the probability of an accident but that was how he drove; always like the madman.

The lay-by was fortunately dark and empty. He pulled in and stopped, intending to wait for the co-ordinates he expected to be texted to him shortly. He also wanted to fix something across the broken window. First he turned to look at Kim, properly, for probably the first time since they had left the café. She had certainly sobered up quickly. Maybe, he thought, their product was not that strong after all. He shrugged. Whether it was or was not would be irrelevant to him now. From within the darkness of the back of the car, her eyes glinted brightly back at him. They were still angry and wild. She had done what he had told her to do, as she always did, but he knew that for the first time in their relationship, she bitterly resented it.

'How are the boys?' He asked. It was a token gesture, he did not really care and his voice did not really sound concerned.

'Not good.' She replied. 'We gotta take 'em to A&E! They need to see a Doctor, like now!'

Lord frowned. He did not have time for this. Their job had been to protect him, not the other way around. He shook his head silently and saw the gleaming slits widen and burn brighter as his gesture merely fanned the flames of her rage. Lord just did not understand this British expectation that a hospital was the first point of call for any injury. A trip to the hospital was definitely not on his agenda. Too many awkward questions! Too long a delay or so he thought. He briefly considered kicking her out here and now but he selfishly decided to keep her with him. A part of him knew that Kim would not stay without "her boys" and to keep her sweet they must be looked after! His mind raced for a solution. If O' Neil was what he feared him to be, the police would be the least of his worries. Then again, he reflected, suddenly hopeful, O' Neil had been in such a bad way, maybe he would die! Lord wondered if he was dead already. All their futures depended on what O' Neil had already reported to his superiors.

Lord thought on. O' Neil did not look like an efficient man, but then that might just have been his cover. Lord would have to get his own man on the force to find out. That man would have more than a vested interest in getting involved and reporting back to Lord. The one thing he could trust about his man was that he would not want Lord arrested. He would hope but not know for certain that Lord would not talk. The arrogant policeman dismissed Lord as a mere criminal. A source of extra funding and it had suited Lord to maintain that delusion.

Just then Lord's mobile phone bleeped. The simple noise indicated that the expected text had come through. The directions were in the disguise of an order number and time. Lord extracted the post code. He entered every third number or letter from the long reference into the Mercedes built in Satellite Navigation system. Within seconds the route was planned and Lord could see that it should take 30 minutes to get there, wherever there was! No doubt it was a "safe house!" The red route-line ended deep in the blank shaded space on the electronic map that had appeared on his dashboard screen. It looked to be an almost empty, probably rural zone, south of the motorway, somewhere between Newport and Cardiff.

For a few seconds Lord reconsidered the advantages of

395

dumping "the boys" out of the back seat and leaving them in the lay-by. No! Kim would not like that and he valued her, almost, above everything else that he had acquired in this country. He got out and walked to the back of the car. Opening the large back door he raised the false floor in the boot compartment and extracted two large blankets. He handed one to Kim over the back seat. He looked into her wild eyes and spoke softly, telling her that it would not be long and when they were safe he would send for a doctor to get the boys checked out. "Privately! That will be best." He rather ambiguously added.

Watching Lord fix the second blanket over the smashed passenger window, Kim began to wonder where they were going and why they were running. She asked Lord and he firmly told her to "wait and see!" She was not happy but did what she was told.

Once the blanket appeared to be firmly trapped by the closed passenger door, Lord walked a few metres away. He was soaked through now by the drizzle but he was not cold. Pulling his mobile phone out of his trouser pocket, he tapped in the number of his contact on the police force. The call proved to be brief and fruitless. Lord was not really surprised at this time on a Friday evening, to hear that the man sounded drunk. No doubt another golfing afternoon had taken its toll on the senior officer. Frustrated, Lord chose not to waste any more time and quickly warned "his" man, the most expensive on his payroll, to sober up and be ready for an important call in an hour. Lord got back in the car and without a word to Kim, pulled on his seat belt and clicked the automatic transmission from Park into Drive. A few seconds later he was leaving the lay-by and accelerating along the road towards the distant orange glow of the South Wales conurbation, which lit up the distant horizon. He was driving fast, too fast, but the thoughts in his head were now spinning faster than the wheels on his car. He had new options in mind and oddly, he was look forward to his new adventure, with or without Kim, but definitely without the two heavyweights in the back.

Less than the anticipated thirty minutes later, the Mercedes was about to reach its destination. The car's wide tyres were splashing through muddy water along a narrow country lane, which was more like a stream than a road because the raised rough grass verges had stopped the overflow escaping into the deep ditches that ran parallel along each side of the poorly tarmacked road surface. There were no lights on anywhere in the dark marshlands and Lord felt he was about to drive off the end of the world until finally he had spotted in his car's full beam, just ahead on the left, across the flat landscape, a familiar black and white patterned Mercedes taxi. It was parked in what seemed to be the centre of the gravel laid farmyard. Almost immediately a giant shadowy shape moved out of an open barn doorway, right into the headlights of Lord's Mercedes SUV. The bright lights showed that the large man was dressed in the traditional garb of a devout Pakistani tribesman. He made a clear gesture with his massive hands, directing Lord to drive into the open and unlit barn. As soon as the car was inside, the giant reached out grabbing the single big wooden door and easily swung it shut behind him. The world outside the barn was plunged into darkness.

Chapter 40: Interview Room 2

In Interview Room Number 2, Superintendent Charles was feeling sorry for himself. His head had been sore long before the truncheon blow and he knew only too well that he should have been sleeping off his hangover instead of being stuck in Aberfoist Police Station. He had achieved little since first arriving in the dark at silly o'clock on a Saturday morning. To make matters worse the bruising was now beginning to swell up right across the back of his head, just where it would be most visible, thanks to his thinning hair line. The young WPC, who was gently dabbing away at the naturally widening cut with a damp ball of disinfected cotton wool, was not really helping sooth his stinging irritation. Nevertheless, he remained extraordinarily polite to the blushing blonde in the perverse hope of impressing her with his personal bravery. Although immature and inexperienced, WPC Gould had the looks and certainly the figure to interest him in advancing her career, but only if she would prove to have the right aptitude and sense of discretion required to work closely with him in the future, and that would be very closely if the Super had his way.

Aside from such fanciful delusions, Charles was particularly concerned about how he could extricate himself from this unexpected and increasingly awful mess in time to get to his next vitally important appointment, another golf match, later that afternoon. Well, this one was especially important to him because it would not only allow him to represent the Force in public, and fulfil his otherwise onerous duty to be seen as active in the local community, but also increase his network of extremely wealthy (and therefore highly influential) businessmen; if such an elite group could be truly considered a valid part of the otherwise brassic local community. However, such people were definitely an essential part of his networking ambitions, mainly because they were usually happy to subsidise his expensive hobby, by paying his various club memberships, covering his costly green fees, and of course, settling his exorbitant golf club bar bills, all for the merest hint of assistance and occasional personal advice in how they and their businesses might avoid certain inconvenient legal issues. Such people were so unlike the awkward Mr. Lord, who could never be part of such grand society. Such a vulgar and uncouth man, well he was foreign wasn't he! Just because he made large regular payments into an offshore trust account set up for a "charity" run by Mrs Charles, Lord seemed to expect Charles to be at his beck and call, day or night. It was Lord who had aggressively demanded that Charles drop everything and get personally involved in this unsavoury affair.

Charles also begrudged having to commandeer a mere police interview room, especially when it was the size of a broom cupboard. Unlike the recently refurbished Police Headquarters, in the newly created City of Newport, where he was normally based, there were no grand offices in a local "nick" like Aberfoist; which was one of the few that had remained open in Charles's region after yet another cost cutting exercise. Offices in local "nicks" were "real" working rooms and usually in such a dilapidated state that typing up reports (on their own laptop or iPad) in the back of a police car, was a much preferred option for most ordinary officers. The alternative room that Charles had been first shown following his surprise early morning arrival, by the overwhelmed but extremely attractive, young police constable, was a poignant example of such underinvestment in front-line resources. No doubt the constable, who seemed to be the only person onboard the Mary Celeste that was Aberfoist's

"Cop Shop", was expected to include cleaning amongst her duties as and when she had a quiet moment, which of course she never did because she was one of only six police officers on duty in a town and surrounding area of approaching twenty thousand residents. In real emergencies, like today, off duty officers could "potentially" be called in from home or stations in the surrounding towns might even be "emptied" to ensure there was *enough* "plod" out on the street to reassure the public that the thin blue line was taking a double murder seriously. Although Charles was always worried how such demand would affect his budget! At least he was reassured by the efficiency of the attractive young woman, who had on seeing the blood trickling down the senior officer's face, quickly produced a first aid kit and volunteered to clean the wound. She now calmly announced in a sweetly soft sigh that she did not think "Sir" would need stitches, before gathering her kit together and excusing herself to resume her duties on the station's front desk. She was so unlike that dim wit of a custody sergeant, who seemed only capable of hovering about and constantly apologising to him or so Charles thought, making a mental note to invite her out for dinner to say a personal thank you for her work on patching him up!

The junior officer, with a full head of fair hair, and wearing the expensive, bespoke tailored, light blue lounge suit, now sat down across the plain wooden table opposite Charles and placed the Superintendent's cap on the table top halfway between them. Disdainfully sipping at a thin brown plastic cup of vending machine coffee, the younger man appeared to be listening attentively to the rant, which his superior had begun as soon as the WPC had left the room. Occasionally, DC Haymer nodded his head in apparent agreement. At other times, he shook his head in empathy. If he had had the opportunity to get a word in, he might have actually said "Yes Sir!" Or perhaps added: "You are absolutely right, Sir!" Of course, the detective did not need to be a Sherlock Holmes to deduce that the situation was not good but he also did not need the panicky, older man, to keep telling him so. Beneath the calm exterior, he resented the way "The Super" seemed intent on laying the blame for "everything" on "everyone" other than "The Super" himself.

Haymer also hated working for an under funded organisation. Especially one which paid him so little that he had to consort with corrupt officers, just to enable him to enjoy life's little luxuries. He also bitterly resented the way he had been expected to sit on the side of the table that was normally reserved for prisoners! His mind was far more concerned about what germs might filter into his fine clothes from the grubbily stained and careworn chair, than the emotive nonsense being constantly spouted by his so called superior. He felt no loyalty to his fellow conspirators. The more he dealt with them and did their dirty work for them, he realised that they were greedy little opportunists. Men who, with perhaps the exception of that Mr Lord, lacked real ambition or the clear vision required to fully exploit their fortunate situation in life and as such, he had decided long ago, were not worthy of his respect.

***

Having recently retreated downstairs to the basement corridor of the modest two cell gaol, the custody sergeant stared bitterly at the door of the only occupied cell. He felt a fool. After years of distinguished public service, he had let his emotions get the better of him and the man behind the door was, in his biased book, totally responsible for what now seemed to be a career threatening incident. If the prisoner did not press charges for attempted assault, which these days, any duty solicitor, however placid and however green, was bound to insist upon, the sergeant knew that he had hit and drawn blood from a superintendent of police. Even though, in the immediate aftermath, he had been told not to worry about it, he did. Whilst he himself would say and do nothing, and he felt the superintendent would also not want the incident publicised, the sergeant knew these things always got out. He certainly did not trust that young DC. He was a sly one. Always watching and never saying much. The sergeant was also sure that the DC had been laughing at the two older men. He pictured in his own mind's eye, the young man grinning ear to ear as he had helped them get up. The sergeant sighed again. At best he would be a laughingstock. At worst he was finished in the job. A job he really loved in spite of all its recent shortcomings. He gritted his teeth. He knew that he would have to ask Teri, the young constable on the front desk, to help him. He did not like doing that but he was sure that she would show him how to get onto the computer, the one which kept the CCTV recordings. The Superintendent had ordered him to get the footage. Of course, he knew that they both knew that that was against the rules. However, what could he a mere Sergeant do about it! The Sergeant sighed again and worried what a mere WPC would think of such a request.

'Bloody technology!' He muttered to himself, whilst scowling up at the little ceiling camera, with it's constantly blinking red "on" light and lens pointing firmly towards the cell door. Why hadn't he paid more attention to that computer training course, back when he had been sent on it!?! Yes! He told himself again and again. She was a good girl, that Teri Gould. He was sure that she would help him out. Even though, it was against the rules!

***

Back upstairs, in Interview Room Number 2, the younger man was admitting (much to the obvious frustration of his older

402

superior), that he had no idea where "their" Mr Lord was! Their cash cow and his minions had simply disappeared. 'Yes Sir!' Haymer acknowledged. He had made the usual phone calls. He had even called in a favour with the neighbouring force and got one of their patrol cars to call in at Lord's snooker club, just before closing time, where the relief manager eventually gave up an emergency contact number, which annoyingly turned out to be The Aberfoist Hotel. There the hotel manager had, in turn, quickly confirmed that Mr Lord's party had checked in at 2 pm, as expected, but they had not returned since leaving with Mr. Pace about mid-afternoon.

The young detective did know, obviously, that later that evening Lord had left the restaurant for The Copper Kettle. He was with his woman, Kim what's-her-name, Sergeant O' Neil, Pace and Lord's two henchmen. Yes, when O' Neil had slipped outside to prevent the Dylan Francis incident escalating, Pace had quickly managed to communicate his sudden suspicion that O' Neil might be the spy in their midst, the one Lord had warned them all to be on the look out for and fortunately (or so Haymer had thought at the time,) it had been decided that he, Detective Constable Julian Haymer, should make himself scarce, so that he would not be incriminated in whatever the others intended to do to O' Neil. Even at the time, Haymer, had been mildly irritated by this unnecessary need to react immediately. All because some pleb who dealt drugs for Pace, had seen two men drinking a military toast at a funeral. Now he was almost despondent. How stupid! They all should have just waited. Knowledge is a weapon, waiting and watching, knowing that O' Neil was watching them but him not realising they knew he was, would have eventually revealed all they needed to know about what O' Neil actually knew about them. This, in Haymer's mind was pretty obvious! They were all villains and up to no good but what good would that do for O' Neil. Nothing! Or so Haymer believed. Absolutely

403

nothing without hard evidence! It would have been O' Neil's word against everyone else's word. However, the so called experienced "bad" guys had panicked. They needed to act, to strike back right away. They simply wanted to know all the answers right then and there. What did O' Neil have on them? Who had he told? And what a hash they had made of it! Pace was dead. O' Neil was as good as dead and Lord, the paymaster, the man who helped Haymer buy and maintain his luxurious wardrobe, had disappeared off the face of the earth, with his little gang in tow. All because of their impatience and unnecessary reactions!

Haymer had known that Pace was distracted by the presence of this man, Mykee Kane! Just because he had turned up out of the blue! After so many years! So what!?! Mykee!?! What a stupid name!?! Pace reckoned Kane was some kind of big time Special Forces Operative, who had served with Frank John and would be trouble if he suspected his old school friend and army buddy had not killed himself. Yet why should he!?! Pace just had the *guilts*. The Special Forces story did not check out. Ever cautious, Haymer had performed a simple background check, which merely confirmed that Kane had served with John over a decade ago but only as a UK based cadet training officer, hardly Special Forces albeit based up at Sennybridge. Anyway, Kane had been working uneventfully as a High School Teacher since then. Yes, he was a big man but too big now! Way out of condition to be a threat to professional villains like Lord and his two body builder bodyguards.

In fact, Haymer had been forming the opinion that Pace was up to something and his alleged concern about Kane was merely an excuse to distract everyone from whatever it was Pace was planning. Pace was always scheming. Nothing was enough for that man. Haymer was exasperated at that man's greed. He had a sweet deal, if only he realised it and simply needed to keep the

404

status quo. That was the trouble with these so called big fish, the pond always seemed too small for their ego.

When the 999 call had come in to the local station from the ever nervous restaurant manager, explaining that his staff had just found two badly injured men in the lane behind the Himalayas, Haymer had casually gone over to investigate, expecting to find Kane and Francis. He had been starting to suspect that Pace was losing patience with the little man, who had once been one of his most trusted "lieutenants." There were rumours, probably started by Francis himself, that he was messing around with Pace's wife. Haymer certainly did not believe that but Pace might have. For sure, Pace had suddenly started referring to Francis as the "Dull-one" and although he laughed each time he teased the little man, it was a pretty hollow laugh.

Now Pace's man, the really simple one, whom everyone locally called Dai Oaf, perhaps wisely behind his back, claimed Kane had attacked both him and Francis. Haymer thought that was so unlikely given the incident he had witnessed in the Himalayas but the testimony could be useful, especially now that he had caught Kane, red handed, so to speak, at The Copper Kettle. In his far from modest opinion, that fat man could not have taken out Pace and Lord's gang all on his own. His excuse, the one he had given to Haymer, albeit rather unconvincingly, at the scene of the crime, that Martini had had a telephone call asking Kane to pop over and when he got there he found the devastation, had much more of a ring of truth to it than Dai Oaf's claim that Kane was an aggressor. All Kane claimed to have done was to attempt first aid, which Haymer believed was likely to be nearer the truth than any other possible scenario. Haymer also had no doubt in his own mind that Lord would have tortured O' Neil and as a result found out that Pace had been trying to cut a deal or worse, setting them all up so that

405

Pace could take over the whole operation. Hence Pace's brutal killing! That certainly fitted the profile of a gangster's revenge attack, rather than the work of the fat, unfit looking, and middle aged high school teacher.

If only Lord would answer his damn phone! Or even Martini would answer hers! Haymer could help solve all their problems and no doubt be handsomely rewarded. He simply could not believe that a man like Lord would abandon his investment, to cut and run so to speak, over killing Pace. Haymer had smirked slightly as he said as much to Charles, who had shook his head and began cursing.

'Bloody Foreigners! No grit or gumption! These Pakis are all the same!' Charles had said unconvincingly, with his hands shaking, and the cold sweat of his own fear dripping from his furrowed brow. Charles did not like not knowing where Lord was! That man had called him at home and made demands on him. That was not the way Charles liked these relationships to work. Maybe it was time to wind up Lord's operation but how? Charles kept wondering, hoping for an answer to his dilemma.

Haymer was a lot more confident of his position. What with O' Neil unlikely to come out of his coma and Kane fitted into the frame for multiple murders, business could get back to normal and a most grateful Lord could continue to fund to "their" lavish lifestyles. The only problem perhaps with his interpretation of events, was the strangely conflicting evidence of broken glass and blood, found outside in the backyard of the Copper Kettle. Yet this was no more than a slight concern to him. Such evidence could disappear. Probably Pace had tried to escape in Lord's car. Yes! Haymer congratulated himself that would all fit in nicely with his theory. He could see Pace panic. Realising that he was about to be found out, he would have made a dash for it. Yes! Haymer smugly told himself. If that happened, Lord may have stabbed Pace outside or not. Perhaps Pace had cut himself trying to break into the car. Pace had certainly been getting too big for his own boots. Whatever nonsense Kane came up with could be overwhelmed by circumstantial evidence and of course Dai Oaf's willing testimony. Haymer did wonder about motive. He was also concerned about Mrs Pace's whereabouts! He had sent a pair of female patrol officers to find her and break the bad news of her husband's murder, first to the Pace's town house and then to their farm, but Martini Pace had disappeared. Haymer was beginning to wonder if she was with Lord.

'Yes! That's where they are! They're all bloody well in on it together!' The too eager young detective confidently concluded. Superintendent Charles agreed. He was slowly beginning to warm to Haymer's twisted version of events. It seemed to be the way out, one that he had been trying to come up with himself. Although in truth, he had only been focusing on saving his own neck. One way or another, Kane and O' Neil were the only ones who would have an interest in disputing the "official" version of last night events. The "official" version would be the one that he, or rather Haymer, was cooking up.

Kane was not saying anything, at the moment. Worryingly, he was not even repeating his original statement to Haymer. If that changed!?! Charles briefly lapsed into mental despair once more. If only they could get hold of Lord! Did the man think they were going to arrest him for a bloody crime of passion! Lord could have the sexy Mrs Pace if he wanted her! He could do whatever he liked, just as long as he kept making the payments. Maybe they would have to demand more money from him. Yes! They bloody well would! That thought comforted Charles, because the one thing for certain in Charles' book was that both Kane and O' Neil needed to be disposed of quickly to stop any possibility of them challenging the reality he was creating.

Disposing of two people was going to be expensive and perhaps the only other certainty in life was that Charles did not expect to pick up the bill himself for those types of expenses. Then again Charles thought that they might only have to dispose of one! 'Have you heard anything more from the hospital?' He suddenly asked the young man sat in front of him.

'No, Sir. O' Neil is in an induced coma and they don't intend to bring him out of that for 24 hours.'

'Have we a man at the hospital?'

'Yes, Sir.'

Who is it?'

'Hughes, Sir.'

'Hughes!?!' Charles cringed. 'He's not the brightest is he!?!' The level of panic surged out again, making Charles' voice quiver.

'No, Sir but that's useful to us. Remember, that's why we let him join our little club!'

Charles grimaced at the mention of their "club" but he nodded. He thought of O' Neil. He had liked the funny Irishman. He had met him only half a dozen times perhaps and he actually smiled briefly at the thought of his banal banter. The smile quickly turned into a frown as Charles tried to recall if he had ever said anything incriminating to O' Neil. Probably! He concluded. Charles looked Haymer directly in the eyes. His voice had steadied slightly by the time he said: 'Maybe, given his injuries, it would be a blessing if O' Neil were to never wake up from that coma. What do you say Constable? That would certainly leave an opening for a new Detective Sergeant!'

'Living with the trauma of those burns would be no picnic, Sir. I just couldn't imagine it, myself, seeing the scars each day.' The young handsome detective flinched as he thought of the horror of being even slightly disfigured.

'Yes! It might be a real kindness if he just didn't come

round.' Charles continued with genuine (self) concern in his voice.

'Yes Sir.' Haymer nodded.

'Perhaps you should go and check that everything is alright down at the hospital. I mean it would be awful if a wire came loose or someone was to flick the wrong switch on the life support system!' Charles's eyes narrowed trying to convey his real meaning.

'Yes Sir.' Haymer nodded again. More dirty work for him to do, he might have muttered but instead he said: 'Of course, he will never be able to tell us what happened to him or how successful his apparent investigation into police corruption turned out to be, Sir!'

'No, that would be a pity.' Charles was almost convincing in his disappointed tone of voice.

'Yes, such a pity, for as far as I am aware and I am an "active" member of the advisory board to our esteemed local Crime Commissioner, no report of any sort has been filed yet and even if the Sergeant has discussed his initial findings with someone, no formal report means no evidence and no evidence means no formal action can be taken! All rather frustrating don't you think Constable? Such a waste of time and resources!'

Haymer grinned at his superior. 'What about Kane?'

"The Super" was so deep in his own thoughts that he did not realise that the young DC had not bothered to address him as Sir!

'Oh, I think I'll arrange for him to be transferred to HQ!' Charles said casually. 'It's pointless keeping him here, so inconvenient for a long interrogation.' He allowed himself a smug grin. 'Unfortunately, what with the murder enquiry underway, we haven't the spare manpower on duty today, so we will have to "contract out" the transfer.'

'Oh dear!' The younger man broadened his own grin. 'I hope

we won't have to use that shambles of a private security firm. The one our political masters always force us to use!' He exclaimed in mock exaggeration. 'They are a complete shower, Sir! Remember!?! The last time we used them they actually stopped for kebabs en route and even gave the prisoner one, which he promptly choked on! Appalling eh!'

'Yes, tragic!' Charles tutted even though he retained a look of glee on his normally agitated face. 'Especially as that particular prisoner was prepared to talk to me and had wanted to give me the names of corrupt officers on our force in exchange for a more lenient sentence!'

'No good deed goes unpunished it seems! Sir!'

'Yes but these contractors have strong political connections.' Charles feigned a sigh. 'And they were eventually cleared of any real wrongdoing in, er, my investigation into the matter. Yes our government advisor insists we still use them. They must be big donors to the party eh!'

'Big donors or *big doners* Sir?' The young man started to laugh at his own effort at a joke.

Charles cracked a smile too as he began to really believe in their short-sighted plan. Things were going to be alright. Mrs Charles would be able to take the family back to Dubai again this year after all and he would be able to spend the holiday enjoying those excellent desert golf courses.

'Well that kebab thing won't happen again but I do hope they keep an eye on Kane. Given his military background and all, I expect he is an escape risk! And someone with his training would, if they got out, simply just disappear, never to be heard of again!'

'Yes, I can imagine! Just disappear and go to ground, never to be heard of again.' Haymer confirmed softly.

'Yes, disappear underground I think is the term we might have to use!'

Both men nodded to each other.

'I'll get off to the hospital then Sir!' Haymer got up and left. His superior now alone in Interview Room Number 2 produced his personal mobile phone from his uniform jacket's right hand side pocket and began scanning through his contact list, ready to make the necessary arrangements for Kane's immediate transfer out of this life.

Chapter 41: Thud! Thud! Thugs!

It was not unusual for the good people of Aberfoist to hear the thud thud thud of helicopter rotor blades cutting through the sky above them. So few stopped what they were doing that Saturday lunchtime to look up. Some did wonder briefly whether the sound was made by minor royalty visiting their Welsh estates, others assumed it was just another military exercise, for there were many as pilots trained by following the river north or south, to and from the various military base camps scattered across the Brecon Beacons. The odd concerned resident feared that it might be the air ambulance, which often brought badly injured ramblers or critically ill traffic accident casualties to the nearby hospital. Those that did look up were disappointed, seeing only a thick blanket of low grey cloud covering the sky. At least they were consoled that last night's rain had stopped and the temperature was rising. Still somewhere high up above the clouds, a helicopter was flying in bright sunshine, its pilot constantly checking his controls. After a quick mathematical calculation he spoke into his mouthpiece and warned his passengers: 'Five minutes to landing.'

DC Haymer was one of the few who looked up to the skies for the helicopter. He was fascinated by them and was considering taking lessons for he had ambitions to own one himself one day soon. In the meantime, he was enjoying the fresh air, albeit sat on a damp wooden picnic table, in a dreary beer garden outside a riverside pub. Well, the only riverside pub in Aberfoist to be exact. He had been on his way to the hospital when he decided that he needed a little Dutch courage before doing yet another dirty job at the bequest of Superintendent

Charles. However, Haymer had been there almost two hours now, mainly because he also needed a little more time to consider his options. Siding with Charles, he had begun to consider, might not be in his own best interests. Now sipping nervously at his second tall glass of gin and tonic, with a slice of lime, not lemon, floating around the top of the otherwise clear liquid, Haymer was busy reviewing his situation.

DS O' Neil obviously knew that he, Haymer, was on the "take!" They had after all worked together as "partners" for a good few months now. So the Irishman had made a right fool out of him. Haymer was quite bitter about that, for in his own mind, he was nobody's fool. Yet, he had never suspected that the seemingly greedy buffoon, who had allegedly been kicked out of London in disgrace, could in reality, be an undercover Internal Affairs agent. Haymer had simply not believed Pace when he had first suggested it to them yesterday evening at The Himalayas. Lord had been easily convinced, and in his anger, most eager to interrogate the traitor or spy or whatever O' Neil really was.

Haymer shivered at the thought of the brutality that the big man had inflicted on his former partner last night. He was convinced that the Irishman must have broken and told Lord everything. Just thinking about suffering that kind of torture made him feel sick and more than a little worried about meeting up with Lord in the future. Haymer was well aware that Pace had planned to double cross Lord, eventually. Ever the schemer, Pace had even recruited the two detectives into his plot and had suggested they could, in due course, get rid of both Lord and then maybe even Charles, making themselves much wealthier in the process. Pace had actually suggested to them that Lord might suffer an accident on that motorbike he used to tear about the place on, the one he used to carry his samples to and from his supply depot, wherever that was! Yes! Haymer concluded, Pace was a devious bugger, too clever by half, and now very dead.

413

Haymer slowly sipped his bitter drink, remembering the schemer's butchered body. Pace would have also told Lord everything and now Haymer feared that the big man would want to have a similar discussion with him, unless he could show Lord that he was loyal and more valuable too him alive than dead. If only O' Neil had been able to talk to him before the medics had taken him away, he would have a much better idea of what to do. Then he remembered that his co-conspirator was not his friend but someone who would ultimately send him to jail. Haymer finished his drink with an undignified gulp. He looked at his expensive wristwatch. It was almost midday and perhaps the fact that not only Lord, but all of his gang had disappeared, without a word of warning or reprimand to his fellow conspirators, must really mean that their game was well and truly up. Maybe it was time for Haymer to disappear too. He had a nice pile of cash stashed away and he had always wanted to travel. He sighed. If only Lord would reply to one of his numerous text messages. Nevertheless, whatever the reality of his situation, Haymer knew, deep down, that a fully recovered and free-talking O' Neil, just had to be bad news for him. So he decided, there was nothing for it! He must get on with his next unpleasant task, because the young and handsome DC certainly did not see his future behind bars.

At that very moment, up in the sky, the noisy helicopter broke through the cloud cover and followed the river almost flying directly towards the pub before suddenly banking right, turning away from the river, towards the hospital, with the charity funded multimillion pounds helipad on its roof. Haymer watched it go amazed at how low the dark green military helicopter was in the sky, hovering dangerously just above the tree tops.

'Ah good!' Haymer exclaimed out loud to no one but himself, recognising that this was finally a bit of luck for him. Some poor grunt must have been injured on exercises or so

414

Haymer assumed. An emergency arriving at the understaffed hospital would prove to be a suitable distraction. This was obviously the opportunity he had been waiting for. He could ghost in and out undetected. Haymer wanted to toast his good fortune but his glass was empty. He did not have time for another. Later! He told himself confidently. Putting the empty glass down on the wooden table top, he got up from the bench and picked up his copy of The Times, which together with it's numerous Saturday morning supplements, was still sealed in the plastic cover, that whilst thin had made a perfectly adequate padded protector from the damp seat, still wet after last night's rain.

Unfortunately for Haymer, it took it him over half an hour to cover the three miles to the hospital. Firstly, he had not noticed that the brewery's delivery lorry had arrived and inconsiderately blocked his car in at the pub car park. Then, after a mercifully short delivery, he had been caught in the traffic, as the seemingly hordes of Saturday morning shoppers queued to get into the nearby supermarket car park. He cursed, where was a traffic policeman when you needed one. He almost rang the station to report the problem but then he realised that it was the time for the afternoon shift to take over and he certainly did not want to take the chance of speaking to Inspector Davies, who should be starting at twelve. Davies was a thorough man and a proper policeman, who was bound to want a full report on last night's murders. Ringing the station was definitely not a good idea.

Then finally Haymer struggled to find a space in the hospital car park. When he had eventually parked in a disabled spot and began walking towards the main entrance to the four storey, rectangular, seventies concrete, glass and steel building, he was surprised to hear the helicopter's engines turnover and spark noisily back into life. The rotors began to spin as it prepared for

415

take off. Of course, he attempted to reassure himself, that that did not mean the panic was over inside. However, then he was even more appalled to spot PC Hughes, the policeman responsible for guarding O' Neil, skulking around in the smokers' Perspex shelter, having a not so crafty cigarette.

'What on earth are you doing out here?' An exasperated Haymer roared.

On seeing the detective, Hughes quickly stubbed his smoke out and rushed over. Despite his closeness, Haymer struggled to hear what his man had to say and signalled, by raising his long index finger, attempting to indicate that Hughes needed to wait one minute until the helicopter had gone. It really was incredibly noisy, especially as it was quite a distance away. Hughes kept talking. Haymer did not try to listen. He was distracted, truly surprised and curious, to see that the helicopter seemed to be heading out towards the town centre, rather than banking right, back towards the river.

'Well! What the hell are you doing down here Hughes?' Haymer asked again, trying to contain his sudden and overwhelming frustration, when he felt that he could actually hear his own speech. Why could not anyone do what they were told to do!?! He should put Hughes on a disciplinary charge, desertion of duty. Then all of a sudden he thought, he hoped rather, that Hughes was about to tell him some good news. Maybe Hughes had been sent away by the doctors because O' Neil had died. However, such optimistic hopes were about to be crushed, in the most unexpected way. All Haymer could say after making his man repeat his story was the word "soldiers!?!" He said it really as more of a question than a statement.

'That's right Sir!' Hughes confirmed again. 'Two soldiers are guarding him now! They've got real guns too, machine guns Sir!'

For the first time since his world had began to unravel, Haymer actually looked shocked. His face paled as he digested

Hughes' report. The PC insisted that he had sent regular texts to the station, asking for instructions but received no replies. Haymer was not surprised. The system back at the station was always going down, probably due to a lack of investment or a lack of expert maintenance or both. Back in the day, when the police used two-way radios, at least they knew when they had lost contact. Now most officers were issued with mobile phones, yet they never rang each other! Just like everyone else they simply sent text messages and once sent they assumed the message had been received.

Now it seemed that Hughes had reported that just before being put into an induced coma, the badly injured O' Neil had rallied slightly and insisted he call his own doctor, or that is what Hughes believed he had meant by insisting he speak to a "good" Doctor! Hughes had rolled his eyes when he told Haymer that the local "Quacks" weren't much impressed by that request. However, they gave O' Neil a phone and he had dialled a number before simply saying "balderdash" just before passing out. Hughes reckoned that O' Neil was probably delirious, what with all the drugs they were pumping into him or the pain. Anyway, everyone was surprised when a few minutes later the phone rang and there was actually a doctor on the line wanting to speak with O' Neil. He must have been an important one, because the locals actually revived O' Neil so that he spoke to whoever was on the phone but according to Hughes, once again all O' Neil seemed to say was a load of gibberish. Anyway, "our Docs" spoke on the phone and explained what was wrong with O' Neil and what they were going to do and that was that. It was a quiet night. So quiet that Hughes managed to have a bit of a kip, as he put it to Haymer, before assuring the visibly flinching detective, that no one, "absolutely no one" could have got passed him! In fact, Hughes continued confidently, every time the nurses checked in they disturbed Hughes. Apparently they were all good girls and even made Hughes a cuppa first thing this morning! Then of course, all hell broke loose at lunchtime, when this Dr Packwood turned up with a bloody armed escort. Finally Hughes shrugged and said: 'His papers seemed to be in order. Blimey! You should have seen who signed them!"

Haymer went a shade whiter, when Hughes further explained himself. Haymer was wondering why the Prime Minister and Her Majesty the Queen would both sign a Doctor's identity card.

'Bloody Hell!' Hughes continued to exclaim, his eyes rolling this time for dramatic effect. 'And to be honest, even if they were faked I wasn't going to argue with those guys with the bloody machine guns! SAS or what! I know my limits!' He smirked, before adding: 'Like I say I texted but with no new orders I had to use my initiative. So they kicked me out!'

'Right!' Haymer began, whilst glancing nervously up at the hospital building, wondering if someone was looking down watching him. 'You've already texted your report, so you'd best knock off now! I'll, er, see you back at the station for tonight's shift, okay!'

'Yeah, alright!' Hughes said informally, looking particularly relieved. The PC wondered about asking for a lift back to town but then he remembered he had actually driven over in his own car. Haymer simply nodded a curt goodbye and headed over towards the main entrance. He stepped inside and waited five minutes before leaving the building quickly. As he strolled out of the door, he subconsciously removed his Police Federation tie. Haymer had decided that it was definitely time for him to leave Aberfoist and South Wales for good! He would simply follow Lord's example and disappear. Decision made, Haymer powered down his police mobile phone and cautiously walked back towards his car, which was conveniently parked in the nearby disabled driver bay.

Jason Powell suddenly sat up in the front passenger seat of the prisoner transport vehicle and scanned the skyline, excited for another glimpse of the military helicopter he could hear but no longer see as the Iveco box van joined the long queue of Saturday shopping traffic, which was hopefully leading them into Aberfoist Town Centre. He had chuckled to himself when he had first seen the Merlin break through the cloud line and follow the river that flowed to the right of the town's bypass. 'Poor bastards!' Powell had muttered to the unshaven and scruffy looking man beside him, who was far too busy watching the screen of his ancient portable SatNav device and cursing quietly to himself as it began replanning their route yet again, to pay much attention to either the noisy flying machine or his travelling companion. 'You ever been in one of 'em?' Powell asked, remembering the times, a few years ago now, when he had been feeling sick and scared, huddled down in the back of similar helicopters as they weaved around the Afghan skies.

The driver hadn't but he did not communicate that information. Like Powell, he had been briefly in the forces and like Powell his dishonourable discharge had been conveniently hushed up to avoid any unwanted bad publicity for the Armed Forces, because it was a particularly sensitive time. Unlike Powell, Luke Jenkins had never seen active service. Mind you, he still walked with a limp but that was after being badly beaten up, in the Guard House, by an unseen assailant, just a few days before his charges for theft and assaulting an officer had been dropped. After that work had, perhaps not surprisingly, proved hard to come by, until he had had the good fortune to meet up with his old cell mate Powell, following a night out in Swansea, coincidently in a very similar van to the one he was now driving,

419

only they were both locked in the back and the van was white, rather than blue and had Police written on the side.

Powell had somehow managed to get them both off yet another drunk and disorderly charge, because his boss was an ex-copper, who saw the advantage in employing dishonourable ex-servicemen, who were under an obligation to do whatever was required and ask no questions about it, unless of course they wanted to find themselves back in jail or worse, out on the streets. Both men had little ambition left in life and were grateful for the odd jobs that funded their heavy drinking.

They had not expected to work that Saturday and both were struggling with hangovers after yet another heavy "session" the night before. Nevertheless, they were eager to earn a little extra cash, with a simple collection and drop off. They were not the type to worry about why they were being asked, at such short notice, to take a man from a police cell in Aberfoist and drop him off at an isolated industrial unit just up the heads of the valleys; they were only concerned with getting back to the pub in time to see that night's big "pay to view" boxing match. The one they had a big bet on.

'How long now?' Powell had asked oblivious to his partner's obvious navigation error.

'Oh, about twenty minutes!' Jenkins had lied. They had been on the road for an hour and a half already. Doing a journey that should have taken them less than an hour. In Interview Room Number 2, at the Aberfoist Police Station, Superintendent Charles was almost hysterical, as he waited impatiently for the men to arrive.

Chapter 42: A New Shift Begins

Inspector Paul Davies waited patiently for the black metal, thick barred, security gate to fully open. Only then did he drive his modest but perfectly practical, beige coloured, Ford Focus Titanium, four door saloon, carefully into the small private car park, which was well hidden from prying eyes behind the whitewashed concrete boundary walls of Aberfoist Police Station. Once inside, he pulled up and checked using his car's rear-view mirror that the gate was closing securely behind him. Satisfied by the loud clunk of metal on metal, as the magnetic locks finally joined together, that it had, he then began to glance around for a suitable parking space, only to let out an immediate and uncharacteristic groan of frustration on seeing the big black BMW X5 4x4. The luxury SUV was casually straddling a white line in the middle of two designated disabled parking spaces; the only two in the limited capacity parking facility. There was no disabled badge displayed on the vehicle and each generously marked out parking space either side of the line should still have been big enough for the oversized car. Seeing such callous disregard for those less fortunate members of society always made Davies angry. Indeed, one of the reasons he had become a policeman in the first place was to be able to legitimately address such obvious injustice. Yet, much to his personal chagrin, he knew that in this instance he was powerless to do anything about it; for the car's owner, who was well known to be a difficult and ignorant man, was also most depressingly, his senior officer.

Gritting his teeth, Davies began to mentally prepare himself for yet another irritable encounter with that black car's driver. A part of him really wanted to park his car equally inconsiderately. Maybe, just maybe, squeezing into the remaining space, right next to the extravagant, top of the range vehicle, and thus restricting access to the driver's door, would send out a strong message to the errant parker. However, Davies also knew that even such an obvious and unsubtle hint, to consider others, would be totally lost on such a selfish man as Superintendent Charles. In fact, Davies worried that Charles was more likely to see such a "message" as an opportunity to exert his own authority and increase his own remuneration, by deliberately bashing his car door into the obstructing vehicle and belligerently booking his own car into the police repair shop, for a full respray. All in order to satisfy personal greed and gain further (obviously unwarranted) benefits, which Charles constantly felt entitled to, merely by being a senior public servant. The Inspector truly despised the man.

The Superintendent was possibly the worst policeman that Davies had ever known in his twenty years of policing and he had known some bad ones! Nevertheless, Charles seemed to have Carte Blanche to stroll around Gwent and call the shots, bullying and intimidating other less senior but more diligent and definitely more able officers. Generally doing absolutely nothing of worth himself, whilst taking all the credit, should any of his "underlings" hard work produce noteworthy results, certainly seemed to be Charles' mode of operation. Perhaps Davies was still bristling about the way Charles had mysteriously set up the hugely successful (and expensive) cross border "Palm Sunday" operation, within hours of the recent, (and to Davies) extremely embarrassing, Aberfoist plant and equipment robbery. All this at a time, when any investigations Davies tried to pursue, particularly with regard to the recent spate of suspicious domestic accidents suffered by local drug dealers, were quickly curtailed on either financial or public interest grounds.

422

No doubt the next irritation that Davies was going to suffer today would be Charles questioning Davies's timekeeping. Even though Davies was only late because he had stopped in what he considered to be the line of duty, coming to the aid of an elderly lady, whose equally ancient car had broken down on the junction of a busy main road. Yes, his shift should have started half an hour ago and technically in his opinion it did, as soon as Davies saw the potentially dangerous incident. Even so, he could now hear Charles crowing that that sort of dalliance was not the responsibility of a Police Inspector.

'It is your duty to arrive at your station on time!' Davies griped to himself, quietly parodying the senior officer's pompous tone. 'Unless, of course, you have a round of golf or two to finish, can't let people down you know!'

And yet Davies felt that if he had not stopped for the old lady who would have!?! Charles always assumed some other officer would be available to deal with the mundane everyday problems faced by the public but Davies knew that the handful of officers on duty at any given time in the area was usually stretched too thin. Davies also knew that most officers within Charles' jurisdiction, were probably stuck indoors, dealing with paperwork, probably writing up pointless reports for "The Super" instead of being out there, policing the streets and heaven forbid, actually helping the public.

Logistics! Inevitably, someone would be off sick. Stress related no doubt but nonetheless certainly debilitating! Davies cringed, remembering how Charles would insist that the all staff, especially those who were "genuinely" sick, receive written warnings or gentile "reminders" of their obligations to serve the public, as Charles liked to call the veiled threats he forced Davies to sign, so that "good old" Charles did not appear to be the unreasonable bureaucrat, who was ratcheting up the pressure on all, to keep performing the seemingly impossible, at least on paper, so that the Super would meet another political rather than practical target. Davies, himself, was almost buckling under the stress of dealing with the fall out from Charles' poor leadership. He tried so hard to stay in the job he once loved, and "manage up" being a policeman rather than a statistician, but each week the security consultancy role recently offered him by his friend at the Welsh Office, seemed more attractive. No! Davies shook his head defiantly; he could not abandon his team or the public, for if not him, who would police the police?

Davies attempted to park his frustrations, like his car, well out of the way of his "so called" superior's extravagant choice of "company" car. However, he was still muttering to himself as he locked his car and strode around the corner of the building, into a little courtyard, no more than three by six metres, that led up to the station's back door. Standing there, bellowing out an immense cloud of white mist, vapour or smoke, was Sergeant Bob Dwyer, sucking hard on one of those new, trendy Vape pipes. Davies knew the veteran custody sergeant was not a follower of fashion. He, like so many other nicotine addicts, was desperately trying every which way to wean himself off the filthy habit, in the hope of living long enough to see his grandchildren grow up. All the same, the lines on Dwyer's forehead were creased; making him look much older than his actual age, and Davies doubted Dwyer would enjoy the long retirement he should be entitled to, whatever healthy choices he made at this stage of his life.

The normally fixed frown lines narrowed briefly when Dwyer's face broke into a warm, natural, smile of greeting, on first seeing the Inspector. Yet they almost immediately rose again into a full on frown, as Dwyer realised that he must now attempt to explain all that had happened to the man he considered to be his only "real" boss; and those happenings would include his own less than glorious reaction in the cell earlier that morning.

424

Dwyer knew that he could not trust Charles to relay an accurate version of events. Davies in turn knew something was up as soon as he saw the usually meticulous sergeant. Dwyer rarely stayed late after his shift but here he was, hanging around obviously waiting for Davies and stressed enough to need his nicotine fix.

Listening supportively to the sorry tale, Davies had only just managed to suppress a chuckle or two, when he first heard about Dwyer striking Charles, and although he knew that he looked far too pleased at the news of Ellis Pace's demise, he had attempted to disguise that inappropriate reaction as a response to the good news that they had the suspect in custody. However, his disappointment that now he was never going to be able to "nick" Pace for any of the crimes he had suspected him and his so called organisation of committing over the years, paled into insignificance when he heard that this suspect had actually been caught red handed by DC Haymer. Davies blinked at that news. He needed to think about this. Charles and his apprentice Haymer. This could not be truly good could it!?! But his increasing subconscious irritation was also being racked up by the fact that he could hardly hear what Dwyer was saying now. Gradually, he had become more and more aware, that a distant buzzing was growing louder and louder, as the helicopter from the hospital flew closer to them.

Like most people in and around Aberfoist that lunchtime, Davies had heard the helicopter passing somewhere up above him. Unlike most people he, being the local Inspector of Police, had spared more than a passing thought or two for the reason behind the flight. When he had spotted the impressive military helicopter breaking cloud cover and heading towards the hospital, he had actually sighed and even said a prayer, for the injured soldier, whom he assumed was being ferried in from some exercise gone horribly wrong. He also began to anticipate

425

the extra paper work the helicopter's arrival in his jurisdiction would bring him and he had sighed again briefly at the thought of the time he might waste driving up to Brecon or even across the border to Hereford, to chat to some disinterested senior soldiers before filing a brief report on an inevitably sanitised "no blame" accident. Davies had then wondered if, in spite of all the increased professionalism and Health & Safety requirements, these so called "training" injuries were becoming more common place; or perhaps the drama of a helicopter rescue, made them appear more prevalent, than for those poor souls, who in the past, would have been stretchered into the back of an army truck or Land Rover, before being driven for hours over bumpy fields and twisty country roads, to some quaint cottage hospital. No! Things had to be better these days, Davies had concluded.

With such thoughts suddenly back in his mind, Davies finally, tried to reassure his trusted colleague that things were surely not as bad as Dwyer feared. However, Davies found that he was actually shouting this out most indiscreetly. Well, he would have been indiscreet, if anyone could have heard his voice, over the racket now coming from directly up above them. Both men immediately glanced upwards to the sky, just in time to see the large helicopter fly less than a few metres over the station roof. Apart from the noise, the down draft rocked them, worryingly, almost off their feet. For a second or two, Davies thought they were under attack as the building rattled and cars rocked. When a car alarm went off, he had almost dived to the ground. Even the fact that it was the big black Mercedes that was emitting a shrill noise and performing an expensively disconcerting light show, did not ease his concerns. Davies was convinced that the flying machine was in difficulty. Maybe it was attempting to make an emergency landing on the nearby river meadow. Quickly raising his hand, to warn Dwyer that they should stop talking, Davies began to rush around to the front of

426

the building. In any other circumstances, he would have been furious to find the side gate unlocked. Although mentally cursing whoever was responsible for such an obvious breach in security, his mind was beginning to focus on what he considered to be an imminent emergency. Yet such concerns vanished as soon as he reached the front of the building. There, Davies was amazed by what he saw next and simply froze in a confused mixture of concern, awe and wonder.

The road outside the Police Station was quite wide and flat. On the other side of the road was a grass verge rather than a pavement. Then a metre or so in, a short hedgerow provided a low obstacle before the field beyond the hedge, gently sloped down towards the much wider river meadows, which would have been spacious enough for the helicopter to make its emergency landing. However, the chopper was hovering above the road. The side door slide open and a thick length of rope thrown out by an unseen hand. The rope must have been weighted and obviously tied fast to something inside the cockpit, for it hung straight down in a twisting line, possibly fifteen metres long, dangling just a few centimetres short of the ground. Then a man, a soldier, in full combat uniform, stepped out and expertly slides down the rope. As soon as he landed another soldier emerged and did the same, then a third and finally a fourth. All four executed the manoeuvre perfectly and it was only when they were all moving their separate ways on the ground, that Davies realised they were armed. He instantly recognised the short-barrelled carbine, with its pistol grip as the standard issue service rifle of the British Armed Forces. This recognition was more from his general knowledge than any specific security briefing. He thought it was called the L85 or was it the L86. Whatever this version's name actually was, he was also well aware of what a powerful weapon each man was holding up and pointing forward, professionally and purposely, in both hands, albeit casually supported by a

427

shoulder strap, as in front of him they appeared to be securing the area. This was not an emergency landing but a deliberate and planned descent.

For a few seconds Davies could only think "flight or fight" as his eyes watched the men spread out securing the road and stopping the traffic, which in fairness had already ground to a halt as soon as the drivers saw the scary war machine appearing from over the roof tops and hovering relatively so low above their pathway. The third soldier was now approaching Davies. He was shouting something to him, trying to raise his voice above the deafening engine noise. The soldier had to repeat his message twice, in quick succession before Davies realised that he was being told to: 'Step back a bit please Sir, if you wouldn't mind Sir!'

The gun, rather than the polite but firm voice, made sure that Davies did step back as soon as his confused brain processed the instruction, whether he minded or not. Dumbstruck he continued to watch as the helicopter slowly touched down and more soldiers disembarked. They seemed to be helping a short, well rounded, white haired and bearded, bespectacled man, dressed in a long dark tan trench-coat, disembark. Even under the constant roar of the rotors, Davies was suddenly aware of Sergeant Dwyer's deep voice somewhere behind him. It sounded like Dwyer was saying: 'Bloody Hell! We're being invaded! I wonder what "The Super" will have to say about this!?!'

For the very first time, Davies was suddenly relieved. He almost smiled as he realised that he was not the senior police officer present. Nonetheless, the white-haired man in the trench-coat approached him. He was flanked by two tall soldiers, who wore smart officers' uniforms, rather than combat kit. Each carried holstered side arms rather than rifles. Davies instinctively returned the old-fashioned salute he was given by the three men.

428

Behind them he saw the helicopter take off. It hovered away towards the river meadow. Almost immediately the two combat soldiers released the traffic, which had suddenly built up either side of their road block. Not surprisingly they had to encourage the rather shocked locals to move and keep moving.

Three vehicles down, in the queue approaching the town centre, and therefore heading towards the police station, was the blue security prisoner transport van. Jason Powell had watched the helicopter landing with admiration at first but when he saw the soldiers approach the two ashen faced policemen, who were standing in front of their police station, he turned to his driver and said apprehensively: 'Change of plan Luke! I don't think we'll call into the station just yet, it's time for our lunch-break!'

'But we're bloody late!' The younger driver had said slightly confused.

'Well we're going to be bloody well even later mate! I don't want to get involved in any of this, whatever the fuck this is!?!' Powell nodded towards the discussion taking place to his left. 'Keep on fucking driving!' He urged bluntly once again.

Luke needed no further encouragement and slowly drove passed their original destination, as directed by the soldier cradling a machine gun.

It seemed that Inspector Paul Davies would need a little more encouragement. The man in the trench-coat was speaking to him slowly. Davies could hear the man's firm but polite voice quite clearly, in spite of all the noise from the helicopter. However, Davies was suddenly rather lost for words. 'Good day Inspector.' The chubby bespectacled man had said. 'I understand you are holding a prisoner in your cells. I need to speak to him rather urgently!'

Sergeant Dwyer it seemed was not lost for words. The sergeant's deep voice inappropriately exclaimed: 'Oh shit!'

Chapter 43: The First Protocol

Pacing around Interview Room Number 2, Superintendent Charles was huffing and puffing, almost as if he were a children's party entertainer, pretending to be a steam engine. Inspector Davies would have been the first to admit that he himself was sat rather too smugly beside the empty interviewer's chair, enjoying the pathetic performance. Indeed, for the first time in his career, Davies was actually happy being in the same room as his so called superior. The tables had certainly turned so to speak and the only one left flustered in the room was Superintendent Charles. Davies knew there was nothing he could say or do to change the situation. Even if he had been inclined to, which he was not! Neither he nor Charles were in charge and therefore the weight of responsibility had lifted from his own shoulders as he watched "The Super" being interrogated by the sharp eyed Military Intelligence Officer, who sat bolt upright in the "prisoner's" chair across the table from him.

'So why exactly did you rush up here earlier this morning Superintendent Charles? Who informed you about the incident? Why did they call you at home instead of informing the duty officer at division?'

Charles grunted feeble but possibly plausible answers to all the questions. Unfortunately for Charles, the much younger officer in the khaki jacket was having none of it. He did not just look as if he doubted the word of "The Super", he told him so, regularly, in brutally blunt, one word responses, the politest of which were: "Rubbish!" "Nonsense!" "Lie!"

'I don't have to put up with this!' Charles had raged at one point, only to be uncompromisingly told: 'Yes you do! Now sit down please or I will call in my man and he will make you!' The man in question was probably the taller of the two thickset soldiers, the ones with the semi-automatic rifles, who stood to attention, on guard, just outside the room.

Davies almost laughed out loud when Charles turned to him and in a desperate appeal said: 'Paul! For God's sake tell this man who I am!' It may well have been the first time ever that "The Super" had used Davies' first name. Despite the shock of sudden over familiarity, the Inspector had managed to reassure "The Super" that he believed the soldier knew exactly who they all were. Perhaps it was then that Charles realised that the game was up and he slouched back over to the empty chair and finally slump down in it. His shifty eyes did not look at his interrogator, who was sat staring across at him from the chair where Haymer had been sat earlier that day. Charles wondered what had happened to the young blonde detective. His man had been gone far too long to have been successful in his mission to silence O' Neil. Had he already betrayed him? Or maybe he had seen the helicopter arrive and thought better of walking in to this mess. Haymer was always a clever sod. Too clever! Charles had often thought.

Given the extraordinary circumstances Charles found himself in, any sane man would have realised that the game was up. Unfortunately for all present, Charles was not in his right mind. He probably never had been. So he persisted in deluding himself that he really had more authority than these military interlopers and this was all just an inconvenient mistake. Davies, on the other hand, thought that it was Christmas combined with his birthday and he was struggling to contain his glee, whilst watching the blunt, humourless bear of a man, squeezed into the immaculate light brown jacket and trousers, slowly unwrap his presents, question by question.

Although Davies himself had initially mistrusted the credentials presented to him outside the police station, simply because they were so imperious, a second look at the men's faces, the guns, the multi-million pounds worth of military helicopter, as well as a dim and distant recollection of what at the time had been an almost laughable security briefing on the extreme and arbitrary powers gifted to certain government agencies within the newly sanctioned Anti-terrorist legislation, convinced him to comply with the polite but firm requests, because in any event, he concluded that there would have been only one other short lived and most likely painful, alternative stance available to him. And he had no reason to choose that option, for unlike Charles, Davies knew that he had nothing to hide, and he was, like the men with the guns, an officer of the crown.

***

At the same time that Superintendent Charles was foolishly trying not to help Military Intelligence with their enquiries, Mykee Kane was enjoying a more civilised conversation down in his cell. At first he had wondered what was going to happen to him this time, when the heavy boots of Sergeant Dwyer approached the cell door. Kane had expected more trouble, especially as he could hear two extra pairs of feet accompanying Dwyer's clump clump clump. Both pairs sounded as if they were wearing much softer leather soles than standard police footwear. One pair seemed to march briskly behind the sergeant. The other pair seemed to shuffle, scuffing along the tiled corridor floor, as if struggling with a heavy weight and unused to keeping pace with the others more purposeful stride. Kane listened to the key turning in the lock but he had been surprised when the door simply swung open without the viewer being clunked down.

However, this break from normal procedure was nothing compared to the sheer astonishment he felt on seeing who was standing in the open doorway. Old instincts die hard and Kane found himself automatically leaping up, off the uncomfortable bunk to stand to full attention.

'Ah Captain Kane! I see civilian life has not agreed with you!' The man in the trench coat spoke with a refined but jolly voice, definitely Received Pronunciation and no trace of any regional accent. 'It has not agreed with me either!' The old man chuckled at his own observation and tapped his brown leather gloved hands on his broad stomach.

'Major Packwood!' Kane exclaimed, almost stuttering. He may have stood to attention but after ten years he was rusty or perhaps it was the shock. Kane did not salute his former commanding officer.

'Quite right Kane no need to salute, just two old friends, and former comrades in fact, meeting in strange circumstances!' Packwood continued gently correcting the error, as his sharp eyes critically examined Kane with the precision of a surgeon. 'I am no longer a Major and like you I have also been enjoying the comfort of civilian life a little too much.' He sighed. Kane could see that Packwood, like himself had put on weight, a lot of weight. Unfortunately, Packwood was a shorter man and much older than Kane. With his white hair and beard, the chubby Packwood now resembled a real life Father Christmas, rather than the small, wiry man, Kane remembered well from just over a decade ago.

'Sergeant Dwyer!' Packwood called behind him.

'Yes Sir?' Dwyer responded immediately, slightly surprised and more than a little concerned that this visiting VIP somehow knew his name. 'Can you get me a chair please and perhaps something for us all to drink? Tea preferably!'

'I wouldn't if I were you!' Kane cautioned.

'Oh dear,' Packwood sighed. 'I hope you can find something better than what you may have been serving your over night guests!'

'I'll do my best Sir!' Dwyer eagerly responded, much to Kane's obvious amusement.

'Now, Captain Kane, I see that you chose not to take Captain O' Neil's advice; I presume he warned you of my involvement in all this! Yes?' Packwood continued softly reprimanding his former charge, once the Custody Sergeant had quickly stomped away and was out of earshot. Kane actually blushed in front of his former commander.

'I actually tried not to complicate things ... Sir!' Kane, his cheeks still warm, actually shrugged by way of an almost but not quite sincere apology before continuing: 'But then perhaps my involvement was necessary, given the temporary difficulty Calamity, er, Captain O' Neil, found himself in last night!?!''Hmm' Packwood smiled slightly. Kane had forgotten how worrying it was to see that thin thoughtful grin. Even though Packwood had aged, the eyes confirmed the old man was as sharp as ever. 'Of course, the local plod has got themselves all excited over you. They want to charge you with murder!' Packwood's smile widened. 'Two murders actually!' He continued, suddenly beaming as if he was highly amused by the situation he found Kane in.

'Really! On what evidence?' Kane tried to ask nonchalantly but perhaps betraying a certain resignation in his tone of voice. Whilst not entirely surprised by the information supplied, it was not good news. However, he refused to show any signs of panic as there was very little he could do about the situation at present, and in any case, his focus was being distracted away from the polite conversation by his curiosity about Packwood's silent companion.

Kane had noticed with interest that the soldier stood next to

434

Packwood wore a holstered handgun on his belt. This Kane concluded was most odd, unless the man was considered to be on active service. Yet the man was dressed impeccably in the light brown jacket and trousers of a British Army officer, rather than the loose fitting camouflage battle dress fatigues such an officer should wear on a mission. The khaki braided tie, light brown shirt and highly polished brown toecap shoes were pristine. The insignia on his jacket's epaulettes announced him as a Captain and the rose and laurel badge, together with the cypress green beret, firmly placed on his head, confirmed that he was a Captain in the Intelligence Corps. Kane knew all this because just over ten years ago he too had dressed in the same uniform.

The Intelligence Officer's stance was confident and relaxed but not overconfident or too relaxed. He reeked of a fitness that Kane could only dream of achieving these days. The bright brown eyes were busy, watching Kane but also watching for, waiting for and anticipating any threat, from anywhere in the environment around the much older man, whom he was obviously silently guarding. Kane deduced that this man, despite his casual air, had been pulled away unexpectedly from a desk job. Nevertheless, he looked more than capable of escorting the old man through any tricky situation, and of course, that was why he was here. This was certainly a tricky situation. What Kane could not understand was why such a senior officer was acting as a bodyguard to an alleged civilian. Still, three captains. Kane was flattered to be included in the conversation at his old rank. He was also slightly amused that Calamity had made the rank of captain. His tendency for catastrophe had always restricted his progress in the past.

'Hmm' Packwood's smile faded slightly as he felt a tinge of disappointment that his teasing had not provoked a greater reaction from Kane. 'Yes!' He nodded almost sympathetically. 'All circumstantial really! Unless, of course, witnesses come forward!

But then they all seem to have rather conveniently disappeared! Well apart from one, that is!'

For a moment, Kane pictured Martini, where he had left her, tied to the radiator. Then as Packwood continued, Kane realised that the old man was talking about Dai Oaf or whatever Pace's pet thug was really called!'

'Hmm' Packwood sighed again. 'This chap apparently has been left in a bit of a bad way by all accounts. I told them that was so unlike you! I mean, you were always one to finish off the job, back in the day! I did suggest that you might have gone all soft, you know, in civilian life. Then again, I can see you really have!' Packwood put on a pained look of regret. 'And I also seem to remember that on occasion you could be rather sentimental about some people!' The stout man's face assumed a sad expression. 'I suspect that was why you regrettably resigned your commission, and chose to work with children, eh!' Turning to the uniform man beside him, he shook his head slowly and shrugged. 'That must be awful eh! What do you say Captain Brown! Then again, a bit like us working with politicians, eh!' Packwood suddenly brightened up as if cheered by his ironic comparison. Captain Brown said nothing, although his lips parted slightly in what may have been the start of a smile just seconds before his head snapped around to see what was coming back down the corridor. An instant later, Kane heard the first heavy foot step on the stairs and then recognised it as the familiar tread of Sergeant Dwyer, stomping down the corridor, slightly out of time, because he was carrying a large padded desk chair for Packwood to sit down on. 'Ah there you are Sergeant Dwyer!' Packwood greeted the man benevolently. 'Thank you!'

Packwood then made a big fuss of undoing his overcoat, before sitting down on the chair and announcing that it would do fine. The police sergeant then assured the "Brigadier" that a WPC was making a fresh pot of tea for them. Packwood thanked him dismissively and then as the sergeant withdrew, Packwood suddenly called out as an afterthought: 'Remember now Sergeant, three cups please!' Kane heard the sergeant almost miss a step as he realised that that included his prisoner in the tea party. Dwyer's thoughts darkened not out of resentment at serving a prisoner but more out of the realisation that his earlier, attempted violent response to Kane was so misjudged. 'Mugs will do!' Packwood added quickly, which prompted a most subservient: "Yes Sir" from the blushing policeman, who already had one foot on the stairs at the far end of the corridor.

'Now, all this nonsense, with the Police, would just disappear if you had actually been working for me!' Packwood met Kane's widening eyes with his own, twinkling grey blue behind the thin round lenses of his sparklingly clean spectacles. Kane sensed that behind the jovial front there was a sudden tenseness in the man as he waited for Kane's reaction.

'I'm flattered by the offer, Sir!' Kane felt it wise to say, whilst involuntarily shaking his head slowly. 'But I don't think you are being serious!' He was suddenly aware that there was a certain irony in the fact that Kane had left the "service" because he had grown disillusioned. Truly burdened with the limitations he had faced in trying to run operations for an under resourced outfit, which also suffered from constantly changing political constraints. Yet he soon found similar frustrations in his current job; as a teacher, he was now regularly facing more constraints than he had could ever have anticipated ten years ago, so many unreasonable demands from constant curriculum changes, to regularly revised "guidelines" and worst of all, in his view, an unnatural insistence to adapt basic learning to include whatever trendy politically correct theory was flavour of the month, that he had often thought about jacking it all in and going back to his old job; but then, at least, however bad it got in education, nobody died, usually!

437

'I'm not saying you are wasted in education, after all it is a very noble cause, but I think, given your rather unique aptitude (and skills), you could make a more useful contribution to the future of this country at the moment if you were working for me.' Packwood continued, sensing the growing confusion in Kane.

'Teaching is what I do now!' Kane answered unconvincingly.

'Teaching might have been what you did!' Packwood grinned mischievously once again. 'I mean let's be fair, even if you got off with last nights little lapse, I suspect the General Teaching Council might consider you a risk in the classroom or at least guilty of bringing the profession into disrepute and as I have suggested already, if the boys in blue upstairs get their way, I really do dread to think what might come back on, oh what do they call it Harry?' However, before the Captain beside him could respond, Packwood answered his own question. 'Oh yes! A CRB check! That's it isn't it!'

Kane shrugged, determined not to rise to the bait. He was wondering what exactly Packwood was doing there and why, given the circumstances, this important man seemed to be in such a good humour. Especially considering the mess Kane must have made of what had obviously been a painstaking planned undercover mission involving the now seriously injured Captain O' Neil. 'So what exactly are you suggesting Major!' Kane eventually asked.

Packwood laughed. This time because the normally stalwart and poker-faced Captain Brown had first grimaced, then visibly paled at the way Kane had mistakenly addressed his superior.

'Look My-Key, if you insist on using titles, I suspect my Adjutant would be more comfortable if you referred to me as Brigadier!' Packwood seemed to blush slightly at revealing his real rank.

'Congratulations, Sir!' Kane coolly acknowledged, more than

slightly impressed at the value such a promotion placed on his former commander; who back in the day had suffered more than his fair share of slights from well-connected self-important high ranking but incompetent commissioned twits.

'Well as you may recall I'm not big on the privileges of rank but it can prove useful outside of my own department. Inside, I prefer my colleagues to call me Dr. Packwood, because that reminds me that I am meant to be the clever one!' The sharp grey blue eyes narrowed slightly, almost challenging Kane to make some quip. Nothing was in fact further from Kane's mind, for he knew that Brigadier Dr Paul Packwood was probably one of the most cunning men whom he had ever met.

Captain Brown suddenly cleared his throat noisily interrupting the conversation, in a polite warning to the two men that someone was listening to their conversation. Seconds later, Kane heard footsteps on the stairs and was impressed by the adjutant's awareness. A middle aged WPC carrying a tray, with three mugs of milky brown tea, a cup of sugar with a teaspoon sticking out of it, and a plate of chocolate digestive biscuits on it, had begun her cautious approach down the corridor, having carefully descended the stairs.

'Ah how nice!' The Brigadier Doctor greeted her efforts approvingly. 'I do hope we have not inconvenienced you from any important police work Constable?' He apologised charmingly.

'Oh don't worry Sir!' She replied, smiling sweetly at his apparent courtesy. 'I'm putting this down on my time sheet as crime prevention duties. If any of the boys had made you a drink you might have had them arrested for attempted murder!' She suddenly blushed on seeing Kane and recognising her perhaps inappropriate casual informality, she quickly added smartly: "And heaven help you if you had tried anything from the vending machine!' The WPC pulled a face which exactly mirrored Kane's

439

expression when he had attempted to drink last night's offering from Dwyer. Captain Brown politely took the tray from her and offered first choice to Brigadier Dr. Packwood.

'Ah!' Packwood's eyes twinkled. 'I am rather partial to a chocolate biscuit or two or three even!' He let out a little chuckle in self-appreciation of the awkwardness of his joke and smiled up at the rather tall WPC, before dismissing her with another warm "Thank you Constable Reilly!"

WPC Reilly retreated down the corridor behind them, surprised that the visiting VIP had taken the time to notice her name. Meanwhile Packwood ordered Kane to sit down. It was time to stop pussyfooting around. Between sips of tea and munches of chocolate biscuit, Packwood began to brief his new/old man; for Kane realised pretty soon after his bum touched down on the bunk bed that the opportunity to work for the man that he would soon learn was nicknamed "The Good Doctor" was not really a suggestion or even a request but an uncompromising, if politely put, command and expectation.

***

'Are you familiar with Article 1 of the First Protocol?' "The Good Doctor" eventually asked Kane. The two men were now alone in the open cell. Kane sat awkwardly on the edge of his bunk and Packwood sat comfortably on the chair provided by Dwyer. After the pleasant tea and biscuits and some straight talking, during which Kane pretty much accurately relayed his actions in Aberfoist since Wendy's phone call, Packwood had dispatched Captain Brown to find Sergeant Dwyer, with the intention of commandeering the Police Station's internal CCTV. The cool manner of his report had fully satisfied Packwood that Kane was not mentally unstable or the crazed killer that Superintendent Charles had attempted to portray. So as the

440

conversation moved deeper into the shadows cast by The Official Secrets Act, it became essential to prevent any record of the events taking place inside Aberfoist Police Station that day mysteriously leaking out and appearing on YouTube or some other "indiscreet" public access media. They were certainly not likely to feature in any official reports, which would inevitably guarantee unwanted public exposure at some time in the future.

'The First Protocol? Isn't that what they bang on about on Star Trek?' Kane had quipped.

'Oh! The television! A joke! How very droll!' Packwood smiled briefly, as his razor sharp mind cut through the obscure reference. 'No, I think not!' The alert grey blue eyes behind the thin round lenses again fixed Kane in a steely glare, telling him that it was time to be serious, time to listen and learn. 'The First Protocol is one of the basic principles of the Human Rights Act and since 1998 it has given me, and of course whatever Government is in power above me, the freedom to run my Department in the way I deem necessary to protect the good people of our land.'

Kane listened silently.

'Unfortunately,' Packwood had added apologetically, 'it did take almost ten years since the law was first passed, to convince the then powers that be, that my interpretation of the law was correct. Thank heavens for Human Rights and a few wars eh!' He gave Kane a little wink with his right eye. 'Now I am not impaired, in any way, from enforcing such laws as I deem necessary to ensure that every natural or legal person is able to enjoy the peaceful pursuit of their happiness.'

'Key words being "peaceful pursuit" I assume!' Kane contributed, trying not to sound flippant.

'Exactly!' Packwood acknowledged. Then with a sad look on his face he sighed. 'Far too many people misunderstand personal freedom these days! I remember the good old days, when we had

441

personal responsibility and a sense of public duty. Don't you?' Packwood sighed again, not expecting an answer..

'Suicide bombers have a strong sense of duty!' Kane suggested.

'Poor misguided fools!' Packwood frowned. 'I hope you are taking this seriously Captain!' The eyes bore into Kane's daring him not to. Then suddenly Packwood's face changed, brightening up, as if he had just made up his mind about something and he lent forward, staring at Kane, with the look of a man who knew he was right. 'I need you to help me get at the people who pull the strings of such dumb puppets. That's what we are about in my Department these days! We won't be wasting your time having you train allies for foreign currency, as one of my politically ambitious predecessors once did! We'll be acting in our own interests! Yes! That is what the First Protocol means to us!'

'I'm not a policeman or someone who can pretend to be a crook, like O' Neil!' Kane said flatly, instantly worried about what he was expected to do.

'I wouldn't expect you to arrest anybody! And I know you cannot be anyone but yourself, Mr. My-key Kane!' Packwood rolled his eyes comically before they straightened and stared back at Kane intensely. 'But I want you to sign back on! You'd work exclusively for me!' He insisted his eyes suddenly serious again and once more determinedly staring straight at Kane.

'How long for?' Kane asked.

'Life! Mine or yours!' Packwood said simply, before winking again. The eyes instantly back to their usual jovial glow. Then full of mischief, Packwood added: 'You know you'd get 30 years for murder wouldn't you!'

'What about time off for good behaviour?' Kane asked, only slightly joking.

'Oh don't worry about that! I don't want any good behaviour from you! That's not what we are about!' Packwood smiled confidently.

Chapter 44: The Guest Who Did Not Stay

Mrs Sarah Wilson was busy peeling potatoes when, quite unexpectedly, the electric doorbell chimed. Digitally enhanced to replicate the mighty tones of Big Ben, the grand sound echoed around the Mountain View Guest House. In fact the device rang out so loudly that the chimes made the proud proprietor jump and drop a half skinned spud into the warm muddy water, which almost filled the impressively large, country kitchen style, white rectangular enamel sink in front of her. The resulting splash caught her straight in the eye.

'Bugger!' She exclaimed to the empty room. Then the landlady began frantically dabbing at her now stinging right eye with the bottom corner of her faded red and white Liverpool FC apron, whilst muttering a silent prayer that this remedy would not ruin her colourful two-tone pink mascara. The makeup had been expensively applied earlier that morning by the young and chatty Brittany, during Sarah's regular Saturday morning "touch up" session down at the local beauticians. The doorbell rang out again and Sarah felt compelled to rush out of the kitchen and into her immaculately clean hallway. There she almost tripped over her two Highland terriers, Keegan and Dalglish, who were excitedly patrolling the hall, sweeping nervously up and down the polished wood block floor and emitting low menacing growls at the dark man shaped outline, just visible through the brightly stained glass window of the Guest House's front door.

Sarah made a shushing hiss-like noise at her beloved pets but this only served to inspire them into deeper growls. She tried to compose herself, nervously wiping her wet hands in the still attached apron. A brief glance at her reflection in the large ornate heart shaped mirror, set in the dark wood frame, which hung on the wall to her right, left her frustrated by the lack of bounce in her romantic curled, auburn highlighted, shoulder length, meant-to-be-wavy hair. She paused for a closer, if slightly blurred, inspection and frowned. It was her fault. She had rushed Chantelle, her preferred stylist down at the Figurehead Hair and Beauty Salon, in exclusive Upper Foist. The urgency had been all because the salon's gossip that morning had unsettled her. Everyone was talking about the murders. Not just one but two murders in town last night! She shivered as she remembered the speculation. Drug dealers!?! Gypsies!?! Probably just the usual Valley Commandos, as some of the women liked to call the Friday night drinkers who regularly visited Aberfoist from out of town. Nobody had really known much about the crimes but that had not stopped feverish debate.

"Oh my God!" Sarah had joined in dramatically at one point, letting her rehearsed posh voice slip into pure Scouse. "I jus' can't believe it!" This of course was true. Sarah and her husband, Mark had not moved away from the overpopulated Northern conurbation to find their escape to the country blighted by this type of urban nightmare. However, her understandable concern at the sudden crime wave was a lot more personal than she could let on to the girls at the salon. Sarah was panicking with good cause and just had to get back to Mark. She wanted him to ring the police and tell them about their guest. The no show! Well the one who had actually turned up, briefly to park his scruffy old car, in their nice recently gravelled, rear car park. "Thank God!" She had thought and repeatedly told Mark. The man had not left it around the front, on their newly paved forecourt. Yes, she had thought, she had overheard the man who just dumped his bag in his room, telling Mark that he was going

445

to a funeral! Well he did have a smart dark suit on, which made a change from their normal clientele. The Mountain View seemed to only attract two distinct types of guest. Ramblers, usually cheerful geriatrics, who insisted on telling her all about their long walks from one ruined castle or abbey to the next, and the scruffy building contractors, who moaned constantly about the funny names on the sign posts. Perhaps it was because she had been so impressed with the smart gentleman that she had become so fuming angry when this tidy bloke did not return at all last night. After all she had waited up until midnight and that's no joke when you have breakfasts to cook at 7 am!

Mark had laughed at her nonsense, when she had rushed in on her return from the salon and told him that their posh guest had been murdered! He simply suggested that the bloke had just got lucky! She did not understand what Mark had meant at first and then when she did she was more shocked than if the man had been murdered. He just did not look the type for one night stands, and after a funeral, disgusting! He certainly was not her type and she doubted whether that even in Aberfoist, especially in Aberfoist, such a dumpy middle-aged man could "get lucky!" Now it was mid-afternoon and the man had not come back to collect his belongings, which she had insisted Mark move out of the room dead on 10:30 am, her normal checking out time.

"Oh my God!" Sarah Wilson suddenly thought. This might be him now and Mark was out! She gritted her teeth. Well he was not having a refund! 'No refunds!' She muttered defiantly under her breath. She would tell him. Yes she would! The cheek of it! Staying out all night! She ran a respectable place! Finally, Sarah was ready. She had flicked up her hair and was satisfied that she looked tidy enough to greet whoever had rung the bell. She was certainly pumped up enough to argue against any demands for a refund. She could see the shadow outlined against the frosted glass panel of the inner porch door. She hoped it was a new

446

guest and not some time waster trying to sell her advertising space in tourist brochures or worse still, charity goods! She had wanted to put a notice up, on the front door, warning that cold callers were not welcome but Mark had said that it might confuse potential guests. Those people who had stopped after spotting the "Vacancies" sign that regrettably had been a permanent fixture in their front window, since they had taken over the guest house late last year.

The bell chimed again and she jumped again. Her dogs erupted into snappy little barks again and she had to shoo them into the guest lounge and shut the sparklingly clean, interior frosted glass door, to keep them at bay. However, just as she did, she glanced out of the large rectangular double glazed front bay window, hoping to see a nice new car outside, not a tradesman's van or a team of impatient salesmen, and to her absolute horror she saw the immediately recognisable bright yellow and blue chevrons of the police car that was pulled up on the road outside, just beyond her low perfectly manicured hedgerow.

'Oh my God! Oh my God!' Sarah's heart fluttered in time to her whispered exclamations. It was a Police Car! 'Oh my God!' She said out loud again. That poor man! She began to stress herself silly. He must have been murdered. 'Oh my God!' What would she do! It would be in the newspapers and all over the television. 'Oh my God!' Then she suddenly thought that it might be really good for business!

Eagerly opening the door, Sarah Wilson's sudden optimism deserted her. She was disappointed and confused. There stood her missing guest, as large as life. Mykee Kane smiled apologetically. He opened his mouth to speak but he did not get a chance.

'What happened to you?' Sarah snapped. She just about managed to stop herself from adding the "I thought you were dead" bit and Kane finally got the chance to begin his rehearsed

447

apology. He used the one where he said he had met up with an old friend and one drink led to another and then he went back for a night cap and ended up sleeping on the sofa, etc. Whilst he spoke she looked him up and down. He certainly looked rough enough to have slept on a very uncomfortable sofa. In fact, he looked as if he had not slept at all. She was also slightly confused by the tracksuit that he was wearing. She assumed that that nice suit he had had on yesterday was in the black bin bag he was carrying. She wanted to say that it would get ruined in there but instead she simply blurted out: 'No refunds! I'm afraid we can't! I mean we lost the chance to let the room. Maybe I can give you something back for not having to cook you breakfast!' Sarah suddenly bit her lip and paled. What on earth was she saying? "You idiot!" She silently told herself. Luckily for her the man seemed to be reassuring her that he did not want a refund. He only wanted his bag and he would be off!

Mark had checked the room that morning. The man had not even unpacked. He had touched nothing, and just left his bag on the bed. Mark had brought the bag downstairs and put it in the hall. It was just behind her. When she handed it to him and Kane had finished saying, once again, how sorry he was for putting them out, Sarah Wilson could not help herself.

'My husband said that you got lucky last night! I told him he was wrong! You didn't look like that type of bloke!'

Kane laughed. 'You were right!' He said. Then he added with a smirk: 'Tell him I got unlucky!' He gave her a wink and said 'Goodbye!' He turned to leave and then stopped. Turning back, he smiled again.

'Mrs Wilson, should you have any problems, er, I mean should anybody ask you about my visit please contact me on this number!' Kane reached into his tracksuit jacket side pocket and picked out one, from a dozen brand new business cards that he had been handed by Captain Brown. Sarah Wilson looked down at the card and pulled a slightly confused face. Kane smiled once more. 'I really am sorry that I did not get to stay at your lovely establishment! From the smell of whatever is cooking in your kitchen I must have missed out on an excellent cooked breakfast!'

He turned away and walked down the path on the left hand side of the Guest House towards his car. Sarah Wilson watched him go. She was blushing slightly, briefly charmed by his manners. After all he had referred to her Guest House as "an establishment!" Sarah turned her head back, just in time to see the Police Car pull away from the front of her house. That, she thought, had been a strange coincidence. The presence of the Police Car had in the end, oddly, reassured her whilst she was talking to that strange man. She now looked back down at the business card in her hand, which Kane had just given her. The card simply said:

Mykee Kane
Change Manager & Logistics Expert
Whitehall Resources Limited
0800 666 747 184

Shutting her front door and ignoring the frustrated yelps of Keegan and Dalglish, who wanted to be let out of the front room, Sarah Wilson rushed to find her mobile phone. She just had to tell Mark all about the guest who came but did not stay.

Chapter 45: Someone's Idea of a Joke

By the time Kane had reached the M4 motorway, he was satisfied that no one had followed him on this particular journey away from Aberfoist. The twenty minutes guarded drive in the confined space of his car had also made him realise that he needed a bath and regardless of his surprisingly high spirits, a few hours sleep in a bed. Kane chuckled, suddenly very pleased with himself as he decided that that was exactly what he would do. Relaxing for probably the first time in forty-eight hours, his subconscious natural auto pilot took over driving the familiar route home, instantly freeing up part of his mind to enjoy considering the meaning behind both fake job titles accredited to him on his new "business" card! He was no longer a teacher. Now he was a "Change Manager & Logistics Expert!"

Of course, he understood the job titles were someone's idea of a joke. Yet he could not stop himself over-thinking why this had been chosen to describe his new role. Management implies control and change is an inevitable occurrence. So he concluded that according to the boldly printed words, blacked on the pristine white cards supplied to him, possibly in an effort to give him an air of legitimacy or perhaps merely baffle most casual readers like that "nice" landlady, his new job was to simply "carry out and control reactions" obviously in line with Brigadier Dr Paul Packwood's crafty schemes, which were themselves a reaction to "threats" against this nation.

Kane laughed again, amused at the humour employed in setting up his cover. Given his recent briefing, he pondered that perhaps "execute" was a more appropriate term to apply to his

450

new work requirements! Ah well, Kane decided, it probably all amounted to the same thing and he had better just accept the situation he now found himself in, for there was no point in creating unnecessary complications. After all it was a situation that he felt would only get more difficult when he sat down, in the far too near future and tried to explain to his wife, why he was making such a sudden and obviously unlooked-for "career" change!

At least Jill might appreciate the increase in salary and a company car, or so he hoped. Yes, Kane thought with a hint of regret, she would be happy to see his old beloved Mazda go. He really could not depend on the power of prayer or wait three turns of the key for his car to start every time he was sent out on a mission by Packwood. Kane also reflected that a new car was only one of the advantages his new employment would bring her. However, he hoped that Jill would not benefit from the enhanced "death in service" scheme, which his new employers had briefly skated over during their most informal induction talk; the one rattled through by Captain Brown, whilst they were sat in that open cell back at Aberfoist Police Station.

Nonetheless, she, like Kane, would have very little choice in the matter, a reality that should have actually worried her husband an awful lot more than his coerced career change. Indeed, the realisation that the efficient Captain Brown had apparently travelled to Aberfoist that morning, with pre-printed named business cards and such an obtuse cover story, firmly in place, for Military Intelligence's newest recruit, should certainly have alerted Kane to the fact that he had been set up! Yet, after almost ten years "enjoying" the normality of a real life, and with what had begun to look like another twenty plus years "trudge" as a wage slave at the "chalk" face ahead of him, if he was lucky, in what had become, if he was truly honest with himself, a rather lacklustre teaching career, Kane was suddenly exhilarated by his unexpected recall to arms.

In addition to the boxed set of smart business cards, Kane had been given three items by the ever resourceful Captain Brown. The first was a small credit card sized Military Intelligence security pass, perhaps not now so surprisingly filled in with Kane's personal details and a bafflingly up to date passport sized photograph. This, on careful inspection, looked to Kane as if it had been taken at the graveside during Frank John's funeral. Calamity! Kane assumed.

The second item was a familiar looking but oddly unbranded and allegedly fully encrypted mobile phone like device. It appeared to function like a fairly standard mobile phone. Although he had been assured that the software applications downloaded on it were a bit special, if compared to standard commercially available software. It came with a pack of four nondescript, magnetic, plastic coated, metallic strips. Each strip was about the size of a fingernail, which Kane had been told incorporated personalised tracking devices. When activated they would, apparently, automatically link to an App on his new "Government" issue mobile phone. He was warned that when operational the devices would also appear on a monitor back at HQ and all such movements would be saved on an operations history cloud for future review, if required.

The third item was perhaps the most essential bit of kit given his mission instructions. Inside a small metallic case, no bigger than approximately 40 cm by 30 cm, Kane had found a dark grey, Glock 17, 9 mm, semi-automatic handgun, with one spare magazine clip. Thirty four bullets in total! There was also fitted into the cream coloured, soft cushioned lining of the case, a waistband clip holster and a dark grey bulbous cylindrical tube, which Kane knew, when screwed into the end of the open nozzle, would almost silence the explosion made when he squeezed the trigger. The gun was remarkably similar to the one he had been issued with more than a decade ago. However, it was a newer model of course, and felt much lighter than his old Glock. It looked uglier than his original pistol but then if it was as accurate and did not jam, he would be satisfied.

Although, there appeared to him to be no direct logistical process in the random flow of the events that had occurred since he had first left his car at the rear of the Mountain View Guest House, a little over twenty four hours ago, Kane could not be anything but amazed by the anticipation of the real Logistics' Expert and Change Manager, that was Brigadier Dr. Paul Packwood. How that man had calculated the probability of Kane's subsequent and definitely haphazard frustration of the intentions of criminals like Lord and Pace was truly frightening. And now he simply expected the far from up to scratch Kane to complete the mission and as he had commanded: "Go get Lord!" The killer of his once best friend!

***

Unbeknown to Kane, it had been Captain Brown who had pointed out, with a smug smile on his otherwise implacable face, as he carefully strapped Packwood into the stiff upright seat of the specially commissioned military helicopter's draughty rear passenger compartment, that the shape Kane was in might prove an excellent disguise for future covert missions. More seriously Brown had added, now shouting above the increasing roar of the engines, that in spite of his need for a new diet and exercise regime, Kane's "talents" had certainly been evident in his brief but key involvement in the events of the last fortnight.

In response Packwood allowed himself the brief luxury of one of his rare smiles of genuine satisfaction, whilst watching Brown stumble backwards into the empty seat opposite. These days the "Doctor" was loathed to travel far from his London "clinic", located within one of the uniformly dull buildings found around Whitehall, but the personal discomfort suffered on this trip had been worth it, for he had got his man.

Packwood had also had fun, especially when exerting his authority over the hideous Superintendent Charles. The "Super" had paid for the classic mistake of trying to get all high and mighty with Brigadier Dr. Packwood. Kane was not the only one sat in the room who had failed to keep a straight face when Packwood had simple said one word in response to Charles' histrionic demands to know, "on what charges" he was about to be detained. "Treason" the Brigadier had almost whispered, before raising his voice slightly to instruct his soldiers to take Charles away.

Inspector Paul Davies had looked pleasantly surprised as Charles had been frog marched off. The crooked policeman would occupy Kane's old cell until secure transport could be arranged to take him under the military escort of Packwood's men, to London for further interrogation. Davies had briefly opened his mouth to ask if Packwood was serious about the treason charge but the senior man merely talked over him, pointing out that Davies now needed to find out "where on earth" this Detective Constable Haymer was hiding! Packwood also announced uncompromisingly that Davies must make enquiries into who exactly Charles had contacted, since arriving at the police station, earlier that morning; and then Packwood added with the thinnest of smiles, "arrest them all!"

'On what charges?' A concerned but increasingly giddy Davies had eventually managed to ask.

'Conspiracy' Packwood had said matter of factly.

'Conspiracy to do what?' Davies had asked doubtfully.

'Conspiracy! That will do, for now!' Packwood had simply replied.

454

People could often be manipulated or so Packwood thought as the helicopter took off from the river meadow and began its flight back to London but as Ellis Pace should have realised, outcomes were never guaranteed.

Chapter 46: A Different Mountain View

In spite of the early morning sunshine and the fact that he had worn more than enough layers to model the entire men's adventure clothing page of a Mountain Warehouse catalogue, Kane was cold. Regular gusts of chilly air blew in from the north, rustling and teasing the polyester of his supposedly "triclimate" coat, so much so that he was never in no danger of ever overheating inside the expensive and allegedly environmentally aware imported garments. Nonetheless, the discomfort was worth it, for his vantage point high up on the fern covered slopes of the South Wales hillside, the one that the locals insisted on calling "The Mountain," even though it was technically well under the required height of 610 metres, afforded Kane a fine panoramic view of the valley below.

With his cheeks continuing to redden in the wind, Kane began to wonder whether he should have worn his old full face balaclava. Although itchy, the wool would have given him added protection against the elements, but he was also sure that this mask, combined with his tightly fitting green jacket hood and heavily tinted sunglasses, would have freaked out the many dog walkers, who were surprisingly out and about in large numbers that fine Sunday morning. Even without the extra knitted headgear, Kane was finding it hard work to waylay the constant interlopers' suspicions, as their curious pets sniffed out his presence in what should have been a concealed observation point just above the main pathway along "The Mountain's" ridge.

456

Unfortunately, his open flask of coffee and poorly wrapped pack of corned beef sandwiches, were proving to be an unexpected attraction to all passing dogs, especially those on extendible leads. Ever keen to escape their bondage and eager to explore any odd scent, particularly if it smelt like food, man's best friends constantly contrived to not only physically drag but also verbally entangle their owners in unexpected and embarrassingly banal conversations with the bulky stranger, unintentionally discovered sat on the olive green camping chair, clutching the rather professional looking binoculars in his gloved hands. The constant banter as the canine carers tried to drag their fur coated, four-legged, child substitutes away from that strange, slightly malevolent presence, was getting tiresome. Even worse, the pets and their owners were proving to be a regular distraction from Kane's real purpose up on "The Mountain" that morning. Still, he insisted with a cheerful grin to all who encountered him, that rare red kites had been reported to be in the area, and after a quick glance up to the empty sky, most dog walkers went on their way, completely satisfied that he was no more than a harmless, if somewhat deluded, *twit of a twitcher.*

Of course, the dogs' fascination with him and their constant desire to sniff him up close was his entire fault. Scoffing that fried sausage, bacon and egg sandwich, was perhaps not the best decision Kane had made that day. Yet how could he resist the "heart attack in a roll" as it had been wittily billed on the black smeared, dry wipe, white plastic board, which hung next to the open hatch of the sizzling catering van, so cleverly located in the nearby visitor car park, at the designated start of the Mountain Trail. Kane was certainly not the only one tempted to live dangerously that morning. The smell of bacon in the pan and sausages griddling on the caterer's Calor gas range, was drawing dozens of ramblers, all willing to compromise their intended healthy exercise in the rare spring sunshine, with an impromptu grease soaked sandwich.

Still, living dangerously was something that Kane had signed up to do. Less than a fortnight ago he would have anticipated spending this Sunday sat at home, surrounded by schoolbooks, red pen in hand, ticking or crossing pupil assignments in readiness for the dreaded return to school on Monday morning. A day spent writing down well meant advisory comments, which sadly nobody would read, unless the work became one of the low percentage samples selected for internal audit by senior management, or even better, an external review by Estyn, the Welsh Schools Inspectorate. All things considered, marking was never really what he wanted to do in his so called spare time but somehow it had become so much an expected part of his life, that his wife and son had planned their regular escape from the inevitable stressful homework environment, by spending their weekend away, staying over in Bristol with his in-laws. They would not normally return until later that evening, which as it happened turned out to be very much to Kane's advantage, now that *living dangerously* had taken on a much more literal meaning than poor dietary choices and stressful paperwork; all since the unexpected phone call from Wendy John just before the start of the Easter school holidays, a lifetime or three ago.

Having set up his modest camp at first light, Kane was not only cold but now very bored. Sipping the lukewarm coffee from his flask, he welcomed a further distraction from his task, when his new mobile phone throbbed into life, announcing the arrival of an electronic message with repeated vibrations. However, he could not read the official email on screen because of the sunshine beaming down from behind him. At least he was grateful that the brightness would disguise his position, dazzling all those who dared look east, up from the narrow valley below, at what passed for a beauty spot when compared to the

458

otherwise blighted local landscape; which still showed the scars of historic heavy industrialisation from the last century.

Eventually shielding the screen with the back of his cup holding hand, Kane gradually worked out that the message was a copy of one which had been sent to his school's head teacher. The text as Mr Kane the teacher might have commented, if he had been marking it, was a load of baloney! A work of pure fiction! Allegedly sent from the Department of Education but probably composed by Captain Brown or another of Packwood's minions. It informed the school that Kane had been seconded to the Ministry of Defence, for the rest of the year, with immediate effect! He was to help set up their new Educational Resources Department. The (hopefully) bitter pill of his sudden and unexpected departure from classroom routine was sweetened somewhat by the offer of a Government grant, intended to mitigate any costs incurred in recruiting suitable supply teachers to cover his classes. Kane actually felt guilty at leaving his pupils in the lurch, well a few of them maybe, especially when he thought of the cramming still needed to be done by his examination classes. However, that sensation was eased somewhat when he considered the fact that he was escaping the long hours of tedium that revision lessons usually involved this time of year. He certainly would not miss the panic and dismay felt by those who finally realised how much work they should have been doing, including the angst of his own self-critical assessment on recognising how easily the pupils had fooled him into thinking they had actually been learning the lessons that he had been teaching them for the past year! "Yes!" He suddenly reflected, sat in the strange chilly sunshine, high on the hillside, his life had changed, possibly for the better. "Like a breath of fresh air!" Or so he told himself, shivering slightly, as another gust of that really fresh air rippled tiny waves across the surface of the coffee in his cup.

Apart from the wind, his only other pressing concern at present was the question of how his wife would take the news of his new job, when and if he actually got around to telling her! He could have, should have told her last night. Kane sighed and tried to concentrate on the valley below but his mind filled with nervous reflections on the last 48 hours.

***

After an uneventful journey home, on Saturday afternoon, (was it really only yesterday, he thought), Kane remembered dumping his bag, unopened for the whole trip, together with the wiffy black bin liner, next to the washing machine in the kitchen, and plugging his battery dead mobile phone into the spare socket beside the kettle, before heading straight for the shower room upstairs The warm water had revived him and twenty minutes later, dressed in his own comfortably sized towelling dressing gown, he sat on his bed, and risked going through the voicemail on his own now recharged mobile phone. There were only a few calls, and they were pretty much as he had expected really, all from Jill. He listened uneasily as they deteriorated in tone from a cheerful "give us a ring" to a rather resentful "don't bother if you're hammered!" Eventually Jill had cracked and she sounded nervous, maybe even slightly concerned, rather than angry, as her recorded message asked him if he "was alright?" After a pause he could tell the unmistakable irritation in her voice, when she had said that she hoped he had not "gone and done anything we are going to both regret!?!"

Kane closed his eyes and took a deep breath. Jill had always been someone whom he had found it difficult to lie to, so he really did not want to ring her back. There was no way he needed to have that "worrying" conversation over the phone. The one that he knew they had to have sooner or later, all about the

460

unavoidable changes to his lifestyle that his reactions to Frank John's death had brought about. So he simply took a moment to justify the lie to himself. It was a lie but one that he would tell her, just to stall her until she had returned home with their son, on Sunday evening. Then he could tell her. Except of course, if things went wrong for him earlier on that Sunday, he might not get to tell her about it at all! So inevitably he had decided to take the easy option. Convinced that he was definitely doing the right thing, he went downstairs and found the family lap top, exactly where he had left it last Friday morning, still in the kitchen. Kane sat at the breakfast bar and used the computer rather than his phone to email her the lie.

This was, of course, still a mistake, something that he had not fully thought through. Although saying that he had dropped his iPhone, whilst drunk on Friday night and that it was not working properly, had seemed like a perfectly good idea to stall her and put off hastening the awkward truth of "that" inevitable conversation, he was left cringing, when the house phone began ringing less than a minute after he had sent the email. Answering the landline, Kane found himself speaking directly to Jill anyway. Perhaps he was lucky, for his natural hesitation fitted in, well in her mind at least, with his pretence of the hangover from hell!

Maybe the hangover was not such a big lie! After the dramas of Friday night, and the long Saturday, mostly spent at the police station, he was pretty tired anyway. Whatever, Jill sounded relieved, just to speak to him. She also sounded slightly distracted. She was ringing from the front seat of a taxi, on her way out for a rare girls night out on the town or so she said, and her companions, her sister and their girlfriends, were in the back of the cab, sounding appropriately high spirited and in a real Saturday night fever as risqué taunts and loud outbursts of laughter thankfully drowned out any attempt at a sensible conversation. Kane said he was off to bed as he needed an early

461

night himself, (certainly not a lie) and wished her a good night out. He hoped to be fully recovered by the time she got home tomorrow. Jill hoped she would be too! They laughed and she rang off.

***

Back up on the hillside, Kane shivered again. The wind was getting colder, even though it was approaching midday. A man of his experience should have realised that the deep groove in the hillside must have been cut out by a persistent and harsh wind, which habitually blew down the valley and that a wind trap was not the best place for a stakeout. Still his position served its purpose and the fresh gusts kept him from dozing off. Obviously, he had not slept well at all last night, guilt at lying to his wife rather than killing two people or suffering nerves about his planned Sunday morning activity. Well, maybe he had not exactly been lying to his wife, but he had certainly avoided telling her the truth. He sighed and placed his flask's detachable plastic beaker securely into the webbed cup holder on the right arm rest of his camping chair, before once again lifting his sunglasses up onto his forehead, and then raising his trusty old field glasses, a souvenir from his army reconnaissance days, to his eyes. The powerful binoculars were proving particularly useful in scanning across the valley; especially now that something was actually happening over at the tall grey old building, directly opposite him on the heavily urbanised western slope.

Kane was not sure what he had been actually looking for that morning. Maybe he hoped to see a bright green motorcycle leave the dual carriageway and tear along the solitary "A" road towards the old Baptist chapel. Of course, that would have been too easy. Yet at last, he had spotted something odd. Or rather something he thought might be out of the ordinary for midday

462

on a Sunday. A large black and white saloon, its panda markings making it stand out from the more colourful silvers, blues, reds and whites of the other vehicles that normally used the road, was slowly beginning its climb along the valley's western slope, having just left the dual carriageway. Even though the traditional star shaped emblem was missing from its usual top front central bonnet mounting, Kane recognised the car was a Mercedes. He felt a tingle of excitement watching the elegant saloon glide silently along the road, for he knew that the black and white markings on a Mercedes meant this car was likely to be one of Cardiff City Council's licensed hackney cabs and as such its presence on this particular road at this particular time was all the more extraordinary. These taxis rarely left the streets of the capital city. Even if the driver was working, Kane wondered, why would they abandon the city centre? There the constant pick ups and put downs would pay better than one long expensive fair out to the badlands of the valleys.

If the driver was not working, Kane thought that surely he would have let the car out to another taxi licensee and borrowed a less ostentatious and more practical car to visit friends or relatives. Just for a moment Kane worried that it might merely be a group of students, who could have pooled together, to get a ride back to their Halls of Residence after a late night and early morning of clubbing in the city centre but then he doubted they would have chosen an expensive Hackney taxi, when a private hire taxi company, like Uber, would have been much cheaper. Kane continued to speculate about the panda cab, until it had safely passed the University buildings and finally stopped, just before the old chapel, with its unlit neon sign hanging on the stone wall, which thanks to his powerful lenses, he could make out read "The Potting Shed!"

Focusing the binoculars on the now stationary taxi, Kane watched as a giant, dressed in flowing biblical robes, emerged from the front passenger seat. This huge man, his long beard flowing in the wind, gently closed the car door behind him, before stomping purposely over to the large five bar gate, set in the middle of a small stone wall, that was attached to the old chapel and whilst it may have surrounded a small grave yard in the past, it now gave access into a smartly tarmacked car park. However, the giant seemed to struggle with the gate's lock and eventually, after what seemed like ages, obviously frustrated, he turned back towards the cab and gestured his obvious confusion by waving his large hands. Kane lowered his binoculars in an attempt to see the bigger picture. For a moment nothing seemed to happen, then, at last, the back door of the taxi opened. Slowly a more conventionally, if not fashionably, dressed person got out.

Kane raised the binoculars to his eyes again so that he could see the tight white leggings, and what looked like an old fashioned, faded denim jacket, which accentuated the person's broad shoulders and strong build. A matching baseball hat was pulled down, over their head but the sun glinted on what had to be expensive gold chains worn around their neck and wrists. This person seemed to briefly remonstrate with the giant, before pushing passed, crouching down and instantly unlocking the gate. Kane's smile broadened, for as the new gate keeper stood up and began to haul what must have been an extremely heavy five bar gate to one side, the baseball hat blew off in the wind, to reveal a crop of bright blonde hair.

With the gate open, the taxi immediately pulled into the car park and drove slowly down the slight incline towards the back door entrance to the grey building. It was quickly followed, on foot, by the blonde and the giant, who on reaching the now stationary taxi, stooped and opened the back door with great ceremony, almost bowing further down as he did so. Meanwhile, the blonde appeared to unlock the building's back door.

Only when both doors were open, did another passenger exit from the back of the taxi. At a distance, the passenger looked to Kane, to be almost as tall as the giant, but he was dressed in casual light blue trousers, probably double denim. Kane tried to zoom in and refocus the binoculars on the flap of red material clearly visible as being wrapped around the neck line, like a scarf or neckerchief. Kane spotted that this person also wore a dark beard. It was enough for Kane.

Anyone watching closely would have thought that the twitcher had finally spotted what he had been waiting so patiently for and they would have been right. Although what Kane had seen was not a red kite. Kane's smile slowly widened. He knew that it was time to make a move. The Lord and his lady were back in residence.

Chapter 47: Going Chopping

Kane cursed as he was forced into changing down yet another gear by the slow pace of the double-decker bus in front of him. His car's small engine also grumbled angrily at the strain placed on it by the steady incline and even though the road was straight, there was a constant enough threat from the few cars coming down hill to make overtaking unwise, if not impossible, given the Mazda's limited acceleration.

The charabanc had actually cut him up, when it had pulled out without signalling, from the bus stop for the ultra-modern building that appeared to be the Halls of Residence for the local college. Such an inconsiderate manoeuvre may have proved fatal had he been driving a faster car.

In one way, the bulky double-decker's presence was probably an advantage to him. It would shield his small coupé from any prying eyes that might be watching from the imposing three-storey, grey rubble stone building, which he knew was somewhere close up ahead.

When Kane had started his ascent up the far side of the valley, he had spotted the sun glinting on the neat circular window, fitted into the highest point of the south facing gabled end of the tall, polygon shaped, old chapel. He had recognised that that was the perfect spot for a look out. Now he could not see it and hopefully anyone up there could not see him.

Instead Kane was staring up into the cheery faces of a conveniently multi-racial group of students, who featured in the colourful poster plastered all over the back of the bus. After ten years of teaching, Kane did not know that learning could be such fun but then if he believed the stylish advert for college life, these suitably diverse scholars were not concerned about crippling student loans and unlike many local teenagers, were free to escape from the social disadvantages created by an era of austerity to live their higher education dreams.

Shaking off his growing irritation, Kane concentrated and tried to remember the road layout that he had been studying for most of the morning. This effort helped him touch his brakes just in time, shrewdly anticipating the bus slowing to almost a standstill, right outside the club, in order to make the wide swing necessary to take the sharp left up the hill. The bus driver had obviously driven this route many times before and was using his gears and gravity to slow down, rather than applying the vehicle's noisy airbrakes, with their bright red warning lights.

Once again without signalling, the double-decker seemed to want to catch Kane out and swept right, crossing the worn white lines that had once streaked up the middle of the road, before swinging sharply back to the left and finally rounding the tight bend, and beginning the even slower climb up the steepest part of the hill. Kane followed the bus around the bend, feeling suddenly exposed to the upper floor windows of the chapel-come-snooker club, but his need to focus on the road prevented even the slightest glance right to see if anyone was watching him. Just after the bend, he took a chance and darted left, making an immediate turn without signalling, into the narrow dead-end street, squeezed between two rows of uniform terraced houses. Given the relative height of the houses on the rising hillside, Kane could only hope that they would block the view from the highest windows in the neighbouring clubhouse and prevent any spying eyes in the taller building from spotting him. He then drove slowly down to the blocked off end of the street, executed a tricky five point turn in the narrow space between parked cars and the concrete bollards, before pulling up in the only available parking space, albeit clearly marked as residents only, with his car wisely pointing towards the only way in or out of the street. He would risk a parking ticket. At least if he did not make it back to his car, someone might report it and eventually someone, somewhere, would realise this was where he had disappeared.

Boldly undressing whilst standing at the rear of his car in full view of the whole of the street, Kane began dumping most of the outer layers of his outdoor clothing in the boot of the car, along with his field glasses, wallet, empty flask, uneaten sandwiches, and private mobile phone. He certainly did not want (a probably hung-over) Jill to ring him at an inconvenient moment. Kane then ran his hands over the zipped pockets of his thin black North Face fleece jacket in a final check of the only outer layer he had decided to keep on. He could feel the gun, heavy in the pocket on his right side, its weight almost balancing the combined drag of the silencer and Military Intelligence "works" mobile phone in the left. Kane had abandoned the waistband holster as impractical. It was far too awkward a fit given his unfortunate girth and the elasticity of the waist on his olive green Gore-Tex cargo trousers. He wondered, for a moment, how those fat cops in America managed to wear such things, and eventually decided that perhaps that was the reason why they shot more people instead of chasing after them, like the popular TV cops always seemed willing to do!

For a moment, Kane considered fitting the silencer, and then dismissed the idea. It would make the gun too bulky for his pocket and knowing his luck, one of the residents might spot him doing it, and the next thing, the whole place could be swamped by armed police. He grinned at the idea of uniformed back up. Now that he was an official agent of the state they should be on his side. However, he knew that the reality of his situation was much less black and white. He also wondered how many armed police units were actually on duty within an hour's drive of the Welsh valleys that afternoon. A lot less than most people would have thought he concluded. No he was definitely on his own for this mission.

After checking that his car was locked, Kane made a great show of taking out the MI mobile phone and putting it on silent. He hoped that if any local villain was watching him from behind the net curtains in the nearby houses, this display would convince them that he still had all his valuables on him and not in the car. He then took several deep breaths. Maybe car theft should be the least of his worries given what he was about to do, but the thought of returning to a smashed window was nonetheless a distraction. He could not risk taking his wallet with his real driving licence and home address on it and yet he worried about the inconvenience of its loss. He took several more deep breaths. In through the nose, down to the pit of his stomach and then out through his mouth. That helped settle his nerves, gradually blanking out all thoughts, other than the process of breathing in this particular way. Eventually, a dozen in/outs later, he felt ready and began walking casually to the end of the street. He carefully crossed the road, there was no traffic to dodge at that moment, and then he strolled along the pavement, down towards the large grey building.

If anyone had looked out from the terrace houses opposite, they may have briefly wondered why a man dressed in rambling gear, was out for his Sunday lunchtime walk, amongst the rows of houses and not up amongst the natural beauty of the undeveloped hillside on the other, eastern side of the valley. Then again, given the large number of satellite dishes fixed to the nearby houses, most residents were probably watching the "Super Sunday" televised football, or so Kane hoped. He stopped on reaching the shuttered front door to the snooker club.

He was grateful to find the place shut. That would limit any

469

innocent locals getting involved and unintentionally complicating matters. Sunday lunchtime snooker was once big a thing in the Valleys and Kane wondered if any locals had been surprised to find the club shut when they popped out for a few frames and a quick pint before dinner. Trying not to look too shifty Kane pretended to be a frustrated customer, whilst casually studying the locks which secured the metal roller shutter in place. He was sure that someone would be watching him but he hoped that they were a neighbour rather than one of Lord's men.

Little did Kane know that most of the club's neighbours knew not to take too much of an interest in the comings and goings at the club. Of course, they were well aware that there were often lots of strange people, appearing and disappearing, at all times of the day and night at the club, a bit like this oddly dressed bloke, who was currently looking over the place. Yet, they turned a blind eye because you see they'd say, there was never any trouble at the club. Not these days! The owner just wouldn't stand for it! Like! Unlike the bother from drunken students down the road! Yes the locals would say that "since 'what's-his-name' had taken over, things had been quiet there. Fair play! He seemed a tidy bloke. He had been a particularly good neighbour, for a foreigner!"

Although a few onlookers may have noticed that the club had closed surprisingly early on Saturday night and they may now be wondering if the visit by the police, earlier on yesterday, had had anything to do with it not opening this Sunday morning. Nevertheless, they would have been shocked if they had kept watching, for the casual pedestrian turned around, as if to walk back up the hill, obviously disappointed that the club was shut! Only he stopped at the end of the building, just before the bend in the road, and leant back against the metre tall boundary wall that ran up and around the bend, sealing off what had once been part of the old chapel's graveyard from the pavement and main road. Suddenly, the man rolled back, disappearing right over the wall, so quickly that any onlooker may have thought that the sun was playing tricks with their eyes. Well, perhaps it was! The man's movement was most odd, given the size and shape, and age of the man! It was a strangely gymnastic movement, almost a perfect backward roll. So agile, so fast that if they had been really watching, they would have certainly thought that they had imagined it all. Maybe they did!

Squatting down below the wall, Kane hoped nobody had been watching. He waited a minute and tried to regain his composure, slowly steadying his breathing. When he heard nothing, other than his own panting, not even a car travelling along the road, he began to edge his way forward. The rubber soles of his walking boots gripped tightly to the thin stone ledge as he balanced along the side wall of the building, just a few centimetres above the long overgrown rough grass that filled the unkempt side space between the chapel building and the neighbouring terrace boundary. Luckily for Kane there were no windows that side of either building and he made it to the end of the wall without discovery.

Still crouching, but now leaning against the corner stone, he listened again. He could hear a sound that he had heard a thousand times before, on trains, school buses and in the playground. The familiar tinny muffled thump, thump, thump, as somewhere, someone was listening to music, through headphones. He chanced a glance, popping his head around the corner to see the back of the building, his head visible for only a second. Hidden behind the wall once more, he replayed the scene in his mind's eye. A young man, in his early twenties, dressed in trainers and jeans but wearing a long baggy shirt, a Kameez, the traditional garment popular with Pakistani men, was standing at the back of the taxi, having a smoke whilst looking up towards the scenic eastern hillside. Kane thought he could smell the

471

tobacco now, oddly floating his way in spite of the breeze. Kane assumed the young man was the taxi driver. Like all the youngsters these days he had the latest wireless earbuds, pressed tightly into his ears. Hopefully these expensive little white sticks, would block off all surrounding noise, with the constant assault on his ear drums of the bass heavy beat from whatever electronic music that was slowly but surely deafening the young man.

Kane chanced another look. Propped on top of his head, a head nodding to the beat, the driver wore an off white or possibly tobacco stained, Kufi prayer cap. The young man still had his back to Kane but was now leaning against the rear of the Mercedes. He was looking across the black roof, staring up, towards the mountain, on the far side of the Valley, seemingly entranced by the beauty of the distant green hills. Kane followed the young man's gaze and saw the tiny dots and slightly taller dark shapes, moving about, as people were still walking their dogs along the ridge way. There did not seem to be anybody else in the car, Kane checked that carefully, relieved that this Mercedes did not have any privacy glass. Nor were there anyone anywhere else to be seen in the back of the chapel club's car park.

Kane stepped back into his hiding place and thought for a moment. The young man may have nothing to do with Lord or his gang. They may simply have been his fare for the day. However, Kane could not take the chance. Taking a deep breath, he stepped out silently and stealthy crept across the tarmac, closing in on the taxi driver. Raising his left arm in an arc, with his hand flat, left thumb touching his right cheek bone, Kane took the final steps forward. Then when he was less than a foot behind the driver, he swung his hand around and down, executing a brutal short range karate chop, onto the young man's unprotected neck.

Lao Fu, Kane's old Kung Fu teacher, would have been proud of the perfect technique and the direct contact with the targeted pressure point, which was found at the base of the neck, just above the collar bone. However, the old man, would not have been pleased with the result of the blow. For all of Lao Fu's skill, the years of training, dedicating himself and others to his art, the old man viewed it all as a non-contact, spiritual activity, a method of avoiding fighting. Kane had learnt to be a lot more practical with his own interpretation of this martial art, than his old master had. In any event the young man collapsed, immediately unconscious.

As soon as the knees had bent, Kane had managed to step in and break the fall, stopping his victim from hitting the tarmac below hard and noisily. After lowering the body to the ground, a quick check confirmed that the driver's pockets were empty. A step forward and a glance in through the open front window, confirmed that keys were still in the ignition and that the taxi was unlocked. Kane stepped back, carefully avoiding tripping over the felled man. He popped the boot of the taxi open and then with surprising difficulty, he struggled to man handle the unconscious driver up and over the back bumper, until eventually he was able to roll him into the large empty storage space of the boot. Gently pushing the lid back in place, Kane next removed the keys from the ignition and took the risk of locking the car. Fortunately it did not bleep but the loud click, as the central locking bolted in to place, left him nervously glancing towards the building. Had someone heard? Would they investigate?

Kane quickly took another deep breath, then six more, steadying himself again before silently but confidently walking over to the open back door. At the threshold he waited, listening for a few seconds, whilst staring into the darkness ahead. He heard nothing. He saw nothing. He stepped inside.

473

Chapter 48: Gym-nast-hits

An unseen sensor reacted almost immediately to Kane's presence in the building, triggering a burst of light, then another and another, as a line of thin florescent strip-lights turned on. The first tube was set directly above him and bathed him in bright white light. The line then ran on at roughly two metre intervals, all along the unpainted, pink plastered, ceiling. Its sudden brilliance shone down illuminating a straight pathway ahead, across the grey concrete floor, until the trail reached a windowless red brick wall, which he presumed must form the front end of the building, possibly just below street level. Kane could also see at the far end of the room, the start of a wide wooden planked, open sided, staircase, which had been built into the wall. The steps rose steeply to the right, disappearing up into the unlit darkness, and undoubtedly providing access to the club above. Aware that he was somewhat exposed, Kane quickly sort refuge away from the light by moving into the dark shadows to his right. There he stood still, silently waiting for a challenge to be called out. None came. His entrance seemed to have gone undetected by anyone or anything, other than the automatic sensor.

The row of strip lights also revealed that the left side of the illuminated pathway was sealed off by a partition wall, formed of large rectangular plaster boards. Pinned and taped together, these rough unpainted boards appeared to have divided what once must have been the chapel's cellar or crypt. Unlike a church crypt, there was no evidence of tombs or other religious memorials here. Although Kane thought that the concrete floor and plaster ceiling appeared to have been the result of fairly recent building work, and he wondered if the area had been cleared of old artefacts as part of an ongoing refurbishment. As Kane's eyes continued to adjust to the varying shades of light and darkness around him, he spotted one area that had not been modernised. Two huge metallic water tanks were lurking in the darker shadows of two large arched alcoves to his far right. Thanks to the brightness of the single row of strip lighting, Kane could just about make out that each rectangular tank was tipped slightly forward and had a small tap fitted low down, front centre, to allow whatever liquid was held inside to be drained out. He bet these were once used for full emersion baptisms, one for men and one for women.

Curiosity got the better of him and he crept diagonally through the darkness into the first storage bay. He ran his finger under the first tank's tap. It was damp. He sniffed his finger. The smell reminded him of the sickly sweet scent that he had first smelt clinging to Martini Pace. However, Kane assumed that these tanks did not contain a vast vat of her expensive perfume. He suspected that the tanks might be perfect for storing the vapour fluid used in electronic cigarettes or such like devices. A little voice whispered, deep within in his head, telling him that there was probably nothing illegal in that! And then he remembered his conversation with Lao Fu in the Coliseum pub and the suggestion that vapes were now used to disguise drug use.

Kane was just about to move on to check the second tank when a strange metallic clunking noise started up somewhere behind him. He swung around but saw nothing. Kane listened hard. The noise seemed to be coming from behind the plaster board wall. The noise was increasing in volume, and the beat had become rapid, almost like a machine, a pile driver perhaps, urgently thumping metal against metal, with regular, precise tinny blows. As he starred at the partition, wondering what lay beyond it, the lights switched off, presumably timed out and he was plunged into almost total darkness. Almost, only because at the bottom of the stairway, to his far right, there was still an electric light glow, coming from an open doorway, which Kane could now see from this angle, had been cut out of the plasterboard, at the far end of the partition wall, just opposite the stairwell. There was also a small pool of natural light spilling through the open back door, creating a modest semi-circle on the concrete floor inside the building, a bit like a tongue, poking out into the otherwise dark interior. It was teasing him into thinking he should take that route and escape whilst he still had time. Instead, Kane took another deep breath and moved away from the tanks to investigate the source of the clanking noise.

With his back almost touching the left hand side of the gap in the partition wall, Kane slowly unzipped the right pocket of his fleece. This was the pocket that contained the gun. He should have taken time out to fix the silencer on the gun but as suddenly as the noise had started, it stopped. Kane reached into his pocket and took hold of the gun with his right hand. His thumb found the safety catch and his index finger rested on the trigger guard. Had someone heard him? He peered up the wooden stairs into the shadows above. From his new position he could just about make out the top of the steps due to a hint of natural light, possibly from an upstairs window. There was nobody waiting or guarding them. Then, much to his relief, the strange noise began once more behind him. Only this time it sounded slightly different. The clunks were deeper. Somehow they sounded heavier. Slowly, hopefully silently, holding his breath and the gun, Kane lent forward, head first, to look around the corner of the partition.

He found himself looking at an impressive weights room, which given the space and variety of equipment laid out, would be the envy of most local professional gymnasiums. At the far end of the room, thankfully with his back to the doorway, Kane saw the giant. Still wearing his traditional robes, Goliath or whatever his real name was, had crouched down into a large silver/grey metallic frame structure and was using the equipment that Kane had heard, once, a long time ago, described as a Power-Rack Multi Gym. The man was too big to use the equipment properly but he was playfully tugging on the pulley system and pumping up and down a full load of metal brick weights. Hence the clunking noise, when they were lowered back into place before being hoisted aloft again and down and up again and again. It was an odd site to behold. An enormous man, uncomfortably fully dressed, in layers of traditional clothing, hunched down into a tight space, to use ultra-modern equipment. The giant was not even sweating, as he tugged on the pulley and the heavy bricks flew upwards as if made of plastic, like a child's toy. Kane might have been impressed with the man's casual physicality, if it were not for the almost overwhelming sense of dread that Kane had, knowing that in some way he had to tackle this giant of a man, who seemed to be training for an Islamic State Olympic weightlifting team.

Once again, Kane thought that the Islamic clothes and potentially shared heritage did not necessarily make this man one of Lord's men. He may simply have been helping out somehow and bored with waiting, had ventured inside to play with the weights. However, his brute strength and willingness to serve Lord so subserviently, as Kane had witnessed upon the taxi's earlier arrival, indicated to Kane that he had best treat the giant as a potential foe rather than a misguided friend. So Kane's left arm rose silently, twisting backwards in a familiar arc, hand flat, thumb touching his right cheek bone. Kane stepped forward, controlling his breathing. Hoping each nervous step was hidden under each matching weighty clunk as the multi-gym was exploited to its limits. Less than a foot behind the crouching man, Kane swung down, executing an equally brutal surprise chop, onto an unprotected neck. However, this time, even though he connected right on target, it was like hitting thick rubber. The blow jarred Kane's hand, which bounced back off the neck, pain reverberating deep to his bones. In one sensational movement, the giant turned, emitting a little growl as he grabbed hold of the shocked Kane and lifted him up as if he were a small child. The giant then began shaking Kane, as if he were a rag doll rather than a heavily built man of too broad a stature. Briefly the giant stopped shaking and for a second or maybe even two, he starred angrily at Kane, before suddenly hurling him away, back against the plasterboard wall. The board crunched under the weight of Kane's impact and stunned, he rolled off, tried to stand only to slump down onto the floor, followed by a light dusting of chalk, loosened from the cracked boards.

Four metres in front of him, Goliath, the giant, rose up to his full height. More like a bear than a man, his dark face was full of hate. Kane watched as the large hands opened the baggy overcoat. One reached inside and from some pocket or belt, produced a large curved ornamental dagger. Like a fantasy character from an Arabian Nights fable, the giant used his left hand to pull the embroidered red and gold scabbard off, revealing a sharp-edged steel blade, with flowing Urdu characters, engraved into the shiny metal. The dagger glinted in the shafts of electric light, which dotted down from the numerous spotlights fitted into a plain whitewashed ceiling.

'I thought I smelt bacon!' The giant roared in a suitably deep voice. 'I'm going to make you squeal like the pig you are!' He promised, his eyes sparkling with glee. He began to sway forward, carving the air as he cut the cruel blade from right to left. 'Come on little piggy! Squeal!'

Kane was naturally terrified but his survival instinct took

control. Somehow he managed to roll his aching body over onto his left side. Whilst his right hand, still in the unzipped right pocket and gripping the gun, blindly pointed the pistol up against the fleece's pocket lining. Maybe he should have shouted a warning but the knife was cutting through the air, swinging closer and closer. Kane squeezed the trigger, once, then almost instantly once again.

The gun's explosions sounded much louder than Kane had remembered. His own body jumped, twice, in reaction to the noise. The first bullet hit the giant in the middle of his chest. The second just above the large hooked nose, directly between the eyes. The force of the double impact managed to lift the heavy man off his feet and he fell backwards with a hefty crunch that rocked the steel multi gym almost off its bolted fixings. Kane hoped the man was dead, for he was far too busy rolling on the floor, trying to put out the flames, now burning their way up his fleece and scorching his right side, to think of any further self-defence. The Glock was obviously too hot for the "triclimate" synthetic material of his jacket and T shirt. Kane should have read the instructions a bit more carefully for the material might be suitable for three different climates but it was also highly flammable!

Chapter 49: Pack Up Your Troubles (and Strife)

'I loved this place!' Ed Lord, alias Sardaar Sarbaah Sar sighed. He looked around his private office, on the top floor of the converted Welsh Baptist Chapel, with an almost whimsical expression on his face. It might not have been much but he had been happy here.

'Do you really have to go?' Kim turned away from the circular window to look at him, a soft pleading in her normally harsh voice. He tried to smile reassuringly at her but it was all too much for him. She was his strong Western woman, blonde and tanned, always fashionably dressed in tight fitting clothes that showed off her fit muscular body. He decided that he would miss her far more than the bricks and mortar of his club!

'I want you to come with me!' He almost pleaded, staring at her with his sad dark eyes. He was standing behind his imposing double pedestal mahogany desk, whilst his hands distractedly caressed the soft dark red leather of his high-backed executive chair. On the desk in front of him, a large Adidas kit bag was unzipped. Almost spilling out of the open gap were bundles of tightly bound navy coloured bank notes, all adding up to thousands of pounds. The not so petty cash float of an extremely successful business recently emptied from the office safe was the main reason for Lord's risky visit back to the place that had been his home for the last few years.

'No! I can't do heat! You-ssh do know vat!' Kim spoke, her voice high with emotion. Her face, however, remained taut, inflexible, like her attitude when it came to leaving her hometown. Botox may have helped iron out her wrinkles but at times like these it hide her emotions and left her with an unnecessary stern appearance. All the same, a tear appeared at the corner of her eye and began to trickle slowly down her cheek, leaving a wet trail in her heavily applied foundation make up. She turned her back on him, rather dramatically, and she stared blankly, back out of the round window. Her gaze blindly scanning the empty street below and then following the rough tarmac road that would take her man out of her valley, down passed the University Halls of Residence, where a double-decker bus waited, pointing up the slope towards her and the village beyond. The dirty red bus was plastered in adverts, all showing trendily dressed teenagers, clutching books or folders or lap top computers, all smiling confidently at each other, and seemingly having a great time, under the tag line "Learn in Wales!" She wished that she had been clever enough to go to college. Perhaps then her life would have been different. Maybe she would have learnt how to leave the valleys.

In spite of the bright sunshine, that warmed the normally dull view and really showed the spring greenery of the valley at its best, Kim saw nothing of the potential beauty of her surroundings. She was still emotionally blinded to it all. This was all she knew. It was just where she lived. There could be no escape. Her life was what it was! She was a bit like the grumpy middle aged, bus driver, who impatiently waited for someone, anyone to get on his bus, in the bay outside the Halls of Residence. He had the skills and experience to drive a bus anywhere but he settled for the same routine journey, day in day out! He simply could not imagine working anywhere else. Nor could she, somewhere else was for someone else!

At this precise moment in time the man sat behind the large steering wheel, was lost in a fog of frustration, fearful that his job was in jeopardy. If the students did not start to use this service it would get cancelled. He would be out of a job and then how would he earn a living!?! How could he keep up the payments on his home!?! The small circle of fear surrounded him. He could not see the opportunities all around him and he had settled for what little he already had and all he could think about was the worry of losing it! Like Kim, he looked but he did not see. He had certainly not noticed the little Mazda coupé, as it sped around the bend and up the straight steep incline behind him, just seconds before he chose to pull out of the bus stop. Only the sharp reactions of the car's driver prevented an accident. The bus carried on, its driver oblivious to the near disaster, making its way slowly up the road, with the car now hidden in the blind spot, right behind it. The car's driver muttered dark threats in a cold sweat. Somehow he had resisted thumping down on his car horn but perhaps that was only because he really did not want to make a show of himself on this particular road at this particular time. Kim was also blind to the approaching disaster.

'Look! I'm not going back home!' Lord shrugged. His voice was soft and reasonable. 'They might be expecting that! Instead, I'm going to take a nice cruise, maybe to Portugal or Spain and then lie low in North Africa for a bit. I have "brothers" there! They will look after us! It's not too hot this time of year! Come with me! We'll have fun!'

'It'd still be too hot for me! No!' She sniffed determinedly. 'Anyway, I gotta stay for the boys! You know they'll all cut up at the moment! Your doctor friend said it'll take a couple of weeks for them to be right! Whose gonna look after 'em! I mean they can't go to the hospital like!'

'They are big enough to manage on their own!' He said, a little unsympathetically, striding over to her and resting his big hands on her broad shoulders. She sniffed again and relaxed, as his hands caressed her tense muscles, through the soft denim.

482

She lent back, resting her head on his broad chest.

'No let me stay! I'll look after the club for your'ss. Maybe you-ssh can come back, in a bit like, and it'll be, you-ssh knows, like it was before!'

He sighed, his right hand gently massaging the back of her neck, whilst his left moved away to stroke his own beard, as he struggled once more to think of an alternative way forward. 'No!' He began firmly, directing his words to himself rather than her. 'These people are after us now! My little "brother" warned me! It's my duty to follow his advice! It's only a matter of time before they turn up here!' He glanced instinctively out of the window. All was quiet outside. The road was empty. Except down by the Halls of Residence, three or four students, were standing at the bus stop. Even at this distance he could see that they were agitated about something. One of them began kicking the glass shelter. The others began to argue with the vandal. Lord sighed deeply. He certainly would not miss the stupidity of the young people around here!

'They! Whoever "they" are! Ain't got nuff-ink on me!' Kim spat out bravely, bringing his attention instantly back to her. 'And I ain't gonna tell 'em nof-ink! Don't you-ssh worry about that! Like!'

'No I know! I trust you!' He said softly, deftly wrapping his red neckerchief around her throat and suddenly using both hands to tug back violently, he began to throttle the life out of his lover. Kim gasped in surprise as her airways tightened. She tried to say something. Then too late, she tried to fight back.

'Shush!' He whispered, through his clenched teeth. Even for a strong man like him it was quite an effort to resist her struggles. 'Women always talk! It's in your nature! Isn't it!' He said soothingly as he pulled harder on the reinforced material. 'Now shush!' He hissed, warming to his task, enjoying the struggle.

It was all over too soon and he exhaled slowly, before gently lowering her lifeless body down onto the thick pile carpet. Even now he remembered her being thrilled as she stood in the local carpet store, proud to be trusted to choose the carpet for him. It was the first time she had ever bought something so expensive for cash. For a moment or two he was sad. He indulged himself in more nostalgia, mainly about their nights spent together. Then he chuckled nervously to himself as he saw her lying there. Her contorted face had turned purple underneath the heavy makeup and she was suddenly quite ugly to him. Stepping casually over the body, he headed towards his bedroom annex. He did wonder whether it was worth the bother of stringing her up. Well, yes, he decided, for appearances sake. For the boys benefit maybe. Another sad tale of a lover spurned. Yes another tragic valleys suicide. That Ellis Pace had had some good ideas, Lord concluded.

On entering the bedroom Lord saw her pink, kimono style, silk dressing gown, slung over the wicker chair in the corner. Yes that would do! He thought. Moving slowly over to the chair he allowed his hands to caress the soft material. It was cold like her. Then he began carefully unfastening the silk belt from the garment. It was at that moment Lord heard the unmistakeably sound of the shots. One! Two! Then silence. He breathed deeply and gritted his teeth, suddenly angry, with himself and the men downstairs.

Dropping the gown, he rushed over to the tall wardrobe that stood beside the bed. He had only just emptied it, bundling up his precious western clothes into the large suitcase that was now waiting on the bed, all zipped up and ready to be taken to the car. Reaching inside the wardrobe, Lord pushed the false back panel loose. A minute later he had the antique "coach gun" in his hands. The short double-barrelled shotgun was always kept ready, fully loaded, with a 12 gauge cartridge sat in the breach of the each of its two parallel, neatly shortened, 18 inch barrels. Lord turned and cautiously headed back out across the office towards the door to the stairs. He stopped for a few seconds to look out of the window. All was quiet on the street outside. He suddenly felt good, now he had his second favourite toy in his hands. Back in his homeland this type of gun was seen as a prestigious weapon, favoured by wealthy landowners, and used as a sign of authority. The wide spread of pellets helped poor marksmen hit small fast moving targets, such as game birds. Known as a *dunali*, which literally meant "two pipes", it was a most effective weapon against snakes. Lord wondered what snake had slide into his lair.

Slowly he cocked the hammers back and then quietly opened the office door. This was his weapon of choice, not just because of his assumed status as Sardaar Sarbaah Sar, a noble head lord of The Brotherhood, nor due to his painfully average shooting skills, but obviously because he was a fan of cowboy movies. The gun reminded him of his heroes, when they used similar weapons to "ride shotgun" on stagecoaches racing across the prairies. Yes, he had once wanted a Winchester repeating rifle, just like the wonderful James Stewart, but alas, he knew that if he was to hit anything, Lord needed a fully loaded Coach Gun. Doc Holiday was said to have used one in the gunfight at the OK Corral! What better gun to use now that he had to defend his premises. Twin barrels pointing forward, he began his hunt.

485

Chapter 50: Snookered

Cowboy boots are not the best things to wear when you needed to sneak down a bare wooden staircase. At least Sardaar Sarbaah Sar or Ed Lord as he was used to being called in this building, was able to console himself that unlike his Wild West heroes, he was not wearing clunky spurs above the hard block heels at the back of his boots. Nevertheless, Lord chose to teeter on the balls of his feet, like a child sneaking downstairs after bedtime, and exactly like such a naughty child, he hovered halfway down the stairs, suddenly anticipating the difficulties he would encounter should he descend all the way to the bottom and step into the cellar of his building.

Lord had found the second floor, the actual snooker club part of the building, an open plan playroom, eerily empty, as expected. The tables all deserted, apart from the coloured balls, perfectly laid out ready for the next frame to be played. The first floor was also deserted. Well at least the accessible area around the open stairwell. Most of that first floor awaited redevelopment, sealed behind securely locked doors and shutters. Lord had gambled, perhaps recklessly, that the intruder or possibly intruders would have little interest in picking the locks and so he had not looked in there. This could only mean that now he must be close to his prey, for they had to be somewhere down in the cellar or possibly in the gym, where he had left Mohammed to amuse himself, whilst Lord collected his things and dealt with Kim. Unfortunately for Lord, the cellar would be in darkness, apart from the stairwell immediately below him. There at the bottom of the stairs, an almost theatrical spotlight

486

had been created by the combination of electric light escaping from the open doorway to the gym and the natural light now shining down from the first floor above after he had opened the door from the club above. Lord also knew that as soon as he reached the foot of the stairs, a sensor would turn on the row of florescent lights. All in all this would make him an easy target for anyone lurking out on the darkened floor space below.

Who could it be? Lord wondered as he waited just out of sight, now crouching down on the middle stair, twin barrels pointing down into the cellar below. He suddenly realised that he had been rash, in rushing to investigate the shots. The gun was loaded but he only had two shots. Upstairs in his office, was a full box of shotgun cartridges and a bag, with a considerable amount of money in it! If he had brought the bag down with him he could have simply fled. Above him, next to the shuttered front door on the ground floor, was his beloved Kawasaki motor bike, ready and waiting on its stand in the hallway. For a moment Lord envisaged escaping on the bike to fight another day! But fight who? He wondered to himself again. Who could it be? He dismissed the idea of flight. The intruder or intruders would surely be on him before he had raised the shutter to the front door. There was no way he could sneak back up and grab the money and cartridges without making a telling noise. Lord also worried that there could also be others, waiting outside! What had become of Mohammed and his driver? Lord silently asked himself. He was tempted to call out to the giant but he knew that he had heard two shots and it did not take a mathematical genius to work out what might have happened to the two men whom he had left casually on guard below. Lord could also smell something odd. It was hanging in the air of the stairwell, a faint burning smell perhaps. Maybe it was the acrid waft of melted plastic or possibly the unpleasantly pungent aroma of singed man-made-fibres, mixed with a hint of something else, equally repulsive. Whatever it was he had smelt it before but in the stress of the moment he could not quite place it.

Down in the cellar, Kane was crouched in the shadows beside the first metal tank, the one furthest from the stairs. He had a clear view of the stairwell and a fair view of the back door. If he glanced that way the relative brightness of the sun made him squint. His back ached but not as much as his left hand throbbed from the impact with the solid muscle that had covered the giant's collarbone. The right side of Kane's stomach also tingled from his scorched skin. He really should have poured more cold water on it to try and stop the skin blistering. He had been lucky though. Amongst the state of the art gym equipment was a water fountain and he had hurled a few plastic cupfuls over his side, after franticly beating out the flames. He could have done with more water but he had been acutely aware that the non-silenced shots would have been heard by everyone in the building. That meant, to him, that at least two dangerous adversaries were alerted to his presence. So he now suffered in silence, with only the cool dampness of his ragged T-shirt as a modest comforter. What was left of his black fleece was draped over his head and neck in a feeble attempt to help him blend in with the darkness but he could smell the singed material and he was sure that anyone with a half decent sense of smell could work out his position.

Kane had heard the initial clicks of heavy shoes on the wooden stairs and he was now pointing his pistol, complete with fitted silencer, towards the top visible stair. Patience was his only tactic now that the element of surprise was gone. Intelligent waiting or so he had heard it called during sniper training and military leadership courses. The theory told him the person who moved first or rather next, was only going to make themselves a target. He assumed, correctly, that being on home ground, Lord had to be armed. To show himself was to court disaster. So he waited.

Up on the stairs Lord knew that he could not wait much longer. He needed to do something but what he wondered. His motto had always been "who dares wins!" Somewhat ironic, given that he had adopted it from the SAS soldiers he had once so admired and then learnt to despise after they had abandoned him and his homeland. Dare he use one of his cartridges to blast blindly into the darkness and rush the switch to turn all the lights on. He would have one shot left and he was sure to spot his target with the cellar flooded with light. No! He told himself that was simply ridiculous risk taking. He even found himself thinking that if only he had fitted traditional lighting to the gym, instead of those trendy spotlights! One shot at a traditional lamp might have given him an advantage by hiding his charge to the light switch but then he was forgetting about the natural light shining down from behind him. Lord knew he needed a distraction.

Kane remained perfectly still and carefully controlled his breathing. He was wishing that he had a grenade. That would be something to request on future missions, if he had a future that is! He wondered what type of weapon Lord had. A machine pistol could spray bullets all around the cellar and with only the cover of darkness to protect him, he had no chance. Darkness was not very effective against red hot lead!

Both men persisted in dreaming up a load of nonsense, their minds working overtime, screaming out the different worse case scenarios but both remained physically still whilst daring the other to make the first move. Then, outside, things changed.

In the boot of the Mercedes taxi, the driver must have come round, for all of a sudden, the car started to rock and through the open back door the noise of him kicking the inside roof of the boot could be heard, punctuated by the pitiful cries, in a thick

Cardiff accent, of: 'Oye 'elp me! I carn't breathe, like! Get me out!'

The voice was so pathetic that Kane actually found it funny and he had to bite his lip to stop himself from giggling and thus giving his position away. Sat up on his stair, Lord wondered whether the racket that the driver was making might cause a passer-by to investigate. If they came into the club, they might switch on the lights for him and then bang! Kane thought of that too. He had fifteen rounds left. Maybe he should just rush the stairs. No he decided he would try something else. It was a difficult shot, especially given that until a few minutes ago Kane had not fired a gun, apart from in a fairground, for a decade.

Nevertheless, it worked. He had realised that Lord or whoever was up on the stairs, had guessed that someone was lying in wait for them, so they were anticipating his ambush. He had to attack but a charge would be suicidal so he attempted a ricochet. Aiming at the large foundation stone, which was laid at the base of the front wall, Kane squeezed off two shots. The first bullet rebounded and hit the third stair, splintering wood. The second missed the stone but made one hell of a noise as it thumped into the grouting of the wall and sent dust into the air.

In fact both shots had had an unsettling effect on Lord because he did not hear them due to the fitted silencer. Perhaps he had been distracted by the driver's cries, because the bullets seemed to come out of nowhere. Despite whistling through the air, their explosive impact was the first thing he truly heard. He had missed the firing light or spark and now a third bullet rebounded off the wall and pinged diagonally in a zigzag motion far too close to him for comfort. The shots made up his mind and Lord pushed up into a standing position, turned around and fled, quickly and noisily, back up the stairs, determined to get up to his box of spare cartridges before the intruders caught up

490

with him. He told himself, as he ran away, that he could set his own ambush further upstairs!

Kane allowed himself the luxury of a groan as he rose up from the hard cold concrete floor. He found it a comfort and it helped him channel his energy into the effort of pounding over towards the stairwell. He knew that he was not fit but his body hurt anyway, mainly from the unaccustomed trauma of being thrown into the wall and the minor burns suffered when his fleece caught fire.

Yet he felt better when he fired another blind shot, roughly up the middle of the dark stairs, before risking a glance up. There was just enough light at the top of the stairs for him to make out a plume of dust hanging in the air, no doubt after the bullet hit home into the crudely plastered wall. To his disappointment, he also saw that the stairs climbed up no more than a dozen steep steps before reaching a small square landing and immediately turning at a right angle for another ascent towards the upper floors. Somewhere up above, he heard a distant door slam shut.

Believing the noise was a sign that the way up head would be clear of any immediate sniper, Kane forced himself to lurch upwards and onwards, climbing both sections, two stair steps at a time, his gun hand pointing up, just in case. The risk was worth it and on reaching the top step he discovered he was in a long hallway leading to the building's main entrance. His breathing was heavy so he paused momentarily shielded by the wall to regain his breath.

Glancing around he could see the club's double doors were firmly bolted together from the inside, and immediately above them, through the coloured glass of a semicircular fanlight window, he spotted the top of the external roller shutter guard, the one that he must have checked out early, when he had stood on the street outside. Kane also saw the bright green Kawasaki

Ninja motorbike. It was propped up on its jack stand, at the far end of the hallway.

There were other doors on each side of the hall, leading to side rooms. Kane tested them, just in case one of them had been the door that he had heard slam shut. They proved to be locked and the cobwebs along their door frames indicated that no one had used them for a long time. Kane concluded that the noise must have come from the door at the top of the next flight of stairs and the only way was up.

He prepared himself for the effort, slowly inhaling six more deep breaths, before starting a rather cautious ascent up the wide and worryingly straight stairway. Thirty four steps later he was stood on another flat rectangular landing, about four metres wide and six long. At the end of the landing he could see a frosted glass panel wall divider and a matching part glazed door, with the words "The Potting Shed" etched into the glass. This was a perfect place for a trap. Anyone on the inside would probably see the outline of his shape as he approached the door. Nevertheless, approach it he did, albeit in a low crouch.

'Oh for a stun grenade!' Kane actual whispered to himself as he foolishly opened the door. Immediately an unseen sensor device bleeped an extra electronic warning to whoever was waiting on the other side of the doorway. On hearing the bleep he amazed himself, instantly reacting by diving into a forward roll. Somehow he rose out of the head-first flip onto one knee, assuming a standard two handed shooting position. Training! Muscle memory! Whatever! He thought! He felt slightly giddy as he continued scanning the room with his gun pointing out in front of him.

Kane was even more amazed, than the fact that his survival instincts had kicked in yet again, when he realised that no one was shooting back at him. His eyes darted around all the possible hiding places, but he saw no one. Nobody was crouched behind the furniture or underneath one of the many snooker tables. He could not understand why that was! Unless, of course, there was a much better place for an ambush deeper in the room.

His attention focused on the small drinks bar to his right. He aimed his gun at the opening, created by the raised hatch at the near end of the dark varnished wooden bar. For a moment he tried to use the mirrored tiles, those fixed behind the spirit drink dispensers, which hung below a high shelf stacked with glasses and more bottles, to see behind the barrier, but the angle was not good enough. He squeezed the trigger twice and watched the bullets thump through the wooden panel. There was no cry from anyone hiding behind the wood so he glanced back down to the far end of the room where another staircase rose up into what must have been the third and top floor.

The stairs disappeared straight up into the ceiling. Anyone putting a foot on the stairs would be blown away by an unseen shooter standing at the top. Kane would not be able to see up the stairs until he was exposed at the bottom. That must be where Lord was waiting for him. That was exactly where Kane would have chosen to wait.

Buoyed by this realisation, Kane stood up slowly. He cautiously approached the bar area, gun still at the ready and he even leaned over the top, gun first, just to see whether he was wrong and someone was crouched down behind the varnished wood. He knew there were two people in the club. Both need not be upstairs. Kane would never have taken such a risk if he had a grenade or two. He would have simply tossed one over the bar and carried on. He shook his head and decided that he really needed to requisition some grenades before he did anything like this again! His throat was dry with tension and he looked at the tempting range of spirits conveniently fitted into their wall mounted optics. He smiled to himself, as a wicked voice within said "Why not!?!"

A few swigs later, Kane was striding boldly down the middle of the large rectangular snooker room, right through the central pathway between the symmetrically arranged tables, until at the end, he sneakily veered away from the open staircase and squatted down, underneath the last, oddly placed snooker table, which stood on it's own, as if on sentry duty, guarding the stairs.

'If you think I'm coming up any more of these bloody stairs, you are having a laugh!' Kane called out. The reply was instant. Two blasts from the shotgun peppered the bottom of the stairs with lead pellets. Then Kane heard the forced laughter from above. It was followed by a deep voice, putting on an American cowboy accent. 'I sure am boy! I sure am!'

Chapter 51: Retaliation

Who the hell's up there? Yosemite Sam!?!' Kane called out, with his tongue firmly in his cheek, from the relative safety of his position under the snooker table.

'That'll be the day!' The deep voice had changed slightly, and was now attempting to mimic John Wayne's distinctive drawl. Kane also heard the unmistakeable click of a break action shotgun snapping back into place. The sound conveyed good news. Kane now knew that the shooter, at the top of the stairs, would only be able to fire two shots at a time, before needing to reload. This should give Kane valuable seconds to act. The bad news was that the click had told him, the shooter now had another two shots, of devastating force, ready to fire down into the narrow stairway, which would certainly become a death trap, for anyone foolish enough to attempt a charge up the stairs.

'Well if you like your Westerns!' Kane paused for effect. 'Let me remind you of the end of Butch Cassidy and The Sundance Kid!'

'Wu-a-ell thank'ee kind-lee stranger, but yer jus' ain't the Bolivian Army down there! Rrrr yer!?!' The voice from above had assumed a general mocking tone as it attempted another parody. This time it sounded, almost, like the traditional old timer, a character essential used to lighten even the darkest of Westerns, and usually played in John Ford movies by that fine actor, Walter Brennan. However, the impersonator did not quite carry it off and the accent came across as a kind of fusion between the intended Western old timer and a West Country pirate!

Another double blast from the shotgun followed. Let loose as if in frustration for the shooters vocal failings. A smattering of pellets suddenly thudded into the walls, floor, and some, actually split the wood of the bottom stair, causing sharp splinters to fly up and impale themselves in the carpet and lower legs of the nearby tables. Kane suddenly did not feel so safe in his position and used the valuable reload time to move, but not before firing off two shots of his own. A nifty side roll later, he was pressing himself against the back wall, well away from the central gap at the base of the stairs that had been targeted by the shotgun.

Kane's two shots were obviously ineffective. The bullets probably buried themselves into the plaster wall, much lower down the stairs, than the shotgun shooter's dominant upstairs position. Nevertheless, the exchange of fire had served Kane well, for he had made his shots through a bar towel, which he had already soaked in almost a whole bottle of brandy, taken earlier from the behind the bar. A blue flame now burned along the sodden cloth, which Kane had stuffed into the top of a three quarters full bottle of vodka. He had another large bottle of whiskey, similarly prepared, and stood on the floor beside him. After applying the safety catch, he tucked his pistol into the elasticated waistband of his trousers. Kane then used the blue flame to ignite the other sodden bar towel in the neck of that whiskey bottle. He did not have any grenades but he now had two, lighted Molotov cocktails, one in each hand.

'You know, I think we must have the same taste in films!' Kane shouted out.

'So what!' Came the blunt response, this time spoken without a put on accent and Kane recognised the strong hint of the North West Frontier perfectly merged with the music of the Valleys, in the tone and expression of Lord's two words.

'Well, in the old movies, when the bad guys were holed up in a log cabin, what did the posse do to get them out?' Kane asked at the top of his voice.

Lord knew, as well as Kane did, that they smoked them out, but he ignored the question and just shouted back down the stairs: 'I always thought of the bad guys as the good guys!' He laughed at his own twisted sense of humour.

'So! Do you think you've got a white hat or a black hat on then?' Kane shouted back.

'No! I don't wear a hat!' Lord yelled out and then whooped, fanning his mouth with the flat of his hand in a mock Native American war cry. 'I am more likely to be miscast with the Indians! Wouldn't you say!?!'

Kane could see the rags were now burning down close to the bottle top and he needed to throw them soon, if they were to work. Nevertheless, he risked one more call out.

'And there's me thinking you were waiting for the cavalry!?!'

Lord laughed at that. He had always enjoyed a genuine bit of banter. 'Who are you?' He called down, sounding truly curious. 'Who are you working for?' He added, more than slightly puzzled by his dilemma. He had expected the police or even a team of Government Agents, not an individual, who seemed unwilling to follow the normal protocol of arresting warnings.

Kane was surprised but then he realised Lord had not seen him or really spoken directly to him, outside of the bravado on Friday night in the all too brief incident at The Kettle. 'Why don't you throw down the gun and then we can have a proper chat!' Kane said without any real optimism in the appeal.

'No! You just *come up and see me!* Lord let out a hearty laugh at his own truly awful Mae West impersonation.

'I will, eventually!' Kane muttered and then raising his voice he shouted. 'Look! If you want to stay in the attic, that's fine with me. But, why don't you send down the woman? She doesn't have to be a part of this! I'll let her go! Or is she loading your guns for you?'

'Oh, she's gone on already.'

Kane was puzzled. There was no other way out or was there!?! His mind raced back over the memory of his morning observations. Of course, what a fool he had been! There was a wrought iron fire escape, clinging to the east side of the building. She could have left when he was in the cellar. He glanced around and saw the fire doors behind him. He then nervously looked back along the snooker hall towards the main door. Maybe she was already coming up behind him, with a gun, intending to shoot him in the back. However, Kane thought that if that was Lord's plan, he would have stayed downstairs. No, Kane deduced something was not right here. The fire doors were firmly closed and the opening device had one of those safety pin security contraptions fitted, which would set off an alarm should the door be pulled open. He had not heard any alarm.

The Molotov cocktails were getting too hot to hold any longer. He had to use them now and he did! The first one landed on the shattered wooden step. The sound of glass breaking was actually louder than the cough like explosion as the liqueur lighted. The varnish on the stair instantly caught and began to give off a dark smoke. Kane switched hands and tossed the second bottle at the same target. His second throw was stronger and the bottle was lobbed passed the step and smashed into the wall. When the glass broke, the whiskey lit up, making a slightly louder noise, almost a burp! Flaming contents splashed up onto the wall and down onto the carpet. Small, clear flames, almost instantly rose out of any damp patches but the fire did not spread. It did not go out either and simply burnt and smouldered away, in a small patch at the foot of the stairs. He could hear Lord clearly laughing at his pathetic effort.

'Are you getting cold down there?' The man at the top of

the stairs asked. 'You should have said! I'd have put the heating on for you!' Behind the jovial tone, Lord was working out his next move. He had had a plan all along, well as soon as he heard the warning bleep, from the snooker hall door. Yet he worried he would not have enough time to see his plan through. He needed a distraction. And now, the fire was his friend. It might stop someone running up the stairs after him, if only it burned a little brighter.

'Don't worry; I'll put another bottle on!' Kane called out.

'Be my guest!' Lord called back down. 'Put a couple more on if you think it will help!'

Kane doubted that he could get over to the bar and snatch a few more bottles before Lord made a charge down the stairs in what Kane now hoped would be a desperate attempt to blast his way out. Naturally, Kane had his gun out again and was slowly unscrewing the now redundant silencer, to allow him greater freedom of movement when the final fire fight came. He slipped the heavy silencer into his fleece pocket and tied the jacket, by the sleeves, back around his waist, in a loose knot, so that when it can to it, one tug would release it. It hung heavy, with the extra weight of the phone and car keys, all now in the left hand pocket.

'Why do you hate my Snooker Club?' Lord called down, not really interested in the reply.

'It's not the club I hate!' Kane began, suddenly sounding bitter. 'It's the man who killed my friend! He's the one I want to burn! You remember Frank John, Mr Lord? If that's your real name! Frank was my friend and you killed him! Didn't you!?!'

There was no reply to that threat from the top of the stairs. No comic voice. No cowboy anecdote. Just silence. All was suddenly very quiet; apart from that is, the strange noise of the short flames devouring oxygen along an irregular patch of carpet at the bottom of the staircase. Kane had noticed the silence. He also noticed that, fortunately for him, the flames had not spread back along the carpet. In fact they were getting smaller. Without more fuel they were likely to burn out completely very soon; so much for his idea of burning Lord out of his lair.

Whoever had fitted out Lord's Potting Shed had done a good job, using the latest flame-retardant material. At least a few modest plumes of dark, hopefully toxic, smoke were rising up the staircase into the attic. Kane suddenly made a decision. He did not want to be poisoned along with Lord, whom he presumed was trapped upstairs. So Kane edged quietly backwards along the wall towards the fire doors. He used his left hand to push the locking bar down and slowly the double doors opened. Of course, the safety pin popped out and swung down on its chain, as it had been designed to do, and almost immediately an alarm bell rang, above the door. Even though he had been expecting it, the ringing startled Kane.

The noise also startled Lord. He was two thirds of the way down a rope ladder, which hung from his bedroom window. The rope ladder was one of those emergency escape lightweight ones. It was not really rope, but was made of two strips of linked chains joined together by plastic coated steel bars. Two large red plastic coated hooks clung to the internal window ledge and Lord had tied his money bag to the bottom of the ladder to weigh it down before dropping it towards the more substantial fire escape that Health & Safety regulations had required him to fit so that customers could, in an emergency, escape from the second floor of his club. Lord had always kept the supplementary ladder under his bed, just in case he needed to make a swift exit, like this one, from his attic office and bedroom. Now, he had been caught out. His flight had been so desperate that he had not kept his shotgun on him. He did not have the time to fix a strap on it. So instead, it was out of reach, safe and secure in his bag, resting on top of all his cash.

Kane could see the bag, through the gap between the open

fire doors. It was hanging a metre off the steel floor of the fire escape landing. Almost two metres above it, Kane could also see a pair of snakeskin cowboy boots. He did not know about the shotgun being in the bag. He only knew that everything that happened next happened fast.

Lord realising that the game was up, immediately dropped down onto the landing. He hit the steel fabrication flooring with a tremendous bang and tried desperately to use his strong legs to push himself up, probably to attack Kane or appeal, surrender, or even try to do a deal, but the angled heels on his boots, designed to keep feet in stirrups rather than grip flat grid-like steel surfaces, caused him to slip and slide into a forward leaning diving motion. Kane, with the gun still in his right hand, raised it, took aim and fired twice in quick succession, before he even realised that Lord did not have a gun or any other weapon in his fast moving, fanning hands. The bullets hit Lord in his torso and sent him spinning backwards, over the landing's vertical steel bar barricade. Somehow, Lord's head got trapped in a section of the escape ladder. The force of his body hitting the ladder caused it to twist and Lord was left hanging, by his neck, in thin air, over the edge of the fire escape.

The big man began to kick his legs against the barrier, trying desperately to get a grip on the steel frame. The smooth leather soles slide off twice. Kane knew that it was only a matter of time. There were two great big red patches, growing bigger by the second, across Lord's denim jacket. The big man's eyes were bulging and he was making horrendous gurgling sounds, as his legs did a little dance, frantically treading air. Kane resisted the human instinct to try and help him. It was too late and this was after all, only what Kane had come here to do. The perfect revenge for Frank John!

A few seconds later, Lord or whatever he had really been named gave up the fight and died.

Chapter 52: Loose Ends

Although tempting, leaving the big man dangling outside the building was perhaps not the neatest of knots to use when tying up loose ends. No doubt the hanged cowboy would alarm the neighbours. So Kane rather half-heartedly set about untangling the corpse from the twisted chain-ladder. Unfortunately the body proved too heavy to haul back in over the fire escape's metal railings and a combination of clumsiness and unhelpful gusts of wind resulted in a final humiliation for Lord as his body slipped from Kane's grasp to plummet into the long grass of the chapel's graveyard and hit the ground with a surprisingly heavy thud. Looking down from the top of the fire escape, Kane realised that the distorted remains would be hidden from street and he could let Lord rest in peace for a while.

With the dead weight gone, Kane finally managed to haul the heavy bag onto the gantry. He was able to untie it and drag it inside, before cautiously unzipping it and being pleasantly surprised at the rich contents.

The fire at the foot of the stairs had burnt out and whilst there remained an acrid smell, all was eerily quiet inside the club. There was certainly no sound of movement upstairs and Kane began to wonder where Lord's woman had gone. Even though he was expecting an imminent visit from the local police, Kane knew that he had best investigate Lord's attic lair before reporting in. What with multiple shotgun blasts and him actually firing his gun twice outside, he knew someone must have heard something, on what should have been a quiet Sunday afternoon. However, Kane did wonder who amongst the locals may have been brave enough to make the call and risk the possible wrath of their dodgy neighbour.

After checking his gun, Kane approached the stairs and cautiously began another ascent. He was sad and angry too, when he discovered the woman's body. He wasted too many thoughts about why she had been killed. He would never know the real answer and whatever it was he doubted that it could ever justify her death. Perhaps she had just been a victim of bad company and poor lifestyle choices, he supposed. Taking the MI mobile phone out of his pocket, Kane made the call.

Captain Brown had answered and after listening to Kane's brief, slightly cryptic report, he agreed that three deaths were more than enough in one day. So it was jointly decided that Kane should give the young driver the benefit of the doubt.

By the time Kane had returned to the car park behind The Potting Shed building, the young man had stopped kicking or banging on the inside of the Mercedes boot. Wondering if he had suffocated, Kane hid around the corner, quite close to where Lord's body lay and remotely unlocked the car, deliberately releasing the catch, so that the boot lid popped open. Kane had already secreted one of his magnetic tracking devices inside the car, and now lobbed the keys onto the tarmac, where they could be found by the driver, if he recovered. He did and a few minutes later he climbed out rather timidly. Kane ducked down back behind the corner, gun in hand, just in case the man was more than he had seemed. He was not!

Looking around the car park the young man suddenly let out a scream. Kane assumed that he had somehow spotted the crumpled body in the long grass. There was panic in the young man's voice as he screamed the name "Mohammed" several times into the building, through the open back door. It then went so quiet that Kane chanced a look around the corner. The driver had disappeared. When the faint sound of wailing started to escape from the building, Kane realised that the young man had gone into the cellar and must have found the giant's body in the gym. That was enough. He came running out of the building and got into the car. Kane hid again and heard the car door slam and then a few minutes later, open again, when the driver realised that he did not have the keys anymore. The strange noise that was a man pathetically whimpering could be heard for what seemed like minutes but was probably only a few seconds, until in his distressed state, the driver must have looked down and seen the keys on the floor. Kane heard rushed footsteps and then the door slam shut again. Seconds later the diesel engine spluttered into life and the wheels spun wildly on the tarmac as the Mercedes sped out of the car park.

Taking his time, Kane picked up the sports bag, which he had previously liberated from the bottom of the "chain-ladder" and rather casually strolled around the back of the building and out of the car park, through the main gate. He had stuffed his burnt fleece jacket on top of the cash, having first removed the shotgun and left it empty of shells, on the top landing of the fire escape, just as if it had been dropped by Lord, and just as he had been told to do so by Captain Brown. Kane wondered if the subsequent police report would state that Lord had been murdered or would they erroneously ignore the bullet holes and consider that, just like Frank John, he had committed suicide. Such irony was highly likely, for following his report, Kane suspected the police would make whatever public statement Brigadier Dr. Packwood's office told them to make and local businessman throws himself off rooftop full of remorse after killing his girlfriend and her lover was a rather neat story.

No one seemed to notice the middle-aged man in the torn T-shirt return to the Mazda. However, someone had sneakily placed a "Fixed Penalty Notice" on the car! Well, Kane was certainly guilty having parked in the "Resident's Only" zone.

Kane picked the sealed plastic bag containing the ticket off the windscreen and tossed it into his car boot, along with the full sports bag, before quickly swapping his T-shirt for the extra thin top, the one he had worn between the t-shirt and his fleece that chilly morning. Whilst changing he glanced up at the windows of the nearby houses. No doubt someone was watching him, probably the person who was such an eager volunteer with the neighbourhood watch. Such a shame, Kane thought, that the good citizen had not taken a more righteous interest in what went on at the local snooker club! Then Kane thought that maybe they had and their complaints were under investigation by a senior policemen like Superintendent Charles. A part of him wondered if that was why the police had not yet arrived; because the neighbourhood parking warden would certainly have reported the shotgun blasts if they had heard them!

The Mazda started at the third attempt and Kane was about to drive off when the MI mobile phone began to vibrate. When Kane answered it he heard the precise and educated voice of Brigadier Dr. Packwood congratulating him on completing his first mission "back on the team!" Packwood went on to tell Kane that they were tracking the young taxi driver, who was "absolutely flying" back down the dual carriageway towards Cardiff. Anyway Kane was not to worry but "that young man" was already under surveillance by another authority and they would be "progressing" the matter.

There were a few questions Kane wanted to ask Packwood. Such as what had happened to Martini, Haymer, Lord's bodybuilders and that accountant Khan? He was also curious as to whether Superintendent Charles had actually been charged with treason. However, Kane knew that he would have to wait for his final debriefing for that opportunity and if his previous service in Military Intelligence was anything to go by, such information would probably be restricted on a need to know

505

basis, and his superiors in the past used to decide that field operatives like Kane, never needed to know!

'Time to go home now, Captain Kane!' Packwood said, sounding worryingly jolly. 'Take a day or two to write up your full report and we will be in touch after that.'

Kane glanced up and down the empty terraced street and wondered where the Neighbourhood Watchers were. He sighed as he noticed the lace curtain in an upstairs window across the street move slightly.

'Well done on surviving, Captain Kane! We'll get you in shape for some more serious action in due course.' There was a brief pause and then Kane heard his superior's voice again, it sounded slightly more thoughtful in tone. 'It may not have been quite what I had anticipated, at the start of this mission but your intervention has got things over the line, so to speak. Now, good luck with the final part of your mission. Telling your wife about your new job as an, hmm, Educational Consultant for Whitehall Services Limited!' Packwood then laughed as if he had heard a most amusing joke, before adding almost sincerely: 'Best of luck with that!'

Kane swallowed hard by way of a response, for he realised that he had already used up his share of luck for the day!

***

Border Force Officer Geen's face rarely reacted when he looked at travellers' passport photographs. He prided himself on his impartial professionalism. The subjects always looked miserable or stern in them because they had been told not to smile. However, even he blinked at the sour looking face in the burgundy covered book just passed over to him as he sat in his booth at Cardiff Airport's Passport Control. Raising his eyes to the face in front of him he was equally surprised to see the large man wore a perfectly matching frown to the one in his photograph.

'And what is the reason for your visit to the United Kingdom Mr. Irmão?'

'Business,' the thickly accented tall man answered unemotionally.

'What type of business?' Officer Geen asked equally matter of factly, although he was already deeply suspicious of any man of obvious Arabic descent travelling from Portugal on an EU passport. Criminal profiling by race might be considered ineffective and offensive by some of his younger colleagues but Geen had years of experience, which made him doubt why a businessman would choose to suffer the indignity of travelling alone on a rowdy cheap flight full of package holiday makers to a provincial airport. Accordingly, Officer Geen had casually pressed a hidden button to alert his supervisor, who arrived by his side just in time to hear Irmão finish his long (well rehearsed and honest) explanation of how he was here to liquidate his late brother's affairs.

Senior Officer Maryam Asghar nodded sympathetically and handed Irmão back his passport.

'Creoso Cymru, Welcome to Wales! Mr Irmão.' She said before repeating the phrase in Portuguese and Arabic. Mr Irmão did not change his expression but he may have just about nodded his head in polite acknowledgement as he walked passed the booth and followed the signs to Baggage Collection.

Turning back to Officer Geen and giving him one of her most disapproving looks, Senior Officer Asghar said quietly: 'We must have another one of our chats later Dave!' She then moved away slowly shaking her head.

Officer Geen tried not to show his frustration as he got on with his job processing the next person in the queue of brightly dressed holidaymakers. He gave them a thin smile and brisk greeting. He knew that in spite his current supervisor being a relatively recent graduate entry to the service, Senior Officer Asghar's membership of the Civil Service's award winning "Fast Stream" leadership development programme meant that she would be moving on soon, so he quietly consoled himself that this clever lady's rapid advancement was imminent and certainly not dependent on the fact that she was the only woman of colour working in the region.

Twenty minutes later, in the Arrivals waiting area, Mr Irmão was greeted by a nervous looking young taxi driver who was holding out a large white card with the words "Armadid" written on it. The young man was dressed in a culture clash of expensive Addidas trainers, tight western jeans and a long eastern Kameez shirt. He led the frowning businessman to a black and white Mercedes parked in the short-term car park. He respectfully opened the near side back door and quickly moved away to collect Irmão's bag and place it carefully in the large boot.

Irmão silently got into the car and sat stiffly next to a much smaller and younger man who had been waiting patiently for his arrival. This young man was smartly dressed in a three piece pin-striped suit.

Only when the driver returned and shut the door did the small man in the suit turn towards Irmão and bursting into a broad smile he said: 'Khosh Amadid!'

The End

Look out for the next exciting thriller from Wayne Edwards in the 'Unnecessary Reactions' series.

Lightning Source UK Ltd.
Milton Keynes UK
UKHW020732191021
392466UK00012B/861